potomac fever

also by henry horrock

Blood Red, Snow White

potomac fever

a novel by

henry horrock

LITTLE, BROWN AND COMPANY

Boston New York London

First Edition

Library of Congress Cataloging-in-Publication Data

Horrock, Henry.
    Potomac fever : a novel / by Henry Horrock. — 1st ed.
        p.   cm.
    ISBN 0-316-35472-4
    I. Title.
  PS3558.06973P68   1999
  813'.54 — dc21   98-45240

10   9   8   7   6   5   4   3   2   1

MV-NY

Printed in the United States of America

We are always at the heart of a scrimmage. There is no safe seat.

— D. H. LAWRENCE

acknowledgments

This book would not exist without the scoundrels, greedy politicians, deceiving lovers, and crooked lawyers the author has had the good fortune of knowing through the years.

Nor would this book exist without the mutual respect and collaboration of our agent, Alice Martell, our editor, Bill Phillips, and the other editors at Little, Brown who labored in this creation. We applaud their exceptional talents and dedication.

Most of all, we cherish our readers with profound appreciation. Thank you, comarados.

potomac fever

1

"This is a forty-nine-year-old male," said a voice. "He was admitted at three twenty-one. He has contusions in his midsection, two broken ribs on the left side, contusions and lacerations on his face. On his arm is a laceration caused by a gunshot. On his right leg is another laceration, quite deep, possible cartilage damage. The ambulance crew said he could not form words.

"An MRI disclosed a subdural hematoma on the left side of the skull, above his ear, that presses onto brain tissue. That is my problem, ladies and gentlemen. I want his head secured to prevent movement when he awakens. I want a five-minute visual watch and a constant monitor of vital signs. I don't like the continued growth of the hematoma, so let's keep alert."

Cal was lying under a very bright light. He could see it through his eyelids, but if he tried to open his eyes, the light was too bright.

"Did you see his back?" whispered a woman's voice. "The scars?"

Cal opened his eyes. The bright light was gone. He could see the ceiling and the tops of curtains on rods to his left and right. He could not move his head; he was held by something soft but firm. There was a bag of fluid hanging on his left, a clear liquid was dripping down a little tube.

He wondered where he was. A hospital, of course.

The phone rang. Cal knocked over the side table trying to answer it, throwing off the recorder and leaving the telephone dangling halfway between the bed and the floor. Vivian was not there, but he could feel the indent her body had left in the bed.

"Terrell," a strange mechanical voice broke the darkness. It was not a human voice, but a voice that sounded as though it were a record played at the wrong speed.

"Who is this?"

"Are you Terrell, the police officer?"

"How did you get my number?"

"Don't mind about that."

"So okay?"

Cal had crawled off the bed and was trying to start the recorder on the floor.

"Do you really want to find who killed Mary Jeanne?"

There was silence on the line for a moment.

He knew this wasn't some crank, some crank who had found his number, listed C. Terrell, listed only in a rural phone book in a county fifty-five miles from Washington, D.C.

"If someone killed her, I want to find him."

"Don't be so quick. There may be things you don't want to know."

"Try me."

"Mr. Terrell, can you hear me?"

She was a gray-haired woman with a heavy face. She was right above him. Maybe five inches from his face. All he could see was her head.

He tried to speak. To say, "Yes. I hear you." But he couldn't hear his words. His tongue and lips didn't seem to work. He could hear a voice, but it sounded muffled, as though his mouth was full of marbles, the words coming out garbled.

"Just blink your eyes," said the woman.

The woman's face pulled away. He tried to follow it, but he couldn't move his head.

"You are in a hospital. You have been seriously injured," said a male voice. "One of your injuries was a blow to your left temple. A large blood clot has formed between your brain and the wall of your skull. It is pressing onto the brain where speech is formed; that's why you can't form words. Do you understand?"

Cal blinked.

"For the time being, this is of some concern. If the clot subsides in the next twenty-four hours on its own, it will reduce the pressure. If not . . . we'll take more aggressive action." The voice did not elaborate. "Do not become frightened; we are watching you closely. If you understand, please blink your eyes."

Cal blinked.

The temperature had changed and there was a chilly breeze whipping in from the bay. Cal's sweatshirt and shorts were not enough. Cal shivered when he went outside. He had heard the horses as the mysterious caller hung up.

He saw the small white envelope long before he reached the truck. It was stuck under the windshield wiper on the driver's side. He hadn't noticed it before. Somebody had just left it, and yet Cal had not heard a car. The dogs were quiet too.

Cal stood for a long time near the truck, listening to the crickets and probing the dark with his eyes. Was the person who left the envelope watching him?

He opened the envelope in the stable, by the porch light.

There was Mary Jeanne in life. Dark glasses hid her eyes, but it was unmistakably her — the smile, the long dark blond hair, her full breasts obvious in a striped sailor shirt, and long legs, in white shorts, drawn up against the side of a reclining chair. Her image was a cut corner of what had been a group photograph. On a piece of paper someone had pasted cutout letters to form two words: MY BONAFIDES.

Suddenly the horses shifted in the stalls. A fox maybe? He stood listening. He still couldn't hear the dogs.

Instinctively he leaned forward and dipped his hands into the oats, pushing the picture and the envelope way down. The smell of the oats came up warm and fragrant. Now the horses were slamming the side boards.

He quietly closed the oat chest and ducked out the far door to the exercise rink. Maybe the person who delivered the picture had waited to be sure he got it?

There was no one. He could hear nothing. He went back inside. Bristol Boy was in the far corner of his stall now, turning his head from side to side. Comet was walking circles in his stall, the whites of his eyes showing.

Cal didn't turn on the lights but scanned the inside of the stable in the light from the porch lamp.

Nothing.

"Shush," he said to Comet. "Shush." He moved silently through the darkness to Bristol Boy's stall, reaching for the horse's neck through the rails.

The first blow, low and brutal, hit him in the kidneys.

He went to his knees. Then someone took his head from the back, twisted it sideways and smashed it into the floor. He saw the floor coming up as though it were moving to him, not he to the floor.

Someone pulled a feed bag over his head and shoulders. He smelled the grain, and the dust filled his nostrils.

They pulled him up to his knees with the bag. He could tell there were two. Sweat was one, stale and moldy. Underarm was the other, a sweet, cheap deodorant, the cream kind, not drying, just covering the body smell.

Sweat was the hitter. Underarm held the bag.

Blow one: stomach. Blow two: kidneys again. Blow three: face, through the bag. Blow four: stomach. Now face. Now stomach. Now two to the kidneys, quick and hard. The tequila and the food came up into the grain bag.

The hitter grunted as he worked, as though he were in a gym, working on the bag.

Cal fainted.

When he came around, he was bent over a saddle in the tack room like a sack of wet feed, the grain bag hanging loosely and filled with vomit and blood. His hands were handcuffed behind him.

Cal tried to get the corner of the feed bag up by shaking his head. He did not know how long he had been unconscious.

He tried to wriggle out of it, but he could find no leverage, no place to brace. His wriggling caused him to roll sideways, and the bag dropped all the way off.

There was no one in the stable but the horses. He started to slither toward the feed door. There was a harsh laugh. He couldn't see, but he sensed that the two men had come in behind him.

One was moving toward him. Cal rolled over and kicked out one boot heel. It hit testicles. The man doubled over. The second man jumped back, but Cal swung his legs around like an alligator thrashing and hit the man, knocking him sideways.

Cal rolled left as hard as he could, avoided a kick, and made it to his knees by the stable wall. Bristol Boy was slamming into the side of his stall with terrible crashes. The men were dark figures framed by the porch light behind them. They seemed frozen by the rearing horse. Cal rolled. The stall gate crashed open and the big gelding was out, looking wildly at the humans around the floor. The horse's right foot came up, the one with the white ankle, and one man jumped back. His gun went off, deafening Cal. Bristol Boy screamed, crashing through the half-latched stable door with his shoulder, knocking it from the hinges. Cal struggled up the wall to his feet and went behind the horse as fast as he could.

Cal could hear the men's feet pounding across the wood of the stable floor. He ran wildly down the ink black path, the handcuffs holding his arms behind his back making him unbalanced.

"Are you awake?"

It was Vivian. She was wearing burgundy lipstick. Her full lips looked moist and inviting.

Cal tried to smile, but he felt as though his face didn't work.

"They say you can't talk."

He blinked.

"You never talked much anyway."

He blinked.

Vivian's head went up out of sight.

"Why is he blinking? Is there something in his eyes?"

"No," said a woman's voice. "That is a signal he understands you. If he rolls his eyes to the left and right, call us. It means he needs attention."

Vivian leaned back, and her lips closed over his. He could feel her tongue caress his teeth as she kissed him.

"They said I have only two seconds, but you won't be alone. I'll be just down the hall."

Cal was in the swamp, off the path, but not in the water. He could see the men up by the stable, framed by the light. Both had pistols, large automatics, which they held in both hands above their heads, pointed upward. They were looking the wrong way, watching for the car they'd heard.

The summer Cal turned fourteen, he and his father had built an egret habitat. God, how long ago? Thirty-five years? They had put the nests on four-by-fours, set in concrete, in a zigzag line, down through the marsh to where it widened to meet the bay. He could follow the nests in the darkness! Cal tried to recall their locations. His father had mapped and named them. Shangri-la, Capistrano, Majorca, Cozumel, Grand Tortuga, Little Dix, places his father had seen in travel magazines but had never been to.

The water was incredibly cold for September. The trees above never let the marsh warm in the sun the way the bay waters warmed. He was waist deep in a few moments. The darkness was complete. He felt something slither by his leg. Snake? Crab? Eel? He leaned against the wood pillar of the first nest. Capistrano?

Cal heard the crashing then. The noise of men unfamiliar with their terrain. They had one light and he could see it swinging back and forth.

He slipped down, his face next to the nesting box. The first nest still had straw and bits of twig. No eggs. There would be no eggs. It was months too late. Cal let himself down farther and crouched at almost water level and inched forward until he bumped into the second nest. Shangri-la! He fell against it.

The light passed from his left to his right and was disappearing. He knew that when they reached the bay, they'd know he was hiding behind them. *They'll think I am in the woods to the left,* he decided reassuringly. City people are afraid of marshes with crawly things.

He heard crashing brush and saw the light moving crazily through branches and trees like a drunken firefly. *Boom!* A shot was fired. No flash. The pistol must have had a muzzle depressant. But the light was swinging back and forth, looking for a target. *Boom!* A second shot was fired. He felt the pain in his arm. How could they even see him?

Cal went under the water; it was filled with algae and leaf particles, as thick as porridge. He crept along the bottom, finally coming up for air. Now there were three shots. They went wild, ripping through the trees.

Cal felt numb with cold, as though he had been in the water for an hour, but it was minutes. Hardly more. There was pain in his arm near his elbow, and he felt the warmth of blood in the cold water.

The light was back on the trail bobbing up and down.

"Shut up," a voice said. He could make nothing of the voice. No accent. No age. Nothing.

Boom! Another round.

Cal could hear them enter the water.

Cal pushed off from the nest and went instinctively to the deep water, scratching himself on the branches. He was near the bay and the water was deeper, up around his neck. There was sharp pain in his knee, like someone had driven a spike into it. He realized his knee had hit a nest pole. He pulled back and felt his knee tear.

The marsh and woods became silent. Slowly natural sounds resumed. Cal heard crickets and a bobwhite, in Montaigne's field. Then he heard a car motor starting, quite far away.

He waited what he guessed was twenty minutes before starting back to the house. He was shaking all over and strangely his left hand felt numb and tingled. When he tried to close it, the fingers didn't seem to work, as though his body was shutting down like a computer without power. He fell to his knees. He knew one thing. They wanted something. Otherwise, they'd have killed him and been done with it.

2

"Mr. Terrell." The voice was young and hesitant.

"There is good news and bad news." The man speaking gave a little laugh. "We think the paralysis in your left arm and your trouble forming speech is caused by the pressure from a hematoma. That would be manageable. What we can't tell right now is whether there is cell damage to the area within the brain. It will take some time, some repeated MRIs, and possibly an exploratory."

The voice stopped as though he wanted that to sink in.

Cal could now see the man's face. He looked like Woody Allen, a young Woody Allen. He kept squinting at Cal.

"My two worries are your brain and your kidneys. The blows you received could still prove to have caused permanent damage to the kidneys. You have a catheter to assist you in urinating. If you have pain, I want you to signal the nurse."

Cal thought he looked too young to be a doctor.

"You are probably suffering a great deal of general pain. Normally I would sedate you, but we need your brain alert. Can you stand it? Just blink."

Cal blinked rapidly. What was there to say?

The face disappeared.

Cal looked up at the ceiling. It was institutional green and needed washing. Obviously he was not in one of the nation's leading medical facilities. He wondered if this ceiling would be the last thing he would see in his lifetime.

He had had a good run. He had done what he wanted and went where he wanted. Devil take the hindmost, as his mother used to say. He had survived a war and a helicopter crash. He probably should have died in the crash. His mother thought he had wasted the twelve years in the army. He was not even sure why he had stayed that long. Travel, good money, cheap booze, no responsibility. Jesus, there was a life achievement: no responsibility.

Police work had been all right, before he and Vivian split, but lately he didn't care. Really, what did he have to lose, if he died? His marriage was gone; he had no kids, no mother, no father, no brother; and he drank too much. What was the old song they sang in the Manila bars? "We are the battling bastards of Bataan, no momma, no poppa, no Uncle Sam."

There was one real joke, though. He was a homicide detective who wasn't sure who had nearly killed him. Maybe the Mary Jeanne case? Why did they bother? He wasn't getting anywhere anyway.

Cal remembered the day he first saw Mary Jeanne. It seemed like a million years ago, but it was only August. Cal's mother hated August. Her mother and her sister had died in August, struck down, she used to say, by the fevers. His brother, Jimmy, died in August, admittedly 3,000 miles away in the cool late summer of Seattle, but to his mother it was the final evidence of the month's evil. August had taken her baby.

The room was white with white porcelain wall tiles and white tile floors, lit with glaring old-fashioned white lights. Everyone was white and everything was white. White Formica tables, white curtains, and a white cadaver lying on a white plastic sheet.

Actually, Mary Jeanne's skin was the chalky, pale greenish white of the dead. She was oblivious to the four men and a woman inspecting her nude body. The coroner had closed her eyes, but the left lid was up, giving the impression that she was peeking at them.

He and Bobbie were there because it was a white case. Nathaniel and the other blacks wouldn't deal with county cops. Nathaniel was pushing him out anyway. Fifteen years on the Metropolitan Police and he was out in the burbs checking out yet another corpse with a couple of twenty-five-year-old game wardens because he was white, because Bobbie was white.

"The actual cause of death was coronary thrombosis, possibly resulting from ingestion of a sufficient amount of cocaine to cause fibrillation." The medical examiner motioned with his pencil at a dark green garbage bag on the nearby table. "After death, the bag was used to cover the upper part of her torso and was wrapped closely around her face before" — his voice rose on the word *before* — "before she was in the water."

The medical examiner was a thin and nervous-acting man. *Prissy* might be the word. Cal thought the man's head was far too large for his body.

"At some point shortly before her death she may have had intercourse. The vagina is bruised, but there is no semen trace, which suggests no ejaculation or a condom."

Intercourse? The girl looked too young to have intercourse. A child's face on a woman's body. Skipping maybe or playing jacks, not intercourse. If he and Vivian had had a child, the way he wanted that first year, he or she would be a teenager now. He wondered if this girl's father knew that his daughter was on a metal table in a Maryland morgue.

"I found eight bruises. One on her face, on the right side above the jawbone. Another is here, on her left temple, and here" — he pointed to her right arm — "and several along the outside of her forearm as though she were holding her arm up to protect her face from blows."

"When?" asked Cal.

"Maybe twenty-four or thirty-six hours before she was pulled out of the bay."

In D.C. even a baby coroner could do better than that. Cal just closed his eyes.

The medical examiner put down his clipboard and rolled Mary Jeanne onto her stomach. He did it dramatically, like this was the pièce de résistance of his lecture. It was.

Right on her butt. High on the crest of a very luxuriant right buttock was the letter *B*. The capital letter *B*, two inches high, blazing red and puffy against the skin. The *B* was quite ornate and detailed. It left little ridges of scorched flesh at the edges. Someone had centered it perfectly, as though they had used a ruler.

The police officer wearing the tank top sucked air through his teeth. "Jesus," he whispered to no one in particular.

"This was probably done with a hot, rounded metal object," the coroner was droning on. "Maybe a soldering iron. You can see" — he beckoned the police officers closer — "how deep this burn is. I suspect the person who branded her daubed the skin and periodically repeated the motion, to be sure the brand took. It was a very professional job."

"In the branding business," asked Bobbie, "what is a professional job?"

He looked at Bobbie's face. He could see the anger. Bobbie hated the callousness of death and those who worked around it.

The medical examiner ignored her. "The woman was securely restrained, possibly over a chair, so her body could not move much under the branding. But the pain was so great that she did move, and you can see marks where she twisted and wriggled for all she was worth. Her mouth was gagged with some kind of tape."

"If she didn't die in the water," the small cop asked, "is there any evidence that you think came from the death scene?"

"Besides the traces of adhesive around her mouth, we've got two fibers that were hooked under toenails. They look like carpeting. Maybe when she was tortured, she dug her nails into the surface of a rug. We've asked for a lab analysis from Baltimore. We also found some oyster shells and gravel imbedded in her side. We think it's from the road near where she was found." The medical examiner looked around at the police officers. "This must have been awful," he said very softly. "I bet it took forever."

They were at a Krispy Kreme Donut Shop. Cal could see the rows of doughnuts coming off the bake line through the glass windows. The two young investigators in their funky clothes and little round dark glasses were seated on one side of the booth, and Cal on the other. "We are not game wardens, Lieutenant Terrell, we are marine police," the serious one said. *Maybe fish wardens,* Cal thought to himself. He didn't say it.

Bobbie had pulled a chair up in the aisle. She was wearing that tight blue-and-white pullover that left nothing to the imagination. He wondered why she wore such tight clothes. The black officers called her Jugs behind her back. Cal was conscious of her breasts and wanted her to put her jacket on, but he said nothing.

The big marine police officer read off the details to Cal, but all the time he was looking at Bobbie, eyeing her chest. *He's going to make a pass,* Cal thought. *A dumb pass.*

"The body was recovered by our patrol unit near the mouth of South River. It was caught on a mooring off the Bayville seawall Sunday, August third. That's kinda strange."

"How so?" asked Cal.

"It's an old-time black beach community, two miles upstream from Mayo Beach. Mostly retired. There isn't a white person in Bayville. Not a one. All black and most of them are over sixty.

"She could have floated in from the bay with the tide, but we don't think so. We guess that someone put her in the water along the seawall. We think the gravel in her side is from the roadway."

"Did you guys find her?"

"No. Two kids visiting their grandparents found her. They saw a leg sticking up near a mooring buoy. It scared the hell out of them. The tide was low and running when our boat got there. She would have floated out if she hadn't been caught in the mooring cable."

The cop took a sip of his coffee and gave Bobbie a smile with his perfect teeth. "If you follow our idea that she was dumped from the shore, you can speculate that it was in the dark and the person did not know moorings were out there. Everyone around here knows there's a forest of mooring rods twelve feet out.

"There was no ID. She was wearing a white bikini with a Neiman Marcus label and a blouse over it. Two buttons on the blouse were torn off as though it was pulled open. Blouse had a label from Talbots. The bag over her head was a Hefty brand garbage bag. They're marked and we'll send them for lab analysis. We'll ship them down, if it's your case."

"Her assailant pulled on her bathing suit bottoms after branding her?" asked Bobbie.

"I guess you're right," the big Maryland cop said. "When our boat pulled her out, she was wearing the top and bottom."

"Neiman Marcus," said Bobbie. "Nice stuff."

"The FBI returned on the fingerprints late yesterday," the cop continued, reading his notes. "They found a no-contest plea to a disorderly conduct charge for one Mary Jeanne Turner." The cop spelled out her name.

"Social Security number two two three two nine oh five oh six, born September twelfth, nineteen seventy-eight." *Social Security number is Virginia,* Cal thought. *So the kid was from around here.* The blond investigator's eyes were squinting at his clipboard, "Arrested D.C. February sixteenth, nineteen ninety-seven. Address at the time of arrest, Seventeen sixty-three Columbia Road, Northwest D.C. Superior Court eighty-six dash three six oh one."

Cal pictured the building at 1763. It had once been a big heroin pad back in the '70s, a raid a week.

But Columbia Road was yuppified, and he was pretty sure 1763 had been condoed. Maybe ten years ago.

"Why wasn't she stripped by crabs?" Cal asked.

The two Maryland cops went silent.

"You must be from around here," the blond one said.

"Calvert County."

The blond investigator nodded. "That bothered us too. I figured that she was dumped not long before she was spotted, sometime early Sunday. We put the tide in our report because you can never be sure, but this has been a good crab season. Shit, I've seen crabs strip a hundred-pound deer carcass in two hours. Little ones swam right in the mouth."

Cal could hear Bobbie make a choking sound.

"Anyone in the area see anything?" Cal asked.

"Nope. We canvassed. Nothing. Zip. There are no houses close by to those ramps or the service road. We flashed her photo across the whole shore area up to Mayo Beach, but nobody made her or saw any other white woman. It was a nice day too, so everybody was out and about. Like I say, a white woman would have been noticed."

The detectives munched doughnuts in silence. Cal had put away his notebook. He was thinking of the girl. More than likely a hooker, one freak show too many.

"If he just wanted to mutilate her, why the ornate *B*?" said one detective.

"Maybe," Bobbie offered, "maybe it was a sex thing, and he didn't figure she'd die."

The nurse put a dropper to his lips. It was broth. He hadn't realized how hungry he was. "Slowly, slowly," she said. She gave him little squares of bread to eat and switched to a spoon when she realized he could accept the broth.

She put a pad in his hand. "If you need to know something. Try to write."

It was very hard. His left hand only partially responded, and he had to lock his hand around the pencil and hold the pad above his face. The letters were shaky.

Bobbie here? he wrote.

"Nobody here by that name. Your wife is the only one here," the nurse said.

He wrote, *Wife?* on the pad.

The nurse leaned down, and her face looked alarmed. "She said she was your next of kin."

He had thought he dreamed that Vivian had kissed him, but it must have been her for real. He'd never changed the insurance form.

"Others want to come," the nurse said. "But Dr. Griffin forbids it."

Cal scratched a question mark.

"Dr. Richard Griffin is the best neurosurgeon in Maryland," she said as though that answered his question. She leaned over him, and her expression showed her impatience.

He wrote no more.

He wondered where Bobbie was. For some reason, he couldn't think when he had last seen her, but as he fell asleep he could remember the stadium parking lot and the snow. That was the night he inherited Roberta Marie Short. They were making a buy in the Redskins stadium parking lot. When was it? Six years ago? Eight years? Eight years! Definitely eight, when they were both in Narcotics. She was brand-new, six months out of the academy. "You're the only guy I can trust to work with her," the squad commander had said. "Don't hit on her!"

They had worked the stadium three home games in a row with Redskins security, looking for a guy moving party drugs from a van with Michigan plates.

The guy finally made his move at the Hawk and Dove after the Giants game. The Redskins had edged New York, 17–14, and everybody was getting a buzz on, cold from the snow and warming up fast.

"I saw you at the game." What he meant was, he'd seen the young policewoman's nose. Cal had showed Bobbie how to make her nose look raw, like a cocaine user, rubbing it with alcohol and red lipstick. It had worked more than once.

But the peddler said his stuff was in his van back in the stadium parking lot. He was just in from Detroit. "I don't know the local customs."

They gave him a ride to the stadium. The parking lot was totally empty now, the stadium dark.

The man entered the van through the back doors, and they could see a flashlight. Cal thought that it was funny he didn't use the interior lights. By then it was snowing hard. Bobbie moved forward with the money in one hand, her gun held down behind her with the other, just as Cal had taught her, ready to grab the packet and fade left, so Cal could call the warning.

Cal saw her hand with the money go up like slow motion and come down. He dropped into a shooting crouch. "Police! Police!" he yelled.

"Out of the van and on the ground." He was holding his shield high, with his gun in his other hand. "Out of the car," he repeated.

It went bad then. For a fraction of a second, Bobbie moved right instead of left, blocking Cal.

Before Cal heard the shot, the bullet hit Bobbie as though somebody had taken a baseball bat and knocked her down. She was in the snow, motionless, her arms flung wide, her pistol still in her right hand.

The shooter was out of the van aiming for a second shot at Bobbie, and for an instant — just an instant — Cal could see Bobbie's eyes staring into that muzzle.

He squeezed the trigger firmly, the way he had been taught when he took pictures of wild birds for his father, quick but sure. "One single motion," his father used to say. "One single motion."

The hole appeared in the man's forehead. It looked like a priest had daubed him with ashes for Lent. He went backward, his arms flung wide next to Bobbie. His gun never discharged. The medical examiner said he was dead before he hit the ground.

For the first few years afterward, Bobbie dogged his every moment. It was as though by saving her life, he had acquired her. After Narcotics, she went to Sex Crimes and he went to Homicide. When she got bored in Sex Crimes, she got Cal to make Nathaniel take her up to Homicide. She introduced Cal to every man she ever dated, once getting him up in the middle of the night to move out a boyfriend who'd turned unpleasant.

Her father had come from Dallas to visit after the shooting, a nice man, wealthy and confident but fearful for his only daughter. "I know she'll be all right as long as she's working with you," he said. "Will you watch out for her?" In effect, he willed Cal not only his daughter's safety but her phobias as well.

There was a problem about the whole thing. Bobbie never spoke of it; Cal didn't either. The doper had been nothing but a holdup man; he didn't even have any drugs. Cal knew he should have spotted it. Never would they have used a sting on a holdup man. Cal was the veteran, she was the rookie. He should have spotted it! So he had tolerated her all this time, like he had tolerated Jimmy, like a kid brother. It was one of the main reasons he had no amorous interest in Bobbie. Thoughts of Bobbie and Jimmy had no romantic cadence.

A long time ago Cal had stopped talking to Bobbie, not more than he had to. He wondered if she noticed. Bobbie had a way of talking right past you anyway, as though you weren't necessary to the conversation.

In a way, Roberta Marie Short wore on him, like a partner in a marriage in which there is no divorce. In the beginning they had been very close. He could remember Bobbie night after night on stakeouts, one leg thrown up against the dash and, in her manly way of sitting, reading German poetry to him out loud, debating the plight of women in America, or extolling the qualities of good wine. She was literate and interesting, lively and beautiful, the product of private schools and art studies in Florence.

But lately she often came across whiny and complaining, a thirty-five-year-old woman whose life had run aground. Though she wore on him when they were together, he invariably began to miss her when they were apart, and he realized that he looked forward each day to seeing her dark eyes and wry smile. Maria Callas in a squad car.

She had become a police officer, she told him, filled with the fervor of social service, only to find out what Cal had learned as well: it was coarse work done by crude men. Bobbie's father begged her to quit, but she had persevered.

Bobbie spent her money on expensive clothes and useless boyfriends. She had a fantastic body to display the clothes on. Her father's money paid for a lifestyle her salary could not afford, and it attracted the useless men. The men she chose invariably had two characteristics: they played the guitar and they were having trouble coping with the twentieth century.

Police work had suited her at first. Bobbie had a sharp, inquisitive mind and a tall, athletic body. After she was shot, she began working out three evenings a week and competed in marathons, triathlons, and mountain-bike races. Once on a bet, she'd gone to the D.C. Fire Department Testing Facility and carried an inert 160-pound man up three flights of stairs on her back.

Saying at the Politics and Prose bookstore that she was the first woman police officer shot in the line of duty had been a conversation-stopper in those days, like saying she was a stripper or an astronaut. But now her being a police officer was old hat to her friends and old hat to her, and she didn't know how to move on. If she quit now, she once told Cal, she would have to admit to her father that he had been right. She could never do that.

Now, lying in the hospital, Cal wondered where she was. She would have been good at the farm with her ankle gun and her kickboxing. She would have come through. He knew that.

3

"Can you hear me on this phone?" said Vivian. "I have to whisper. . . . They think he's getting worse. They drained the blood clot. They didn't want to, but they thought a blood vessel in his brain would burst. . . . Now? Now he's back in his room. . . . What would that mean? That would mean a stroke."

Silence.

"Jesus. You're losing your mind! He's half dead now, what more do you want?" she asked petulantly. "This man cannot walk! This man cannot talk! . . . That's right, he can't talk. Can't —"

Vivian was silent for a long time. Finally she said, "Last night, when they thought he was going to die" — her voice caught for a moment — "they asked me what his religion was and if he had a living will."

She was silent again.

"No. I'm not getting sentimental."

Cal heard a telephone receiver slam. He wondered who Vivian was talking to.

The newspapers immediately dubbed it the Reggae Club massacre, except for the editorial pages, which called it Martin Cameron's worst nightmare. It was a drive-by. But in the way of Washington crime, it didn't quite measure up to a Los Angeles drive-by, sort of a tinny copy of the real thing. The shooter, in the BMW, started firing with a MAC 10 just as his car turned the corner from Benning Road. Cal guessed that the shooter was aiming his MAC 10 at the silver Jaguar and managed to hit several young bystanders in the crowded parking lot of the Reggae Club.

The attack came two nights after Mary Jeanne was identified, landing on Cal and Bobbie's plate by the chance of shift rotation. The crime scene stretched a city block long, south along Oklahoma Avenue from the parking lot toward the stadium and marshes of the Anacostia River. More than a dozen victims, the nearness to the Robert F. Kennedy Stadium, and the wild scene quickly took it from the eleven o'clock news to national television.

Emergency services had rigged giant floodlights, and detectives were marking the location of the spent cartridges with burning emergency flares. With the Capitol dome rising twenty-five blocks to the west, the whole thing looked like a painting of the British burning Washington.

A historic heat wave, even for Washington, had brought twenty-one straight days of temperatures over 100, the weatherman said, with no respite in sight. The heat hung over the scene, the air thick with it and with thousands of tiny gnats nurtured by the river dampness.

Cal moved to where the ambulance team was working, stepping neatly over the chalk marks of the fallen victims. The target of the attack, a nineteen-year-old black man, lay slumped half out of the driver's seat of the Jaguar coupe.

A thousand yards across open parking lots, distinguishable through the trees only by a different circle of floodlights, Cal could see where the shooter ran out of luck by the stadium ticket windows.

An area patrol managed to stop and get off one round with a 12-gauge riot gun. It tore out the rear window and the BMW went out of control, careening across the open space and smashing into the stadium's entrance for upper-deck ticketholders. The driver had been declared dead at the scene.

"That's all we need." Bobbie's voice startled him.

Cal followed her gaze. The mayor's Lincoln Town Car nosed through the barricades and came in behind two ambulances. Martin Cameron was out before it stopped.

Cameron spotted the Channel 9 cameras and elbowed his way in front of them with only a nod to the police officers.

Angrily Cal put the bullhorn to his lips. "Eight fifty-two, pull your car in front of that barricade," but 852 wasn't fast enough and Channel 9's truck slipped in behind the mayor's car.

The television reporter wasn't going to miss a bet. She was clearly ready to go live, and Cal could see the techs in the van raising the cherry picker. The woman thrust a mike in the mayor's face and literally pulled around the soundman.

"Mr. Mayor, have the police told you what caused this shooting?"

Cameron affixed a serious and determined look as he scanned the macabre scene.

"It's early, Susan. They're still sorting this out, but it's street crews. The gangs. Probably a territory fight. I would guess the Crypts were involved and maybe the Benning Terrace Crew." He swept his hand toward the stadium and the river beyond. "If I were Moses tonight, Susan, I would let the waters close over here and cleanse this sin," painting the unlikely picture of the garbage-strewn, sleepy old Anacostia River roiling over its banks and rushing toward downtown Washington with its cleansing power.

Susan, the TV woman, looked a little nervously at Cameron, as though the mayor might have slipped a cog. But Cameron hauled in his rhetoric as he often had in the pulpit. Having now ensured that he would be in the lead of the broadcast, he continued, "We need to retake this city. Like Beirut or Bosnia, we have to end this senseless killing! Two-thirds of these youngsters were here to have a good time, but one-third rule the streets. That one-third will be stopped!"

"What a piece of work," Bobbie whispered. "For all Cameron knew, the Martians landed and gunned the place."

Cal smiled. "Honey, there are no Martians living on Benning Road."

The mayor now turned and strode toward them, a big, agile man, muscular and trim at fifty. He was the son of a sharecropper, great-grandson of slaves, the first man in his family who had not had to work stooping over. Now he was the first Republican mayor in Washington, D.C., a historically Democratic city with virtually no local Republicans. Cal marveled at the amazing strength of a Republican president's coat-tails.

Cameron had grown up fifteen miles from Cal, in St. Mary's County, and like Cal and other southern Marylanders, Cameron had come to Washington to find work. Cameron took the strength built picking his father's tobacco and molded it to become the most powerful running back Morgan State had ever had. He'd gone to the Redskins for six seasons, played right there in the stadium to the cheers of the fathers and older brothers of the teenagers killed tonight.

From the playing field he went briefly to the pulpit and finally to politics. After Clarence Thomas, he was the most prominent black conservative in the Republican Party, with a voice like James Earl Jones and a build like O. J. Simpson. And like O. J. Simpson, athletics had made Cameron graceful and quick, as good on the dance floor as he was on the tennis court.

It was Cameron's magnificent presence that had recommended him to Philip Winston a decade ago. Winston, the cerebral architect of the GOP's urban economic plan, built a bridge to black voters on Cameron's shoulders. At the same time Winston took the White House, Cameron became mayor.

At first the whites loved Martin Cameron. He had rid them of Marion Barry. They had thought he would keep the blacks in line, keep docile the maids, laborers, government clerks, and cabdrivers who ran the nation's capital.

But when he finally achieved power, Cameron had fooled them. He ignored the developers who financed his campaign, ignored their plans to displace blacks and bring whites back to the city, fought for black housing and black jobs. He taunted the power structure as well, challenged the whites, insulted their values, and laughed when they excoriated him.

Now he was in trouble for the first time. *That is why he is here tonight,* Cal thought, *here in this desolate parking lot, here in the floodlights, trying to turn this tragedy around.* The city was out of hand, black and white agreed, gang violence is drowning us. Why isn't something being done?

Cameron's way with women didn't help him. Unlike Marion Barry, he never used drugs, never drank, kept his body as he had when he was playing football. But women were a different story. Cameron was drawn to them, young and old, and they to him. He liked to touch women and flirt with them, to pat their arms and hold their hands. For a woman to spend a few moments with him was to find his arm around her waist, a hand grasped and squeezed.

Cameron made little attempt to hide it. He had the flamboyance of a great athlete. Women had flocked around him when he was running the football, and he had come to expect it. It was his due.

But the proclivity kept the gossip columns filled, resulted in strange, unexplained absences from duty, and, possibly most politically dangerous, infuriated the white men who had backed him.

As he walked toward them, Cal could see that Cameron was riveting Bobbie with his gaze.

"You mind if I borrow these officers?" Cameron said to Cal, grabbing Collins and Bobbie and pushing them in front of the cameras. The eleven o'clock news wasn't going to show a black mayor talking with a middle-aged white male cop, not in Washington, D.C.

Walking with the television reporter, Collins gave a rundown of the attack. Cameron stayed in step, leaning in closely so he'd get in every frame. The audience would know that the mayor of Washington listened to the men and women on the line.

"Have we got everything we need down here? How are we handling the injured?" Cameron asked.

"We're moving them out pretty fast." Collins's head bobbed up and down. The ambulance teams had been so slow to respond that one person nearly bled to death, but the ambulance service was Cameron's baby, and Collins was not about to criticize it on TV.

Cameron questioned them about when the call came in and how many officers were on the scene. The inquisition didn't take thirty seconds.

"I know you-all want to get back to work."

Cameron proceeded to lead the camera crew through the scene, scuffing the chalk marks, trampling the carefully laid-out shell casings, and giving the very pictures Cal knew the U.S. Attorney wouldn't want.

Cameron circled the scene once. He never stopped talking and the TV reporter never had to ask a question. He finally ended by suggesting a camera angle. "Get up high there, shoot down on the ambulances." Dutifully the crew, now in his grasp, put their cherry picker up by the club's wall.

He was motioning for Cal to join him at the car. Cal recognized Ophelia Cameron in the backseat, wearing one of those dramatic wide-brimmed summer hats Vivian always favored. Even in the darkened car, Ophelia Cameron was a knockout. Everyone always asked why Cameron played around when what he had at home was so sensational. Cal had never heard a good answer.

"You still work for Nathaniel, right?" Cameron asked, never casting his wife a glance.

"Yes, sir," Cal answered.

"Is this too small a shooting for the illustrious chief of Homicide?" Cameron roared at Cal. "The chief of Homicide I made out of whole cloth."

Ophelia reached out and put her hand on Cameron's arm as though to quiet him. He was shrill now, and the touch did not seem to calm him.

"How come there was no patrol or security at that club tonight?"

"I don't know yet," Cal said. "The area car told us he was ordered two weeks ago to increase his loop across the bridge, so he was at the wrong place for sure. The district commander told me he had no idea six hundred kids were going to be here."

"Shit!" Cameron said, not to Cal, but in general. "How many people you think got shot tonight?"

"Right now, if you count the shooter and his driver, we'll hit at least seventeen dead or seriously wounded."

Cameron shook his head back and forth. He said *shit* again, very slowly.

They crowded in, the car's tiny wall lights casting little glows over the mayor and the woman. Cal sat on a jump seat.

"Is D.C. General the best?"

"Best?"

"Most victims! Tonight!" Cameron said impatiently.

"Oh. Sure. We've transported six already."

Cameron hit a number on a phone console between the jump seats. There was a sound of a phone ringing, then a sleepy voice answered, "Wha —"

"H.C.? Get on over to D.C. General emergency. I'll meet you there. Also get Channel Four, Five, and Seven. I've got Nine. Set up some kind of telephone number parents can call to check on their kids. Yeah, coordinate with —" He turned to Cal. "What's your name, fella?"

"Terrell."

"Yeah, Terrell."

H. C. Johnson was the city's health and human services director. Once he heard the mayor's voice, he never asked a question. He didn't even ask, What shooting? Cal was impressed.

"How many dead?" Cameron asked.

"I figure the driver's dead, the main target's dead, probably the girl with the target. The area car said the shooter might live. We'll end up with three or four dead."

"What happened?"

"We don't know, but my guess is, you were right, it's a shootout over territory. The shooter and his target were both in fifty-thousand-dollar cars. Neither of them stolen. I've got Juvenile and Narcotics teams working. If the shooter hadn't been using an automatic weapon, we'd be dealing with three or four."

"Take this number." Cameron handed Cal a preprinted card with a mobile phone number. "Call me at the hospital administrator's office in — how much, Rodney?"

The burly driver turned halfway round. "Twenty."

"In twenty minutes give me an update. Don't patch through the department." By cutting out the department, the mayor made himself the sole news source. Cal couldn't help grinning.

"And call up Mr. Nathaniel Bench and ask him why the mayor can get to a scene where our children are dying and he can't."

Cal called Nathaniel from his car, getting Dispatch to put it through on the telephone. Ylena answered, her soft German-accented voice filled with alarm.

"Where's the boss?"

"He's out with his brother. I was in no mood to go. They always stay out too late for me."

"If he calls, tell him Cameron is on the warpath, okay?"

"Oh yes, I saw on the news."

Cal told Bobbie to call Nathaniel on his beeper. He didn't mind saving his ass, but he didn't want to talk to him about it.

It was funny how they found it, after Cameron and the press had left, in the dawn's early light. Actually Bobbie found it, five hundred yards out, while walking to where she had been shot that time.

"You better come out here," she had whispered into the radio. "There's something strange."

Nearly 1,500 feet from where the Jaguar and its driver came under fire, beyond the overpass where the subway line skirts the stadium, five feet into the tall grass of the river marsh, a second shooter had knelt and fired seven rounds of 7.62mm ammunition. The bright new cartridges lay like sparkling pieces of gold in the hazy early sun. "They've been fired in the last few hours," Bobbie said, holding one in a plastic-gloved hand. "You can still smell the cordite."

The shooter had been lazy or stupid, leaving the cartridges lying in a half semicircle just as a weapon with a left ejection port would spew them out. Maybe he thought they would be covered by the grass. The shooter had chosen that spot for the same reason the holdup man had chosen that end of the parking lot the night Bobbie was shot so many years ago. There were no floodlights there, only dark shadows.

The soft ground showed that the shooter knelt on one knee to fire and rested the butt of a rifle on the ground to pull himself up, putting enough weight on it so that a dent on the butt plate left an imprint in the dirt.

"Why here? Why another shooter?" Cal asked, turning back toward the Reggae Club.

For the next two hours they worked the question, mapping the fields of fire, examining slugs in both the BMW and Jaguar. Unless the second gunman could shoot around telephone poles and the corner of a building, there was only one conclusion: he was in the grass aiming for the shooter in the BMW.

"But how did he know the BMW was going to turn toward the stadium? It could have gone down C Street," Cal asked out loud.

And Bobbie, in the way she had over the years of finishing his thoughts, answered, "That's the point. He was a sniper. He was there to kill the shooter. Our man had to know ahead of time that he's going to have a target near the stadium."

For a long time they stood looking at each other.

4

"Cal, honey." It was Vivian. "Are you awake?"

He stared at her.

"Do you remember where your pistols are?"

Cal fluttered his eyes violently.

"Shush. Shush. I just want them so no one steals them. Jeremiah's watching the house, but the state police said he can't go in, they'll get them for me." She reached down and touched his forehead. Her fingertips felt warm and soft. "Trust me."

Trust Vivian?

She gave him a pad and a little pencil.

Under sink, he wrote. *Rag pail.* He knew what she asked didn't make much sense, but he was in no position to argue.

He wondered if he had ever really trusted Vivian. He lusted for her, yes, loved her, maybe. Trust? He hadn't trusted her when they were married. When push came to shove, Vivian had her own agenda. He remembered when he left her, when he walked out, his greatest feeling had not been sadness or anger, but relief.

Vivian had ridden into the yard the first time they met, bold as brass. "I see you board horses." She had just moved from California, she said, worked for NBC, and was looking for an occasional riding companion and a place to keep her horse.

"I keep Victor at Green Landing, you know, the Montaigne estate, but it's awfully expensive," Vivian said, waving her hand toward the bay.

They had ridden that day along the Old High Road. Vivian was very good in the saddle, more elegant than Cal, strong and assured, rising and falling in a flawless post, an athlete. He had taken her horse in for $100 a month and cost of feed.

Over most of the winter she would come, without calling, and ask if Cal wanted to ride. Cal couldn't figure out how she knew he would be there; maybe Jeremiah told her. They would work Cal's horses or Vivian's gelding. At first he really hadn't grasped who she was, but one night he saw her on television, doing a stand-up outside of federal court. Later, she told him stories about covering Hollywood for television and he told her about being a cop. She liked cops, the way a lot of women do, the suggestion of danger and violence.

Cal didn't recall that Vivian ever asked a question, but he soon found himself talking about Vietnam and how he ended up a police officer. She listened well, which had made her a good reporter. If Vivian wanted to, she could charm your socks off.

One day he was reading the *Washington Post,* and there she was, in a six-column picture, standing in the NBC newsroom, to the left of Tom Brokaw.

Vivian Welldon, the story said, is the daughter of one of California's oldest political families, a former anchorwoman for Los Angeles affiliate KPIX who is now taking over the justice department for NBC.

Cal asked what "oldest political family" meant, and Vivian laughed. "It means they're dead or broke."

That first winter he was alone on the farm in a weekend snowstorm. Cal had not expected anyone. The television said it would be a blizzard. Washington people usually didn't come to the country when it snowed, but just after noon Vivian came through the flakes wearing a wide hat and a blue cape.

They rode for an hour, watching the footing of the steel-shod horses, giggling over the cars abandoned up on Route 4. Vivian's teeth were chattering when they got back, and she was shivering.

"Can I give you some coffee or a drink before you go home?"

They drank Wild Turkey straight with no ice, more than one, leaning back in the wooden chairs and talking as close as family.

Vivian had pulled off her poncho and sweater but water had run down her neck and her blouse was soaked, outlining her breasts. The cold had made her nipples stand out. Cal noticed Vivian for the first time, really noticed her.

"Do you have something I can change into?" Vivian had said. "I'm freezing."

That was the first time Vivian had been in the house and she walked through, following Cal, looking, touching the silver and dishes, reading the titles in the library.

"Why so many books on birds?"

"My father was an ornithologist" — Cal paused — "for the Smith-sonian. I studied migratory birds in college. Some of the books are mine."

"Do your parents live here?"

"Nope. They've gone on, died within a year of each other." He didn't say they died within a year of Jimmy. It was strange; except for him, the Terrell family had disappeared.

He gave Vivian one of his shirts and took her to his mother's room to change. Later he had heard the music. Vivian had found his parents' old 78s.

"God!" he heard Vivian exclaim. "This Victrola is worth a fortune! Listen to that tone!"

As he entered the living room, Vivian stood in only a bra and riding breeches, fiddling with the record player. Suddenly she swept Cal into her arms. The Victrola was playing Glenn Miller's "Danny Boy," and they danced and swirled around the room for twenty minutes, stopping only to put the needle back to the right groove. He had felt good in Vivian's arms, warm and excited, like at a college dance.

They made love on the floor, the wood hardly softened by the old Oriental rug, a draft coming in through the fireplace. He'd had a dog named Roger then, a Chesapeake, who came in and licked her ear. "Jesus, that's erotic," she'd teased him later. "How'd you train your dog to lick the girl's ear?"

She had stayed until the plows came Monday, wearing his old shirts and his mother's riding breeches and his big wool socks.

Vivian said the storm was an omen. They'd become lovers. She knew it. He thought it was strange too. Glenn Miller's "Danny Boy" had been his parents' favorite song. They danced to it every New Year's Eve, his father in his old evening jacket and his mother in the dress she always wore to the Terrapin Club.

As the months passed, he and Vivian grew more to be happy lovers, whispering and laughing, sharing confidences and tribulations. They would go to the National Gallery or the string quartet at the Library of Congress, lunches in Georgetown and sometimes on the wharf, or theater at the Kennedy or the National.

Once they flew to Paris on a whim, went to a little hotel on the Left

Bank where Vivian had stayed when she was at the Sorbonne. Another time they spent a week in Cozumel, tearing another hole in his savings. Cal rented a helicopter one day and took her to one of the little sand keys, where they swam nude and scuba dived until the sun went down. He had scared and impressed her then, maneuvering the helicopter back through the tropical night and onto Cozumel's main runway, chatting with the tower and dodging around a Mexicali Air flight.

It was the life Cal had dreamed about in the army but never lived. With Vivian, his life was sophisticated and elegant, a giant step away from the crudeness of his work. The first time he had met Vivian's brother, Charley, was for tea at the Four Seasons. He could tell it thrilled Vivian to present her police officer. "Cal's the top detective in Narcotics," she had said.

"Read that, one of the detectives in Narcotics," Cal said.

Charley was a lobbyist-lawyer with a house in Georgetown. Often Vivian would bring Cal to Charley's dinner parties. Before each party she would tell Cal what to wear, how it would go, not patronizingly, he felt, but gently, as though she wanted Cal to have a good time.

When she had said she wanted to marry Cal, Charley had not been so warm. "You're really worlds apart. Vivian is a brilliant and talented woman. She's still exploring the world, don't tie yourselves up in marriage," Charley had said to Cal one night. "You two will not wear well over time." Cal had ignored him and they forged ahead, Charley or no Charley.

In the end Charley wouldn't even give his sister his home for the wedding. They were married at St. John's, the little Episcopal church across the park from the White House, and Cal and Vivian paid for the reception at the fancier Hay-Adams hotel.

Cal had still been flying in the reserves then, and Vivian had made him wear his dress uniform. Charley had been surprised. "I didn't know you were a major," he had said at the reception. "I was in ROTC, but I injured my leg playing squash. I always thought I missed something."

"The North Vietnamese were accelerating the army advancement program in those days," Cal told him, laughing. "You would have had all sorts of opportunities."

They had moved to a town house in Woodley Park, virtually on Vivian's money. She brought her family's rich furniture from California. She decorated the house herself and did the entertaining, sort of positioning Cal like a piece of art, where the guests could enjoy him.

There were already little cracks appearing though, tiny anxieties, disputes over what sort of life they would lead. They went to the farm less and less and for shorter and shorter times. Being a prominent Washington television correspondent was a full-time job, day and night.

After a while, Vivian patronized him. He was a trophy, a person from a hard world that she could show off, like she was a rich woman fucking the chauffeur.

Vivian ran their lives, dragging him to a million dinner parties and social events. She put calendars on his dresser, showing where he should be on what days and what he should wear. He still had the suits she'd bought him in those years. She viewed his job as an inconvenience. When he called from a case running late and long, she'd pout. "Couldn't somebody else do that?"

Vivian rewarded him with sex when she was happy, and punished him by silently withdrawing when something didn't please her.

As she grew more important in television, she seemed to exclude him from all things consequential, as though they were beyond his grasp. At parties, she worried that he would say or do something that would embarrass her. By the last year they went hardly anywhere together. Vivian brought him only to things that were necessary, dinners or places where his absence would show there was trouble in paradise.

Cal pulled the pin, out of pride really, like quitting your job before you get fired. He took his stuff to the farm right before Thanksgiving five years ago and never came back.

Edward St. Denis had always been in the wings, a friend of Charley's, "President Winston's alter ego," Charley used to say. "The man who delivered California for Winston," Vivian once said on television. Vivian moved into Edward's town house within three weeks of Cal's leaving.

5

"Mrs. St. Denis, we're doing all we can," said a man. "I'm not going to lie to you. The brain is very tricky. It may be that the pressure of the blood on the surface of the brain did some damage that I can't see. Once we get his fever down again and a new MRI, we'll be able to give you a better assessment."

Then there were words Cal could not hear.

Cal lay motionless under the sweltering covers and kept his eyes closed. They obviously thought he was asleep.

"If there are other family members . . . He keeps writing the name *Bobbie*."

"That's crazy. She's . . ."

Cal couldn't hear what they said about Bobbie.

After a while, he heard Vivian say, "No. Calvert has no one else." Their voices faded then, as though they were walking away. When Cal awoke again, it was light, but early and gray, which made the green walls even more dreary. He tried to say "quick brown fox" to himself, but his upper lip and tongue felt swollen and enormous, and he sounded like Muhammad Ali after the brain damage.

He wrote Vivian's name on the pad. "She went to the White House," the nurse said.

The day after the Reggae Club massacre, Cal didn't awaken until afternoon. The old farmhouse was sweltering. He had fallen into bed too exhausted to pull the shades against the sun or crank the air conditioner in the bedroom.

At 3 A.M. Nathaniel had taken over the case, angry and chagrined at being caught out by the mayor. "You could have at least said I was on my way," he bitterly told Cal.

"I didn't have a chance to say shit, Nathaniel. Your buddy the mayor did all the talking. I thought I was doing you a favor by tracking you down!"

"Just finish up your report and give your papers to Collins," Nathaniel said, averting his eyes. "I'll take it from here."

"That idiot?"

Nathaniel grimaced. "I know he won't get anywhere, but he'll make the mayor of the city of Washington happy and that's what we're going to do."

After finishing the report, he'd downed tequila shooters at Stoneys, playing the jukebox and fuming over Nathaniel. In the days when they had been partners, they had been so close that they knew each other's thoughts, but now Nathaniel saw Cal as one of the obstructionists, trying to resist Nathaniel's efforts to close cases and make statistical records.

Cal lay in bed, knowing if he moved his head too fast it would be worse. He lay staring at the ceiling. There were two water stains by the window. The room needed to be painted.

The Reggae Club shooting made headlines in the first Saturday editions of the *Washington Post* and *Washington Times*. Television was going crazy. Every news outlet had a different version. The Road Runners from Division Avenue were fighting for turf. Jamaicans gunned the whole place to establish control of the Benning Terrace Crew. The Colombians had hired gunmen from New York to collect from gang guys in D.C.

The *Washington Times* had a rare front page editorial calling for an end to violence and the *Washington Post* said the Speaker of the House wanted hearings on whether Washington needed to come under martial law.

The mayor was all over every story. He had gone to the hospitals, prayed at the AME Zion Church on Division Avenue with the family of one youngster, and ended up in front of D.C. General with that idiot Collins, who was trying one more time to kiss the mayor's ass while standing up.

Now as Cal lay in bed, turning it over in his mind, he was glad he held the sniper lead out of the reports and from Nathaniel. The mayor would have leaked it in a heartbeat, telling the sniper that they found his spot.

He wanted that for himself. He wanted to work it. Later, he could fix the report. Kid gangs in D.C. were depraved and lethal, but he'd never heard of one of them sending an assassin to take out the gunman in a drug shooting. They weren't that organized. Who then? And why?

He got up and threw the undershorts he was wearing into the hamper and went down to make coffee, naked, letting the breeze on the first floor cool his body.

He wondered where the dogs were. They must be dying to go out, but he couldn't hear them, which seemed strange. In the kitchen he went straight to the coffee maker, pulling out the coffee and beginning to spoon it into the filter. He noticed that his hands were shaking.

The voice startled him. "Well, look at you. I forgot you like to roam around in the altogether. A fine figure of man, I might add."

"What in the hell!" Cal said.

There was Vivian, sitting in the corner chair by the window, her long, tanned legs on the windowsill, sipping iced tea as cool as if she'd never left.

"You ready to pick up where we left off five years ago?" Vivian asked. "I'll get naked." She reached out to grab his thigh, but he jumped back.

"How did you get in here?"

"The key, remember, over the doorjamb in the stable. By the way, your dogs looked a little thirsty, so I gave them some water and let them out. Was Daddy a little under the weather when he got home?"

Cal ignored her. He went back upstairs and put on some swim trunks and a T-shirt. "What are you doing here anyway?" he yelled down.

"Waiting for you, sweetheart. Waiting for you."

When he got downstairs again, he finished making coffee without talking to her, walking around her as though she weren't there.

Vivian wasn't fazed. She sipped iced tea, gazing lazily around the old kitchen. "Something has Edward all wrought up. My God, he was out half the night." She nodded toward the paper. "I was looking to see what it might have been."

Silence.

"I see you were busy," she said, thumping the front page. "The taciturn Lieutenant Terrell would not comment!"

Silence.

Vivian kept right on. "Of course, Edward won't tell me anything either! We were at dinner and his beeper went off. He went running out of the restaurant."

Silence.

"Maybe he was on the same thing you were?"

Silence.

Finally Cal spoke, working on the coffee, not turning around.

"Honey, I don't think the White House gives a shit how many black kids kill each other! Meanwhile, I've had only four hours' sleep. I have a tequila headache, and I have a lot of chores. And also, please don't come in my house when I'm asleep! We aren't married anymore."

"My goodness, Cal. I gave you my best eight years. You're so ungrateful!"

He petulantly pulled the coffee pot off the maker before it was done, burning himself.

Cal looked at her over the rim of the cup. He hadn't seen her in — what? Two years? She was looking good, the way the rich look, as though everything was perfect. Vivian took off her dark glasses. He could see her hazel eyes with pale centers that gave her a dreamy look. They were set in a quite strong face with high cheekbones and smooth skin that never needed makeup. She had hardly aged since Cal first saw her. With her golden hair and her golden tan, she was a golden woman of the Golden State. It was the look and the skin of the wealthy and the well cared for.

"Vivian, what is all this?"

"Let's go for a ride, like old times."

"I don't have time."

"Sure you do. Go for a ride with me, and I'll do half the chores."

They rode south, ducking on and off Route 4. August in southern Maryland, hot and hazy, nothing stirring, the heat making little wavy lines over the meadow. They cantered a lot to keep the bugs away. He gave her Bristol Boy, so she could lead. Bristol Boy wouldn't ride behind Comet. Ever.

Vivian was silent, riding as she always did, erect, like a cavalry officer. With the wide hat, she reminded him of his mother. He expected to turn in his saddle and see Jimmy bouncing along behind on Zombie, uncomfortable and angry. Cal's mother made Jimmy ride, but he hated it. He did it because he was Momma's baby.

Cal and Vivian bought cold bottled water up at the 7-Eleven outside of Solomons and took the horses down to the little estuary east of the navy dock, letting them wade out in the water to keep the flies off.

She sat by the bank, her shoes off, dangling her bare feet in the water, not looking at Cal. The serious Vivian.

"I know this probably isn't the right time to bother you, but I need your help."

Cal didn't answer.

"Something's gone awry with Edward."

"With Edward?"

"With us. With our marriage." She stopped to let that sink in. "I know this sounds silly, but you're the only one I can turn to. Since mother died, I'm all alone. There's no one I can even talk to."

Cal started to laugh. "That's like asking the captain of the *Titanic* for navigating instruction. You married Edward of your own free will. Biggest wedding in history, right? Bishop of Washington officiates at St. Matthew's! I don't know how you managed being married in the Catholic church, your being divorced and all."

"Just let me explain. Okay?"

"Does Edward know where you are?"

"Right now?"

Cal nodded.

"Edward doesn't care."

Vivian took her feet from the water, and an inquisitive expression came over her face. "I don't know what happened. I have an idea, but that's part of why I need your help," she said mysteriously. "Anyway, six months ago something changed. Abruptly. Boom! We were close and then we were not!

"Lately, Edward is a tortured man. It's nearly impossible to spot from the outside, but sleeping next to a man, feeling his body, listening to his breathing, listening to him when he doesn't know you can hear him, watching him at night when he thinks you're asleep, you learn things.

"Now Edward cannot sleep through the night. Never. He has to have liquor even to go to sleep. He's not a drunk, far from it, but there are demons, things on his mind. He has terrible dreams, thrashes around, flails his arms, cries, begs. Very few words are intelligible, but it is awful to watch.

"You remember you would sometimes have dreams about the crash. I would hear you talking to your copilot in your sleep, but this is nothing like that. I could reach out and pat you, and you would calm down again. But I can't calm down Edward. He either wakes up and has to go get a drink to get back to sleep or he calms down by himself."

"Does Edward know that you're worried?"

"I don't think so. Edward has always been consumed with himself. As long as you're not intruding on his interests, he really doesn't pay much attention."

Maybe God does even things out, Cal thought.

"Do you have relations with Edward?" Cal asked. Why did he say that? That was a stupid male question. Why did he care who Vivian had relations with?

Vivian grimaced. "After a fashion." She didn't elaborate. Her hazel eyes shifted gaze to the open water, to a sloop anchored a ways out. They sat for a while in silence.

"What are you doing here, Vivian?"

"I still have something for you, Cal," Vivian said softly, her gaze fixed on the sloop. "I never lost it. I realized that I think about you all the time, and when things started to get dicey, I realized you are the only one I could turn to."

She stood up from the bank, walked around Cal, and put her hands, her beautifully manicured hands, on his shoulders, the way a person does who is positioned to massage tight neck muscles.

"You know we have something. That's why you've never found any-one else, that's why you're all alone."

Cal felt her fingers on his neck.

"I am the lover and the loved," she began. It was a second before Cal realized she was reciting something.

"Home and wanderer, he who splits firewood and she who knocks . . ." She stopped and turned Cal's head gently toward her breasts. "I am knocking."

At the water's edge, at this moment, basking in the August sun, her hands felt good to him. They were warm and comfortable, as though she was still familiar, as though he had never left her. There is a fantasy about divorce. Every divorced person shares it. It is the fantasy that you will get back together.

"When she was good, she was very, very good," he said out loud to himself.

"What?" Vivian said.

"Nothing, an old rhyme."

He looked up at her.

"Listen to me."

Interrupting, he looked into her eyes, very steadily, the way he looked at suspects, not glaring, just steady.

"We had a great thing for a while. Right? Best love affair in the eight-ies. Right?"

Vivian nodded.

"Then leave it be! Let it alone. I've got a life. You've got a life. Five years is a long time. Leave it alone."

"You don't have a life, Cal. Nobody who knows you thinks you've got a life. You were living here with a couple of dogs when I met you and nothing's changed. You know what I found in the house this morning?"

He started to speak, but she was already telling him.

"I found eleven bottles of assorted booze, all open, half a case of Rolling Rock, thirty-five pounds of dog food, seventeen unopened cans of tuna fish and three that were open — incidentally, throw *those* out — two loaves of moldy bread, and cold fried chicken from Colonel Sanders. This is a life?"

"Be that as it may. I like it. Leave it alone!"

Vivian moved around to Cal's front, took a deep breath, straightened her shoulders, and placed a hand on her belly. Vivian was one of those women who could display her body with total naturalness. She was proud of it. Cal guessed she spent a lot of Edward's money on it. Cal remembered how often he'd seen Vivian run her hands over her flat stomach, as though she wanted to reaffirm that the astounding attributes were still in place.

"Help me. Maybe I made a mistake, maybe I've made a lot of mistakes, but it's because I can't get you out of my system. When I'm with Edward, I close my eyes and make believe it's you. Did you know that?"

"Bless your heart, honey," Cal said gently, slowly shaking his head. "I hate to say it, but that song doesn't play anymore."

"You've got to help me, Cal. I don't know where to turn."

"What do you want of me?"

"I want you on my side. I want you with me. I want you to help me get away from Edward."

"You've got to be crazy — you want *me* to help you get out of your marriage? How in the hell would I do that?"

She was using her hazel eyes the way she did best, as though the person she was looking at were the most important person in the world.

"I'm in trouble here. Edward is doing things he never did before." She spoke in a low tone, conspiratorially, almost in a whisper. "I am forbidden to go into his study, I am forbidden to answer the White House telephone in the den, I am forbidden to be around when he talks to the president. *My father* knew the president before Edward did."

"So?"

"Edward shreds everything. One day I found him shredding Publishers Clearing House. He said it was good security procedure."

"What's that got to do with anything?"

"Six months ago, when Edward got that special telephone and the shredder, everything changed! He has become obsessive, secretive. I can't even be in the room when he's talking on it.

"I know the phone ties in to the White House. Once I picked it up when he wasn't there. For a while there was a dial tone, then a man came on the line and asked what I wanted. That night Edward knew I had picked up the telephone. That's when he told me never to touch it."

"It's a security line, that's all," said Cal. "They put them in top officials' homes. It is so they can reach him quick. It may code the calls too."

"If that's true," Vivian said, "we must be at war! He's on that telephone day and night."

Her voice was all business now — the business Vivian. "There is a man. Edward says he is the National Security Council security officer, but I covered the White House and I never saw an NSC aide like this. Valasquez. Carlos Valasquez.

"He is very smooth. Very fit. Black hair, black eyes, manicured fingernails. Beautiful suits, handmade, box jackets, British cut, expensive. He wears enough gold jewelry on him to stock Tiffany's."

"Maybe he was stationed overseas," Cal cut in.

"Wait. Wait. It's not only his suits. It's his manner. He drives Edward home, and they go into the study and Edward pours him a drink! When did you ever hear of a security officer having a drink every few nights with the White House counsel?

"Another thing. I think he is interested in me."

Cal took a deep breath. Vivian had always thought men were interested in her. Many were.

"He watches me. You know, checks me out. When I'm in the pool, he never takes his eyes off my body. He watches my rear end when I walk. Once, he patted me, right on the butt! He made a joke of it when I jumped. When we make drinks or when I'm cooking, he is right next to me. Touching, whispering, telling me what great perfume I have, suggesting recipes."

"Tell Edward."

"I did. Edward said Carlos is just Latin; 'that's his nature.' Two days later he sent a beautiful silver dagger from Morocco. 'I did not mean to offend you,' the note said. 'Now you can defend yourself.'

"Valasquez and Edward go to Latin America all the time. At least six times, maybe more. White House planes out of Andrews Air Force Base, all very hush-hush. They almost always stop in Cartagena. Valasquez has a hotel there or something. Edward's very secretive about it. Edward said Valasquez planned that whole drug-summit thing that Winston did in Cartagena last year. He put the media up in his own hotel! I recognized the name. He and Edward call somewhere down there late at night all the time, after dinner, from the study. I can hear Valasquez talking to someone in Spanish."

Vivian paused to let that evidence sink in.

"Maybe they are planning a state visit you don't know about, maybe they're private emissaries for Winston on something," Cal said.

She didn't answer.

"It's also the money."

Cal recognized that. Vivian had always paid attention to money.

"When I got married, Edward had Charley draw up a prenup. I was to get a regular stipend, banked in my own account and available when I wanted. Five years and I'm still waiting."

"Maybe Edward didn't have as much as you thought?"

Vivian shook her head hard, her blond hair sweeping back and forth.

"Edward's got it. I think he's afraid I'll leave if I have enough money."

"You do have enough money. What are you talking about?" Cal was getting exasperated. She ignored it.

"I went to Charley. 'Where's my money, Charley?' I said. 'Get Edward to tell you. He won't tell me; maybe he'll tell you.' You know what Charley said?"

Cal shook his head at the preposterous idea that Charley would ever tell his ex-brother-in-law anything.

"'We've got it invested abroad. You'll be wealthy when we're done. Trust us.'

"*We!*" She was shouting. "Did you get that, Cal! Edward brought Charley into some deal. Edward isn't supposed to be managing his money. When Edward took office, he made a big deal out of putting all his money in a blind trust."

"You need a lawyer, not your ex-husband."

"I can't go to a lawyer in Washington. It would get back to Edward or my brother in a minute."

Vivian was flushed and breathing hard from the excitement of her story. Suddenly, she pulled him around and kissed him, full on the mouth, hot and long.

"I need you," she whispered. "Don't send me away. Help me!"

When they got back to the farm, she was as good as her word. They did the chores together. Not talking. Cal thinking about what she had said. When they were done, they drank cold Rolling Rocks, sitting on the hay bales. "Can I take a shower here? I don't want Edward seeing me all dusty."

"Can I ask you one thing before you go up?"

"Sure," she said.

"Why did you marry Edward?"

"Not for the same reasons I married you, darling." Vivian patted his cheek. "Not at all." She looked at him with that cool, level gaze she used on field producers when they asked stupid questions, and started up the stairs. He watched her. This man Valasquez was right, it was a great butt to watch.

He sat outside on the porch while she showered, listening to the water running and thinking about her body. "I'll call you," she said as she guided the big Mercedes down the drive. "Soon."

6

The state policeman had such a big head with his hat that it shut out Cal's light, and that was what awakened him.

"Lieutenant Terrell. The doc gave me only a short time. We found a Jeep Wagoneer abandoned over in Salisbury. It matches tire tracks at your farm. It was stolen in Richmond the day before you were attacked."

Cal knew it was green, but he didn't know how he knew it. He wanted to say, "Green," but he couldn't. He couldn't do anything, and he wasn't sure the state police knew his blink code.

"Your house is a wreck, but I'm afraid we can't establish if anything's missing without you. I've secured the house. Jeremiah up at the Montaigne estate said he'd feed your horses. We gave Mrs. St. Denis your pistols, like she asked."

Cal blinked furiously.

A woman's voice behind the policeman said, "I think he wants to ask you something."

She gave Cal the pad and a little tiny pencil like the ones for scoring miniature golf.

Dogs, Cal wrote.

"I thought you knew." The state officer looked anxiously down at Cal. "They were poisoned. Strychnine.

"Can you give us anything that will help?"

Cal wrote, painstakingly, *Two men. Hard plastic ski masks. Black clothes. Black athletic shoes. Professional.*

"What do you mean, 'professional'?"

Cal wrote, *Quick — quiet.*

He still couldn't remember why he thought the Wagoneer was green.

Cal's hooker idea went out when they saw Mary Jeanne's apartment. It was simple but decent. No sex paraphernalia, no thigh-highs, no garter belts, no black fishnet stockings, no vaginal jellies, no incense.

Also no friends or relatives. Not even a starving pet. It was not at all as Cal had imagined it, the messy pad of a streetwalker.

It had been furnished by someone who read decorating magazines and didn't have a lot of money, Pier 1 wicker, secondhand furniture, pieces of driftwood and swatches of linen and silk.

It was a woman's apartment, but a man had been in mind. There was a big club chair, used and worn but inviting too, a makeshift entertainment center with television, compact disc player, and Bose speakers. A thousand bucks, easy, was tied up in the sound system. The pièce de résistance was the walk-in closet with enough clothes for a small shop. On one wall, by themselves, were six evening dresses, not one Cal figured worth less than $2,000 new, and six pairs of matching shoes.

"The place has been wiped. I mean, wiped." Bobbie's arm swept the room. She had just finished the kitchen.

"Are you sure?"

"Somebody took Formula Four Oh Nine, I can smell it, and they went over everything. I bet we don't find any prints on normal surfaces."

"Maybe she was just real neat?" Cal asked.

"Did Vivian clean the inside of cabinets around the latch?"

"Vivian never cleaned at all."

They appeared as a macabre medical team, wearing plastic surgical gloves, moving wordlessly around the rooms, faces glistening with perspiration. It felt like the air-conditioning had been off for a week, the second hottest week in Washington's history.

The Reggae Club shooting was all over television and the front pages again. A twelve-year-old girl who had been hit by a ricochet died unexpectedly, and now the massacre had the dynamic that drove it into white homes and white hearts.

Nathaniel had called a meeting that morning, still angry, chagrined and clearly under pressure from the mayor. "Why didn't you tell me this kid was on critical," he asked Cal bitterly.

"Nathaniel, we didn't know. I gave you the body count myself. The little girl wasn't even listed critical."

Nathaniel grabbed Cal's arm and propelled him out into the hall. The other detectives looked ill at ease. "What in the hell are you trying to do to me," he hissed. "My deputy is supposed to make me look good!"

"Jesus, Nathaniel. You're getting the Washington disease. Paranoia. I was trying to control a massive crime scene. I called the department right away and asked for assistance. Normal procedure would be for you to be alerted. Where were you?"

For a moment, just a moment, Nathaniel looked chagrined. "Aretha Franklin."

"Aretha Franklin, what has she got to do with it?"

"She was at Wolf Trap. I forgot to turn on my beeper after the concert."

Cal shrugged. He knew Nathaniel's real problem: the Reggae Club shooting put Martin Cameron in desperate political trouble.

Spotting a new opportunity to embarrass city officials, the House District Committee escalated the battle over who should run the city and ordered an investigation of the Reggae Club massacre. President Winston's wife had met with the parents of the dead girl at the hospital. A delegation of parents had picketed the Reggae Club, demanding it be closed permanently and saying it should never have been licensed in a residential neighborhood. Cal and Bobbie had wondered about that too.

The momentum had shifted overnight; now the mayor was on the run, and even the White House of his own party seemed to be talking around him.

Cal and Bobbie had had only five hours' sleep over two days, but the Maryland police had been leaning on them about Mary Jeanne, so they had to go check out her apartment.

Bobbie bagged personal items in plastic freezer bags, dating and marking them. Cal went through the clothes, the drawers, and cabinets, cataloging the belongings and searching for the unusual.

There wasn't much. No purse, except two empty ones in the closet, no wallet, no money except a jar of pennies, no identification papers, no checkbook. There were pictures, one whole drawer full. Mary Jeanne Turner smiled a lot, an extraordinarily pretty young woman, athletic and robust.

Some were at the beach — Cal guessed Rehobeth, from one backdrop — one on the Mall playing softball, one with four young women. It looked like a slumber party; they were in pajamas. In others Mary Jeanne was alone. She posed well on the bike or stairs, at the Capitol, by a car, looking directly into the lens and holding her body as a model might pose, enticing if not provocative.

"There aren't any pictures with men or of men," Bobbie said.

"So?" Cal asked.

"A pretty girl who has pictures only of herself? No men?"

There were paycheck stubs from the River Club in Georgetown and pictures of a poodle in an envelope with an Arlington return address.

They marked and sealed the apartment with a big yellow Metro Police crime scene tape and a warning that it was a felony under D.C. law to enter the premises without police permission.

"Do you have to do that?" The resident manager looked painfully at the sign.

"At least until her family is notified." Bobbie was clearly sizing up the manager. *That is her type,* thought Cal: bearded, tight blue jeans, nice buns, and a look of vulnerability. He probably owned a guitar.

"If a man plays a guitar," Bobbie would say, "he has gentleness in his heart."

"Or he's musical," Cal used to counter.

Bobbie was undeterred. She had been humiliated by at least two guitar players Cal knew about.

"Where is Mary Jeanne? Is she all right? I mean, nothing's happened?" the manager asked when they got to his office. It was a ridiculous question. Why else were detectives there?

"Not exactly," Bobbie said. "She was found dead in the Chesapeake Bay."

The guy gasped, sucking air between his teeth.

"Drowned?"

"We're working on that." Bobbie didn't mention the brand.

"When?"

"We don't know," she answered, deliberately obfuscating. "When did you last see her?"

"I think it was about two weeks ago. In the laundry."

"Can you remember the day?"

"It was near the first of the month. She gave me her rent instead of mailing it."

"Anything unusual?" Now Bobbie was taking notes, all the pose of the good detective.

"No. But she's been real chirpy for weeks."

"Chirpy?"

"You know, happy."

Bobbie looked at Cal. She shrugged and went on.

"How long had she lived here?"

"Six months." The manager put on glasses that suddenly made him look like what he was, a well-worn forty-two-year-old guy who had to work as a resident manager. Cal wondered if he'd tried for Mary Jeanne.

"Own or renting?"

"Renting. She paid five seventy-five a month, was late twice."

"Is that her furniture?"

"Oh yes! She decorated herself."

"Did she have any friends?"

"You mean, men friends?"

"Any kind."

"She knew some of the girls in the building, and different men brought her home. I don't know if there was anyone special."

Bobbie wrote down names and addresses of everyone in the building the resident manager thought might have known Mary Jeanne.

"Is coke a big deal here?"

"I don't think so. . . ." The manager seemed truly surprised. "Not Mary Jeanne. She was a nice kid." The guy looked painfully at Bobbie. He knew the word *kid* had made him seem older. He probably would like to change it.

He snapped his fingers suddenly. "A couple of times I've seen Mary Jeanne arrive here in a limousine. A big black car."

"Did you see who she was with?"

He shook his head. "Not really. All I saw was a black man in the back of the limo with her. I couldn't describe him. I didn't get a good look, just a glimpse."

The manager didn't get the license plate or make or model. "You know, a limousine."

"There are two zillion limos in Washington," Cal said.

"Is there anything else?"

The guy shook his head. He was trying to please Bobbie and was running out of ways.

"What does the letter *B* mean to you?" Bobbie asked.

"What . . . why?"

"Please, answer."

"Nothing."

Cal watched Bobbie. He had long ago guessed it was the Age of Aquarius quality that attracted a certain type of man, the San Francisco catalog clothes, the black hair hanging down her back in a single braid, the soft, throaty voice, and the kind of mysterious look her dark eye shading gave her.

The rental application form listed Mary Jeanne's job as dining room manager at the River Club, former residence as an address in North Arlington — the same one on the envelope — and two references.

Bobbie ostentatiously left her card. "If you think of anything that can help us in this investigation, give me a call. Anytime. I put my home number on the back." She smiled her warmest smile. "This matter is confidential, of course, until we contact her next of kin."

Bobbie was looking around his small office apartment. "Do you play?" she asked, nodding toward the corner. Cal followed her gaze. There it was! A guitar in a large black case.

"Not as much as I'd like to," he said, looking into her eyes. "Sergeant Short," he read her name off the card.

"The only thing short about me is my name." Bobbie stood up, her six-foot frame towering over the seated man. He laughed.

Cal wondered how many times Bobbie had delivered that line.

Trying to form words had tired him, and Cal was dozing on and off. He realized he ought to remind Vivian that he was entitled to burial in a national cemetery with full honor guard. Shit, he'd done twelve years in the regular army.

Madeline Turner's balcony looked right over Arlington National Cemetery and Marine memorial.

It was the day after Vivian showed up at the farm that he notified Mary Jeanne's mother. Or was it the next day? Bobbie couldn't go. She was testifying.

Arlington County sent a uniformed sergeant to meet him. Cal was relieved. Notifications were bad enough with kid officers. Notifications made people of the deceased, you knew their lives then. They weren't just corpses; if you met their loved ones, they were people. Cal hated this part of his job.

This one was worse than most.

The woman who opened the door still had a briefcase in her hand. She must have just come home from work. A woman of Cal's age, heavy and worn looking. The likeness to Mary Jeanne was there, the facial features unmistakably similar.

When she saw the Arlington officer's uniform and Cal's identity folder, she said two words: "Mary Jeanne."

Cal told her as gently as fifteen years on the job would permit, but it was no good. The woman went to her knees on the carpet, the sobs were so deep, Cal thought she must be hyperventilating.

Suddenly she rose, brushing them aside and running along a hall. They could hear her vomiting into a toilet, great heaves of noise.

The Arlington sergeant said, "Oh shit," very slowly and precisely. He and Cal looked out over Washington. A summer storm was coming up over National Airport, and the Lincoln Memorial's pristine white was now half darkened by clouds and half asparkle with late-afternoon sun. Personally, Cal hated apartments, but this was a great view.

The vomiting stopped.

Cal walked slowly down the hall. "Mrs. Turner, are you okay?"

He could hear the woman breathing, a gurgling sound.

"Can we call your husband?" Cal knew there was no man living here. He had known from the moment they entered. Maybe he lived nearby.

"I have no husband."

She came out holding the wall, a towel over the lower part of her face, the vomit running down the front of her very expensive suit.

"Is there someone, a friend or someone . . ." Cal felt awkward and stupid. He should have found out more about the woman from the clerk downstairs.

"No. No. I'll be all right."

When she finally came out to the living room, the storm had begun and wind and rain lashed the balcony and the French doors.

"Where is she?"

"At the Anne Arundel County mortuary near Annapolis."

"Can I see her?"

"Certainly. But you don't look well enough to do that now. It can wait."

"No, it can't!"

Cal had made another mistake. He wished he had let the Maryland cops do this.

"Can we call someone to drive you? A friend?"

"No. I'll be all right. Just give me the directions."

"Mrs. Turner, I can't do that. This is just something that you can't do alone."

The Arlington sergeant wasn't helping. He didn't volunteer a car or an officer. Finally he whispered something about vacation overload. They had no one to spare.

She looked dazed. "I don't know who . . ."

When Cal went back down the hall, he passed what must have been Mary Jeanne's room. It was full of her childhood as though she were coming back any minute.

All the way to the mortuary, Madeline Turner spoke not two words. She had cleaned herself up and changed into a blouse and skirt. Now she sat on the far right of the seat, resting her head against the glass of the side window, staring unwaveringly at the road.

Mary Jeanne was there as they had left her, waiting for her mother, looking cold and stiff in death.

"May I be alone with her?"

He took the mortuary attendant's arm and guided him out.

The guy walked to the parking lot, pulling out a box of Marlboro Lights. "Give me one of those," said Cal. He had quit smoking ten years ago, but there were moments when a cigarette seemed the way to go.

They had three cigarettes each, blowing the smoke into the dusk of the parking lot, before she came out.

7

When he got back to Arlington, he bought some take-out Vietnamese soup, some spring rolls, and lemon chicken. Up behind the cash register was a calendar for Air France. THE NEW VUNG TAU, it said. WORLD CLASS BEACHES, CASINO, LEISURE VILLAGE. He wondered if the scuba divers ever bumped into *Amazing Grace,* lying there with her nose in four feet of sand on the bottom of the bay. Maybe the Vietnamese had dredged the harbor.

"You like to go to Vung Tau," said the old lady behind the register.

"No. I've been to Vung Tau."

She giggled.

Mrs. Turner looked awful. Her eyes were sunken, and crying had left her face splotchy. She wore no makeup, and her hair looked flat and hung tight to her head. Cal laid out the supper in the dishes she showed him.

She clutched the robe about her with both hands, sitting hard into the corner of the sofa as though she needed the armrest to hold her upright. Her little black poodle nestled like a muff against her body. Cal saw the glass dressing table and the open vodka bottle on the dresser.

"Tell me why somebody does such a thing," she said in a belligerent way.

"God knows, Mrs. Turner. I sure don't, and I've been doing this work for fifteen years. I don't know." He waited, watching her face. "We could do this tomorrow. You've got to take it easy."

The woman got up and brought the vodka bottle and poured a drink in a fresh glass. Neat. No ice. She didn't offer Cal a drink. She didn't touch the soup he put before her, but she nibbled on a spring roll.

She wanted to know it all. She could not look at Cal as he talked, staring out over the city instead. The heat had built up again after the rain, and the air was so thick with haze you could see it.

When Cal was done, she didn't speak. They sat in silence for maybe sixty seconds.

"Who did it?"

"We don't know."

"Why . . . why Mary Jeanne?"

"We don't know."

"What kind of man does that? How could he do that? How in God's name could somebody do that!" Her voice rose until it was screaming; the poodle jumped.

Cal spoke in a low voice, trying to answer the unanswerable for her sake, to help her.

"There are a lot of sick people out there. They go along and we don't recognize them and nobody does anything about them and then suddenly . . ." Cal let the sentence dangle. "Half the time what they do isn't even directed at the victim. They're acting out rage against someone else in their lives."

"How did he get Mary Jeanne?" Mrs. Turner asked.

"We don't know. The Maryland police have notified other police departments to see if there have been random attacks with the *B* brand, or the letter *B,* or brands at all, something like that, but we don't have anything. We don't know if it was somebody she knew or somebody just picked her up," he said. He didn't tell her what he thought. He thought it would be somebody she knew. "What about the letter *B?* Mean anything to you?"

She shook her head.

"Did you know Mary Jeanne used cocaine?" Cal asked.

"No." Her voice was flat. The question was no surprise.

"Other drugs?"

"I once found some marijuana in her room when she lived here." Mrs. Turner now seemed less sure, less adamant, filled with denial.

"Are you sure you can handle this?"

The woman nodded dumbly, still not looking at Cal. "Could I have another drink?" She nodded toward the bottle. Cal poured one for her. "Do you want anything?" she asked.

Cal shook his head.

Cal used an old technique, going back to the innocuous, something he already knew.

"What's Mary Jeanne's date of birth?"

"September twelfth, nineteen seventy-eight."

"How long did she live at Columbia Road?"

"About half a year."

"Where was she living before then?"

"Here."

"Why did Mary Jeanne leave home?"

For the first time she looked at Cal directly.

"The abortion."

"When was that?"

"Two years ago."

Mrs. Turner waited a heartbeat as though gathering her strength. "In her senior year."

"Where is the man?"

"At Annapolis. The academy."

Whereas Mrs. Turner had been reluctant before, she was now eager, and the story came out in a rush, like water tumbling down a streambed. There was no need for questions; she wanted to talk now, to explain.

Mary Jeanne had known the baby's father all through high school. "I never would have guessed, he was not even a special boyfriend."

"His name?"

"Chris Hudson."

He was the best football player at Washington and Lee High School. His parents had been terrified it would ruin his future. They had paid the costs. "'We don't want to hurt his chances,'" they had said. "The boy's father is a big lawyer," Mrs. Turner said. "He sent us to Germany."

She graduated along with her class; the diploma was freedom. She moved out the next day.

Her most recent job was at the River Club.

"She wanted to be a model. She'd get occasional jobs, but not enough to live on."

"Had she kept in touch with you since she moved to D.C.?"

"Through Togo." She clutched the little poodle.

"She would call to check on Togo, and we would talk. Togo was my little helper." She squeezed the dog tightly, and Cal could see fresh tears. "Only for two weeks she hasn't called. I was getting worried."

"Where is Mary Jeanne's father?"

"I don't know. I think Fort Worth."

"Should we try to reach him?"

"He left when she was two. Years ago I tried in court to get child support, but he's never paid a cent, never called, never sent her a gift, a card — nothing."

Cal worked around slowly back to the hard part. Had Mary Jeanne ever been out of control on alcohol? Did she suddenly seem to have a lot of money?

Mrs. Turner was ruthless on herself in grief. With no husband and no money, she had gotten herself a college degree, a GS14 job, a condominium, a new car, good clothes, the works. Mary Jeanne had paid as a young girl with latchkey loneliness. It was a stiff price. Madeline Turner was sure it had come due.

"It made her develop far too early. When she was twelve she acted eighteen. She loved clothes, loved going out, loved expensive things. She developed early, big as a grown woman, but really a little girl. It wasn't only her body — somehow living alone with me made her older, you know, like my sister instead of my daughter."

There had been one ominous incident, a harbinger of what might come to pass.

"When she was sixteen, we were living over in the River House." She nodded her head out toward the Potomac.

"I was dating a very attractive man. A Parnell, from the real estate family. He had just gotten divorced and had the penthouse, and we hit it off right away.

"We often took Mary Jeanne along. He kept a boat in the marina. It was quite fancy, a big cabin cruiser. She loved it, loved the way Greg entertained, loved to go on the bay, everything.

"One day I came home early" — Madeline Turner went silent for a moment — "I went into her room to put some clothes away. She had a little jewel box where she put her treasures. It was open and there was a ring I'd never seen. A diamond ring! It had to be worth a lot of money. There was a note."

"A note?"

"A love note."

She had confronted the man that night. "She is only sixteen. I'll have you charged," I said. "Charged in court."

"He moved out of the building the next day. Mary Jeanne never forgave me. You know what she said?"

Cal shook his head.

"She said I did it because I couldn't stand the competition. She got pregnant three months later, around her birthday was my guess. I always wondered if she got pregnant on purpose."

"On purpose?"

"Yes, you know, to try to prove something."

The mother seemed to be studying the answers as she gave them, chewing them over, deciding now how much she would say.

"Do you have children?" She was looking at Cal's left hand, looking for a wedding ring. He shook his head.

"Then how can you understand all this?" She shook her head.

Her whole body crumpled on the couch as though the bone structure was no longer holding it up. The little poodle jumped off her lap in alarm.

Cal moved to the couch and took her in his arms. It was an awkward gesture for him; he didn't do it easily. The woman curled into Cal like a child, burying her face in Cal's chest as though to shut out the light.

She was crying now, slowly and steadily — not hysterically, but like a good, slow, steady rain that really waters the garden.

"She was too beautiful by half. She grew up too soon. I wanted to stop it. When she was a little girl, those were the happiest years of my life." Cal could hardly hear the words mumbled against his clothing. "I never would have believed, back then, that we could ever grow so far apart.

"I . . . Oh God, if I could have only stopped time. I couldn't stop it. I couldn't stop it."

Finally Mrs. Turner sat up, her face tear-stained and puffy. She leaned back and let her head fall back on the couch and looked at the ceiling.

"She was terribly excited when she got the job at the River Club. She told me, 'Momma, I'm on my way. I'm meeting all sorts of important people! People who can help me.'

"She'd call me at my office and tell me she'd met this senator or that one. Football players. Kevin Costner came there for dinner once, and Mrs. Moray introduced Mary Jeanne to him. She was ecstatic. Once the president was there, and she worked with the secret service agents.

"What I couldn't understand was what she could have done to be made the manager? She wasn't even twenty! She didn't know anything about food or managing employees or budgets."

"Did you know that she was arrested last year?"

Mrs. Turner looked at him sharply, her face full of disbelief. "No."

"We don't know much about it yet, but the record shows she was arrested for disorderly conduct."

"She never said anything. I would know if she was in trouble!"

"The record shows she pleaded no contest. Possibly it was a party or something where a lot of kids were given disorderly summonses," Cal said. He realized he was breaking a cardinal rule. He was answering questions for a witness. "Was she dating anybody? Did any man seem special?" Cal continued.

Mrs. Turner shook her head. "I don't know. . . ." She clearly knew little of her daughter's private life, and it pained her; the vacuum was an indictment of her indifference.

"She was so hard to talk to, so prickly, so prideful."

"Did you notice anything recently, anything at all that seemed unusual?"

There was a long silence.

Mrs. Turner stood and walked down the hall. Togo looked frightened. Cal thought Madeline might have become ill, as she had earlier. But in a moment she was back, holding a letter addressed to Elizabeth Pender c/o the Wilderness Ranch in Bisbane, California.

"Liz is an old friend from high school. She's hiking in the Sierras for a few months. I kept forgetting to mention it to Mary Jeanne. I didn't know if she wanted me to drop it in the mail or what. I found it about a month ago after she'd come to get some clothes."

Cal opened the one-page letter.

Full of girlish gush, Mary Jeanne told her friend about meeting "a great guy." No name. "He's super! Real down to earth, intelligent, a stud, a good sense of humor. God, I'm crazy about him. He knows everybody and I guess you'd say he's got a pretty strong ego. Now the downside — he's married. And he's a lot older, as old as Mom! Mom would have a fit if she knew about him. But, oh Liz, he treats me sooooo well. We have the best time and he spends a fortune on me. We went to the opening of a fabulous new disco called the PINGA and we ate the biggest lobsters you've ever seen at the Palm. Some nights he gets a little weird, but I think I can handle all his moods. Sometimes I worry about getting used again. God knows, this man can have all the women he wants. Can't wait for you to get home and meet him. How's your love life? Find any handsome mountain men to wrestle with in a sleeping bag? Write. TTFN"

"Do you know who this is?" Cal asked, handing her the letter. Madeline Turner shook her head.

"What does 'TTFN' mean?

"Ta-ta for now. It's a phrase they've used since they were little girls."

"What would *weird* mean to your daughter?"

"She used that all the time." Suddenly the woman understood the question. "I mean, to her it meant silly or different, not —" She stopped short.

8

The day after Cal saw the Turner woman, Bobbie ran down the two most likely leads, the midshipman father of Mary Jeanne's baby and Parnell.

The cadet had been on maneuvers in the Adriatic all summer. When Bobbie hung up the phone with the academy, she started laughing. "I had 'em shaking in their boots. They thought this might be another scandal on their hands. The guy was so relieved. He said this kid has been at sea for sixty-one days!"

Mary Jeanne's girlfriend had talked to Mary Jeanne two months ago. She told Bobbie that Mary Jeanne had said something strange. "Older men are very gentle."

"What is an older man to a nineteen-year-old?" Cal asked.

"Thirty-five," said Bobbie.

Parnell had spent the entire weekend of August 2–3 playing golf in Arizona at a fund-raiser for Dan Quayle. He was chagrined at being called. "Who told you I even knew Mary Jeanne?"

"What now?" asked Bobbie. "We got zip from all those people I interviewed in Mary Jeanne's apartment building. Nothing left to try there."

"Let's track down the officer who booked Mary Jeanne."

They found him in the Robbery Division, two floors down.

He thought he recognized the photo Cal had taken from the girl's apartment. It took him twenty minutes to find his old book.

His fingers leafed through the carbons as he talked.

"One night my partner and I were eating lunch up the alley behind Martin's. Our car was dark, so nobody noticed us.

"After a while we see this stretch limo pulled up by the back door of TJ's, and the driver goes inside. Then a waiter comes bustling out with a bottle of wine on a tray.

"We finish our sandwiches and get ready to go, and the limo starts to rock on its springs like a buffalo is loose in it." The cop's voice falters; he tries to avoid a smile.

"My partner went over and yelled for them to open the door. Nothing. When he pulled open the door, this guy has this girl down in the back. She's stark naked, not a stitch."

"So how come you charged only her?" Bobbie said impatiently.

"Wait. I'm coming to that. Shit, at first we weren't going to charge anybody. We were going to tell them to take this stuff home. But when Billy — that's my partner — picks up her clothes to hand them to her, she comes at him with the wine bottle, calling him names, swings at me, hits him in the nuts, takes out the limo's side window. It took us two minutes to restrain her."

Cal's face showed his skepticism. The uniformed cop grew more ill at ease.

"We asked her if she wanted to make a complaint against the guy. But instead, she's sitting in the cruiser, putting on her clothes, spitting out the window at us, threatening a lawsuit and telling us she could take care of herself. Since they were drunk . . ." The officer had come to the right page and Cal could see Turner printed in large letters on a carbon.

"The guy said he'd met her at a party. He said she agreed to take a ride home, but instead they'd been riding around in the rental limo drinking wine. The only reason they stopped was they were running out of wine.

"The guy said he figured she was game for a little fun" — the cop made a gesture of copulation — "but she teased him along. The limo driver told us he was getting scared of them, so when he stopped for the wine he was on the phone to his office to get a supervisor out."

"Any drugs?"

"Nothing. We searched them and the car. We thought maybe PCP, the way she was acting."

"Did you have her tested?" Bobbie asked.

"It was busy as shit. We put her out on personal recog right here."

"No AIDS screen?" Bobbie said.

He shook his head.

"You had possible intercourse in a disorderly arrest and there was no AIDS screen?" Bobbie was raising her voice.

The cop sat in defeated silence.

"Give me the guy's name," Bobbie said.

The uniformed cop looked sheepish.

"Tony Frohlo."

"The running back?"

More sheepish.

Bobbie and Cal looked a long time at the uniformed officer. He grew nervous.

"You find a giant football player wrestling with a naked eighteen-year-old girl" — Bobbie was shaking with anger — "who might be on PCP. You charge her but not him. You don't order a drug test? You don't order an AIDS screen? You don't detain him? You don't detain her? What were you doing? Holding the Redskins and ten?"

"Come on, Sergeant! Frohlo had a lawyer at the district before we processed 'em. He talks to him, to her, next thing I know they're all lovey-dovey, and restitution of limo window, personal apology, a little too much to drink, blah-blah-blah."

The MRI closed around him, and all he could see was the white plastic of the tube he was lying in and the whirring noise of the camera process. It took longer than he had expected. He was not claustrophobic, but lying in the white tube with its walls two inches from his face suggested a coffin. Cal did not dwell on this thought.

What he needed, he decided, was a good belt of Stoli.

Max the bartender was talking fast. He looked like the late John Candy. Cops clearly made him nervous and he felt the need to entertain them, as though to stop talking would let their attention wander to crimes real or imagined.

"How would I know who she dated? We just worked together. That's all. She was way over my pay grade."

Bobbie leaned over and patted the bartender's hand. It was a reassuring gesture.

"Tell me a little more about Mary Jeanne."

"Well, like I said, she was the dining room manager. She directed the waiters, made sure the tables and silver and everything were ready, but most important of all she greeted the customers if Celeste wasn't here."

"Celeste?"

"Celeste Moray. This is her place. You know, Mrs. Harry Moray. Celeste's number one rule is: If a customer has been here once, the second time you'd better know him by name. Every reservation is reviewed. If it's a prominent person, Celeste wants the dining room manager to know about that person, title, claim to fame, the whole thing. Harry's office runs their background on a computer — bio, credit history, financials."

"How could a kid with no experience get to manage this dining room?" Cal said.

The bartender scrubbed his glass a little harder for a moment. "You ever see Mary Jeanne?"

"So she was here because of her body?" Bobbie said.

"It ain't really like managing. I do the managing."

"What's it like?"

"Like maybe greeting. Celeste always dresses formal for dinner here, and often she stands at the entrance with the dining room manager." He nodded to the broad entranceway. "She and the manager are in evening dresses, like two wealthy dames welcoming you into their home."

"We found ten thousand bucks' worth of gowns in her closet," Bobbie said. "Did she pay for those out of her salary?"

"Naw. We own them. Celeste issued them like uniforms. The girls had to sign a lease for them."

"Was the Turner girl especially friendly with any customers?" Bobbie asked.

"That's what you want. You want your regulars to feel like they're well known, you know?"

Bobbie nodded.

"These are wealthy men, right?" she said.

The bartender gave her his John Candy look, as though he marveled somebody could belabor the obvious so well.

"There are eighty thousand lobbyists in Washington." His hand swept a half circle in the air. "Most of them got an expense account."

"Did she date any of them?"

"Celeste don't like it. It ends at the door."

"What about Moray . . ." Bobbie let her voice trail off.

The bartender laughed nervously. Celeste was Harry's fifth wife; talking about Harry Moray's marital fidelity was not healthy for one of his employees. Moray's fourth wife had tied him up in a divorce settlement for five years; half of his vice presidents had been called to testify.

"Not here, for sure. Celeste is here every night he's here. She'd kill him."

"Was there anybody regular in Mary Jeanne's life?" Cal asked. After a long silence, he tried again: "A black man?"

Max had begun washing glasses again, furiously spiking them up and down on a whirling electric soap brush. It was a stall.

Bobbie persisted, a note of irritation in her voice.

"Tell us about it."

"I think that was her preference, if you get my meaning."

Cal wandered off through the cavernous room. The room was set for the evening, peach tablecloths, fresh flowers, sparkling glasses, glistening silver.

Moray had put $5 million into his wife's hobby, the papers said, re-creating a 1930s supper club. It was all Bauhaus, shielded sconces, black lacquer, long mirrors — somehow it reminded Cal of a main dining saloon on a cruise ship.

Celeste had a wall of pictures that looked like every luminary in the world had put his arm around her. There was President Winston with a note to his "precious" Celeste, the attorney general, the secretary of state, Richard Gere looking his Hollywood best, Mayor Cameron, and even Cal Ripkin.

Cal had been here once with Vivian, when Vivian was still in TV, a lifetime ago. That's what Vivian had always wanted. She wanted to be at the River Clubs of the world, to no purpose, just to be there.

What the hell did the Morays want with a kid from a suburban high school out chitchatting with ambassadors?

In the kitchen the cooks were slicing and chopping for the evening meal. Three were Hispanics who looked fearfully at Cal's ID wallet to see if he was Immigration. The fourth cook had an Appalachian twang. He remembered Mary Jeanne as "real nice. She'd bring me a ginger ale from the bar."

"Did you see Mary Jeanne Saturday night, August second?" Cal asked.

"No."

"Did you see her that Friday?"

The cook shook his head. "I didn't see a thing that weekend. I worked my ass off."

"Would Max have seen her leave?"

The little cook shrugged his shoulders. "Help leaves from the back."

"Show me?"

He took Cal past a giant double-door freezer down a dark little hall.

"Most of the girls go out the back. They get cleaned up, change back here. It's easier." There was a door marked WOMEN ONLY!

The other door opened onto the parking lot, which ran uninterrupted up to K Street.

Cal walked back out front. Max was at the bar.

"Did Mary Jeanne work the weekend of August second?

"I'm not sure."

"Have you got a record?"

The bartender wiped his hands on a towel and went into a tiny office at the end of the bar.

He came out with a stained timecard.

The last punch was August 2 at 2:30 A.M.

"Were you here?"

Max shook his head. "I took a guy home."

9

Cal was lying on the gurney outside the MRI office, staring at the ceiling. He was wondering how you live if you can't speak. He'd be off the police force, for sure, living on a 65 percent — or was it 80 percent? — disability. He could handle the horses okay. It was touch and soft sounds. The horses didn't understand words anyway, but to teach riders?

Why couldn't he ever do anything the easy way? He wouldn't be lying in a hospital frightened, wondering if he was going to die, if he had just taken the job with Moray. The easy life. Funny, it was the first positive thought he had ever entertained about Harry Moray. From the moment Cal met him, he distrusted him. Washington was full of Morays, skipping between the raindrops, making a living selling pieces of the Republic.

Harry Moray looked his part, like central casting had sent him down with a label that said "U.S. senator." He wasn't a senator anymore but had been: two years, appointed by the governor of Oklahoma to fill out the term of old Kincaid. That was enough for Harry, that was all he needed. He never ran for reelection.

Harry saw that the opportunities in Washington were in a different direction, that the rewards of government were not in governing. He went "downtown," as they say, down to K Street, down to money. He wasn't as big as Jody Powell or Tommy Boggs, but he was still a man worth knowing.

The term *lobbyist* was distasteful to him. He liked to think, he would tell reporters, that he was a man who "put things together." He had put together the Union Station project. It was also Harry Moray who thought up a one-paragraph change in the Tax Reform Act that earned the insurance industry $10 billion. They still talk about that with awe at the Cosmos and the Metropolitan Clubs, the way you speak of Cal Ripkin surpassing Lou Gehrig.

A newspaper profile of Moray once said his real money came from "foreign special interests."

"The only interest I represent," Moray had replied in a letter to the paper, "is my own. It is, however, very special to me."

Two years ago he had put together a consortium to bring the Redskins back to D.C. from Landover and rebuild Robert F. Kennedy Stadium. His gift to the city, he had said. But it had been perfect for him too: the skybox on Sunday, dinner at the River Club after the game.

Now if you spotted the guests in his box on Sunday, you could figure out the deal on Monday. The president and his wife were there two home games out of every four, the vice president damn near every weekend, unnumbered senators and cabinet members. What made Moray's box interesting was the number of foreign guests. "One would never guess," wrote one columnist, "how many Saudi princes, Chinese tycoons, Japanese executives, and Singapore brokers have a love of the game of football."

For the past two years Moray had been working on his biggest deal: Rivergate. They said it would be the most sweeping redesign of the city since Pierre L'Enfant. Everybody said it would be a permanent monument to Harry Moray.

It would change the eastern end of the city, make the new Redskins Stadium the center of a $20 billion business-and-office complex that would stretch nearly to the Capitol to the west and down beyond the old *Washington Star* newspaper plant to the south, from the National Arboretum to the Union Station rail yards to the north.

His biggest problem was the working people of the district. They said Moray was trying to drive them out of decent housing. They said they had nowhere to go.

Moray had a giant-scale model of Rivergate just outside his office, done in sparkling white imitation marble with perfectly crafted little people and lights in the windows and little cars. Bobbie whistled when she saw it, like a kid at an electric-train show.

Cal and Bobbie walked around it while they waited. Bobbie spotted the place in the parking lot where she had been shot and where they found the sniper's post in the Reggae Club shooting.

Everything was changed. On the model, all the blocks of little row houses, all those neat homes of some of the city's most stable black middle class, were gone.

"Just where *are* they going to move all the people?" asked Bobbie.

"That's what Martin Cameron keeps asking me." Moray had come out behind them from two cherrywood doors, startling Cal.

Moray held out his hand. "You must be Lieutenant Terrell."

"Sergeant Short."

He offered his hand to Bobbie, looking at her like someone who expected women to respond to him, and when she grasped his hand, he placed his other one over hers. "Sergeant, let me tell you a little about my project," he said, drawing Bobbie closer to the model. "We think some of the people will take the very competitive prices we pay for their homes and move to Prince George's County, southern Maryland, or Virginia.

"Our demographics show that there are also a great many people either retired or near retirement, and for them the sale price on their house will allow retirement plans to go forward. Others may move to other suburbs."

"None of them will stay?"

"A few. Professionals. Lawyers."

Cal wondered how many lawyers, if any, were now living more than twenty blocks east of the Capitol.

Moray was now unconsciously massaging the smooth dome of the Capitol's model with his hand. "Washington in the twenty-first century will be the capital of the world. The twentieth century was the American century; we're going into the global century. What happens here" — he patted the Capitol dome — "will determine situations ten thousand miles away.

"We need a city to meet that responsibility. We can't let the official city, the city of leadership, move out to some Virginia county. We need a city like London, a city that can be a world leader.

"This area's already a victim of hodgepodge gentrification. It's not like Capitol Hill; people are stampeding out now. That's what I've tried to make the mayor see. People are being moved out one way or another."

He walked around the table to a different angle and pointed along by the marine barracks.

"The housing stock from here east was built in the nineteen forties, not very distinguished and not worth fighting about. I told Martin. If you and the city government can stabilize crime in this area, my architects can give a mix that will knock your eyes out.

"But things like the shooting of all those teenagers. God! I told Martin, who let somebody build a goddamn drug club when we're trying to reassure people about the safety of the nation's capital. Who in God's name gave them the license!"

As he watched Moray, Cal realized that the Oklahoma twang neatly disguised him, made him less threatening, but it was fake. He was drawn tight like steel wire.

Moray began to disengage. This afternoon he was chairing a board meeting for the Kennedy Center, he said, would twenty minutes be okay? His left hand touched Bobbie's elbow to brush away a nonexistent speck of dust, the cuff links twinkled. Presidential seals. He did not have to say that they were a gift from President Winston.

He led them into the office.

"I told her. You must believe me. I told her again and again. I said, 'Mary Jeanne, honey, you be very careful at night going home, you hear.'

"This city ain't safe, anywhere! I don't mean that as a criticism." He nodded and smiled, as though it was something that was painful and embarrassing to the police officers before him.

Two men were already seated in the room. Cal recognized one as Moray's lawyer, Victor Stein, in one of those big Connecticut Avenue law firms that had its own building, but Moray didn't introduce them. As Moray talked, they silently handed little index cards to him as if he were at a congressional hearing.

Moray said he wanted to be helpful. God knows, this is awful. Just awful. Should he offer a reward? Is this proper? Is her mother well fixed? Could he help with funeral costs? Should he call?

Mary Jeanne had come as dining room manager, he looked down at the card, on February 24, "just as pretty as a picture and smart too." He said it like *smart* and *pretty* were normally incompatible attributes.

"Celeste wants her establishment to be like a very nice private club, a London club. Do you know London?"

Cal said he'd been there twice. Bobbie said she'd been there in college.

"Well, you'd know then. You're not a customer in London, but a member of a club. They bring you right in like it's your aunt's house and she's been missing you something awful.

"That's what Celeste wanted. She didn't want some damn French maître d' looking fishy and asking if you had a reservation." He paused, looking from police officer to police officer to be sure they followed him.

"I still have a problem," said Bobbie. "This girl had held a summer job in a flower shop, no college, never worked in a restaurant. I can't see what she was bringing to the table."

"Herself . . . You see, Mary Jeanne had a quality, I don't know just how to describe it, but she could make you feel twenty-five again. It was a great attribute."

"Can you tell us what you know about Mary Jeanne's whereabouts on the weekend of August second?" Cal asked.

"Celeste and I have racked our brains." He shook his head like his brain was racking. "We just don't know. Celeste's so upset she's taken to bed. Celeste is really the one who worked with her most closely — hired her, trained her, managed her, but she's too distraught now to help you."

"Were you at the River Club on that weekend, Mr. Moray?" Cal asked.

He shook his head. "Celeste remembers it was very crowded for August. The World Bank was meeting here both Friday and Saturday. Mary Jeanne had to do the main room all that night. Celeste was working on something outside, so Max handled the cocktail lounge and the kitchen, and Mary Jeanne was alone on dining."

"Do you know when she left work?"

He looked again at the card.

"Celeste said Max told her it was after the last seating. That would be after midnight."

"Why didn't you report her missing when she didn't come into work?"

"She had three days coming, so this was the start of her weekend," Moray said. "That was why she was not missed right away."

"When were you going to report it?" Bobbie asked.

Moray's face showed he didn't like the tone of the question. He didn't answer.

"When she still didn't come in after three days, was she missed?" Bobbie tried again.

For the first time the lawyer Stein spoke. "I don't think Mr. Moray had any obligation to report her missing. He employs thousands of people in his organizations. Some of them just don't show up."

They went through their litany of questions. Did Moray suspect she used drugs? Was there a drug problem at the River Club? Did he know of any limousine that picked her up from time to time? Had she had a fight with another employee? Did any customer take some unusual interest in her and, finally, had he known about the night she was arrested with Tony Frohlo?

At each question Moray would pause — diffident, thoughtful, and unhelpful — until the Redskins question. The smile didn't leave his face, but Cal saw his eyes harden, and the two other men in the room leaned forward in their seats.

"Let's not bring that whole damn thing up again. Jesus! Tony had just signed a new contract and we had a little party to celebrate. Mary Jeanne was one of many guests, and Tony offered her a ride home. I guess they were a little light-headed."

The two men behind him nodded briskly in silent agreement with this tale.

"That's what often happens with football players. Everybody has their eye on them. Nothing serious happened, but the policemen ran into a well-known athlete cavorting around and just had to take a hand." More nodding in the room, as though this assessment should end the subject.

"I notice that you hired Mary Jeanne just one week after she was arrested with Frohlo," Cal said, glancing down at his notes. "Was there a connection?"

"There's no connection there. None." The homey Oklahoma manner was gone, and the lawyer Stein noticeably bristled. "I don't even know who actually hired her." He looked at the lawyers as though they might have the answer.

"Did she date any other Redskins?" Bobbie asked in that little girl way she had.

Moray looked as if he was going to choke but suddenly beamed again. Celeste had a theory. Mary Jeanne had gone somewhere after work on Friday, and was snared by a dangerous person, someone she had never met, a homeless person or a deranged person, someone who had no connection to her life.

The theory was very self-serving. It took the case away from the River Club, away from his wife, away from any question of negligence or responsibility, away from Redskins and National Football League inquiries about drug and alcohol use. Far, far away.

"He's bullshitting us," Bobbie whispered out by the elevators. "Frohlo held out. I remember reading about how his negotiations dragged on. He was late to training camp and bitched in February about getting only two million. No way is Harry Moray stupid or forgetful. So why is he lying?"

"Maybe Mary Jeanne was part of the negotiations. To keep him focused on the Redskins?" Cal said.

Bobbie looked at Cal.

"You've got it! When Frohlo roughed her up, they had to give her a job. He didn't even remember he told us Celeste hired her."

10

The Monday after they talked to Moray, a suspect popped up from a simple and routine quarter: criminal records.

Richie, the cook for whom each night Mary Jeanne had thoughtfully brought cold glasses of ginger ale, had done a two to five in West Virginia for burglary, with a count of attempted rape dismissed.

Cal had worked with Bobbie long enough to know this was going to be her meat. "Men who rape women," Bobbie liked to say in her rape seminars, "are men who will kill them."

They picked up the cook as he went to work at noon.

"Man, you'll get me fired. I can't be late. Please." They said they would give him a note.

"You're not under arrest, Richie. We just want to talk to you." Bobbie was careful and correct. When and if Richie became a suspect, the record would show that in this conversation, he was not under arrest and that he had accompanied them voluntarily. No Miranda needed, no Miranda given.

Richie's thin, tattooed forearms dropped to his sides. It was a gesture of those in society who are impotent. Bobbie was simply a representative of forces that he could not control.

For the first two hours, Richie was belligerent. He had his rights. But as so often had happened to him in those small bare rooms, his rights seemed so hard to maintain, so remote, as though they existed some-place far away and he was not free to go get them.

Finally there was despair, clear in every gesture as he listened to a mono-tone Miranda and signed the waiver. With despair came compliance.

"Every goddamn guy in that place tried to hit on her. What the fuck do you think? She had a new guy a week. Shit, one was even a nigger."

"Who was that, Richie?"

"Some guy named Virgil James." Richie paused for a moment. "He's a regular, broiled tuna fish steak on a bed of greens without oil, garnished with pine nuts." How did Richie know? "I seen that they was always whispering down the hall by the pay phone."

Maybe Richie tried his luck? No. She wasn't his type. He wouldn't have nothing to do with her. She was stuck up. He knew some girls around better'n her. Well, actually, she had not paid him the slightest attention.

"You thought about it, didn't you, Richie?" Bobbie said in that avenging-woman way she had.

"I had better'n her."

"When?"

"Sure, I thought about her."

"Just thought? Not touched?"

"I never even met her out of work."

Richie grew less compliant and more and more argumentative as time wore on. The bitterness of his lot tumbled out.

"Celeste is only giving me seven ten an hour. I'm the main broil cook. She fucking pays the Salvadorans six bucks."

At this low station he knew Mary Jeanne would not consider him. He had asked her out once, but she had demurred.

Cal watched Bobbie with admiration. Once he had taken Bobbie and one of her languid boyfriends fishing out on the bay. Bobbie said she used to fish with her daddy, the air-conditioning king, in a lake west of Dallas. "Our lake," she had called it. "Our lake." Cal and Bobbie took four big blues that day, glistening and thrashing about in the cooler.

Bobbie said she knew how to cook fish, yes sir, her daddy had taught her. As she talked, she was cleaning the fish, with deft, awful knife strokes. She killed them with the knife, pulling them live out of the cooler and inserting the knife under the head, quick and brutal. Her boyfriend looked on in horror. Later, Bobbie told Cal with surprise, she never saw the boyfriend after that trip.

Today her face was set with the same concentration. Richie was hooked now, thrashing around like that fish.

Suddenly Richie pulled for open water. "I wanna leave. I feel sick. Really sick. I don't wanna answer no more." He was bent over, his brow furrowed in what Richie must have thought was a look of pain.

Bobbie took a sheet from the folder on the side table. "You ever see your old West Virginia file, Richie?"

Richie watched the piece of paper move toward him.

"You remember the file?"

Bobbie started to read the file. "According to the complainant, she awoke because she felt a hand on her breast. She said the suspect, who she identified as Richard Keith Willis, was trying to undress her. It was then the complainant said she screamed, and the suspect broke toward the window. . . ." Bobbie was looking hard at Richie. "You bargained this down, didn't you? Pleaded quick to a burglary stick; that was better than another deuce and a half for rape, am I right, Richie?"

"I never touched her. Fat old woman made that up. I was out of the house before she even got a good look at me."

"Richie, Richie, Richie!" Bobbie said like a schoolteacher who has a reluctant student. "What happened here? Did you go see Mary Jeanne? Just to talk to her? You just wanted to take her out for a little drink, didn't you? Then something went wrong. Isn't that it?"

Bobbie's face was now two inches from Richie's. Cal watched her eyes; they were filled with loathing. The cook began to shake all over, and tears silently flowed down his cheeks. He could see where this was going.

"I swear to God. I swear to God," he kept saying, except he never quite said what he swore to.

Bobbie was relentless. "This isn't West Virginia, Richie. We're talking Lorton now. You're going to be" — she turned to Cal as if for technical advice — "one of maybe five white men in the cell block." She sized up Richie. "You're really sweet looking, Richie. Slim and sweet. Isn't he a sweet man, Cal?

"If they had enough personnel, they could segregate you, but" — now Bobbie was wistful — "but there've been enormous layoffs. Now they'll just put you in the dorm."

Tears rolled down Richie's cheeks. He'd done time in West Virginia's Reformatory for Wayward Youths. They'd been farm kids and runaways mostly; his imagination was now going full force.

"Tell us where you got the cocaine, Richie." Bobbie walked over and stood next to him, looking off in the same direction like a companion or an older sister, like somebody on his side. "The coke impressed her, didn't it, Richie? She liked that idea."

Richie's face was now drenched with tears. For a second he actually leaned his head against Bobbie's thigh. She put her hand gently on his hair.

"You want to tell us something, don't you? You want to."

Richie's head was moving up and down now, still leaning against her thigh, but nodding yes. He was nodding surrender.

"I seen her."

Bobbie silently turned on the video camera, checking the tape. She wore a look of satisfaction, an abbess of the inquisition.

Richie stopped as though he knew he must not get out of step in this ritual, as though he knew his place.

Bobbie mumbled into the recorder. "This is an interview with Richard Keith Willis, August eighteenth, by Lieutenant Terrell and Sergeant Short. Mr. Willis has been advised of his rights to counsel and has waived them under D.C. statutes. He has signed waiver sheet number one oh oh two nine seven."

Bobbie looked at Richie.

"What do you mean, 'you seen her.'?"

"In the shower."

"In the shower?" Bobbie's voice was harsh. "What shower?"

"Employees' shower. I seen her most every night."

They called Max the bartender and had him meet them there, trooping through the dining room like a strange parade: Richie, Max, Cal, Bobbie, two lab techs, and the police photographer.

Richie solemnly moved bags of potatoes and onions. He began sobbing again. "I didn't mean nothing," he said plaintively as he lifted the bags and boxes out of the way.

A small hole had been cut waist-high through the wall into the employees' bathroom and shower. Even though the angle was oblique and the toilets out of view, Richie could watch a woman prepare herself and enter the shower stall.

Max started screaming at Richie. "You fuckin' little redneck." He hit out at him, pushing his shoulder, before Bobbie could stop him. "Celeste is going to kill me," he whined. "You're through here. You're fired," he screamed as Bobbie backed him out the door.

They did a complete workup on the hole. Photos front and back and fingerprint work both in the shower area and the storeroom.

Back at police headquarters, Richie sat in dejected silence while Cal talked to the U.S. Attorney's Office.

"How'd you know when she was in there?" Bobbie asked.

"The Salvadorans could see the door. 'Hola, your lady's coming.' I let them watch too. Are you going to charge me?"

Cal shushed them so he could hear better on the phone. The assistant U.S. attorney seemed bored and unsure.

"Unless the West Virginia case has a parole or probation tail on it, I can't see how you can hold him in the girl's death. I'm not even sure I can get a search warrant. Anyway, I can't get it today."

"You've got to get it before we release him. It won't do us any good after he gets home," Cal said.

"Uh-uh. I've got motions and a meeting with the assistant attorney general. No way, José."

"Can we delay his release? Peeping Tom or something?"

"We can't go Peeping Tom, because we haven't got a complainant. Maybe destruction of property. My advice is to cut him loose until you get more to connect him to the woman's death."

Five minutes later he called back. "I've been thinking about this: get a public defender in there so we'll be covered to charge him later if we have to. Tell the public defender I'm going for a warrant tomorrow, and see if you can get Willis to sit still for a voluntary search. Go home with him."

The public defender was a woman. Cal had met her before. She was young and no dummy. She stopped the drug screen, blood work, and semen sample idea at the pass, got Richie a sandwich from the machine, and talked him into demanding to leave. No voluntary searches of his home, thank you.

The lawyer was walking Richie out when Cal stopped him by the door.

"Did Mary Jeanne have a brand on her buttocks the last time you saw her?"

He answered so quickly, it seemed without thought.

"No. Everything was smooth and tan."

The public defender pulled him angrily through the door.

When Cal got home the day they interrogated Richie, the farmhouse had been completely cleaned from top to bottom, the way it was kept when Vivian would send her maids down. The way it was when they were married.

The bedroom ceiling had been painted, the floors cleaned, a new rug was in the foyer, the furniture glistened, and someone had brought in firewood and taken out last winter's ashes. When he opened the refrigerator, it glistened with cleanliness and was packed with food. The offending cans of tuna had disappeared.

Instead of Rolling Rock in the cooler shelves were six bottles of an expensive designer water. Someone had fixed a plate of cheese and fruit, a very pricey Camembert, a cut of Roquefort, and a Stilton. There were also the graham biscuits that Vivian had fed him at the little hotel near Stratford-upon-Avon, lying next to him, one naked leg draped over his body.

There was a rose as well, a single yellow rose with a large blossom, the kind that came from somebody's garden, and a note.

I didn't mean to upset you the other day. I have been having so many conversations with you in my mind that when I saw you, it all tumbled out as though we'd been in touch every day.

What I need is the safety of your strength and the peace of the farm for a while. Can I come occasionally, at least; if you prefer, when you're away?

Vivian had drawn a girlish little circle happy face, like the ones she drew when they were married.

When he went to get a drink, all the hard liquor was gone. There were two bottles of a good Riesling and a merlot. He smiled to himself. Vivian had not changed.

11

Cal drove down to the Haven Inn, bummed a bottle of tequila and some limes, and went home and turned on the O's and Oakland. He had to laugh. Vivian never could resist readjusting Cal like the fine-tune button on the TV. Wine was more genteel than beer and hard liquor. "You are a trained ornithologist, a war hero, a decorated police officer, a championship dressage rider. Why do you try so hard to be uncouth?" Vivian would ask.

He heard the upstairs toilet flush. He realized that either Vivian or her maid was still in the house. When he turned, Vivian was coming downstairs in tennis clothes. "Going to a game?"

"They're for Edward's benefit."

"The house looks beautiful. You didn't have to do that." Cal stood. "Would you like a drink?"

She looked at the tequila bottle on the coffee table.

"You never change. I buy you a Riesling that has won every award in Europe, forty-two dollars a bottle, perfect for the cheese I selected, and you go get a seven-dollar bottle of tequila."

"That's because you threw out about three hundred dollars' worth of booze, including my tequila."

She went over and sat down next to Cal on the sofa. "Do you know why I got you the Riesling?"

He shook his head.

"Riesling emboldens a man." He felt her hand on his thigh. "Tequila makes a man sleepy."

They sat out in the pasture, where they could see the bay, and drank both bottles of the Riesling and ate the picnic supper. Vivian put her car radio on and left the door open, and they listened to the hope-filled melody of Mozart's *Jupiter* Symphony.

"How do you explain this to Edward?"

She kissed him very long and hard. "That's my business. Will you let me come here sometimes?"

"Sometimes. If you bring a picnic."

"It's a deal."

They talked a lot and watched the stars come up and fireflies dance. They talked about his cases and her news reports. Vivian had read a small item about Mary Jeanne, she said. She and Edward went to the River Club a lot. "Edward just adores the food." Cal laughed.

"Tell him to eat hearty. We may bust the cook for Mary Jeanne's killing."

"You have a suspect?"

"Yeah. Bobbie's working on him."

"Did he do it?"

"Shit, I don't know. It's too early."

"I think I remember her."

"Who?"

"Mary Jeanne. Was she the big girl?"

"Yes. Tall, dark blond hair."

"That really is terrible. The paper said she was tortured."

He felt Vivian's body shiver next to him.

Cal wanted to touch her. He had wanted to all evening, and she was right — the Riesling seemed to encourage the idea. He hadn't been with a woman in six — or was it seven?— months. He could smell the fragrance on her neck and literally feel her warmth, but he held back. He didn't want too much too soon. He still didn't quite understand what Vivian's agenda was. She always had an agenda.

"You're very decorous," she said, late in the evening. "But you have to muss me up a little, or Edward won't think I had a rousing game of tennis."

They kissed long and hard, Cal's fingers entwined in her hair. He could feel her tongue between his lips. He felt himself becoming aroused. Vivian pushed herself up. "Too late. Your timing's way off, Calvert."

After she left, he had two tequilas and went up to bed. He could hear the dogs racing through the brush.

———

On Tuesday night the telephone woke him from a sound sleep.

For a minute he thought it was Vivian.

"This is Dispatch. I've got a woman who says she's a public defender. She's hysterical. Keeps saying something is awful and somebody's dead. And she keeps repeating your name and somebody named Richie. We've sent a car and an ambulance to the address at Fifteenth and P. You wanna talk to her? I'll patch her through."

He couldn't think. "A woman . . . who is it that wants me?"

"A public defender."

"She's on now?"

"Yeah."

"Patch her through."

It was the young lawyer who'd handled Richie. Her speech was slurred and rambling. Richie was dying. Richie was dead. She had tried to save him.

"Where are you?" Cal said.

"Richie's."

"I'm coming, but it will take a while. There will be a police car there in a few minutes. It was dispatched already. It'll take me an hour to get there."

Cal disconnected and called back Dispatch.

"Tell the responding car to look for . . ." He couldn't remember her name. "A hysterical woman, Caucasian, late twenties, dark hair, named Susan something."

"Will you meet them there, Lieutenant?"

"Yeah, but don't let them wait on me. Tell them we're looking for a twenty-nine-year-old white man. Richard Keith Willis. He lives in an apartment near there."

Even on the empty predawn roads, it took forever. By the time he finally reached the Beltway, he realized this was stupid. He should have just let the district car handle it. Get the woman and get Richie to a detox center, whatever. He tried to remember Richie's address from the arrest form but couldn't bring it to mind.

Twice Cal started to turn around, but he knew after he said he was on the way, the uniforms wouldn't like that. He wondered if they'd tried to call Bobbie. Shit, she lived only twenty-five blocks away. Anyway, if he didn't show, they would just keep calling Dispatch. When he crossed the South Capitol Street Bridge, Dispatch gave him an address in the 1400 block of P.

He was three blocks south of P Street when he saw the lights of an ambulance and a couple of cruisers. They were on the west side of the street in front of a twelve-story brick apartment building. It had been fashionable in 1910, but now it was shabby and worn, cut into small units for winos and the elderly.

A cop standing by one cruiser was talking on his handheld. He never challenged Cal. "Third floor," he said.

The elevator wasn't working and looked like it hadn't been working for a long time. Cal trudged upstairs, fixing his shield on a chain around his neck.

The apartment was awful. The police had opened the door to the hall to air it out, but the stench was still unbelievable.

Richie was in the bathroom. He would never have to face the Cals and Bobbies of the world again. Like everything Richie had probably ever done, it looked like a crude and stupid plan.

Richie was hanging from a rope that stretched out the upper portion of the bathroom window to the metal bar of a fire escape strut on the floor above. After the rope had been fixed, Richie apparently stood on a washbasin, an old one, with white porcelain. Cal guessed it was four feet off the ground.

Of course the jump was not enough to break Richie's neck. It left him dangling from the top of the window sash like a macabre drape. Cal could see that he strangled. His fingers were still hooked in the rope where he had desperately tried to loosen the hold on his throat. But in the porcelain-covered Victorian bathroom, there must have been no place to brace his feet, to get purchase enough to take his weight off the rope. He was probably just inches short of the edge of the basin, and the window behind was flush with the wall. There were marks where he had tried to hook his heels on the window frame.

Cal wondered why he hadn't jumped outside, from the fire escape. This would have been more sure and, to Cal's thinking, the real escape. Maybe Richie was afraid of heights.

Richie's tongue was out, his eyes bulged from their sockets, and his face was now a deep purplish blue. In death he had wet himself and lost his bowels, and his pants thrust out with the erection common with hangings.

"Not a pretty sight."

The officers were kids, maybe twenty-three or twenty-four. The male uniformed officer ran his flashlight beam up and down Richie's body. One was a woman.

"The woman who called was totally whacked out, Lieutenant," she said. "We found her sitting on the floor, talking to the wall. She apparently tried to get him down. She's covered with it."

She pointed to the closet with her flashlight. "He had a cat. It got sick, I think. It's in the closet." The policewoman spoke with distaste. She and her partner were holding their hands away from their tailored uniforms as if to keep their pristine neatness. They had put on disposable plastic gloves.

"Did you call the coroner?"

"Ambulance is rolling."

"Where's the woman?"

"Down in the ambulance. They were going to transport her to GW Hospital, but she wanted to wait for you."

The woman police officer walked over to the window, trying to stay as far away from Richie as possible, and called in, holding her radio out the window to give the transmission reach.

"You got any more of those gloves?"

The male officer fished a box of gloves from a black police bag by the door.

Cal poked through the room using the handle of his flashlight. No branding iron. No coke. No victim's clothes. Nothing but the trash of a marginal man. There were papers strewn about, W2 slips and an expired West Virginia registration for a 1978 Ford LTD. A rent notice warned of eviction.

Cal went downstairs.

The woman lawyer was, as the officers said, covered with urine and excrement. The ambulance crew had wrapped a disposable blanket around her, but she smelled like hell.

"What happened?" Cal squatted down next to the woman. He was trying to remember her name. Susan? Lundorf? Lungren?

"Can you tell us what happened, Susan?"

A patrol car pulled up by the ambulance and a cop got out balancing a paper box with 7-Eleven coffee cups. Even though it was nearly 4:30 A.M., the curious had formed on the far side of the street and others were slowing down their cars. He waved them along and began to hand out the coffee.

"I'm sorry, Lieutenant, I only got six."

"That's okay."

Cal took the coffee he proffered to the woman, opened it, and crouched down. "Let me hold it, Susan."

The woman's hands were trembling, and she bent forward, sipping the coffee without using her hands.

"You want a cigarette or anything?"

She shook her head.

"Can you tell me what happened?"

"He was still alive." Tears began to well up. "He was twitching all over. I didn't have the strength to lift him."

"Why were you here, Susan?"

"He kept calling me. He said I had to help him. All night. Then his wife called me. Long-distance. She said Richie said cops were around asking about him. She said he thought he was going to get arrested." She stared ahead in a daze.

"I decided I'd better come down."

"Why didn't you call the police to see if he'd been brought in?"

"I don't know."

The young lawyer lived in an apartment in Silver Spring outside the Beltway and had had trouble getting her car started, but she was a public defender and a destitute client had summoned her. She couldn't tell how long it took, but when she got there, she smelled an awful smell. "I couldn't stand the smell."

The door was blocked, but she finally pushed it open. There was Richie across in the bathroom, confronting her as he had Cal.

She ran over and tried to lift him up, to get his feet under something, but at first she couldn't. Then she got a chair from near the bed and put his feet on the chair, but the rope had cut deeply into Richie's neck and she couldn't budge the knot.

She had to run down to the street to call, then run back up to try to help Richie. "He was past help," the paramedic whispered. The woman sat there in silence, finishing the coffee. Cal bummed a cigarette. It was Susan Lungren, not Lundorf. She refused medical treatment.

Susan had taken Richie that morning to Celeste Moray to beg for his job back. It was all he had. There were no jobs in West Virginia. It turned out, Susan said, he fed a wife and two children with that job, wiring the money at the Western Union, taking out a little for rent and wine.

She still had the photo of his family. She'd taken it to Mrs. Moray's office. She dug in her purse.

The old photo was wrinkled and grainy, the world of Richard Keith Willis. A woman with a face as gaunt and defeated as Richie's looked seriously at the camera, holding two small children on the steps of a mobile home. The yard was strewn with parts of what seemed to be several cars. The faces of Richie's family wore weak little smiles, as though the picture taking was an unexpected interlude in an otherwise unpleasant existence.

"Richie said they'd run out of money and had no food."

She looked sadly at Cal.

"It was ridiculous to think he could have killed Mary Jeanne. When he got home that night, he sat drinking wine until noon and fell asleep on the back stoop." She nodded toward the building. "He was going to find some of the guys he was drinking with for me."

She said Richie had been sure he could persuade Mrs. Moray to take him back. Let me talk to her alone, he kept saying. But a few minutes after he went in the office, Susan heard Mrs. Moray screaming at him, and he looked stunned when he came out.

"Do you remember what she was screaming?" Cal asked.

She paused before answering. "I think something like 'Don't try it.'"

12

Cal went straight to the office from Richie's and tried to nap on a couch in the ready room, but it was no go. He felt tense and angry without quite knowing why he was tense and angry. As a policeman, he had learned to recognize many forms of human behavior: anger, derangement, drug dependency, alcoholism. Richie was a high-time drinker. High-time drinkers don't kill themselves. They get some Thunderbird and travel on. Life didn't expect anything of Richie. He didn't have a concept of failing. Richie was slow, but by the time he got to the apartment that night, Richie would have guessed the cops really didn't have too much. Even if he had killed Mary Jeanne, he'd have just run. Richie was already on the run in life. Within a month, he'd be cooking in someplace like Amarillo, Texas, using a different name.

But Cal was also sure Nathaniel would want the case. After the Reggae Club and 286 unsolved homicides, Nathaniel and his mayor were on the run like Richie. Nathaniel would love Richie. *In less than a week, our officers identified a suspect.* Cal could hear the news conference.

Cal and Bobbie went to Nathaniel's office at 8:30; Cal really had had only an hour's sleep. Nathaniel ignored them for perhaps two minutes, keeping his head down, apparently studying a group of files before him. It was an old trick Nathaniel used with suspects: he'd ignore them, reading some report until the suspect wondered who called the meeting.

Nathaniel was dressed in an Armani cut double-breasted dark brown suit, a paisley bow tie, and those silly little round Teddy Roosevelt glasses. He looked like he was at a poetry reading instead of a homicide meeting.

Cal and Nathaniel had been partners when Cal first came to Homicide. In those days Nathaniel, six feet two inches of rangy ex-paratrooper, sported black turtleneck sweaters and tweed jackets and had seen every Shaft movie ever made. He rode a motorcycle in his off hours in an all-black leather suit and black helmet. But the motorcycle had been sold, the black leathers disappeared, and his Screaming Eagles coffee cup was replaced by cold bottles of Perrier he kept in a refrigerator behind his desk.

He and Cal had been paired to show the department that white and black officers could work together, and for a long time they were close — not as close as Cal and Bobbie were — but close. The "case busters," they called them. They had complemented each other. Cal could organize a case and make sense of it, but Nathaniel had grown up in D.C., the son of a cabdriver, graduate of Dunbar High School and American University. He knew the city and he knew the streets. He knew the bootleggers, the numbers guys, the bust-a-bank-for-lunch bunch, and the kings of Lorton.

Nathaniel could massage a report to make himself look good for the promotion board, and both Cal and Nathaniel liked to bend the rules now and then, just to get the job done. Once they joined a pimp's funeral in a rented gold Cadillac convertible; another time they racked up a $15,000 bar bill for a sting that netted nine suspects in an arson homicide.

Ambitious, college educated, and on the rise, Nathaniel became president of the Black Police Officers Association. The BPOA was Cameron's baby. There were those who said he wouldn't be mayor without it. The BPOA guarded him at political rallies, kept the drug guys back, and, some said, raised campaign money from merchants eager to please the cops.

Cameron changed Nathaniel's life. The old-timers agreed on that. From the day Cameron took office, Nathaniel's star was on the rise. Cal didn't resent it at first. Everyone — including Cal — expected that Cal would be the next head of Homicide, until Nathaniel got Cameron's juice. Nathaniel had reorganized the mayor's security detail, sold Cameron's politics to both the white and black police unions, and spent untold hours at the mayor's side being his walking encyclopedia on crime. That Cameron would give him what he wanted went without saying.

Cal still didn't resent the job going to Nathaniel, that wasn't it. It was the way they'd done it, never mentioning other candidates, making no pretense of a choice, just announcing it one day and doing the paperwork later. Cal wasn't even interviewed.

Nathaniel patronized him from then on. "Nothing's changed, Cal," Nathaniel said. "We're still the same team." But, of course, that was ridiculous; everything had changed. Now, after four years, Cal knew Nathaniel was set to make his move. He was going to push Cal out. Nothing personal. Cal was the only guy in Homicide with enough experience and skill to disagree with Nathaniel. Nathaniel didn't like anyone to disagree.

For a long time, Cal kept asking himself if the situation were reversed and Cal had been made head of Homicide, would he have treated Nathaniel any better? After all, they were both strong, stubborn, determined men, perhaps able to exist only as equals, never one subservient to the other. In the end he never really settled the question, stuck instead in a sort of emotional rut with the same old question and lots of contradictory answers, none very satisfying.

Slowly Nathaniel looked up at the two detectives before him and began his ritual weekly reminder of how far behind Cal and Bobbie were in their casework. No matter how many cases they were handling, usually seven or eight active ones at any given time, ten in bad periods, Nathaniel would never sympathize with the workload. Instead, he just kept pushing, nudging, nagging.

"What about Division Avenue? What was the name — Parker?"

"Simmons thinks the shooter is a guy at Lorton," Cal said. "He was picked up on a parole violation and was back in Lorton the day after the shoot."

"To build an alibi?"

"Maybe."

"Did Collins talk to him?"

"If he can get free of the Reggae Club shooting, he's going down this week."

"You gonna close Defoe?" Nathaniel changed folders.

"Yeah. Peters said North Carolina will charge Defoe and there are two manslaughter indictments outstanding."

"What about Turner? We going to close that?" Nathaniel slowly drew Mary Jeanne's file over from the left pile.

"Might as well," said Bobbie. "We'll never locate the others."

Nathaniel picked up the red pencil.

"What others?" Cal asked. He looked at Bobbie with real amazement.

"The guys with Richie," she said. She seemed surprised at the question.

"What guys?" asked Cal. He had been ready for Nathaniel, but Bobbie caught him off guard.

Nathaniel looked up in surprise. Cal felt Bobbie swivel in her chair. "You don't think the little cook did her?" Nathaniel said. "The papers said he did." Nathaniel began grinding his teeth, a sure sign that something was irritating him.

"Are they running Homicide?" Cal shot back.

Out of the corner of his eye, Cal saw Bobbie shift defensively.

"Nathaniel, it's what you always preach," Cal said. "Capacity. Willis didn't have it. He didn't have the brains, money, or muscular coordination. We want to believe he could lure a nineteen-year-old, five-foot nine-inch female into a van, brand her, dispose of the body, and clean her apartment. Last night I searched Richie's apartment. There was not a thing in his apartment to connect her to him, not one damn thing."

"Why don't we think he branded her?" Bobbie asked. She sounded tense.

"Because when I asked Willis if she was branded, he never paused, not for a single second; he said the last — repeat, last — time he'd seen her — she didn't have a mark on her!"

"Sure he did." Bobbie's face was reddening. "That was before — let me repeat, before — the first. She didn't have a mark then. Cal, this was a sick puppy. He snatched her, tortured her, and killed her. He wasn't going to tell you about it!"

Cal started to explain that it didn't make any difference that it was before August first; the point was that it was Richie's natural, uncoached reaction.

But Bobbie had turned back to Nathaniel.

"What I figure is, Willis had a friend or friends pick Mary Jeanne up at work. They had some wine, some coke. They wanted some action. Just like Cal says, Richie is a loser, so he wants to impress some old buddies. He said this girl down at his work would be off in a few minutes. 'I seen her in the shower,' he says. He gives them a description of what they can get."

"You mean, Mary Jeanne was going to get into a car at three A.M. with a bunch of smelly, sweat-stained rednecks?" Cal felt his anger rising and knew he was talking too loud.

Bobbie shook her head angrily. "But she would come over to the window. That's all it would take."

"Maybe you're right. Maybe she wouldn't go near him, but maybe, just maybe, Richie and his friends grabbed her by force. She stops, just for a second. Richie leans out. She knows Richie, that throws her off guard. Boom!"

Bobbie was acting out her theory now, standing up, making wrestling and grappling motions.

"They've got a side-door van. 'Come on, honey, let's party.' Tie her up. Go someplace woodsy, isolated, push coke on her, play with her a little bit.

"The van's a good ol' boy's road palace with a rug in the back. So as long as they got her, one of them decides to put his initial on the merchandise."

Bobbie sat down and opened a notebook on her knees. "I did some work on my own last night. . . . Most of the cooks usually leave before the front room help because the kitchen closes at one. One stays to clean up and handle dessert orders. The bartender said that was Richie on the first. Richie left at two-ten, according to the timeclock card. Remember, Mary Jeanne's timecard showed she left at two-thirty. One of the waiters said he saw Richie walking up Thirtieth Street, but he isn't sure of the time. There's no bus stop there. So I guess he was meeting somebody."

"Or walking home," said Cal. "Nathaniel, I was in Richie's apartment when he was still twitching. No cocaine, no branding iron, no women's clothes, nothing. *Nothing.*"

Cal turned with his final argument. "In the hands of three or four West Virginia boys, her vagina would have been badly torn and bruised and we'd have had buckets of semen. You know that!"

Bobbie shook her head. "She died before they could do anything. She died from the pain of the branding."

Nathaniel sat silent for a time.

Bobbie turned around and was facing Cal, no longer talking to Nathaniel. "Cal, just listen to me for a minute."

Cal started to speak, but stopped.

"When you work Sex Crimes, you learn people have fixations or fantasies that control them. Voyeurs, for instance, want to watch from a distance. If a peeper was watching a woman through the bedroom window and she came out and started to take off her clothes for him, he'd walk away. The erotic fantasy of being an *unseen* viewer arouses him, not nude women."

"Where are we going here?" Cal asked.

"Patience. Patience. Richie drills a hole in the women's bathroom, waist-high. What's on his mind? Her vagina and buttocks. He can't have them; he can only watch. Richie burns a brand on Mary Jeanne's body. Where is it? Is there a connection? Hell, yes. He could have branded her breasts or her face or an arm. I talked to this guy out at Maryland University. He says sexual marking is not uncommon, but the marking is usually sexually meaningful or aimed at destroying something that the subject is sexually angry about, like cutting off the breasts on a woman's corpse. That's not Richie—Mary Jeanne wasn't defaced, she was adorned! Richie wanted her, and a brand on her butt was an acquisition sign. He finally had her."

"Is *B* for Richard, Keith, or Willis?" Cal asked.

Bobbie ignored Cal. "With the pain of getting branded, she digs her toes in the rug and picks up fibers. Only now, that rug and that van are probably fifteen hundred miles from here.

"When her heart stops, Richie's in a panic because the others are from out of state. He knows he's the only one who connects to her. He gets rid of everything, gets anything out of his apartment that could incriminate him."

"If the action is all in the van," Cal said skeptically, "why would we find her apartment cleaned? Why do you think he'd clean his apartment? By the way, I've got to tell you, if Richie cleaned up evidence in his apartment, he sure missed every other sort of dirt. So we want to believe he cleaned his apartment, her apartment, but leaves his fingerprints all around that hole in the bathroom wall, then breaks down and leads the cops to it?"

"You see, the problem for Sergeant Short," Cal finally said to Nathaniel, "is that we have no evidence for her theory. No van. No friends. No witnesses. All we have is Richie hanging from the window sash."

Bobbie's voice rose in summation, "Nobody kills himself because he got fired from a seven-ten-an-hour job. Richie took the window way because he knew he was going down for murder."

Cal didn't say that he wondered about that too. He didn't say that Richie wasn't a candidate for suicide. Nathaniel would laugh him out of the room.

"You said you would take care of Richie, right?"

Bobbie nodded.

"So you sent the Second District detectives over to his building to check him out?"

"I didn't have time."

"Bullshit," Cal said. "His wife told the public defender that he thought cops were around looking for him."

Bobbie looked perplexed. "What cops? There were no cops. We didn't do that yet," she said.

"Give me a break," Cal said.

"Anyway," Nathaniel said. "We don't really have anything besides Richie. Right?"

"Correction! We haven't got that much," said Cal.

"We know Mary Jeanne met somebody who became very special to her. Her mother doesn't know who Mr. X is. But no Richie, this guy! Mr. X could take her to the Palm and dancing at the PINGA."

"How do you know?" Nathaniel said.

"She wrote it in a letter."

Suddenly, Nathaniel was leaning forward. He looked very tense. "Did she name this lover?"

Cal shook his head. Nathaniel sat back.

"My guess from the letter is that her mystery lover was older, well off, maybe a lobbyist or something. Mary Jeanne was afraid of being used. She wasn't sure he wouldn't screw her and drop her."

Nathaniel and Bobbie were staring at Cal in skeptical silence.

"Look, this was an extraordinarily beautiful young woman! She had enough poise and style to be a greeter in one of the fanciest places in town. She loved clothes. Her mother says she spent her whole salary on getting the smartest stuff she could. We can establish that she went out with a two-million-dollar-a-year professional ballplayer. We can surmise she was squired to some of the best restaurants in town." Cal was talking faster and faster. "More important, we know enough to tell us that she wasn't going to give a nod to a hillbilly cook."

Bobbie looked up in fury. "I get the picture now. You want this to run true to form, don't you! You want a black suspect, what's-his-name," she paused. "James. Virgil James."

Nathaniel took a sharp breath.

"What's James in this deal?" he said.

"We don't know," said Bobbie. "Richie said he was a regular at the River Club and spent a lot of time with Mary Jeanne."

"You know this guy?" said Cal.

"I know of him," Nathaniel said cautiously. "I guess you'd call him a developer. He put the Shaw redevelopment together."

"What does he do, actually?" said Bobbie.

"Makes money," said Nathaniel. "He was the treasurer of Martin's first campaign."

Cal saw Nathaniel move the Turner file to the actives on his desk. "Take another week. Run it where it goes, but we've got to put an end to this. I need closures! I want you two back on the Reggae Club. That's my problem! Not some waitress. Interview James and maybe get the West Virginia State Police to find Richie's known associates, see if any of them have a van. Okay?"

13

In the car on the way to James's office, Cal and Bobbie got into a furious argument. "How dare you demean me in front of Nathaniel!" she screamed.

"I didn't demean you. You had the wrong fucking cut on the case. You know that as well as I do, and calling me a racist back there to kiss up to Nathaniel isn't going to change that. You were wrong! But in your massive femininity, you can never ever deal with the fact you could be wrong."

Bobbie hit the car brakes with such anger that Cal flew forward and almost hit his head.

"I know you haven't grasped this," she roared. "But this is the nineteen nineties. John Wayne is dead. June Allyson is doing incontinence ads. Men don't shout down women colleagues just because they don't agree with them."

"Sergeant Short, do you want to interview this potential suspect or do you want to take yourself off the case?"

"Do you know why Vivian left you? She left you because you are impossible! You simply cannot deal with women."

"Sergeant Short, try to get some facts straight. Vivian didn't leave me. I left her. You haven't got time enough to hear all the reasons."

The car lurched forward, throwing Cal back in his seat.

He ostentatiously concentrated on reading the database printout. He could feel Bobbie seething.

James had graduated from Howard in the middle sixties, son of a wealthy funeral parlor director. His father's money had bought him a place in the movement, and he had been on the fringes at Memphis and

Resurrection City, a gofer for the men trying to hold together Martin Luther King's achievements after a bullet cut him down.

He had become a Republican in the '70s, gone into developing by re-habbing row houses, and by the end of the Reagan administration, the *Washington Post* was calling him one of Washington's "most innovative black entrepreneurs." He was the mayor's fund-raiser and his connection to many white developers.

"Progress in this city," James told one interviewer that year, "is spelled *Cameron.*"

They went east on H Street, behind the Capitol and Union Station. It was like driving through Dresden after the bombing. If progress was spelled *Cameron,* then failure was spelled *Near Northeast.*

In the 1950s it had been one of the black mercantile centers. But when the riots broke out, it had virtually been burned out. The scars had never healed. Despite the Great Society, urban enterprise zones, housing grants, and tax breaks, the corridor was hardly less bleak than it had been in 1968.

On the left was a giant sign, MARTIN CAMERON IS BUILDING YOU A NEW CITY. It had a picture of Cameron standing by the stadium, looking across the marsh grass and the Anacostia. A bunch of little black children were clustered around, and he was pointing at a city rising from the mist.

In the urban desolation, James's office building stood out like a rock-etship from Mars, all steel, glass, and marble, with giant hanging gardens on the different lobby levels. To step from New York Avenue into the main lobby was to cross into this other planet, away from the gritty and the soiled.

Virgil James too was from a different world than the one around him. He was all Georgetown, a tan seersucker suit, a white shirt with a pin through the collar, a silk paisley tie that must have cost $160, and shoes worth $500.

"I know I should have called you. But we've been jumping here with Balustrade."

"Balustrade?" Bobbie asked.

"Over on East Capitol. First mixed-use development east of the Ana-costia River. You ought to take a look at it."

"Why were you going to call us, Mr. James?" Cal asked.

"Oh! About Mary Jeanne, about that lady!"

"What about her?"

"Well I knew her. I was telling Martin just the other night. I said, 'Martin, I knew that lady! The one that was killed.'"

He had gotten the mayor's name in the first two minutes of their visit. Cal didn't miss it. Moray knew the president, Moray's lawyers knew the U.S. attorney, Nathaniel was close to the mayor, James was dropping names too. This was a crowded case.

"Anyway, when I got around to calling you, I heard on TV that you-all solved the case! I guess that ends it."

Cal didn't answer him. "How did you know her?"

"At the River Club. She was quite something. You did not miss Miss Mary Jeanne." James had a singsong tone like old-time Jamaican music. Cal wondered if he was just putting them on.

"Did you ever take her out?"

"Oh, a couple of times. You know, late evening, for supper or a drink. Once or twice on a weekend."

"Were you Miss Turner's lover?" Cal thought the word *lover* was as delicate as he could be.

He never paused. "Nope."

"Never once?" said Bobbie.

James didn't answer her.

"When did you last see her?"

"Maybe six, seven weeks ago."

"Where were you on August first and second?" Bobbie asked.

"Is that when she died?"

"Yes."

"I'm not sure. I lost my calendar and I'm just not sure."

"Try," said Bobbie.

James sat for a long time, then suddenly jumped up and left his office. "Come on," he said, "I can check one place." They followed him.

He silently took them up through the building by the glassed-in elevator. It was an impressive array. The city's largest black Realtor was on one floor, the main black radio station on the next, the Urban Coalition had another floor, and finally when the door opened they faced a stunning black obelisk under a giant wall hanging that read RIVERGATE DESIGN DIVISION in black stone.

"Ophelia," James called out, pushing past the reception desk. "Darling."

Ophelia Cameron was a big woman when Cal saw her up close, much bigger than she looked in the mayor's car that night. She was handsome, like one of the women in the old James Bond movies. Cal guessed she was six one in heels, and big boned, with a strong, commanding face and smooth dark skin.

"Where was I on August first and second?"

"How would I know?" Ophelia shot back, looking from Cal to Bobbie.

"Could you check your calendar? Didn't we have a presentation that week? Maybe it will show something."

The mayor's wife disappeared, all nylon stockings and tailored dress. The receptionist had recovered herself and was bustling around, asking whether anybody wanted juice or coffee.

Bobbie leaned into Cal's ear. "What's the mayor's wife doing working for Moray?"

Shaking her head, Ophelia called out from her office, "I don't know, Virgil. I remember I was in New York all weekend. I'm sure of it."

"Ophelia, honey, I thought you and Martin and I were together," James yelled back. Cal thought there was a little pleading in his voice.

"How did you lose your calendar?" Bobbie asked.

"Somebody cleaned out my car. Took a briefcase worth three hundred dollars. Tennis racquet. Everything. Took the floor mats." He looked at them quizzically. "What in God's name do you think they took the floor mats for?"

"Homeless," Bobbie said. "Homeless take them to sleep on."

Virgil nodded as though he marveled at such expertise on crime.

"Was that your only copy?" Bobbie asked.

James looked glum and nodded.

"Did you report it?" asked Cal.

"Were the cops going to get it back for me?"

They lapsed into silence.

"I think I may have been on the Eastern Shore," he said, looking nervously toward Ophelia's office door.

Ophelia walked back into the room thumping a thick leather calendar. "According to my book, you and Martin were scheduled to be at Kent Narrows."

"That's it! I remember now!"

"Is that the Eastern Shore?" Bobbie said.

James nodded.

"Do you own a place there?"

"Oh no! Just visiting."

"If it becomes necessary, can the mayor verify that?"

"Sure. We were at a meeting."

He said it with a big smile.

James called out thanks and pushed the elevator button.

"Wouldn't the mayor or Mrs. Cameron know her too?" Cal asked as James ushered them into the elevator.

"Know who?"

The door closed.

"Miss Turner."

James impatiently pushed the button. Now he seemed intent on denying Cal the opportunity to talk to Ophelia.

"Why would you say that?"

"Don't they frequent the River Club?"

"The mayor doesn't frequent anything! I suppose Martin's been there. He goes all over."

James's manner had changed. He was looking hard at Cal. "What are you trying to make of this? Just what? A friend of mine said this was all over. Just what are you after?"

A friend of his! Nathaniel had called him! He hadn't missed the way Nathaniel's head shot up at the mention of James's name. It was a nasty thought. Nathaniel may have evolved into an ambitious bureaucrat, but he was still straight. He'd never bend the rules for this little weasel. Cal tried to push the thought from his mind.

"When you told the mayor that you knew Mary Jeanne, made the connection that it was the same girl at the River Club, what did he say?"

"I don't remember. Something like, 'Really,' or 'Too bad.'"

"But he didn't remember her?"

"He didn't say he did."

"Did that surprise you?"

"What are you getting at" — James looked at Cal's business card — "Terrell? What are you getting at?"

"You just said nobody missed Miss Mary Jeanne," Bobbie interjected. "Come on, Mr. James."

James snorted.

"We're trying to reconstruct events on the weekend Miss Turner was killed. Could the mayor have been in the River Club?"

"You're not trying anything. I'll tell you what you're trying: you're trying to dig dirt on Martin."

James's voice had risen several octaves.

The elevator had now passed James's floor and was in the lobby. A security guard stared at them from behind his bank of television monitors.

"No. We were both at Kent Narrows. We went down together."

"Mayor take the city car?"

For the first time James hesitated.

"Yes."

"When did you leave?"

"Friday, maybe three or four."

"Come back?"

"Sunday afternoon."

Suddenly he reared back, punching a finger at them.

"I get this now!"

"Get what, Mr. James?"

"You don't want it to be a white person."

"What do you mean?" asked Bobbie in her edgiest voice. This guy was challenging her liberalism! It was all right for her to question Cal, but she hated for her liberalism to be doubted.

"I mean, it wasn't enough for you that a white cook killed her. That wouldn't fit. That bothers the hell out of you. Could it be that black people don't do all the crime in D.C.?"

Shaking with fury, Bobbie started to speak. Cal put his hand on her arm. "Let's go."

They rode back downtown in silence. The heat shimmered off the hood of the car, and little kids all laughed and snickered at it. Everyone knew the unmarked old Cavaliers.

"Every businessman uses his calendar for taxes. If he lost it, he'd be going crazy. So there must be a duplicate," Cal said. "So why was he doing that little act with Ophelia about the calendar? He started to lie, and it got stupider and stupider."

"Reality check," said Bobbie. "Calendar or no calendar, we still haven't got a suspect — besides Richie — and we haven't got a motive. For all we know, Mary Jeanne was into kink and it kicked her over. If that's true, we haven't got a chance of tying in James!"

Sometimes Cal felt Bobbie had the attention span of a three-year-old.

"This is a woman who'll get it on with a football player," Bobbie continued. "In a parking lot! That's not too discerning! So if it isn't Richie, maybe she just took an offer she should have refused." Bobbie summed up with classic police logic. "You've got to know when to fold 'em," she said. She knew that Mary Jeanne's death had grown cold.

Bobbie flew down to West Virginia the next day. Cal knew she didn't have to go in person, but he also knew that her pride was hurt. She was going to make Richie fit if it killed her.

14

The day Bobbie went to Charleston, Cal read Collins's report on the Reggae Club shooting. Nathaniel had been right. Collins really never got past what they knew the night it went down. The cartridge casings from the sniper's rifle were 7.62mm ammunition, manufactured in Czechoslovakia for the Kalishnikov assault rifle and sold in the United States.

Criminal records showed that the driver of the Jaguar, Kareem Montroy, had done two terms for assault as a juvenile and one as an adult. He was hit by several rounds from a MAC 10. The Jaguar had been bought at Foreign Motor Works for cash, and although the Narcotics Task Force had investigated the transaction, the cops had no idea where he got the money.

His killer, Leroy "Kitty Kat" Thompson, was in some ways a duplicate of the victim. He too had dropped out of school in the ninth grade, did a stretch at Juvenile and the youth home. His BMW was leased to him for $499 a month after he posted a $5,000 cash down payment; he paid off the lease two months before the Reggae Club shooting. He was on parole from twenty-four to thirty months for burglary. Unlike Kareem's mother, Leroy's mother had stuck with him, and she told the investigating officers that Leroy would have made it in life except for the "damn Reggae Club."

Strangely, Collins had not been able to establish by fact or rumor why Thompson wanted to kill Montroy. They had never had a fight, never "dissed" each other. There seemed to be no dispute over drug territory or a woman and their gangs were not particular rivals. In fact, Collins had concluded, there was precious little evidence they even knew each other.

The Reggae Club was more interesting. It was owned and licensed by one Carter Welding. Welding had no prior police record and, until he opened the club, had been a resident of the U.S. Virgin Islands. He had told the D.C. Liquor Authority that he owned 3 percent of the outstanding shares of BobMar Enterprises, which he had explained was a play on the name of Bob Marley and had absolutely nothing to do with the late reggae star. BobMar in turn, he said, was held by a Cayman Islands nominee company called Teekna.

Welding said he did not know who the principals of Teekna were. A Miami lawyer came to him in St. Thomas, he said, and asked him to open and manage a disco in Washington, D.C. He was offered $150,000 and a participation of 3 percent of a week's earnings above $50,000. The club, Welding said, had never broke even. A week after Collins interviewed Welding, the club was closed and Welding went to Venezuela.

Cal called Collins. "Did you talk to Leroy Thompson?"

"He's dead."

"Dead?"

"Died on the operating table. You were right. He was hit with two 7.62 rounds. They tore out his insides."

Leroy's mother lived in a row house down by the Congressional Cemetery, half a mile from the Reggae Club.

She was a husky woman, maybe forty-five. Cal had picked up that she had a security officer's license, and her broad shoulders and powerful arms suggested that she was right for the job. Leroy was her sixth and last child. Her "failure," she said.

Leroy had a different father than her other five children, and she had concluded that this father's seed was flawed.

"He never listened. Never."

After Leroy dropped out of school, her strength and determination had kept him in line when he was near her, but when he went out of the house, she said, he became what he really was, a hoodlum.

"You said he got money working at the Reggae Club," Cal said. "What did he do?"

"That's what I asked him. He'd say, 'Hang out.' When it opened, Leroy started going there all the time. The next thing I knew, he was sporting a leather coat made in Italy, a Rolex watch, and five gold necklaces. Once I found four beepers — not one, four — in his dresser. Once a woman told me he was living in an apartment on East Capitol. I said, 'That's shit! He's living at home.' She swore she saw him in this apartment.

"I said, 'Where'd you get all that money?' He said, 'Got contacts.'

She-e-et! Contacts. He hadn't turned eighteen. Drugs. That was his contact. Drugs over at the Reggae Club." She had no proof.

The Narcotics Task Force officer had little on the Reggae Club.

"Detective Collins asked the same questions." The task force officer was clearly bored. "Yes, we suspected it was a drug sales point. We put an undercover there for two months. Everybody had drugs, but nobody was selling. The owner seemed clean. The Hispanics were all legal. Salvadorans. Nice little guys."

"Salvadorans?"

"Yeah. Kitchen, bar, the works."

"Have you got anything on them?"

Two hours later, the task force officer called back.

"Atlacatl Placement on Columbia Pike. They all said they got their jobs through there."

"If there was no drug action and Welding said the joint was failing, what was it doing?"

"That's what bothered us. The area is residential. They had to get a special exemption to put the club there. Not ten blocks away was an empty movie theater they could have had with no zoning. The reason they didn't make any money was they were discounting like crazy to get kids to come. There was no cover, no minimum, live groups six nights, beer was three dollars a bottle and wine was two-fifty a glass. You can't get a Coke in the movies for that."

The drug officer said that at first he figured they were discounting to try to build a clientele. "But why do that?" he asked. "All that land is slated for Rivergate."

"That far up?"

"Yeah. Town houses and a marina."

Cal drove over to Atlacatl. The Salvadorans that worked at the Reggae had all gone back to El Salvador. "They were here with the army."

"With the army?"

"Sure. Training. Fort Belvoir. Six months. They can work to get extra money only within fifty miles of their base."

The owner pointed to a framed picture with pride. There were eight young men with wide serious Indian faces under helmets with chin straps buttoned, caught after a parachute jump, with the lines and canopies piled behind them.

"Parachutists?" Cal asked.

"Special Forces. Just like the United States . . ."

Vivian was talking to someone. Someone in the room. He could just hear.

"I don't know much. He never talked about it."

"It's important." The second voice sounded like the doctor.

"Well, I know he purposely crashed his helicopter into the sea. He got a medal for it. For avoiding crashing into the outskirts of Saigon. I know he broke both his legs. He was in a hospital in California for months. A head injury? You'll have to ask Calvert."

There was a murmur Cal couldn't hear.

"My husband could get those expedited," Vivian said. "He's the president's counsel. I'm sure he can help."

Cal started to open his eyes and push the buzzer with his left thumb but decided not to. He did not want to think about Vung Tau. He had forgotten the head injury. When *Amazing Grace* hit the water, the impact had thrown him through the front windshield and hurtled Yancy back on top of him. Yancy's jaw had been blown away. The last thing he saw as he floated up was Yancy looking up at him with half a face.

When all was said and done, he liked the work. Vivian had never understood that. In her world of careerists and courtiers, she had never been able to understand why he had stayed in the army for twelve years or why he had stayed a detective for so long. He liked the physical act of flying. Helicopters were like old prop planes, they flew low over the countryside in graceful swoops. You worked at flying every minute. There was no automatic pilot in helicopters. In the same way, he liked being an investigator because he liked the work.

The real reason he'd taken the lieutenant's exam was Vivian. "I hate to even say you're a sergeant," she would complain. "It sounds awful. You're the best detective they have. Why do you put up with it? Nathaniel pushes himself forward."

"You mean, his German wife pushes him," Cal told her.

When he and Vivian split, Cal quit pushing. Sometimes, when Bobbie was pissed off at something, she'd say that was the real reason he didn't become chief of Homicide, he didn't push.

But Cal liked being an investigator. He liked interrogations and legwork, sifting and searching databases, reading and organizing. He liked solving the puzzles. It was that simple. As time went on, he didn't care whether there was a prosecution, just so he knew the answer.

He slowly typed V-i-r-g-i-l M-a-l-c-o-l-m J-a-m-e-s into the computer and began the file. He was the only detective above the rank of patrolman who did his own research. The others sent routing slips on their dubious course through the D.C. government, bitching and moaning when they didn't get information back. Cal knew you had to do it yourself, so you could notice the little things. Little things made a case, lots of little things.

It was dark in his office and he was bathed in the glow of a single lamp and the computer screen. He felt good for the first time in days. He felt very good. He wondered if it was because he was seeing Vivian again.

Virgil James had seven corporations. Why seven? He didn't know. He listed them all.

A Porsche was owned by Rivergate. A Mercedes by VMJ, Inc. Why not the same firm?

He didn't know.

James had been married in D.C. to a Yolanda Fleetwood, and divorced six months later. No financial statement on file, and the divorce was uncontested. They both listed the same address on the decree. It was up near Howard. Where was Yolanda now? Cal didn't know.

Dun & Bradstreet gave James's total holdings as $22 million but reported that he was heavily leveraged. They listed some Uniform Commercial Credit reports, but the nature of his debts was not described. What were his main sources of income? Of financing? Dun & Bradstreet didn't say. Cal didn't know.

James had been sued seventeen times, little niggly-piggly suits, contract disputes, late payments. Two suits took a strange tack. In one the plaintiff complained that James and the city were colluding to force her to sell a property on Twenty-fourth and E Streets, NE at a loss. It had been settled out of court.

In another, a renter in an apartment off of East Capitol near RFK Stadium had said James rented the two adjoining apartments to drug pushers to force him out. The suit said they were selling cocaine out of the apartments. "My life was filled with terror," the renter said in the affidavit. James's lawyers said their client didn't know of or condone the drug sales. The suit was dismissed when the plaintiff moved to a nursing home out of state. Cal noticed that a partner in Vic Stein's firm had represented James.

Cal spent two days at Housing, ducking Nathaniel. The records were a shambles.

Virgil James had bought ninety-two pieces of property over two years on the west bank of the Anacostia River, not in the areas where he was building, but at scattered sites, all clustered around the football stadium and the D.C. Jail. Cal looked up the plans for Rivergate. All ninety-two properties fell within the broad proposal that Moray had filed.

The acquisitions in Near Northeast were virtually all from private owners or small real estate firms, all row houses or small apartment buildings. There were no mortgages. James was paying cash. Cal could see $1.5 million was paid out in only the records he pulled.

Cal selected ten properties at random and ran them through the housing violation records. Before James purchased them, all ten showed multiple housing code violations. All had been inspected within the past two years.

Cal picked the Twenty-fourth Street property where the owner had sued, and photocopied the documents and the listing. It was twenty-five blocks east of the Capitol, a block from the Reggae Club, a classic 1920s Washington row house: twelve feet wide, twenty feet deep, porch, two stories, postage-stamp lawn out front, and a backyard half the length of the house opening onto an alley.

It stood empty now, the windows boarded up, weeds growing in the garden, wind-whipped city flotsam on the lawn.

A forbidding sign said NO TRESPASSING, VMJ INC., but vandals hadn't been dissuaded and the evidence of their work showed through. The brass was gone, piping pulled out of the basement through broken windows, and somebody had removed a window, casement and all.

The previous owner now lived off Rhode Island Avenue Northeast in a nondescript row house. Cal found the place just at dusk.

The woman who answered was frumpy and overweight, trying to ignore the two small children that hung at her legs and examining Cal's identity folder with the slowness of someone who has difficulty reading.

"What do you want?"

"You owned Eight ten Twenty-fourth Northeast?"

"Me and my mother."

"I'd like to talk about your lawsuit."

"Jesus. What is this big case?"

"Mrs. Mallory. Would you let me in?"

They sat in the tiny living room. Two children played underneath the table, taking little pieces of brick, rock, and wood and building a fortress of some kind. They both had Mighty Morphin Power Rangers; the blue one's head was worn off.

The house James bought had been her mother's, she said, purchased under a housing program in the 1970s. They rented five rooms and lived on the first level, combining the rent with her AFDC and her mother's Social Security.

Two years ago housing inspectors had made a sweep, found fire and water violations, issued a repair warning. Tanya Mallory's former boyfriend, Willy, a sometime handyman, had fixed them "two weeks before deadline."

But the inspectors wouldn't pass the work. Willy went at it again. Nope, no dice. The final housing warning ordered her to evict the roomers if the building could not be brought up to code in thirty days. She went to housing court. "The judge say, Do what housing wants."

It was then that a man working for VMJ Balustrade builders had come to see her. They were rehabbing "certain selected properties." His offer was half what she and her mother had thought they could get if they had to sell.

Willy had been more stubborn, and proud of his work. He went back over repairs, got the housing inspectors out one more time. Still no go. Then Willy suggested they file the suit against VMJ.

Cal could see Willy was the backbone of this union. He wondered if the children were Willy's.

As soon as Tanya filed the suit, a different man had come. "He come to me in the middle of the day. He say, 'Tanya, there's to be a heap of trouble in your backyard'" — she pointed out the window as though she was still on Twenty-fourth — "he say this neighborhood going to change, it's going to change a whole lot.

"I ask him what he meant. He said, 'Tanya, you goin' to beg me to buy this house when we're through.'"

Cal nodded. He thought for a flash of the dead bodies outside the Reggae Club. The man had been right. The Reggae Club's parking lot was a hundred feet from her home.

VMJ sweetened the deal. We want you happy, the man said. It traded them the house Tanya now occupied and made a cash settlement as well. Tanya dropped the suit the next day, but it made her angry. "They were paying off the guy from Housing. Yes sir, paying him bigtime."

"Did you ever hear of a man named Virgil James?"

"Who is he?"

Yolanda Fleetwood had become Yolanda Mack and lived across the bridge up in Anacostia.

It was a big 1930s colonial brick on a large lot. When Cal was a little boy, this neighborhood had been all white, an upper-middle-class area that captured the coolness of the hills overlooking Washington.

Cal saw the woman in the back before he was seen. She was a knock-out, tall, in short shorts, a halter, and big, dangling, beaded earrings. "Mrs. Mack?"

"Yes."

"My name is Terrell." He held up his ID. "I'd like to ask you some questions about Virgil James."

The woman started laughing. "Good Lord, what's Virgil done? I thought he was one of the rich and famous."

A little girl, Cal guessed about three, came trundling down the back steps, barely in control of a pitcher of lemonade.

"Cassandra, honey, take it easy." Yolanda ran across the lawn and was trying to keep the pitcher upright until it got to the table.

"Come on" — she motioned to Cal — "sit down."

"You were married to James?"

"How did you find me?"

"Just regular police work, marriage license, phone books . . ." Cal let his voice trail off.

"I'll be damned."

"You were married to James?"

"If you could call it that."

"What happened?"

The woman turned to the little girl.

"Cassandra, go play on the swings. Okay, honey?"

After the child had toddled off, she turned back to Cal.

"What's this for?"

"We're investigating a woman's death. There was a little item in the *Post*. She was found in the bay. She'd been branded with the letter *B*."

Yolanda's face took on a look of fear and distaste.

"I don't want to get involved in anything like that. You hear, none of that. I haven't even seen Virgil for years." She stood up abruptly as though the interview were over. "I've got nothing to say. Nothing."

"Take it easy. This is background only." Cal became soothing. "We don't think Mr. James did anything; we have to check everything out. He dated the woman who died."

Yolanda snorted, a fast cynical grunt of air.

For a long silence she stood looking at Cal, as though she was trying to decide something.

"You *were* married to James?" Cal asked.

The woman nodded.

"The divorce record said less than a year. What happened?"

Slowly she sat down, cocking her head and raising her eyebrows. "He didn't like girls." Yolanda's breathing got heavier. People sometimes almost pant when they are tense.

"Sexually?" Cal said the word very softly.

"He liked boys."

"Little boys?"

"Young men."

They sat in silence again, looking at the surface of the picnic table as though something were lying there that the two must study.

"Why did you marry him?"

"I don't know. He seemed so nice. We went together almost a year. When he didn't try anything, I thought it was because he respected me, that he would wait until after we were married."

"Why did he marry you?"

"For a long time I couldn't figure that out either." Yolanda's face took a look of perplexity.

"After we were married, I found out what he was really. He had been practicing — I guess that's the word — homosexuality for years. Men called all the time, and he got these newspapers with party ads and personal columns. And he had things. . . ."

"Things like branding irons?" Cal almost whispered the question.

"Jesus. I don't remember that. But God, he had everything else. I don't want to think about it." She shook her head violently from side to side.

"I'll tell you why I think he married me. I think it was so he could run for city council. He and Mayor Cameron were old friends. Cameron had just been elected and he wanted to put his own people on the council. I think Virgil wanted to be married so he would come off straight in the election."

"What happened?"

"He lost. Homosexuality never came up in the election, but he didn't get any ministers to endorse him either. Not one. Maybe he realized he couldn't hide what he was. His plans fell through in November. I walked out in December."

"Did he hurt you?"

"The whole thing was painful, humiliating."

"Well, I mean physically?"

"Physically, it didn't feel good."

Cal dropped it.

"Why didn't you leave him when you first found out?"

"I was scared. I was eighteen, and every friend I had in the world had been at that wedding. My mother still thinks Virgil James is the nicest young man I ever dated."

The crash of the screen door was so loud, Cal jumped. A tall man came skipping down the stairs and swept Cassandra up in his arms.

Yolanda introduced him as her husband.

"Lieutenant Terrell's been checking on an accident out here last week."

The man looked confused. "I don't remember an accident."

"Well, sometimes we get the wrong hundred block." Cal smiled at Yolanda. "You-all have a nice little girl there."

Yolanda followed him to the street. The man was playing with the little girl at the top of the garden stairs. "I don't know why I told you that," she whispered. "If this comes out, I'll say you made it up." She turned hurriedly back to the yard.

The sun was sinking west behind the Capitol, and the city around it had a haze of warm air that seemed to settle just at the treetops. Cal hadn't eaten all day, and his hands were shaking with fatigue and hunger. He could feel the adrenaline; it made his whole body shaky.

James was going to be his man, but how to reel him in?

He pulled the Cavalier onto the grass median near the Library of Congress, put the red light on the dash, and walked over to Sherrill's. He used to go there with his father when he was a little boy, guaranteed to get a piece of pie if he ate everything on his plate. They would walk all the way up Independence from the Smithsonian to "ptomaine row," as his father called it. Cal had to run to keep up with his father's long strides.

He could see his father now, the seersucker suit and the brown straw hat. His father never had a lunch that he didn't bring a book or a paper he was working on. He would lay out the work in a Sherrill's booth and explain what he was doing so Cal could follow it. Sometimes it would be a map of birds' travels or a description of a nesting or mating pattern.

"They had no maps, no radio beacons, no radar-guided flight, no FAA. Birds, with brains smaller than a pea, make intercontinental trips, flying for days in squadrons as tight as the air force, finding landing places with water and food," his father would tell him.

"Do they ever get lost?" Cal would ask his father.

"Sometimes," his father would answer, laughing. "People think that birds can't get lost, but that's because humans don't know the flight plan. But birds do. Once in a while in late fall, I'll spot a flock of geese pass over again and again. That probably means they have had to double back, the navigator bird was off course, and they're looking for a landmark."

Cal had a tuna on white, wolfing it down so fast that when the waitress came to ask how everything was, it was gone.

He knew he had stumbled onto a scheme. Virgil James was a friend of the mayor's and his single biggest financial contributor. This gave him juice with Housing to force repeated inspections. The inspections drove the price down and harassed the owners. The owners sold low so they could get out.

Of course, that was James's business, acquiring property, but he was acquiring it pointlessly. He was holding it too long, paying too much in taxes, letting it sit.

James was either planning to sell it to Moray if Rivergate got going or was buying it for Moray. Maybe Virgil was the straw man for Cameron? Maybe Rivergate was really Moray and Cameron Incorporated? The mayor saw to it that selected houses were forced into a position to sell. The profit would go to James, and James would share it with Cameron. Maybe Ophelia Cameron was part of the deal. She had a job with Rivergate. What was that all about? Could James be the guy who got the license for the Reggae Club? Why would somebody open a disco club in this residential no-man's-land, and who got the special exemption-use permit from the zoning board? James? Or Cameron?

Suddenly he remembered something Moray had said. Gentrification had already started in the East End, but it was a hodgepodge. Maybe Virgil and the mayor were the hodgepodgers. While Cameron was opposing Rivergate in the open, Virgil was profiting from it, behind the scenes.

And in the end, what did this have to do with Mary Jeanne Turner? Nothing? Or something? Maybe James hung around Moray's restaurant on the morning of August 2 until 2:30 A.M. and picked up Mary Jeanne. The sex got rough. *Painful* was what Yolanda said. Mary Jeanne died, and he threw her in the bay up by Annapolis. Simple. Only where did she die?

What did her death have to do with a drive-by shooting at the Reggae Club? Was it coincidence it was located on land planned for Rivergate? Whoever heard of a nonprofit cocaine club?

15

Moray's house sat on the Virginia shore of the Potomac above Chain Bridge and the rapids. It was just beyond the old Kennedy estate on the same side of the road, with a long, winding drive. Cal guessed $10 million at least, maybe more, hard-earned money, of course, mined along K Street and Capitol Hill.

Celeste was a long shot, but maybe that was why Harry Moray had kept her from talking to him and Bobbie. Maybe she knew about James's sex tastes and would give him up in a minute.

Anyway, Celeste probably wouldn't see him. She would call Moray, and Moray would call the mayor to complain. Cal knew this was stupid, but he took a shot anyway. The gossip columns said Celeste was a bombshell. Harry Moray's secret weapon, they said, but unpredictable and flamboyant. Cal was banking on it.

Suddenly Celeste Moray came out through double doors from the left, framed in the sunlight, like a picture layout in *Architectural Digest*. Her beauty was extraordinary. Her jet black hair surrounded a face quite Egyptian: almond eyes, aquiline nose, strong jaw — all set off by flawless skin. Cal guessed that the clothes came from Paris: tan silk, tan pumps, and a wide-brimmed white straw hat.

"I am so sorry. I hope you do not wait. But I was choosing flowers from the garden. We have a dinner party tonight for the Saudi ambassador."

Celeste led Cal into a high-ceilinged solarium with a wall of glass that made the very formal garden behind almost a part of the room.

"This is stunning." Cal walked around admiringly. "Did you and Mr. Moray have it built?"

"No. It was built for the Wrigley heiress. I think in nineteen fifty-five. We have modernized here and there."

She ordered coffee and led him to a conversation center that formed the room's lower level, the level leading out to the garden.

"You are a policeman?" She looked at Cal's card.

"Yes."

"It is so strange. In Egypt, policemen are awful little men with pointy-toed shoes who smoke American cigarettes."

"They prefer American cigarettes?"

"They take them in bribes."

"Our guys just take money" — Cal laughed — "no cigarettes. Most of them don't smoke anymore anyway."

"Do you?"

"Take money?"

"Smoke?"

"I haven't for ten years," he said, lying for no particular reason.

Celeste's English was very American, and her accent had a fetching quality. Her manner struck Cal as direct and forceful. He could see her telling Richie he was finished.

"You were kind to see me on such short notice."

"I can't imagine why you are here. Harry said this was all settled. Had I known what sort this Willis man was, I would never have hired him."

"You are convinced he killed Mary Jeanne?"

"Oh yes! He must have become obsessed with her, I think. Watching her through his dirty little hole."

"When he came back for his job, what did he say to you?"

A look of disgust crossed Celeste's face. "'First he cried . . . like a child. He said he didn't kill her. He asked for a chance."

"Did you consider it at all?"

"Never. I know his kind. When I said he could not come back, he stopped crying. He threatened me. The nasty little fellow threatened me."

"Threatened to do what?"

"He said he would say bad things about me."

"Did he tell you what?"

Celeste drove right past the question. "I was furious. I called Max. I said, 'Throw him out.'"

She sipped from the Limoges cup held in beautifully manicured hands flashing with diamonds. Her face was as cold as the diamonds.

"Harry and I were so sad. Harry has had a hard time getting over it.

Mary Jeanne was such a beautiful young woman. We loved her like a daughter."

Celeste paused, a pouty look now coming over her face. "Harry said his lawyers told him I would not have to talk to the police. Have you checked with them?"

Cal nodded reassuringly. "Of course," he murmured, but he knew Moray's lawyers would have blocked this at the pass. "You know what policemen learn?"

Celeste shook her head.

"We learn women see more, notice more detail than men do."

She seemed to enjoy the flattery. She plumped herself in her chair the way a cat does, as though she were settling down for a good talk.

"Can you tell me a little about Mary Jeanne, why you hired her?"

"Actually, I didn't hire her. Harry hired her. He met her at a Redskins party. Came home that night and said, 'I found this wonderful girl! Do you have something for her?' I didn't, but he thought she would fit in, so I began to look around. I had a dining room manager who was clumsy and stupid, so I tried Mary Jeanne. Voilà! She was perfect."

"Did she know anything about the restaurant business?"

"I taught her," Celeste said emphatically. "It is really better. People do things my way."

"In the weeks before she died, did you think there was anything wrong? A problem with a man or drugs or something?"

"Oh no. We worked very closely. I think I would have noticed."

Cal made a show of furiously taking notes, his head down, looking at his pad. "We interviewed a man named Virgil James," Cal said. "He told us he dated Mary Jeanne on several occasions. Did you know that?" Cal looked up.

For a millisecond Celeste looked startled, but she covered it with a laugh.

"Nineteen-year-old girls are nineteen-year-old girls. Actually, I did find out about that, but she promised me it would not happen again."

"You didn't approve of James?"

"Oh no. It was not that. I do not want the help involved with the customers. It is a rule."

"When did you stop the thing with James?"

"I don't remember. A long time ago."

Cal shifted direction; Celeste's body language told him he couldn't go further with James.

"Did you see Mary Jeanne on Friday, August first?"

"Oh no. No. Harry and I were giving an important party that night."

"A party?"

"Yes. We had a cocktail buffet on our boat and after we sailed, I had to give a sit-down dinner for ten people. I was too busy to go to the club."

Cal took a deep breath. Nobody had mentioned the party or the dinner.

"What kind of boat?" Cal said.

"Why do you want to know?"

"Oh nothing. I live by the bay. I've been around boats all my life."

"We have a motor yacht. The *Potomac Fever.* It is Harry's joy. He says it's the only place he can get people together properly."

"Where do you keep it?"

"Usually at Solomons Island, sometimes at Kent Narrows. We had a deep-water mooring dredged there when we bought it."

Virgil James had said he was at Kent with the mayor! Cal took another deep breath.

"Was there some sort of a meeting at Kent that weekend?" Cal took a flyer.

"What has this got to do with Mary Jeanne?"

"It's routine. We try to place everyone who might be able to complete our report."

Celeste did not look persuaded, a grimace forming on her face. "We ended up at Kent. We usually do. It takes too long to sail back, so Harry lays on cars or a helicopter at Kent to take everyone home." Suddenly Celeste's mask of laughing cordiality dropped away entirely. "Are you sure Harry's lawyers said this was all right?"

Cal nodded. "This is very helpful. Believe me."

"I think this is silly," Celeste said. "You people are all alike. Like Immigration."

They had now talked for ten minutes. Cal had learned something. Celeste answered in two ways. One way she looked right at you, another way she looked out over the garden. She had looked into the garden when she said Mary Jeanne had promised her not to keep dating Virgil James, and she looked into the garden when she said she had not seen Mary Jeanne on the first, a long look into the garden.

Cal ostentatiously put away his pad, as though the interview was over.

"Do you often have sailing parties?"

Celeste brightened. "Harry is most famous for his sailing parties! He says he can knock heads. Is that right? Knock heads together out there.

In the player's strike that's where Harry made the deal — in the middle of the Chesapeake Bay!"

"Can you tell me a little about the party that weekend? Who was there? Was the mayor there?"

"Why do you ask these questions? It had nothing to do with Mary Jeanne."

Suddenly a dark cloud passed over Celeste's face, a look of anger and recognition.

"I don't think you talked to the lawyers," Celeste hissed. "You tricked me."

The heat had broken in the few minutes Cal had been talking to Celeste. By the time Cal got outside, Canadian air had sailed in just as they said it would on TV. He breathed it in gratefully.

The weekend Mary Jeanne died had transformed itself! Harry Moray had said nothing about a party on his boat, Max the bartender didn't mention it, and Virgil James had come up with Kent but conveniently forgotten to mention that Harry Moray had a place there!

Cal had learned in Homicide not to get too tricky. Things are often what they first seem to be. Mary Jeanne Turner was found floating in the Chesapeake Bay. These people had all been on or around the bay. It was a start.

16

The drive down to southern Maryland after he left Celeste's was fun. He opened the windows and let the cool air flow in. He felt the excitement of a new lead, turning it over and over in his mind. Why had they all lied about the weekend? What did Moray care about James? Maybe they all knew something.

He passed the cutoff to his farm and kept on the road to Solomons Island. The old city Cavalier couldn't make very good time, but he pushed it as hard as he could. He turned off the two-way radio so he wouldn't hear anyone calling him and turned off his beeper as well.

He could see Carol long before he got to the harbormaster's dock; she was wearing old, very tight jeans, bent over, tying a hawser, looking brown and trim for a woman with a couple of twenty-six-year-old daughters.

Carol and Cal's brother Jimmy had been in the same high school class. The prettiest prom queen Calvert Regional had ever had, they used to say. Her husband was killed in Vietnam, down in the Delta. Cal had been home on leave then, and his mother had made him put on his uniform and go over to the funeral parlor.

When he broke up with Vivian, Carol had been ending her second marriage. They would have a drink now and then, talking about the old days, ending up at her house or his. After a year, he just drifted away.

Carol stood and turned to look at him as he walked up. She had a weathered face, tanned and lined from squinting into the sun, but the flirty eyes of a twenty-year-old.

"You ever kill anybody as a cop?" she asked.

"Yep. When people ask me such dumb questions, I have to waste them."

Carol started laughing. It was an old joke.

"You here to sweep me off my feet and take me away?"

"I'm too old, too broken-down. No, I'm checking a guy's story. He said he was working on a boat owned by Harry Moray up in Washington, but he couldn't remember the name." Cal made his voice sound skeptical. "I figured I'd come down and check. It was such a great day for a ride, great day to see my favorite harbormaster."

"That'd be the *Potomac Fever*."

Cal looked along the vessels moored in the estuary.

Carol laughed. "You won't find her there. She draws too much to come up here." She waved her hand out toward the bay.

Cal spotted her just beyond the breakwater. The *Potomac Fever* looked like the *Queen Elizabeth*. She was moored in open water where the Patuxent met the bay. Cal whistled.

Moray's yacht was 150 feet if she was an inch, maybe more.

There was a long saloon cabin running from just behind the bow to the stern, a swept-back pilot's cabin, and an open deck behind the flying bridge laid out with deck chairs. The emblem of the Redskins was painted on the forward smokestack.

"You know somebody who can take me out there?"

"Jeez, I don't know. Nobody's on board today."

"Nothing official, I'd just like to see her. That's a hell of a boat."

She took a set of keys hanging on a board and climbed down to a whaleboat with a red light on the bow. "Okay, but you've got to promise not to touch anything. If a crew member comes back, I'll just say we were going out to eat a sandwich on the bay."

She throttled and headed hard out of the estuary, the spray dotting Cal's suit jacket.

The *Potomac Fever*'s main cabin had been designed so it was really three rooms. One outside the superstructure was sumptuously furnished in teak and brass; the side walls and overhead could be opened to the sky. The first inside cabin was a living room that would make any top-flight home proud, double doors opening to a dining room that seated twelve.

The main deck also had a galley, office, and what Carol called the "master suite."

"Something, huh?" Carol grinned. "This ain't the half of it."

She led Cal down a flight of stairs to the second deck. There were four more sleeping cabins forward, a Jacuzzi in pink marble, crew's quarters for four, a laundry, and an engine room that Cal figured had been adopted from a battleship.

"Those engines" — she pointed into the spotless engine room — "are the same size you get in a seagoing tug. This baby can keep headway in seventeen-foot seas, cross the Atlantic without refueling."

"Do you remember if she was here August first or second? Maybe a party?"

"Moray has parties all the time. He sails her down from D.C. overnight, and they stop for fresh seafood and maybe bakery products. We also work on her some of the time."

Cal nodded.

"Is it important?" The boat rocked with a swell from the channel and knocked her against him for a moment. She put out her hand to steady him, and their hands clasped.

"Yeah. Really." He looked into her eyes.

"Let me get my log." She bounded up the stairs and climbed over the side to her launch; an outdoor life and hard work had kept her trim.

"Remember, don't touch anything," she said.

"Never!"

As soon as she left, Cal began searching for the ship log or some kind of guest book that would tell who was on board August 1. Nothing on the bridge, nothing in the desk of the main salon. Carol would be back momentarily. He began taking fiber samples from every carpet he saw, running swiftly along the passageways and up and down the ladders, putting them in Baggies he found in the galley and marking them. He searched as much as he could. In the master cabin he found a slew of color photos on one wall. No Mary Jeanne, no Virgil, but senators, congressmen, and the president. Even Vivian's husband.

When Carol got back, he was sitting in the dining area reading a boating magazine.

"I remember it now," Carol said, opening a big leatherbound ledger. "We stoked it for both a party and a weekend trip. They came in overnight. He was going up the bay to Kent Island. He had it fueled, battery check, running lights, radar and depth finder check."

"Why doesn't it provision on Maine Avenue?"

"Shit, I don't know. Rich people. Probably want fresh seafood."

"Can you tell if anybody came ashore?"

"No. When they come in at night, they usually call the night master as they approach the bay from the Potomac. By the time they get up here, they've called the provisioners or service guys. They go out in their own launches. You know how it is here in the summer. There is so much traffic on the river that we wouldn't know whether people land or leave.

They shot the breeze for an hour, standing by the rail looking out over the open water. It was like old times, listening to the soft southern Maryland twang; it was almost as though she were family.

"Where's the crew now?"

"D.C. today. Immigration check."

"Immigration?"

"Yeah. They're from Curaçao. This is leased from a Dutch company."

"Leased?"

"Sure. The crew said that for the long leases, they'll make it look like you own it, so that's why the Redskin colors are being flown, but it belongs to a Dutch charter company."

"Where does the crew live?"

"All over. Moray charters the crew too, but I know the captain and one other guy have family in Curaçao."

"Have you seen this woman?"

She took the picture of Mary Jeanne and studied it hard. "I thought you said you were checking some guy's story?"

"Cops lie."

She grunted. "I've seen a lot of pretty ladies on this ship, but I don't remember her."

"Hey, look, it's lunchtime. How about a beer, maybe some softshells?" she asked.

He touched her cheek with his hand. Just gently.

"You've been real sweet. I'd love to. I mean, I'd love to any other time. But I've got to get back."

She nodded as though she knew where he was coming from.

"Come on down Sunday. I'll take you out in one of those." She pointed over to a group of cabin cruisers moored in the estuary. "We'll take a picnic, sip a couple of beers, and pull blues."

"Hey, I'd like that," he said, smiling. "Nothing better than that sweet watermelon smell that comes up from the bay when the blues are biting."

Carol always reminded him of the first girl he had made love to, down at St. Mary's, shy but eager. If he hadn't joined the army, he'd probably have married a girl from right down here, a girl like Carol. She would have been better for him than Vivian. He wasn't a Georgetown dinner party, White House, big television star guy. He was what he was:

a kid from southern Maryland who somehow got a college degree and an army commission and ended up a cop.

"You remember anything else about that party now, you give me a call, you hear!" Cal said.

The next night she called him at the farm. "A very funny thing. A few hours after you were here, the *Potomac Fever*'s captain told me to ready it for sea. I thought he must be running down the coast to Hilton Head or the Islands with Moray. But when I asked him where he was bound for to put in my log, he said the Caymans. He said the charter was complete and he'd been ordered to winter mooring. It's awful early for winter mooring."

"Has he sailed?"

"Yeah. This morning. This was the first chance I had to call you."

17

Vivian was reading to him from John Le Carré's new novel. It was extraordinary how well she read, her television-trained voice effortlessly delivering fear, anger, and mirth in the proper places. From his position, he could not see her and he imagined for a moment that she was reading to their children. They should have had children. When they were married, he had thought she was simply too selfish to have a family, but after the divorce, when he thought about her, as he often did, he realized that she may have been afraid, afraid of the pain.

The doctor's voice interrupted Vivian. "I'm glad you're here, Mrs. St. Denis. We found Cal's military health records, thanks to you. Thank whoever your friend is at the White House."

For the first time, they raised the bed, so he was almost in a sitting position.

Now he could see the room and the people from the neck down. Vivian looked terrific. Her hair was pulled back, and she was wearing a pale blue cashmere sweater with wool slacks. She came around the bed and took his hand.

"If you have questions, squeeze Mrs. St. Denis's hand and she'll help you write them on a pad."

"As I suspected," the doctor said, looking down at a folder, "your head was injured as a result of your helicopter crash in Vietnam. According to these records, when you went through the windshield, the Plexiglas shattered and a large shard was pushed through the skull beneath your helmet.

"It left the brain membrane's surface scarred. I think that is where the clot is now sitting." He gently touched the left side of Cal's head with his pencil. "Right along the already weakened surface spot, so even though the size of the hematoma has reduced, you're still having problems."

The wood-paneled dining room was actually two floors above the River Club, in the Potomac Building, but a small elevator and stairs had been built from the restaurant complex. The walls of the room were dedicated to Harry Moray. There was Harry as a young man with Lyndon Johnson, holding a pen for the signing of a bill. He was on a beach with Nixon and Bebe Rebozo and teeing off with Jerry Ford. Jimmy Carter, who had put Moray in the cabinet momentarily, rated three pictures, and Ronald Reagan had two. *If nothing else,* Cal thought wryly, *the display was a monument to bipartisanship.*

Drinks were served in the rotunda with a stunning view of the Potomac looking south toward Memorial Bridge. Moray moved among the guests with a handshake here and a smile there. There was no one in the room whom Cal knew, save Moray and Vic Stein, but he found himself being warmly greeted by name by men he had never even heard of.

The invitation had come from Moray's lawyer Vic Stein the day after Cal searched the *Potomac Fever.* It was ironic because it was the day that the Maryland State Police lab said none of the carpeting fibers from the *Potomac Fever* matched the two found between Mary Jeanne's toes.

When Stein called, Cal presumed it was to complain about his unannounced interview with Mrs. Moray or boarding the *Potomac Fever,* but Stein didn't even bring them up. Stein said he was calling to invite him to a dinner party. "Harry Moray has a regular men-only dinner Fridays at the River Club. He'd like you to come, nothing formal, a business suit will be okay. He wants you to meet some people from the Redskins' organization."

"Me?" Cal asked.

"You," Stein said with a laugh. "Harry has been very impressed how you and your partner handle yourselves. He thinks these are some people you ought to know."

"Will I be able to talk to him about the case?"

"I don't think the dinner party is the right setting. We want to help. That has been Harry's instruction to me all along. Give the police what they need. I've had to advise Harry to go slow. He has civil liability, you know, as Mary Jeanne's employer because he hired that man Willis. We want to help all we can, but if you have more questions, give them to me. Harry wants to talk to you about something else."

Stein spoke as though nobody refused a dinner invitation from Harry Moray. "Be at the River Club at nine, okay?"

Cal started to decline but figured, What the hell, wasn't Harry Moray the biggest name in Washington? He didn't tell Bobbie about it.

At dinner, the Redskins manager was to Cal's right, and to his left was Harry Moray's inside counsel, Billy Norris; across from him was another lawyer Cal only knew of from reading about him in the *Post* Style section. Skip MacLaine, the tight end, was there, and Goober Cobb, the center. At the end of the table were two other lawyers and Jack Lightfoot, the Redskins coach, as well as Stein and Moray.

In the small, beautifully paneled private dining room, Cal was not uncomfortable, not intimidated. He felt good, in fact. He felt, as he did sometimes, that this was what he had missed. A good dinner, good wine, good-natured talk of football and politics and the day's events, understated, murmured, the way he imagined powerful people conducted their affairs.

The room was silent as the two waiters cleared the duck and brought in fruit and cheese. Cal would have thought duck too heavy to serve in warm weather, but it had been so well prepared that it had been delicate and light.

Moreover, the sauternes was excellent, and Harry Moray had suggested the guests keep their sauternes glasses and continue it with the fruit and cheese. Cal had never been a big wine drinker; wine gave him a headache. But tonight he felt relaxed, as though for a moment the edges of his life had been wrapped with gauze.

He had held his own on Redskins lore. Twice Moray had said what good ideas he had. It turned out that Vic Stein was as avid a horseman as he was and owned a farm in Middleberg. By the cigars, Cal felt as if he was admitted to a new club.

Mary Jeanne Turner's death was never mentioned.

It was half past eleven when Moray began to prepare his cigar. He never stopped talking as he did so, but later Cal realized it was a signal because no sooner was the beautiful old silver Ronson put to the tobacco than Jack Lightfoot left, the Redskins lawyer bowed out, the two ballplayers followed, and Moray's counsel said he had to catch an early plane.

Suddenly Cal realized he was there alone with Stein and Moray. Stein was telling a story of his first meeting with Justice Scalia, and the waiters were putting fresh German café filter pots on the table.

In the candlelight Cal felt almost as though he were alone with a woman, the room had become so intimate. He could see the texture of Moray's skin and the soft, pink folds under his chin, glistening with perspiration.

"Cal." Moray took a long pull on the cigar, and its embers became another point of light in the dark, paneled room. "I wasn't sure when I sat down I was going to broach this. Vic here says that his friends on the force tell him you're a first-class guy, and Lord knows, I'd never doubt my chief counsel."

Cal chuckled and Stein laughed.

"But this is so sensitive, at first I figured I'd just pass it up. Just not burden you with it at this time, just wait and meet you later. Now we've had dinner, I know I was wrong. There is nothing, absolutely nothing, better than eyeballing a man."

Cal looked at Moray's eyeballs; they were very clear for a man who by Cal's count had had six glasses of wine.

"I make my coaches bring a ballplayer to meet me before we sign. I can talk to a man for ten minutes, look him in the eye, and tell you more than if I read a thousand scouting reports."

Cal wondered if he should say something; in a funny way this felt like a job interview, like he should say something to compliment Moray's view.

Before he could speak, Moray leaned into him, lowering his voice. "What I am about to tell you must be held in the strictest confidence. This must be what we lawyers call privilege. This can't be Harry Moray talking to Police Lieutenant Calvert Terrell. Can we talk together, man to man? Can we?"

"You've got that, sir," Cal said far too quickly, knowing damn well that there was no "privilege" between them.

Moray pointed his finger at Cal, very close to his face. "I knew I was right. Knew it! Edward said you'd be my man!"

Cal nodded dumbly. His pulse was galloping now. He knew that this was a delicate moment, but he didn't know why. He wished he had not had the third glass of sauternes.

"Edward?"

"Edward St. Denis. President Winston's counsel. He's a big fan of yours, you know. He said I might think it strange that he'd recommend his wife's former husband, but he said you're aces with him. I have to tell you too" — Moray leaned even closer to Cal — "that I admire any man who won Vivian's heart even for a moment. She's topflight!"

Cal found himself agreeing that Vivian was wonderful and exceptional, and before he knew it, Stein was starting to gush about her as well. But something didn't feel right.

Just as quickly, Moray was moving on, with a tone of voice that told you he was imparting startling news.

"Shortly, Martin Cameron will announce the district government's participation in Rivergate!" Moray leaned back as though waiting for Cal to exclaim. "It has been a long fight. But I have finally gotten Cameron to see that this is the best thing for the people of Washington. I can't tell you how important that is."

Vic Stein was nodding furiously, his head moving up and down.

"You see, whites don't understand Martin Cameron. We see an adept politician, a mayor, another government official, but he's more than that. He's the leader of the African American community. I suspect it comes from once being in the pulpit or maybe a tiny taste of a civil rights crusader, but until Martin certifies this project, I cannot get any local support! The African American people of the city are waiting for Martin! They're waiting for Martin to lead them to the promised land!"

Cal found himself thinking of Moses and Cameron in biblical robes.

"Now, with him on board, President Winston can approve a transfer of six hundred acres along the Anacostia and East of Fort McNair to the city. This land, next to the railroad land grant in San Francisco, is the largest government land grant for city expansion in modern times. This will make Rivergate the biggest inner-city development in the United States!" His cigar had not lit well and Moray studied it with a petulant look, as though it had interrupted him. Stein quickly produced a lighter, and the butane surged up. Moray took a long, slow drag on the cigar until the end glowed.

"Two billion dollars in commitments. Canada, Europe," he said as the cigar turned cheery orange.

Another drag on the cigar.

"This will be the greatest transformation of the nation's capital since Pierre L'Enfant!"

The cigar glowed again. Cal wondered where all the smoke was going.

"We are going to lay out a city that will truly be the capital of the free world!"

Finally, Moray stopped and let loose a cloud of cigar smoke, enveloping them both. "Only we've got a problem."

Stein nodded vigorously.

"Crime. Crime is killing this city. Crime scares our investors, crime scares Congress, and crime scares Winston."

Cal tried to picture Winston inside the White House surrounded by armed Secret Service agents being scared.

"Last month I told the president of the United States that I would personally guarantee the safety of the East End of Washington until our project is complete!" He gazed into Cal's eyes for several seconds in silence. "You can be part of that operation!"

Cal was now somewhat mystified.

"When this project is done," Moray went on, "this city will have a new hundred-thousand-seat stadium, six thousand single-family homes and town houses, twelve thousand apartment units, one million square feet of office space, parks, firehouses, and police stations! I'm going to dome the stadium so the president can have his second inaugural ball there, if he's a mind!

"But to achieve that, I and my backers have promised to provide security for the entire area of the project. That's really more than two major police districts. We privately told congressional leaders and the president that we could bring crime to acceptable levels from the Anacostia River west to Lincoln Park in three months."

Again the pause for effect.

"One week after I made that commitment, four youngsters were killed and seventeen wounded at the Reggae Club. That was the straw that broke the camel's back! More than a dozen young people gunned down in Washington, D.C.!

"This could have dire consequences for Rivergate! The investors will pull their money out of a city where the president has to declare martial law."

Cal started to speak, but Moray shushed him.

"That's what brought Cameron around. In a sense the Reggae Club massacre brought everybody together."

"But the mayor hasn't approved it," said Cal.

"Hasn't announced it," Moray corrected. "He needs time to get his people in line."

Again Cal started to respond, but Stein nudged him with his knee under the table.

"What I want to do now is form a private police force, about the size of the forces the city has committed in the Ninth and Tenth police districts plus, let's say a hundred and fifty officers. Since we're private, we can hold down administration costs, use my development firm's infrastructure to handle administration, and keep maybe twice as many police on the street as the police force can. We'll be the law east of Lincoln

Park, and that'll free up police from the department to concentrate on other areas.

"By using saturation tactics, we'll at least drive elements permanently out of the Rivergate area, and by the time we're selling houses, we'll be able to get the middle class back to Washington." He paused, now squinting hard at Cal.

"In the end we may establish that privatizing police is the way to go across the country! Cameron is going to go to the city council and get them to give our men police powers within the Rivergate area. That's legal, isn't it, Vic?"

Vic smiled enigmatically.

Moray nodded. "That's why I pay all these smart lawyers."

He leaned back as though this was all the explanation Cal would need. "What do you think?"

Cal tried to think of a neutral word. He couldn't quite see the city council granting rent-a-cops police powers, but on the other hand people were worn out with fear. "Breathtaking," he finally said. "Breathtaking, but I still don't understand. Why me? I've been an investigator more than an administrator."

Moray smiled, big and warm. "That's why I always listen to Edward St. Denis. He believes we can recruit trained police officers from the armed forces. The Pentagon is still downsizing, and infantry and military police units from the army and marines are being cut in the next round. Not everybody knows that. I want a man with a sterling military record, a former regular officer who has credibility with regular military personnel. I would guess that a Silver Star, a Purple Heart, and twelve years of service would be credibility enough for anyone!

"But enough for tonight." Moray held up his hand. "You young fellas can take it, but I'm an old dog. I need my sleep."

Cal wondered how much sleep Moray got with that woman Celeste. "Vic, give Cal and me some time to talk turkey before I run out of gas."

Cal could tell that unlike the others, Stein had not expected to be asked to leave, and his face betrayed it. But he got up, shook hands with Cal, leaned over to whisper something in Moray's ear, and left.

Moray took a sip of brandy.

"I spent an evening a week ago talking to Vivian about you. I suspect that lady still has a warm spot for you, but she and Edward can go all the way. That's in the cards."

Cal wondered what "all the way" meant. He tried to remember how much he'd told Vivian about the Mary Jeanne investigation.

"The Cal Terrell she described is stubborn, belligerent, sometimes mercurial," Moray continued. "But he's also smart and maybe the best policeman in town. She says you won't take this job, because you have some stubborn idea that doing good means a vow of poverty.

"Prove Vivian wrong. Give my proposition serious thought. Okay?"

Cal nodded.

"Here's the deal: We'll give you an initial two-year contract at two hundred and fifty thousand per year. President and CEO of security services. If the idea survives, five hundred thousand a year over five years to run the police services company and help us market it to other municipalities."

Moray leaned very close to Cal, as if the walls had ears.

"You and I know that a white man's days are numbered on the Metropolitan Police Department. Do the right thing for yourself!"

Driving back to southern Maryland, Cal knew he had been offered a bribe, a big bribe. What he didn't know was why.

18

The next morning he called Harry Moray at the office using the private number Moray had written on his card. "That's a fast decision," Moray said. "So, we have a deal?"

"Nope," Cal said, just like that, short and sweet.

Moray's voice lost the country boy. "That's very shortsighted of you, Cal."

"What can you tell me about Virgil James's relationship with Mary Jeanne?" Cal asked.

The line went dead.

When he hung up, Cal sat for a long time and thought about what $250,000 a year would have been like. He took a paycheck stub out of his desk. After everything was deducted, he took home $1,412.33 every two weeks. He tried to figure out what the take-home would be on $250,000, but he couldn't. He envisioned the nice big office Moray had talked about at dinner and the new car and driver. He would have had dinners like Moray's and business lunches at the Palm, a secretary, and a cellular telephone that worked properly. Cal guessed he was never going to know how much $250,000 a year really was. He didn't like Moray anyway.

He wrote, *Mary Jeanne Turner,* on the blackboard in big, careful letters and stood back, looking at her name.

She was just a kid like his brother, Jimmy. She went off the road in life before she had learned to drive. When Jimmy was little their mother used to say, "You take care of your brother," as they went out to play, but in the end he hadn't taken care of Jimmy, he'd taken care of himself. When his mother asked him that last time to go to Seattle, he dallied. Jimmy's problems were a pain in the neck. When he finally got to Seattle, the little tousled-headed boy he'd grown up with was dead, dead because his big brother couldn't get there on time.

Cal drew a line from the left of Mary Jeanne's name and wrote, *Harry Moray.* He drew a second line and wrote, *Celeste Moray.* He was writing faster now, sketching in arrows. Virgil James, Martin Cameron, Richie. He drew another line to a circle with a question mark. *Potomac Fever,* Max the bartender, Celeste, James, Moray.

He built a time line under the schematic and put in the salient events. A woman was found dead in the Chesapeake, Moray had an important party on a yacht sailing the Chesapeake that same weekend. Teenage druggies do a drive-by machine-gunning of a dance club, and another shooter was set up to assassinate the drive-by killer. Now Moray tells him that the drive-by cleared opposition to his mucho-dinero project.

Cal stood back from the board a minute. The crazy quilt of lines now annoyed him because it broke his cardinal rule: Keep it simple. Was he mistaking coincidence for evidence?

He wrote down the name Ophelia Cameron in the middle of the board under neither list. He didn't quite know where she fit.

Ophelia Cameron was working with James at Moray's Rivergate office. If Moray wanted to rope the mayor, what better way than to employ his wife? When he and Bobbie had arrived to question James, James went to Ophelia to establish his alibi. The transparent little drama with the calendar was puzzling. Maybe Ophelia was covering for James. But why had James hustled them out?

The problem with Ophelia was that to ask her about James, he'd have to get her alone without the mayor, his lawyers, or Nathaniel. He wanted Ophelia alone and vulnerable. Hell, he had pulled it off and questioned Celeste, maybe he was on a roll.

He ran Ophelia through Motor Vehicles. She had a Porsche with the D.C. vanity plate MVNG ON listed in her name at her home address, and she had a lot of forgiven parking tickets. Once the car had been stolen and recovered. The car had been stolen from the tenants' parking garage of the Wilner Hotel in the 3600 block of Sixteenth. Tenant? He called. Sure enough, there was an Ophelia Cameron.

In the 1950s the Wilner had been *the* luxury address: heated pool, two restaurants, a beauty salon, and a view of Rock Creek Park that stretched to Virginia. Jimmy Hoffa had lived there; so had Everett Dirksen and half a dozen other well-known congressmen and senators. Upper Sixteenth Street had gone black twenty-five years ago, but the Wilner was still hob-knobby, the "Black Gold Coast."

When he got there, the desk clerk was snippy. "Mrs. Cameron doesn't actually live here. This is her office." She handed Cal an engraved card from a small box on the counter: Urban Strategies. 707D.

"Should I ring?"

Cal shook his head. "No, I just wanted to verify it for a delivery."

He went back and ran Urban Strategies through D.C. Corporations. It turned out to be a limited partnership formed back in the 1980s. Ophelia was the principal partner; Martin had been the treasurer, but he had been replaced by James when Martin became mayor.

Cal took a shot and did an Internet search. Sure enough, Ophelia had a web site, which said she could assist private developers and public authorities in designing urban habitats for the elderly, single parents, and the handicapped. It gave the Wilner address.

That night Cal didn't go home. At 6 P.M. he picked up Ophelia's Porsche at the Rivergate office, hanging way back and letting the Porsche's bright red color help him keep her in sight. She went around Independence to the Four Seasons and gave the car to the valet. Cal parked on Thirtieth using his red light and walked into the registration desk area, where he could see the lobby lounge overlooking the park. Ophelia was drinking a cocktail with two well-dressed women. He went back and pulled his car up on M where it became Pennsylvania.

At 7:15 they brought up her car.

Ophelia drove back downtown and parked in the Warner Theater garage and walked to the District Building. Her stunning figure and beauty attracted admiring glances from a dozen men as she crossed D.C. Plaza. She went in the side door, and Cal could see through the glass that she entered the small staff elevator.

He pulled down onto Fourteenth and sat in the Reagan Building driveway, watching the exit where Cameron's car would come out. Sure enough, half an hour later, the mayor's Lincoln Town Car came out and turned left toward the Mall. Cal followed them to the Sheraton Park Hotel, where the mayor's car pulled away while Cameron and Ophelia went in.

Two hours later, when they hadn't come out, he took a chance and called Dispatch on his radio to ask if D.C. One was rolling. "Yeah, Lieutenant, D.C. One en route to the Wilner Hotel." They must have exited onto Calvert Street. He floored the Cavalier going over the Duke Ellington Bridge.

It was just before eleven when Cal got to the Wilner. He parked down Sixteenth Street where he could see the driveway and the garage entrance, put his radio on scanner, and waited for the mayor's car. Nothing. *Maybe they'd been and gone?*

But after ten minutes, a male voice using a voice code, calling himself Robin and talking to Batman, came in so close, Cal scrunched down in his seat and turned down the volume on the scanner.

At almost the same instant the mayor's car came up Sixteenth. Cal could see Cameron's driver, Sergeant Maynard, at the wheel, but the tinted back windows kept the rear interior dark. It turned into the half-moon drive. Just as the Town Car's doors opened, the same male voice transmitted, "This is Robin. We're in place."

The transmitter stopped. It certainly wasn't a D.C. police car; in fact, it wasn't on any city frequency. Cal wondered where Cameron's security was. Maybe somebody was tailing Cameron. The transmission was so strong, it was overriding the regular circuits. Cal couldn't see a car, but he didn't sit up and look because it could have been parked right behind him.

Cal's attention had been distracted. He looked back quickly enough to see Ophelia's back as she entered the Wilner. The mayor was nowhere to be seen.

Another radio transmitted, this time on D.C. Main. It was Maynard. He made a time check with D.C. Dispatch. "This is D.C. One. I'm going to go out of service at L'Enfant Plaza." The Town Car pulled out onto Sixteenth and headed south.

Cal knew if he moved and went into the Wilner, the tail car would make him for sure. He decided to pass up Ophelia and figure out the tail car. It hadn't followed D.C. One, so it must be sitting on Ophelia. He waited almost thirty-five minutes, lying down in the seat half dozing and listening to the crickets and the radio calls.

Finally he said it out loud. "This is ridiculous." He looked in the rearview mirror to see if he could spot a parked car with someone in it, but he couldn't. He slid out of the passenger side and ambled down Sixteenth. It wasn't until Cal was a block down Sixteenth that he saw them, just heads in a darkened Ford Crown Victoria. It had Virginia plates IRZ 960. He knew they had made him, at least made his skin color and maybe a description. He couldn't tell if they were white or black, men or women. Just two heads.

He pulled out his shield and his flashlight and headed straight for them, making a gesture for the passenger side to roll down the window. Suddenly he was bathed in a bright light from the dash, and before he could adjust his eyes, the car pulled out.

Back at headquarters, he ran the plates back to a Ford leasing agency in Detroit. He called. "Can you tell me who has the lease on IRZ nine six zero?"

"No."

"This is police business."

"You will need a court order for that information, sir. Have a nice day."

The next morning Cal took a pass up Sixteenth and spotted the Porsche in the Wilner driveway. He didn't stop at the front desk. Using his badge to get in through the garage, he went right up to the apartment. There was a small brass plate by the door, URBAN STRATEGIES. He rang.

Ophelia looked awful. Her face was puffy, she wore dark glasses, and her hair was stringy and lifeless.

"What are you doing here?" she asked.

"I want to talk to you privately about the Turner case."

"I don't know anything about that. Virgil gave you all the information you need."

"May I come in?" Cal asked.

"No."

"Would you rather I schedule a meeting through the mayor's office?"

"I don't have to talk to you."

"That's true. But somebody killed a nice young woman. She had a mother and a dog who loved her. Wouldn't you want me to do my job?"

"I want to call my husband."

"You have a phone, don't you?"

All the while Ophelia had been backing up. She was now well into the apartment, and Cal had followed her. Ophelia walked stiffly, as though she were in pain.

The apartment-office was sumptuous, not personal but lavish the way an interior decorator would do it. It had a sweeping view of the park through a glass wall along a carpeted balcony. The living room and dining room were combined to make one giant room with white couches against a dark blue rug and a white baby grand piano. There were brochures and photos of urban scenes neatly laid out on a table, and a small model of Rivergate and another development in glass boxes.

Ophelia hung on to the piano as if to steady herself.

"Mrs. Cameron, maybe you'd better sit down."

Ophelia shook her head.

"You don't look well."

"It isn't anything. The flu. What do you want?"

"Did you know Mary Jeanne Turner?"

"I met her a couple of times."

"Where?"

"I don't know. At the River Club. Why are you bothering me?"

"This woman was tortured and killed. James said he dated her; your boss employed her at his club."

"My boss?"

"Harry Moray."

"He's not my boss, and anyway, you've already talked to him. I don't know anything more about it."

"Okay. But maybe you can fill in some blanks."

"Were you at Kent Island with James and the mayor on August first and second?"

"No."

"What were James and the mayor doing there?"

"I don't know."

"Did you make the entries for the calendar you showed us?"

She didn't answer.

"Why were James's appointments on your calendar?"

"It's business. We keep track of each other."

"They were written later, though, weren't they?" Her head swiveled toward Cal. Even behind the dark glasses, Cal sensed he had scored.

"I don't know."

"Come on. It's your calendar."

"I tell you, I don't know. I didn't make those entries."

"Who did?"

"I don't know."

"What's at Kent?"

"Moray owns a summer house there."

"Have you been there?"

"Sure. Lots of times."

"When was the last time?"

"July."

"Was James on that trip?"

"I think so."

"Tell me about the July trip."

"It was the same as always — Rivergate, Rivergate, Rivergate."

Ophelia was clenching her lips as though nothing more should pass through them. Cal pressed on.

"What's your role in Rivergate?"

"What's this got to do with Mary Jeanne?"

"You're the one who showed us a calendar James is using to alibi his weekend. You tell me."

"It's simple. Rivergate requires twenty percent minority vendors. I'm the twenty percent."

"Isn't your real job to sell the plan to the mayor and pick up his share?"

"I won this contract fair and square," Ophelia retorted defensively. He was pushing hard now.

"Could Mary Jeanne have been with James and the mayor on the first weekend in August?"

Ophelia didn't seemed surprised at the question.

"I don't know."

"But she could have?"

"Sure."

"Where did you say you first met her?"

"At the River Club. But she lived just down on Columbia Road." Ophelia's head nodded south. "I gave her a ride once."

"When did you last see her?"

"I'm not sure. At the River Club probably. I saw her about a week before. I don't know."

"Are you the cover for the mayor's payoff in Rivergate?" Cal said, switching back.

She stood silent.

"Come on. Ophelia?"

"No, you come on. I've got a degree in urban planning. I managed two planning grants in Baltimore. No white police officer is going to come in here throwing charges around."

"If you've got all these degrees, why did James have you keeping his calendar like a goddamned secretary?" Cal asked, deliberately trying to provoke her.

Ophelia fidgeted as though this bothered her as well.

"How long did Mary Jeanne date the mayor?"

Again it was like a Texas leaguer, the question rose like a pop fly and hung in the air.

"I don't know."

Cal felt his adrenaline spike. He had hit it. He could feel it.

"We were told they met in March. Does that sound right?

Ophelia nodded. "Who told you?"

"I can't reveal our sources."

"Were they sleeping together?"

"I guess so." Ophelia was looking out over the park now. "God, I'd be the last to know."

"Did you talk to him about it?"

"He'd never admit that."

"When did you learn Mary Jeanne was dead?"

"When I read it in the paper."

"Did you ask the mayor about her then?"

"Yes."

"What did he say?"

"He said he couldn't believe it."

"I want you to tell this to a grand jury."

"I'm not going before a grand jury. You get your other witness. You understand? Now get out of here!"

Ophelia started forward, albeit unsteadily. Her voice was angry but fearful as well. Cal knew she had figured out there wasn't any other witness. She'd been bluffed. She stumbled sideways, he reached out to steady her, and she winced.

"Are you okay?" he asked.

"Get out of here!" she screamed.

He went back to headquarters, got a cup of coffee, and sat at his desk watching Nathaniel's office door. He figured that by now Ophelia had called her husband, and her husband had called Nathaniel. He sat there for an hour. Nathaniel came out and went back several times and then left for a meeting. Nothing happened. He called Dispatch to reach out for Bobbie. He'd better brief her before the shit hit the fan.

19

Cal drove Bobbie all the way down to the end of Hains Point, half a mile from the nearest building. This way, he could see someone approaching three hundred yards away. Ever since he'd spotted the surveillance on Ophelia, he had the feeling that he too was being watched.

Twice he'd done evasion maneuvers coming into work, varying his route and choosing interchanges that allowed him to see who was behind him. On the second evasion, he'd driven down into Bolling Air Force Base and pulled off by the gate. No one followed him, but at the last minute he looked back and saw a man in a suit standing by the stone wall along Route 298, looking down at him. By the time Cal turned his car around, the man was gone.

Cal and Bobbie sat in a cruiser with the windows open to the river coolness, eating sandwiches from the deli on Seventh.

"Why couldn't we step out to eat at Melvin's? This car is a mess and stinks of old coffee." Bobbie was petulant. She had broken up with her most recent boyfriend, and since she got back from West Virginia, she had been curt and unpleasant.

He twisted in the seat and looked at her. She was wearing her Spanish countess special: black turtleneck jersey, short black leather toreador jacket, black pants, and black boots with tiny silver tips and silver mountings. With her black hair, the outfit made her look like a horsewoman of old Mexico.

Her Polaroid sunglasses were mirrors in which Cal noticed he looked worn. He glanced down for a moment and could just see the tip of the ankle gun she wore when she had on boots.

After she was shot, Bobbie became obsessed with guns. The ankle gun was a .32 with a spring in the holster that popped the pistol into her hand. He suspected she also had her German-made PPK in a holster in the center of her back under the jacket.

Yet, in the time he'd known her, she'd never drawn a gun in anger. The night she was shot, it happened so fast that she could not get her pistol up to fire. Having been seriously wounded with a gun, Bobbie jumped into weapons training with a vengeance. She practiced all the time. At the Willow range in Virginia, where the targets were a man's silhouette, she was infamous among cops for being able to put six rounds in eight seconds where the target's penis would have been.

"What's wrong?" Cal asked.

"I don't know. I feel like my life is over, you know, like there's nothing else."

"Somebody told me you split with that guy Greg?"

There was silence.

"That's why I suddenly took leave. I rented a little place at Berkeley Springs. Big Bobbie was going to work things out. It was horrible! Two days of my begging and his looking uncomfortable. What he forgot to tell me was that it was over when we got there. He'd been involved with this woman for weeks.

"He's going to live with her! I know her. This means every goddamn party I go to, there they'll be." Her face screwed up. For a moment Cal thought she was going to cry.

"What about the building manager. I could tell you liked him."

"That son of a bitch. He told me he was single. Shit. I found his wife's cosmetics in the bathroom! She's a German television producer. She was away on leave to see her family."

Silence.

"Anything more from West Virginia?" She had already told him on the phone that Richie was a dead end. But he wanted to change the subject.

"That makes me madder than anything else!" she said with a wry grin.

"Why?"

"Because you were right, of course," she mumbled through the sandwich. "I made a few more phone calls. Richie didn't have any friends to speak of, and none with a van. He married his wife after he got her pregnant when they were fifteen. He's stayed with her on and off ever since, and the local sheriff said the most exciting sex escapade he probably ever got into was stealing *Playboy* from the newsstand."

"What about the attempted rape?"

"They had had reports of Peeping Toms and prowlers for years, but the old woman who tagged Richie was apparently pretty weak on the ID. They let it go to a break-in to close the case."

They ate in silence for a while.

"Can I talk to you like the old days?" Cal asked gently. "About some things I learned."

She was biting into the second half of a guacamole on pita bread sandwich, and her face had an expression of surprise that was almost comical. "What old days?" she mumbled through the food.

"When I could tell you something and you didn't know better than I do and start arguing with me. Something really between us?"

She took off her sunglasses and looked hard at him.

Her face changed. The look of sultry innocence was replaced with a look he had never seen before: toleration. It was only for a moment, then it flickered.

"What you don't realize is that I'm all you've got."

She said it matter-of-factly, as though she were ticking off attributes on her fingers.

"The black guys won't work with you because they don't want to work with a middle-aged white guy. The white guys won't work with you because you're arrogant. You ever notice that you don't ever ask anybody about anything? You tell them. Christ, ask once in a while. Also stop letting people know you don't like cops. *You are a cop!* Dumb as that may be.

"It's not just on the job. You know that! Your marriage went down the tubes five years ago, and that harbormaster woman you were sleeping with left you last summer. For all I know, even your dogs have run away."

Cal started to speak, but Bobbie raised her voice. "You know what most of the guys in Homicide figure? They figure they have the something you want." She paused for effect. "A life."

He remembered what Vivian had said. He didn't have a life. He felt like telling Bobbie that he may have found a life, that he was trying to get a life going. He felt like telling her about Vivian's coming around again, but he didn't. Bobbie wouldn't believe it, and he didn't understand it either.

"A lot of the white guys have told Nathaniel they don't think you're management material. Two asked for transfers. You know why? Ever since you made lieutenant, you're nasty all the time. A person can't ask you the time of day without getting some mouth. You disparage people.

You demean them. Collins did his best on the Reggae Club. He heard you went and interviewed the shooter's mother. Why didn't you tell him you were going to do that? Why didn't you tell him you were going to the Narcotics Task Force? Why didn't you tell him about the Salvadorans instead of sending a memo to Nathaniel?"

Bobbie paused for breath. "Did you ever notice that I'm the only officer who actually works with you on cases? Nathaniel probably didn't give a shit when the blacks complained, he expected guys like Collins to, but when the white guys came to him . . ." Bobbie let her voice trail off. She turned away from him and looked out the car window. "Maybe it's time to cut papers for retirement?"

Cal opened the door, threw out his sandwich, and slammed the car into reverse so fast that Bobbie's Coke splashed all over her slacks.

"What the hell!"

Slamming on the brakes, he screamed at her, "Get out of the car! I don't need you either. I've been carrying you for nearly eight goddamn years. I don't need you anymore and I don't need this shitty job. Not one more goddamn day! I need a partner I can trust, and instead I've got to listen to a woman who learned everything she knows about the world from *Vanity Fair*."

He realized he sounded hysterical now, loud and abusive. She was looking at him as though this made her point.

"You're an airhead," he went on. "Do you think I care about what the white cops think? Incidentally, I hate cops, black or white, and I don't care if they know it. Half of them don't do shit anyway."

Bobbie tried to speak, but he shouted her down.

"I've got more overtime than anyone in Homicide! This job cost me Vivian. Just three days ago I turned down a two-hundred-and-fifty-thousand-dollar-a-year job offer. I've got a boss who thinks he's going to have eighty percent completions with fewer officers than we had in nineteen ninety, and now I'm into a nasty, dangerous investigation with not one person I can trust in the whole department."

He was screaming so loud, the car reverberated with the noise. She looked awestruck.

"Go back to the part where you turned down the two-hundred-and-fifty-thousand-dollar job," she said.

Trying to keep his voice calm, he told her about Moray's offer, about how Vivian had recommended him.

"Maybe you should take it, Cal. A lot of people think you ought to pull your time. Do something else, kick back. That sounds like a great deal. Call Moray and say you changed your mind."

He felt deflated, as he had with Vivian. He was angry, but it always came out worse than he meant, it always came out bad. Bobbie was the last person he should be yelling at. He knew she was right too. He'd burned a lot of bridges.

"It's not a job, Moray's just bribing me. I can't accept that job, Bobbie. Maybe my time is up. But I can't go out on a bribe," he finally said. His voice was flat now and tired. "I made a lot of headway while you were off. . . . I think Moray knows I'm breathing down his neck."

Bobbie said softly, "You know what you need —"

He cut Bobbie off. "If you say what I think you're going to say, I'll pull out my gun and shoot you."

"You need a vacation."

"I can't take time off. This case is coming down on me, I can feel it."

He gripped the wheel with both hands. His knuckles were white from the strain.

"You and I are on to something I'm not sure I want."

"Explain."

There was another long silence.

"Can we agree that Richie probably didn't do Mary Jeanne?"

Bobbie nodded.

"Well, there are too many things wrong with Moray's story."

He told her about the *Potomac Fever*, about the land deals around the stadium.

"Ophelia said the mayor was boffing Mary Jeanne!" Bobbie said, giving a silent whistle.

Cal nodded. "She took it for granted."

"Shit," said Bobbie. "Shit."

"Also, I think there's a tail car on the mayor or Ophelia."

"Security?"

"No. I don't think so. It wasn't Metro, maybe the FBI. I couldn't tell. It sure picked me up right away. Now I think I'm under surveillance all the time. That's why we're down here."

"Why didn't you tell me the whole story before?"

"I wasn't sure of my facts, you were away, then you took leave. Now I'm sure. I don't know who killed her, but it has something to do with Moray and the mayor and the *Potomac Fever*! Christ, maybe it was the mayor or Moray."

Without knowing why, he reached out for emphasis and squeezed her thigh, feeling the hard muscles and firm flesh. Slowly and impishly, a grin crossed her face. She reached down and grabbed his hand in a powerful grip before he could pull it off her leg.

"Calvert! After all these years, you're finally going to give me enough to turn you over to the EEOC. Come on, sweetie," she said, lifting his hand toward her crotch. "Go for it."

"Screw you!" Cal was laughing, and so was Bobbie. She was holding his hand, doubled over with laughter. It was the crazy laughter of two people who had had a terrible fight and patched it up, the laughter of two people trying to throw off their fear. They were in dangerous territory and they knew it.

For a moment they couldn't stop laughing. Bobbie was giggling so hard that her whole body shook, and then she was hugging Cal and he could feel her body wrapped around his. Cal pulled back and got a handkerchief out and realized his eyes were wet.

"Why the Feds?" Bobbie countered when she'd stopped laughing. "Maybe corruption? Maybe it's part of the insurance commission case. You get the Crown Vic's tag?"

Cal shook his head. "Lease." He held up his hand. "There's something else I didn't tell you."

He reminded her of how Nathaniel acted when Cal first mentioned James. He told her of his suspicions that Nathaniel might have tipped James.

"From the moment I wouldn't go along with closing the case on Richie, he's been loading us down. There was so much work at first, I didn't notice it, but I figure our section's drawing forty percent of the work by ourselves."

"Why?"

"To keep us off Mary Jeanne."

"Why does he want to do that?"

"If Mary Jeanne was running around with Cameron, Nathaniel's covering for him."

"Maybe it isn't the mayor. Maybe James is bisexual," said Bobbie. "Maybe Ophelia's wrong and it's James who was sleeping with Mary Jeanne. Maybe James likes to go both ways." She didn't look convinced. "Incidentally, why didn't Ophelia raise hell when you questioned her?"

Cal shook his head. "I don't know. I don't think she told Cameron either. Perhaps she doesn't like being played the fool."

"Nathaniel wouldn't take a risk for James," Cal said. "But the mayor's his rabbi.

"If Mary Jeanne wasn't a problem for Cameron," he continued, "why wasn't he on the phone to us saying, How can I help? He wouldn't have to admit anything, but he could have called Nathaniel and said he'd known the woman."

"Maybe he did," said Bobbie.

"Cameron would have to figure out that an investigation would turn him up," Cal said.

"Only you just did turn it up," Bobbie said. She was getting into it now, he could tell, beginning to appreciate the nuances. "If we'd closed it with Richie, they'd be okay," Bobbie reasoned out loud. "So maybe Nathaniel told the mayor, 'Sit tight, be cool, this isn't going very far.'

"What I still don't understand is why Ophelia even talked to you. Why she didn't just call her husband and get you off her back."

"Let's get coffee," he finally said, pointing across the river. Cal threw the car into gear, tires squealing up the river road.

He drove across the Rochambeau Bridge to Virginia.

He could feel Bobbie's tension rise. She was like a African hunter who just noticed that the elephant she was chasing was gigantic. They weren't screwing with James now. They were screwing with the whole hierarchy of the city.

"You've got two years to retirement," Bobbie said. "You could go out of here right now with your military time." She was nursing her coffee, looking intently at the cup. "Why not forget this whole thing. Begin to look for a job, maybe get Vivian back, live happily ever after."

Cal looked up sharply. "How do you know about that?"

"I'm your partner, for Christ's sake," she said. "Anyway, when I got back, everyone knew — Nathaniel, Collins, everyone who pays attention to you."

Bobbie had her head down now, talking into her coffee cup, avoiding his gaze.

"We're never going to get a conviction out of this. You know that. Even if everybody is lying to us about that night, how're we going to place the mayor at the scene? Where is the scene? You said the fibers from the *Potomac Fever* didn't match. We still haven't got a crime scene!"

Cal knew she was right. No witnesses, no forensics, no crime scene, no suspects. Only a cover-up.

"Cal, it isn't like we don't have enough business. Christ, half the cases we never finish. It's like the Reggae Club. That report is due in two weeks. This isn't investigating, Cal — you and I work on a conveyor belt. We just shovel the shit along until it's time to leave."

Cal found himself looking at her with enormous affection. He realized they were very much alike, after all; neither of them came to police work for security or pay, they came to accomplish something. It had just turned out badly.

"Neither you nor I are going anyplace in this department. They think I'm a cranky middle-aged white guy. They think you're an oddity; the rich girl playing police officer. Even if you could pass the lieutenant's exam with a hundred percent, they aren't going to let it happen."

He was punching his finger at her. "So, one way to look at it is that we've got nothing to lose," said Cal. We're the perfect cops for this case."

They drank the coffee in silence. Finally Cal made his last pitch. "Mary Jeanne was just a kid, a beautiful kid. She couldn't even buy a drink in half the states. Like her mother says — Why would somebody tie up this kid, feed her booze and cocaine, heat a metal brand, and push it into her flesh?

"I need your help," he said. "Please."

"Jesus, that's a new approach," Bobbie said. "How do we do it?"

"There are only two ways to break open a conspiracy. You've got to have an undercover inside, or you've got to turn one of the participants. We haven't got an undercover. . . ."

20

Pretexting Moray had been Bobbie's idea, and Cal thought of every reason it could go badly. "You don't cozy up to the most powerful lobbyist in Washington wired like he's a drug dealer! I should have never turned him down, should have at least played along for a while. But to come back now? Moray will accuse you of soliciting a bribe. You'll be taping the evidence for your own prosecution. He's playing serious ball. If he thinks you're setting him up, there's no telling what he'll do. For all I know, he's violent. For all we know, he killed Mary Jeanne."

Cal knew he sounded shrill, but he was daily growing more anxious as well. He'd once again spotted what he thought was surveillance. One night when he stopped for a sandwich at Denny's, a white panel truck had followed his car into the parking lot, but the driver never got out. For two days he thought he saw the same panel truck.

Richie's death still nagged at him. Susan Lungren called to say that she was suing the River Club for wrongful termination on behalf of Richie's wife. She said she found two men who said they were drinking wine with Richie on the morning of August 2. She said when she advised Moray's lawyers, "Vic Stein told me he was sure Moray would consider a settlement. He said Celeste will be out of the country for some time, and they want to get this whole thing behind them."

The next day, Anne Groer in the *Washington Post* reported that Harry Moray and Celeste "were taking a time-out. Moray's friends say he treasures Celeste and doesn't want their marriage to go the way his others did, so the Mrs. is off on an R and R trip and they'll rendezvous in St. Moritz when the snows start."

When Bobbie had come up with her plan, he'd opposed it. "What I told you down at Hains Point is true. This is a very tricky little deal; we stirred up somebody's hornets."

Bobbie cast aside each objection.

"Harry Moray has an eye for the ladies. The first time we interviewed him, I thought he was going to drool. You said yourself that we have to get inside a conspiracy. By trolling a high-paying job past you, Moray gave us an opening to go straight at him. I'm going to tell him we're business partners. That will intrigue him. It may not persuade him, but he will talk to me, I promise that."

In the end, she turned to Cal with that impish grin. "Don't deny me this, Cal. With Celeste out of the picture, I may be able to land myself a multimillionaire."

Bobbie had won out, of course.

On a hot September evening, Cal and Jack Mobus were lying prone in a clump of bushes, a hundred yards from Moray's living room, trespassing on his land, listening to a radio receiver and scanning the house with binoculars.

Jack had been his partner in Narcotics, before Bobbie. Jack had done his military service in the Signal Corps, wiring telephones. A master with a wire, they called him. Jack had retired from the cops right on twenty years and opened a telephone-installation company, one of those companies that sets up your office system with other people's equipment. He made enough money to drive a Ferrari, but he liked a little fun once in a while, like tonight.

Cal and Jack had done this a hundred times in the old days, dressed in black Levi's, black gym shoes, and black turtlenecks, waiting on an undercover, listening to the little transmitter, waiting for the buy, waiting to burst through the door and make the arrest.

Bobbie and Moray were in the cavernous living room where Cal had interviewed Celeste. The drapes were open on the two-story glass wall and as long as they stayed in that room, Cal could see them through binoculars.

Bobbie had come dressed to kill. Cal had never seen her look so beautiful. Gone was San Francisco mod and all of her other costumes. For Moray's dinner invitation, she wore basic black velvet, a demure dress from the front, but one that left the alabaster skin of her back bare from neck to hips. She wore a diamond bracelet that Cal had never seen before and now realized was probably real. She had done her hair in a high French knot so that her neck was bare, and she had diamond earrings to match her bracelet.

Bobbie was so stunning that when Jack Mobus fitted the tiny microphone into the folds of her neckline, his hands were shaking. "Jesus, Jack," Bobbie had teased him, "being retired has given you palsy."

"Sweetheart, don't tease old Jack. If you don't watch out, I'll call your father and he'll put a stop to this whole plan."

Jack had devised a mike from new micro parts that looked, were it seen, as possibly the head of a seamstress's forgotten pin. The power supply and the transmitter were on a pack the size of a cigarette box, which he had taped to Bobbie's groin. "If you get worried, even just a little bit worried, excuse yourself, go to the bathroom and pull the whole thing. It will come off in two motions. Unclip the mike and pull the tape on your groin. Don't leave it in the bathroom! It's as vanilla as I could make it, but the mike can probably be traced."

Moray had gone for the bait like a trout in a Montana stream. He'd love to talk to her about the job offer he'd made to Cal. Cal should have taken it. What about dinner? Friday? Eight? Celeste is in Egypt; would Bobbie like to come to the house? Most of the servants are away, but he'd have a little something whipped up.

Bobbie had driven over on her own. Cal and Jack had crisscrossed northern Virginia to elude any surveillance, changed cars in a Metro parking lot, and ended up in a rental van. Unable to leave the truck on Chain Bridge Road, they'd come up behind the house from the river, a fast, hard climb for a quarter of a mile through heavy brush.

Jack had done his work well. The transmission was clear enough for them to keep the volume down as they watched and recorded.

"You're saying that in matters like this, you and Cal are a team off-duty too." Moray was talking, standing by a cart mixing drinks. He turned and handed Bobbie a long crystal martini glass. "Best martini in Washington!"

Bobbie accepted it and turned toward one of the large sofas. "Cal has no ambition, bless his heart. He wouldn't know what to do with the job you offered. Don't get me wrong, he's a wonderful man. Simple. Straightforward." Cal could hear Moray chuckle. "He was afraid you were setting him up."

"Setting him up? What —"

"When I heard he'd turned you down, I was furious. I said, 'Cal, honey, we've labored in the vineyards too long.'"

Moray poured himself a drink and followed Bobbie, taking a chair close to the couch. Their heads were now together like two conspirators.

"That's what went wrong with Cal and Vivian." Bobbie's voice dropped an octave, a woman imparting a confidentiality. "He's the kind of cop who wants to put in his day, you know, have a little tequila, watch the Orioles."

"And you're not?"

"Nope. My daddy is the air-conditioning king of Texas. He told me making money is its own reward."

They sipped the martinis in silence for a time.

"Oooh. This is nice," Bobbie said. "Daddy makes a really great martini. He said you have to use gin. Vodka isn't a martini! he says, it's just vodka and vermouth!" Bobbie imitated the deep voice of her father.

Moray nodded at her drink. "That's Bombay gin."

There was noise of movement, the tinkle of glass, a soft shurring sound of Bobbie's dress as she moved in her seat.

"Cal said you know Vivian?"

"Through Charley. Great gal! Vivian's brother, Charley, is in Rivergate, you know. Terrific lawyer. He's doing a lot of the land-acquisition stuff. He and Edward were on Northwest's board."

Cal's eyes widened. Vivian hadn't mentioned that Charley worked with Moray. You would have thought she'd mention it.

"If I sell you to my investors, how soon could you get going?"

"Two to three weeks."

"How would this work with Terrell?" Moray said.

"I've thought a little about that since we first talked, and to be frank, Cal and I've talked it through. You hire me. Place a woman at the top of this new force. Placing a woman there will be good publicity for you, you'll get a lot of notice. So I'm gone. Cal's getting ready to retire anyway. So he can cash out when he wants, but for the time being, he'll sort of stay, cover our backs, you might say."

"Terrell is going to retire?"

"Oh. Yeah. He's run his course. He knows that."

"Nobody told me that," Moray said in a perplexed voice. "What do you mean, 'cover our backs.'"

"Protect your interests inside the department. We asked ourselves, 'What are the most valuable services we could perform for Mr. Moray?'"

"What did you come up with?" Moray said wryly.

"Seeing that the Mary Jeanne Turner case doesn't go off the road."

There was a long silence. Cal wondered if Bobbie had not made the deal too plain. Moray had been a lawyer thirty years before; maybe he could spot bribe evidence when he heard it. Cal tried to focus on Moray's face through the binoculars, but Moray was down behind Bobbie.

"How much would these services be?"

"Cal said you suggested a two-year contract. I don't think that's as appropriate as a one-time signing bonus of, let's say, four hundred thousand dollars," said Bobbie, all business now. "Like a football contract. Four hundred thousand on signing, and then if the police thing gets under way, we can talk."

"This includes Cal?"

"Absolutely. This is a joint deal. A twofer. If you think about it, you're saving a hundred thousand dollars and getting more for your money!"

"It sounds like you and your partner are an item too."

Bobbie laughed, a little too hard, Cal thought.

"He's one of those men who likes a strong hand. Vivian used a strong hand with him, and when she left, he was all at sea. Let's just say I'll handle him."

Cal heard Moray whistle. Cal laughed to himself. Bobbie sounded so good that he began to bristle a little.

Moray snorted. "I've got to tell you, honey. You don't mind if I call you 'honey'? I call everybody 'honey.' The hell with political correctness." Moray laughed. "I didn't think much of this idea when you came to the office. But damn! I'm getting to like you. I talked to some people down in Oklahoma who know your daddy. They said you're twice as smart as any of your brothers."

Bobbie chuckled. "It took years for my daddy to understand that."

"You know," Moray said, "you and I'll be working very closely. You know that."

"We'd have to," said Bobbie in her throaty voice. "I've got to understand your concepts of law enforcement."

"I'm going to put you right over in Georgetown with me. Later the police headquarters can be over with Virgil at the Rivergate building, but I need you where decisions are being made."

A Hispanic-looking man in an evening jacket entered from behind Moray and announced dinner.

"Thank you, Raoul." Moray and Bobbie stood up at the same moment. "You know, Bobbie, the name Short doesn't do you justice. How tall are you?"

"Six two in heels," Bobbie said.

Moray took her elbow to escort her to the dining room. "Somebody told me you can carry a hundred-and-sixty-pound man up three flights of stairs."

"Who told you that, Harry?"

"Oh, just somebody I know."

"I did it to win a bet."

"You know, Bobbie, I weigh a hundred and sixty."

They disappeared from sight.

The dinner seemed interminable to Cal. Bobbie and Moray were to- tally out of sight, and without the glass wall, the transmission was spotty too.

He and Jack could make out that most of dinner was small talk, wine, food, gossip, Redskins, politics, and Rivergate.

"Cal made me kind of mad," Moray said. "I invite him to dinner to talk about a terrific opportunity for him, and the next day he calls and tries to question me about Mary Jeanne's death. You know damn well you don't act like that. For Christ's sake! We gave you everything we had. God, I wish I could bring Mary Jeanne back, but we can't. Celeste and I just don't know any more."

"Harry, Harry, relax. Cal's so linear. I'm in charge anyway."

"But if you leave the department, what happens to the investigation?"

"Let's say we make the deal we were talking about."

Moray grunted.

"I'll resign and join you. Cal for the time being will stay on the job — you know, taking care of things. We're already working on a report. We think there's ample evidence that Mary Jeanne had become the victim of people into scarification."

"What in God's name is scarification?"

"People who mark up bodies. You see them all the time, Harry. The women with the rings in their belly buttons and in their eyelids."

"Oh yeah."

"Think back. Maybe Mary Jeanne was already wearing some of this stuff?"

Cal could hear heavy breathing by two people, and he realized that Bobbie and Moray were sitting close, very close.

He heard an "uh-uh" in a man's voice.

"I've been in touch with scarification experts, leather shops, sex em- poriums. I spent two days on the Internet checking porno sites for branding and body marking alone! We know we're looking for a man who likes to mark his sex partners. Unless you know someone like that, we're through with you and your employees."

"But what happens when you leave the force?" Moray asked again.

"Nothing, really. That's the deal. After three months Cal will write a final report, putting this thing on the back burner. You know what kind of a case this is?"

Cal could hear Moray grunt.

"This is the kind of case that breaks open years later. Some police department picks up some nut a million miles from here and he starts telling them about all the women he's done. A serial-killer type."

"You really think so?" asked Moray.

"Sure."

"Why do I get the feeling that I've been had?" Moray said, not unkindly.

"Mr. Moray," Bobbie said in her Texas debutante's voice, "we're just a couple of civil servants trying to do our job."

It was past ten when they reentered the living room. Moray had an arm around Bobbie's waist and led her on a tour of the Egyptian antiquities. His arm rested on her hip just below the open panel of her backless dress.

What annoyed Cal was that he couldn't see what Moray was doing, but he knew the two were whispering.

"Get him back in view!" Cal said out loud.

But Bobbie and Moray walked in and out of the shadows of several alcoves where the art had been placed.

"Harry, could you run and get me a drink while I freshen up?" Bobbie's voice was low and husky, and Cal wondered if the liquor she had drunk was taking effect.

Moray went over to the drink cart and poured liquor from a crystal bottle into two goblets. Bobbie disappeared through a side door. Cal and Jack heard water running and then an abrupt silence.

The transmitter had gone dead.

"She pulled it," Jack said.

"What?" Cal was furious.

"She pulled it. Maybe she thought Moray might feel it."

"On her groin? I don't want Moray feeling anything!"

When Bobbie came back, the two sat in a large semicircular sofa looking out over the garden. Suddenly the lights of the drawing room went dark, leaving only a handful of candles flickering on a piano, and a garden speaker system was playing Placido Domingo. Cal and Jack could hear nothing over the tenor's aria, and they could no longer see anyone at all.

A few seconds later, the entire garden was as light as day and fifteen fountains and watering systems went off all at once, sending cascades of water over both of them.

"Stay down!" hissed Jack.

Cal started to stand up, but Jack held him down.

"They'll see you!"

"What about Bobbie?"

"Bobbie turns thirty-six next year! If she hasn't figured this out, you can't help her!"

They waited there, in what amounted to an Asian monsoon, with Cal fuming, for nearly two hours.

Finally the garden light show ended and the showers subsided. They saw light from the house flood out onto the courtyard and parking area. Moray was walking Bobbie to her car. He had an arm around her waist, and at the car door he turned her around and kissed her neck, held the door for her, and watched her car head down the driveway.

Cal and Jack started to gather their soaked equipment when they saw the other headlights come on, behind Moray's garage. A Crown Victoria pulled into the courtyard. Moray went to the window for a second, then the big car hurtled down the driveway.

"Oh, shit," said Jack. They started running down the hill through the brush, cutting their legs and arms.

21

In the end, they didn't clear it with Nathaniel. No regulation said they had to, but the fact was, you didn't haul important citizens off the street without permission. Cal knew they were way beyond regulations anyway.

They grabbed James two blocks from the White House. They pulled his Mercedes over with their red light flashing, just like the cops on TV, and ordered him out of the car. Bobbie searched him, bending him over the hood of the unmarked. "Just spread 'em, Mr. James. That's a boy."

"What is this? What is this shit! Who do you two think you're fuckin' with. Am I under arrest?"

"No, Mr. James. We just want to talk to you. You said you wanted to help us with Mary Jeanne's death. But you didn't return our telephone calls," Bobbie said.

Virgil looked nervously around. A small crowd had gathered, watching the scene: two white detectives had a black man braced on the street. They looked at the Mercedes and James. He probably stole it, their eyes said. In this white downtown neighborhood, despite his $800 suit and the gold jewelry, James had no allies and nobody was coming to his rescue.

Cal figured Virgil gave a thought to simply getting in his car and driving off, but in the end Virgil rejected it. He really had no way of knowing Bobbie wouldn't shoot him. She had planned the whole deal down to the clothes she had on. Today she was *Miami Vice,* her reflector sunglasses denying James even a look at her eyes. She wore a light linen jacket, which kept opening when she moved, exposing a large automatic pistol in a shoulder holster.

An Executive Protection Service car had pulled up and so did a Park Police wagon, offering Cal and Bobbie assistance. The crowd was growing. James kept swiveling his head, looking for some support but finding none. Bobbie bent him over the hood again to handcuff him, just like they do with the bad boys. She put him in the back of the Cavalier, where the doors didn't have handles.

Bobbie drove the Mercedes. Cal followed in the unmarked. It was a violation of policy, but then again, the whole thing was. Instead of taking him to Homicide at 300 Indiana Avenue, they took him up to the Sixth District interrogation room. The Sixth had the most white cops of any district in the city and a white commander. Half of them were kluckers, the other half had tried to hit on Bobbie. They wouldn't ask questions about a black suspect. They wouldn't question anything Bobbie did.

At the Sixth, Cal read James a Miranda warning and took him to an interrogation room.

Bobbie played it to the hilt. She ostentatiously locked the interrogation room door and took off her jacket. She was wearing the shoulder holster, less the gun now, but with her size and her well-muscled arms, she was an intimidating figure of a woman.

Bobbie often carried a slapjack even though they were illegal — for self-protection, she said. She took it out and dropped it on the interrogation table. The lead-filled leather made an awful noise as it hit the wood.

James couldn't take his eyes off Bobbie.

"You want coffee," Bobbie said to Cal. "We're going to be here a long time."

James didn't say anything. His eyes said he hadn't figured on being here at all. Cal said, "Black with one sugar."

"What about you?" she said to James.

"Just cream," James finally said.

When Bobbie left and locked the door, James leaned forward and whispered.

"I thought everything was straightened out."

"What?"

"Didn't Moray talk to you?" Now James's face really looked wild and frightened.

"What?"

"Harry was supposed to straighten everything out."

"What do you mean, 'straighten'?" Cal said.

James lapsed into a kind of fitful silence.

Bobbie came back and put the coffee carrier on the table. She sat down silently, as though she was controlling rage.

In fact, Moray had enraged and embarrassed her. The morning after her dinner, a videotape was delivered to her apartment building. It had been shot with infrared light and wasn't very good. Bobbie was all entangled with Harry, not undressed or anything, but you couldn't tell where Harry began and Bobbie left off.

The audio was like nothing Cal had on his tape and was pretty incriminating. Bobbie swore it was faked, clipped and re-recorded out of context, but it was nasty, filled with heavy breathing and rustling clothing, the way people sound when they are trying to get at each other's body.

"So I give you four hundred thousand dollars," Moray said at one point. "That's a lot for a little girl. What do I get?"

And Bobbie said, "What about this."

A moment later Moray whispered, "And Mary Jeanne?"

And Bobbie's voice, all husky and soft, said, "Mary Jeanne Turner goes bye-bye."

"For good?"

"For good."

With the video came a note. *You're way out of your league,* it said. *Love, Harry.*

"Let's lean on James," Bobbie had said after she showed Cal the tape. "He's the weakest link. I can break him down."

James must have sensed Bobbie's rage. He never took his eyes off her.

"Do you know my specialty on the police force, Mr. James?"

Virgil shook his head. He was watching her hands fingering the slapjack.

"I specialize in men that hurt women."

The slapjack hit the table with a resounding crash.

"Mr. James tells me he thought Harry Moray straightened all this out," Cal said. "He kinda whispered it, so I guess he didn't want you to know it was all straight." He paused. "Are you straight?"

"Uh-uh," Bobbie said, shaking her head. "Harry tried his best to straighten me out, if you mean as in horizontal. You know what Harry really told me, Virgil?"

James shook his head.

"If the shoe fits Virgil James," she said, "go for it."

The slapjack hit the table again.

"Mary Jeanne Turner was nineteen years old, Mr. James. She should have been going to college dances," Bobbie said. The slapjack hit the table. "Sorority parties." *Crash!* "Homecoming games." *Crash!* "You know, living the kid life."

Bobbie stopped.

"But she isn't. Last August second or third, you or somebody else tied this young girl up and took a hot branding iron and burned a letter *B* into her skin."

Cal sat looking at James with unblinking eyes.

"Did you do that, Virgil?" Bobbie asked.

James furiously shook his head.

"Do you think that would hurt?"

James nodded again.

"When we came to ask you about this the first time, you thought we were funny, didn't you? You thought cops investigating the murder of a young girl were funny. Right? You thought this was a joke? Right?"

The slapjack crashed.

"What time did you get to Kent Island on August first?" Bobbie asked. She turned on the video recorder and was looking hard at James. James didn't notice there was no tape in the recorder. His eyes were following Bobbie.

"I don't remember. Maybe five or six."

"Did you drive down alone?"

James swiveled now to look at Cal.

"What is this? Can she do this?" James said.

Cal could see in his eyes that he was trying to buy time.

"You know what the old-time cops used to do?" Cal nodded toward the slapjack.

James shook his head.

"They'd take a telephone book" — Cal reached under the table and pulled out an old raggedy D.C. Yellow Pages — "and they'd put it on a guy's head. Then for every wrong answer, they'd slam the book with a slapjack. No marks. A little blood sometimes. You know, from the nose and mouth, even from the ears, but no marks. Amazing."

"Did you drive down alone?" said Bobbie.

"No. We went down in the mayor's car."

"Where was Mary Jeanne?"

"How should I know?"

The slapjack hit the table.

"Don't get smart, Virgil!" Bobbie said. "Was the mayor dating her that weekend?"

"Who told you that?"

The slapjack crashed.

"Answer the question," said Cal.

"Was the mayor dating her?" asked Bobbie.

"Ask the mayor."

Crash went the slapjack.

"Didn't I tell you to talk nicely?" Bobbie said.

"I don't know if Martin dated her."

"You saw Mary Jeanne on the first, right?"

"Maybe. I don't remember."

"Sure you remember. You and the mayor and Mary Jeanne actually went for a little boat ride. Tell me what happened on the *Potomac Fever*."

James looked wild. Maybe the mention of the words *Potomac Fever* lit him up. He really didn't know whether Moray had betrayed him or not.

"Who told you about the party?"

"Somebody you'd never guess in a million years!"

The slapjack hit the table again.

"I don't remember much."

"Virgil, Virgil, Virgil." Bobbie sat down next to him and put her face close to his, the way she had with Richie.

She told Cal once that she wore lilac water or a strong cologne for interrogation. Cal had asked why. "It reminds them of their mother." Bobbie would laugh her big, deep laugh.

"You made a terrible mistake, Virgil. You lied to us. Lying to us is a felony, Virgil, a crime. We can arrest you right now. We're federal officers. Section one double-oh one, Virgil. Didn't Moray tell you that, Virgil? Didn't he?"

Silence.

Bobbie was making up facts and criminal code numbers as she went, and the results were impressive. Anger made her a terrific interrogator. Bobbie had no idea whether James had been on the yacht, but she defied him to prove her wrong. Sure, a lot of arrows were pointing to Kent Island and the yacht. There had been a party on the yacht and an overnight cruise to Kent Island. The mayor and James had gone to Kent Island the same weekend by car. Mary Jeanne dated the mayor. But the night of the cruise Mary Jeanne was working until 2:30, according to her timecard. Then just over twenty-four hours later she floated up twelve miles across the Chesapeake Bay.

"What happened on Moray's yacht?" Bobbie said menacingly.

He shook his head again.

"Mr. James is indicating no," Bobbie said into the microphone.

Bobbie turned to Cal. "Lieutenant, could you leave us alone a minute?" Suddenly she grabbed Virgil's right hand and handcuffed it to a chair. He tried to pull himself free in a wild way. Cal stood up as though to leave. Bobbie was reaching for the telephone book.

"Wait. Maybe I made a mistake." James was looking at the slapjack again. "Maybe that was the weekend I was at a party there."

Virgil James was truly scared now, his whole body shook. Handcuffed as he was, he couldn't turn easily and was craning around, trying to keep his eyes on Bobbie.

"Were you on the yacht with Cameron?"

"Yes, yes." Virgil said it with resignation. He watched the picture of himself on the monitor.

"Who else? Harry Moray? Celeste Moray?"

"Of course. It's their yacht."

"Who else?"

"Some businessmen, government officials."

"Miss Turner?"

"I don't know."

Bobbie slammed the slapjack. "You don't know. What were there, a million passengers?"

"I don't remember."

The slapjack hit the table again.

"Come on, Virgil, that ain't going to do it anymore. You took that girl on the boat so you could have a little fun with her, right? Put the mark to her? Make her squeal."

James shook his head back and forth. "You can't do this to me. You can't do this to *me*."

He stood up. It must have taken all his courage to do so. The chair came with him and he made for the door, pulling the chair behind him, grappling with the twist of the lock with one hand.

Bobbie's slapjack crashed the door frame like a boom hitting it.

James screamed as though it were he who had been hit, not the door. He came back, righted the chair, and sat down.

"I want to call my lawyer."

They ignored him.

Bobbie leaned down again. "If you watch your own face on the monitor, you'd see what we see. We see one scared guy. We see a guy who's going to jail. Who are you going to jail for, Virgil? Harry Moray? Or Martin Cameron?"

James shook his head.

"This would be your first time?"

James nodded. He looked nervously at the video camera. "I didn't even know she was dead until later. I didn't have anything to do with it." He paused. "Martin was going to explain everything."

"Why did you lie to us?" Bobbie said.

James looked fearfully at the slapjack again.

"They told me to."

Harry Moray, Virgil said, always had good-looking women available on the *Potomac Fever* and at the River Club: airline stewardesses, Avis rental car clerks, public relations women. Moray's women were slim, smart, smooth enough to spend an evening with. They were well dressed, well coifed, well mannered. That was what Harry meant when he said a London Club. He meant the clubs off Pall Mall where Saudis seemed to have cornered the market on the university-educated second daughters of English civil servants.

The fake timecard that showed Mary Jeanne working was all Harry's idea. "Harry told me to bring Mary Jeanne onboard that night. 'Martin will love it,' Harry said."

Martin Cameron had never dallied once with Harry's women. Never, Virgil said. Martin knew Harry Moray. He knew that anything you got from Harry, you paid for.

Then along came Mary Jeanne. Maybe Mary Jeanne was younger than the others, sweeter, "more vulnerable." Mary Jeanne played the ingenue, Martin Cameron played the roué. It was crazy, said Virgil. Crazy.

"He fell in love. I didn't want him to fall in love. I just wanted him to make the deal."

"What deal?" asked Cal.

Virgil James sharply shook his head. The gesture of someone clearing cobwebs.

"Land. Rivergate. We were behind schedule on acquiring the land. Our investors wanted to close. We needed Martin. Harry said, 'Get Martin!'" But Virgil could not deliver his friend.

All through the spring, Virgil said, Martin had been getting in deeper and deeper with Mary Jeanne, going to her apartment, taking her places. He made Virgil go along in public. "I was the beard."

Virgil thought Martin had deluded himself into believing that Harry Moray hadn't arranged Mary Jeanne, that Harry didn't know.

"It was silly. Harry was using her, just like me, to get Martin. It was the same reason Harry gave a contract to Ophelia. He thought if he bought Ophelia, he'd buy Martin. Martin doesn't care about Ophelia. Ophelia doesn't care about him."

"What happened on the boat?"

"I swear to God, I didn't see anything."

"The boat sailed all the way to Kent. Come on!"

"I didn't see anything."

"Was Mary Jeanne alive at Kent?"

"I don't know. I didn't see her in the morning."

"What happened to her?"

"I don't know."

"What do you think happened?"

"It's a big boat."

"Come on, Virgil!"

Virgil violently shook his head.

Cal asked him again. "What happened to Mary Jeanne Turner?"

"I want a lawyer."

Cal nodded.

Bobbie went out and got a telephone and plugged it in.

"What's the number?"

Terror came over his face. "I can't remember." He opened his wallet with his left hand and clumsily began going through business cards, throwing them on the table.

Cal got up, gently took James's wrist and unlocked the handcuff, handed the cuffs to Bobbie, and opened the interrogation room door. James suddenly realized he was free to go. He stood up. He looked embarrassed. He had wet his pants, and a dark stain on the cloth was spreading.

"Bitch!" James hissed at Bobbie as he scuttled out.

Cal and Bobbie looked at each other in amazement. "Maybe *B* is for *bitch*," Bobbie said slowly.

Nathaniel was screaming, literally screaming. "I thought it was policy in this department that you tell me before you arrest someone." Everyone said Nathaniel Bench looked like Nelson Mandela, but today, pacing his office, Nathaniel looked too pissed-off to be mistaken for Nelson Mandela.

"James was not arrested. He told us he wanted to help, and we wanted to ask him about a discrepancy in his story," Bobbie said.

"Don't jive me. You pulled him off the street, got him in his car like a bank robber, braced him in front of a lot of people. Don't give me any shit!" Nathaniel's voice was raised, and even though the door was closed, Cal knew they would be able to hear in the squad room.

"He says you beat him with a slapjack, handcuffed him to a chair!"

"Captain, James was advised that this was a voluntary interview, he drove himself down to the Sixth, and when he wanted to leave, he left," Cal said.

"He said you told him you didn't leave marks when you beat people. He said there's a tape of the whole thing. I want the tape, I want your notes. You're suspended."

Cal got up and moved between Bobbie and Nathaniel. The gesture said, Nathaniel, you're dealing with me.

"There's no tape, Nathaniel. No one threatened Mr. James. No one had a slapjack.

"Since it was a voluntary interview, there was no videotape. There were no handcuffs. There was no Miranda. Mr. James is too modest. He came to help us. He was a model citizen."

"Where did you say you took him?" Nathaniel was getting ahold of himself.

"Up to the old Sixth. It was the closest place."

Nathaniel's face fell. He and Cal knew there were no witnesses for a black suspect at the Sixth.

"Do you know where James is right now?" Nathaniel said.

Cal shook his head.

"He's sitting in the White House counsel's office talking about a civil rights complaint!"

Cal looked sideways at Bobbie. Tinker to Evers to Chance. There it was: Virgil to Cameron to Edward St. Denis. James had driven straight to the White House, not Cameron's office, not to Harry Moray. He went to the top. The call to Nathaniel couldn't have been more than thirty minutes after he left their custody.

Cal handed Nathaniel a written request for presentation to the U.S. Attorney. They had typed it up at the Sixth.

"We'd like to take this over to the U.S. attorney and see if he will take James to the grand jury and see if we can get a judge to give us a search warrant for his office and house. He said he lied to us. James said he brought Mary Jeanne aboard the *Potomac Fever* on instructions from Harry Moray. He said Moray was using her to induce Cameron to make a favorable decision on the D.C. Land Grant. James said that he did not see Mary Jeanne Turner leave the *Potomac Fever* alive."

"If you got James's statement under duress, it's worthless. Do you have anyone besides James?" Nathaniel looked at Cal with an owlish gaze.

"We have a second witness who also told us Cameron had been having an affair with her."

"Who is the witness?"

"The witness asked for confidentiality."

"Lieutenant, if you have a witness, I want a proper work-up. Who the witness is, whether he or she has direct or indirect knowledge of the events, whether he or she has given you an affidavit, whether he or she has a record or other indications of credibility."

The way Nathaniel said "he or she" made Cal squirm. It was as if he already knew it was Ophelia and it was as if he already knew it was a thin reed.

"Right now, all you've got is one pissed-off citizen who says he's going to file a police brutality complaint."

The three stood there in silence for perhaps a minute. It was eerie to Cal, as though Nathaniel was waiting for him to reveal more of what he had.

"Did you ask yourself why James went to the White House with a police brutality complaint? Doesn't that intrigue you, Captain Bench? Are you part of the cover-up?" Cal asked very quietly.

Nathaniel's eyes blazed.

"You know better than to push me. How can I rely on you? Picking up James was dumb. It could cost the prosecution. Maybe the idea was to fuck up the case, and James was an opening? You see what I mean. For all I know, you're working for Harry Moray."

The remark alerted Cal that maybe Nathaniel knew about Bobbie's meeting with Moray, but there was no time to think. This was the critical moment.

"Nathaniel," said Cal, again in his softest voice. Nathaniel looked startled at Cal's tone. He turned and faced Cal.

"You're the mayor's man. We all know that. Recuse yourself. Turn this over to the U.S. attorney."

For a long time, Nathaniel stared into Cal's eyes. It was a look of sadness. "You should have come to me before. We could have worked together."

In a louder, more affected voice, he said, "This case isn't ready for submission to the grand jury. You should have done a proper work-up, found corroboration. Half the people in Washington are trying to set up the mayor. If you had a lead on him, work it! You should have come to me with more information. Checked with the mayor, requested to interview him, placed the question to him."

Cal looked at Nathaniel with admiration. He was not covering up. He was not protecting the mayor or the White House. The record would show he was trying to rescue a case botched by underlings. Cal wondered where the mike for the recording was, in the desk or behind Nathaniel in the wall files.

"Let's ask an AUSA to take him before the grand jury."

"No. Got it? Not at this time!" Nathaniel threw file papers down on the desk with a *thump.* "You are both suspended pending James's complaint. Give your working papers to Collins."

He got to Stoneys late, just past eleven. The place was packed. Off-duty Federal Protection Service cops, firemen from Number 13, and two tables of women clerks from the insurance building. Cal could see Jack in the back booth, looking out at the world through dark German racing glasses, the kind that cost $300. "How can you see anything in here with those on?" Cal asked as he sat down.

"What would I want to see in Stoneys?" Jack answered. "Jesus, why do you still come here?"

"Old times' sake," Cal said wearily. "The good old days when you and I were heroes in the war on drugs."

Mobus grunted. Jack was wearing a beautiful double-breasted blazer, British cut, and one of those spread-collar shirts you get in London, his throat knotted with a silk regimental tie. He looked as though he belonged in the first-class cabin of the Concorde. Cal felt rumpled and messy in his presence.

"What are you drinking, Cal?" the barmaid called down.

"Jacks and Rocks." He nodded toward Mobus's martini.

"No, I'm good," said Mobus.

"What have you got for me?" Cal asked.

Mobus didn't answer. Instead, he watched the barmaid's back as she went down to the far end of the bar. Slowly, he brought a brown cardboard box up to the surface of the table, but he didn't open it.

"This is as untraceable as I could make it," he said, patting the box. "The recorder is a standard Sony Walkman look-alike. I bought it from a street vendor in London last year. I bought the insides in France. If they try to trace it, they'll find generic materials sold all over Europe."

"Is it going to be easy to mount?"

"Absolutely." Jack liked that word. He said it slowly, letting the syllables play out.

"This is just like the ones we used in the department. I've got a twenty-hour battery, British made, and there are two spares in the bag. Four tape cartridges. They came from England too." He paused, took a sip of the martini, and wrinkled his nose.

"When the call commences, the recorder goes on, but not the tape. I had enough room to load a voice-activation trigger. Conversation starts, the tape goes. Conversation stops, the tape goes down first, no click, and the nice part, the recorder stays on a few seconds. If he makes another call right away, there's no delay, the noise reactivates the tape. That saves the battery. The problem is, the tape is only ninety minutes. At the end it rewinds itself. That's the best I can do and keep the size at six by six, so you or somebody will have to service this every twenty-four to forty-eight hours; otherwise, it's recording over itself. The service will be quick. Reach in, pop the cartridge, put another one in, and go!"

Jack reached into his inside pocket and brought out a long folded piece of computer paper. A large brass key dropped on the table. "This is a printout of the schematic for the box number you gave me. This is the door key. Bell Atlantic keys are generic, so this should work. If it doesn't, you're outta luck. There are three houses wired on this box. Your house is the top." He spread the photocopy on the table.

The printout had *184* written at the top and a dizzying map of wires and numbered connections. "The wires are laced in clusters, but it should be easy to spot the connections. Your house is this one" — his manicured finger pointed to one little cluster — "see: four lines, eight connections. I suspect the newest connection will be the two wires on top, but I don't know, so you'll have to hunt for it. The White House telephone's dial tone will be slightly delayed because it's feeding through a remote switching station. Whether the wires are different, I don't know. Whether there is a line-tampering alarm, I don't know."

"How could there be a tamper alarm?" Cal asked. "The phone company probably goes in the box all the time."

"Maybe, maybe not. The Secret Service may have installed it, or the telephone company may have put it in for them. If it's in, repairmen will find a service note in the computer that they have to alert Secret Service before doing repairs in that box. The alarm's your biggest danger. If they have one on the wire or on the box, it will ring at some nearby police station and at the Secret Service. When it rings, you won't have more than minutes to get away, but you won't hear a damn thing, so you won't know when the cops have been alerted. You have to hope that the responding car uses his siren."

Jack let that sink in, looking straight at Cal as though he wanted to be sure Cal understood.

"The recorder and every part in it is absolutely clean of fingerprints and even dust. Wear plastic gloves and throw that box in a fire" — he pointed to the cardboard box — "as soon as you take the recorder out."

Mobus sipped his drink and Cal scanned the drawing.

"You got a court order?" said Mobus after a while, idly, as though he had asked, *Is the weather good?*

Cal didn't look up. He finished his Jacks and waved his hand. "Claire." He kept his eyes on the paper. He heard Mobus take a deep breath.

"Rumor has it that you and Bobbie were suspended." Cal still didn't look up at him. "Can I tell you something?"

Cal nodded.

"Let it go. This is going to blow up in your face."

Cal shook his head.

"You know," Jack said. "You have turned into a substantial asshole."

Cal looked up sharply, just as Claire got to the table. He bumped Claire, and his drink spilled all over his jacket and down his shirt.

"Oh, Jesus, Cal. I'm sorry."

"Its okay, hun."

"I'll get you a towel."

"Thank God it didn't get on me," said Jack. "I own good clothes."

Claire brought the cloth and a new drink. Cal started to daub himself. He was shaking with anger.

"They picked the wrong guy. I don't give a shit how much juice James and Moray have. It's like I told Bobbie, I don't have a lot to lose."

"This is crazy." Mobus tapped the cardboard box. "What can this get you? You can't use it in court."

"It can tell me how the White House is tied in."

"Jesus, Cal. This is a felony writ large! All I can pray is that you don't give me up."

Cal started to demur, to swear he'd never divulge Mobus's name.

"Shit, I know that. I wouldn't be sitting here if I thought there was a chance of that. What I'm trying to say is, this is serious shit.

"When we were in the department, if somebody had caught one of those wires, all they'd do is bounce us with no pension. Cal, the voices we listened to in those days were Leroy Browns! They were the baddest men in the whole damn town! This is a White House telephone!"

Mobus sat in silence, pulling on a Marlboro.

"I'm meeting a Lufthansa stew at the Hyatt for a late drink. The whole crew is laying over. I'll get her to bring a friend. Come on, Cal. Kick back. Forget this thing."

Cal shook his head. "Nope! Bobbie and I are working surveillance tonight," Cal said. "I don't want to leave her alone too long. Trust me. I wouldn't do this," he said, tapping the box, "except as a last resort."

Mobus smiled with relief.

Cal didn't tell him it was going down tomorrow night. Why worry him?

"Cal, telephone!"

"It must be Bobbie." He went to the end of the bar and took the receiver.

"Don't say my name and don't talk."

Cal stood mute.

"We must work together! Tomorrow go to Air and Space and wait in the navy dive-bomber exhibit. You know where I mean?"

"Sure, but . . ."

"You have nothing to lose by trusting me."

Nathaniel was right about that. Cal started to speak, and the line went dead.

He went back to the table.

"Who was that?"

"Nathaniel."

"I thought he suspended you."

"He did, that's what I don't understand."

Jack started to get up and thrust a finger at the package. "Guard that with your life!"

Cal watched him walk out. He waited for Jack to get in his car, then he gave the package to Claire. "Put this away safely, okay? I'll pick it up tomorrow."

Cal tried Bobbie's cellular when he got out on the street. She had been on James all evening, and he wondered where James had gone. The cellular was on voice mail. He left a message: "I'll meet you at one at the Wyoming Seven-Eleven." He got into the rental car and buckled up. The whiskey he had spilled smelled like hell.

Roaring up Connecticut, he knew he was going to be late. He tried Bobbie's cellular telephone twice, but it was turned off.

The avenue was crowded, so he switched to Seventeenth. Cal felt anxious and jumpy. He didn't even know why he was racing along.

He slowed down on P Street, shifted east on N, and went up Eighteenth Street until he doglegged over to Nineteenth. The 7-Eleven, at the top of the hill behind the Hilton, was the only glow of light on the darkened street. It had been built on a corner where three streets converged, and Cal could see a green Jeep Wagoneer was blocking Twentieth Street at the corner, parked half on the sidewalk driveway, so he parked on the street, next to a stop sign. He didn't see Bobbie's car. The Jeep was parked kind of funny, with its front facing out toward Wyoming Avenue, and he had to squeeze between it and the wall to get to the store.

God, he smelled awful. The whiskey had ripened in the closed car, and he realized it was on his pants too. He tried to shake his pant legs out in the air for a minute before he went into the 7-Eleven.

Mohammed, the regular night clerk, was standing behind the register. Cal went to the coffee bar and began to fill a container.

"Have you seen Bobbie?" he asked over his shoulder.

Mohammed didn't answer, so Cal turned around. "Hey, Mohammed, has Bobbie been in tonight?"

Mohammed glanced toward the employees' alcove.

The man who stepped out was not tall. Cal would guess five foot four, but this guy wasn't relying on physical strength. He had a sawed-off pump shotgun, black and short. He also had a white plastic ski mask that glistened in the fluorescent lights.

Cal stood stock still.

The man motioned him to the counter with the muzzle. Cal walked over and faced Mohammed, slowly putting down the coffee container.

Cal started to lift his arms. "Shsst," the man said, motioning with the muzzle to lower his arms. The man stepped back into the employees' room. Now Cal could see only the barrel of the shotgun and the right eye of the ski mask.

Mohammed started to quiver. His whole body was shaking, and he put his fingertips on the counter to steady himself.

"Take it easy," Cal whispered.

"Shssst," went the gunman.

Tears began to slowly course down Mohammed's cheeks.

The headlights of a car lit up the store, and Cal turned slowly toward it. It was a rental with D.C. plates, which parked directly across the street.

He didn't realize it was Bobbie until she stepped out, swinging that big leather bag she carried over one shoulder, and locked the car door.

She had taken a step toward the entrance before she saw Cal by the counter and waved, her little-girl wave. *"Duck!"* Cal screamed at Mohammed. He threw the hot coffee at the employees' room doorway and dropped to one knee behind the counter, waving and screaming, "Get back," to Bobbie.

The shotgun blast deafened him. It came from the back of the store, not the employees' room, shattering a six-foot-tall window. Another quick round followed. Cal couldn't see where the shooter was. Suddenly a second man was up and running from the back, leaping through the hole the shotgun had made in the plate glass and hitting the ground with a practiced roll.

The shotgun behind him now thundered above Cal. The guy in the employees' bathroom was pumping rounds, the blasts blindly looking for Cal, chopping away pieces of counter and breaking the soft drink refrigerators.

Cal drew his pistol and went up as high as he dared, sighting along the barrel at the man outside. He fired, but the man rolled again, the bullet ricocheting off the pavement. He tried to slither forward for a second shot, but the shotgun behind him roared again, tearing into the linoleum flooring. He slithered back.

Cal could hear Mohammed sobbing Muslim prayers. The little store clerk was down behind the counter, and Cal couldn't see him. From the floor, he couldn't see Bobbie either.

Suddenly, for some reason, Bobbie stood up. There was blood running down her face from two small cuts in her forehead, and she looked dazed. The man on the ground by the storefront motioned for her to raise her arms. She did.

Cal couldn't fire. They would kill her if he did.

"Come up, mister, or I kill her," the man outside said.

Cal couldn't place an accent.

Cal slowly stood up and put his gun on the counter. The man behind Mohammed stepped out and brushed Cal's pistol to the floor with the muzzle of his shotgun, then stepped around Cal and darted out the door.

They frog-marched Bobbie toward the green Wagoneer. She was twisted sideways, and Cal could not see her face. One man ran around and opened the back passenger door. As Bobbie bent to enter, Cal saw her hand go for her ankle gun, so slow-motion that it looked like a football replay. He wanted to shout, "No!" but the words wouldn't come.

The man with the white mask saw her too and fired point-blank. Bobbie's entire body lurched left, slumping against the car's open door. Suddenly there was a siren and glaring lights.

Cal saw the shooter jump into the Jeep. The second man knocked down a promotion sign and followed the first, pushing Bobbie's body out of the door and blasting his shotgun wildly around the street. Cal dropped to the ground. Pellets grazed his leg.

The two Park Police officers were kids and they came out of their car looking terrified, shooting haphazardly from down behind the car door. The Jeep jumped a curb and disappeared.

Cal struggled up, grabbed his pistol, and started to run to Bobbie, but one officer smashed him against the wall, taking the gun.

"On the ground! Hands out flat!"

"I'm a cop!"

"On the ground, motherfucker!"

The two stood above Cal with their guns drawn.

"I'm a police officer," he said from the sidewalk. "Look in my pocket."

One of the officers backed away, squatted down, and aimed his automatic at Cal's head, while the other gingerly fished through Cal's pocket from behind. The officer who squatted down wrinkled his nose.

"Jesus, this guy smells like a whiskey still!"

He pulled out the ID case and handed it up silently to the first officer. They put their guns away.

Cal got to his feet and brushed by them.

Roberta Marie Short's beautiful Maria Callas face was gone. She had turned her head away as the shotgun fired, and the bullets took off her profile. He couldn't tell if she was still alive, but there were little bubbles of blood near where her nostrils should have been and he guessed that she was still breathing.

The young park cops were good. They radioed in and found that a Metro helicopter was up over a house fire in nearby Cleveland Park and they got him down to Columbia Road. The helicopter pilot maneuvered the chopper between the apartment buildings onto a tiny patch of park.

"Hey, Cal," one pilot said as he and the copilot brought up the stretcher.

"It's Bobbie, Vern. She's hit bad. We've got to make GW."

They carried her to the chopper and put her on the floor.

"Come on," Vern said.

Cal sat on the floor and held her hand. One crewman put a headset on him.

"Better to try Georgetown," the pilot named Vern said. "GW got all the victims from the fire."

Cal could feel the chopper make a wide swinging turn, and suddenly the city was a panorama beneath them, the Capitol, the White House, the Washington Monument and the Lincoln Memorial, as clear and beautiful as he had ever seen them, framing Bobbie's head in their light.

Up above the streetlights, the cabin of the chopper was dark, and he couldn't see Bobbie clearly anymore. But he held her hand tightly, her grip firm and warm. He knew she could feel his presence.

Bobbie had great hands, long and elegant. They were her pride. Cal could feel the outline of the ring that she got from the boyfriend who made silver jewelry. The boyfriend was long gone, but Bobbie loved that ring. Cal rubbed the soft back of her hand. He felt her grip tighten on his.

"Shush, baby" he said. "We'll be at the hospital soon."

There was a gurgling sound, and he saw bubbles at her mouth as though she were trying to speak. He leaned in close to her ear and whispered. "It's okay, honey. It's okay. You're going to be all right. Just lie still. Old Cal will get you there."

The 'copter was turning over the Potomac, right over the River Club, to maneuver onto Georgetown's landing pad when Cal felt Bobbie's grip slip. It happened quickly, like a rowboat slipping its hawser and drifting to open water. For a moment Cal wasn't sure she'd let go.

He touched her neck for a pulse and found none.

He started to cry. "Please, please, baby. Please don't do this!"

But Bobbie lay silent and remote.

He tried to rub warmth into her hand, but it too now seemed cold.

Cal took her pulse a second time. There was none.

"Oh, baby. Why did you go and do that! Don't do that. *Please don't do that!*"

Now he was screaming into the mouthpiece, and the helicopter pilots whirled around in their seats. It was like the wounded he'd carried in Vietnam. One minute they were with you, the next minute they were gone.

The hospital team worked furiously in the ER, but Cal knew she was gone and he watched with a kind of sadness as they worked on the faceless woman.

After an eternity they gave up and one nurse gently covered Bobbie with a green sheet. Cal suddenly remembered his mother singing to herself in the kitchen. "Some bright morning when this life is o'er, I'll fly away. To a home on God's celestial shores, I'll fly away."

Nathaniel was crying. Cal tried to remember if he'd ever seen Nathaniel cry. The big police captain had come from home; he was wearing a pajama top stuffed into his trousers and sneakers with no socks, leaning over Bobbie with his tears dropping onto the sheet.

They put Cal in a curtained treatment stall, and a nurse brought him coffee. "Do you need something, Lieutenant," a young woman doctor with kind eyes asked. "To calm you?"

Cal shook his head.

When she left, Nathaniel pulled a chair up close.

"What in God's name were you doing at the Seven-Eleven at one A.M.?" he whispered.

"We were tracking James. Bobbie took the early evening, and I was going to relieve her," Cal said wearily. "She was going to brief me and go home."

"Jesus, Cal. You were both on suspension!" Nathaniel didn't say it angrily, but sadly, as though he were talking to a child. "Did you get either of the guys?"

Cal shook his head. "No. I don't think so. I popped two, maybe three rounds at one, but he rolled too soon."

"The park cops said you had been drinking. They found a rental car smelling of whiskey. How in Christ were you going to track James if you were drunk?"

"I wasn't drunk," he shouted. "It spilled on me!" His roar startled the nurses outside.

"Shssh," said Nathaniel.

The two sat in silence for a moment.

Nathaniel went out and got a piece of paper and a pencil and came back.

"We're working this hard. Collins already has a team over there. It looked like they were robbing the place. What happened then?"

"They had split up. I didn't even notice the second guy. When I got there, Mohammed was standing behind the counter. I thought he was alone, but there was this gunman standing in the employees' room. I figured he'd take the money and leave, and either I'd get him as he left or just call in and get backup. The next thing I knew, Bobbie was driving in.

"I yelled at her to get back and dropped to the floor. Suddenly a second gun fired from the back of the store. She went down. That's when I realized there was a second guy. I think I shot at him three times."

"Was she alive after the first shot?"

"Absolutely. She stood up! I don't know why, but she *stood up* and put her hands up. Once she was up, I figured they could kill her anytime they wanted, so I stood up and put my gun down.

"The two guys were forcing her to get in the car. As she bent to get in, she tried for her ankle gun. One guy shot her point-blank. Shit, he couldn't have been two feet from her."

"Why were they putting her in the car?"

"I don't know. Maybe hostage? I don't even know why she stood up," Cal said.

Nathaniel wrote it down with those same careful notes that he used to take when they were partners, serious, never looking up at Cal, but Cal saw that occasionally a teardrop appeared on the paper.

Suddenly Nathaniel looked up.

"My Lord God," he said. And then they were hugging, two big tough men, hugging and crying.

"Why did she pull the ankle gun?" Cal screamed. Nathaniel was patting his cheeks with both hands the way you do to make a child stop crying.

"I think she was trying to save you."

The nurses outside looked away, sort of embarrassed to see the two big men crying.

He had been in the little alcove for an hour, sitting dazed in a chair. One of the nurses brought him some brandy in a white paper cup, and he drank it slowly, trying not to look across the room at Bobbie.

A nurse opened the curtain. "Captain Bench said the media's all over outside. He asked that you stay in here until he can get a car to carry you home."

Cal nodded.

It was maybe ten minutes later when he heard the mayor's voice coming from the waiting room. It startled him.

"I knew Roberta Short!" Cameron intoned in his pulpit voice. "She was a good cop! That is the proudest epitaph a police officer can have! Good cop!

"Off-duty, on her way home, she stopped for milk and to meet her partner. We all stop for milk, don't we? She stopped in a public store in the District of Columbia for a quart of milk. She wasn't wearing a protective vest, she wasn't expecting trouble. This was the most normal thing in the world, a quart of milk. But in our city a quart of milk can be deadly. Two men were hiding there, holding her partner, Lieutenant Calvert Terrell, at gunpoint. Sergeant Short did not have to take action. She could have hung back, called for help. But Roberta Short was not that kind of police officer. Roberta Short took a hand and saved the life of a fellow officer and an innocent citizen!"

Later he heard a woman's voice. "Why were the two officers meeting at one A.M.?"

Cal heard Nathaniel. "They have been working around the clock on the Reggae Club shooting. Terrell was meeting her to fill her in on his findings of that night."

There was nothing about Mary Jeanne, nothing about James, nothing about him and Bobbie being suspended. Bobbie was a heroine now.

When he got home, the sun was coming up over the bay like a ball of red gold. Vivian was in the living room. She was listening to "Danny Boy" and drinking Cal's Wild Turkey. For a long time they didn't talk.

"Did she suffer?"

"I don't think so."

"Did they catch the men who did it?"

"No. They got away."

He slept most of the day, and when he awoke, Vivian was by his side in bed. She made love to him, not joyfully, but urgently. They had more Wild Turkey and a bowl of soup, and Cal went back to bed. "Thank you," he said before he went to sleep. "Thank you for being here."

22

Cal still had pain, on the left side of his skull, but he knew from the moment he awakened that the operation had done something. Even in the darkness, he felt that his mind was clear, as though dense air had been cleared by a spring rain.

He could form words and he lay still, saying words in a low whisper. "The quick brown fox . . . Peter Piper picked a peck of pickled peppers. . . . Four score and seven years ago, our forefathers . . ."

"Mr. Terrell?" said a woman in a low voice.

The nurse did not turn on the light, but he could see that she was holding a flashlight by her side.

"What is on my face?" His voice sounded weak but clear.

"Bandages and two monitor cups. Can I give you some water?"

She bent and put a straw in his mouth. He drank eagerly.

"They're going to send you home today. Anybody there that can look after you?"

He lied with a nod.

"What time is it?"

"Three A.M."

"On what day?"

"Saturday. The funeral is today."

"The funeral?"

"For your partner. Sergeant Short. The president is going to be there. It was on the six o'clock news."

He felt a sudden sharp pain in his temple. He hadn't been dreaming. Bobbie's faceless face in the helicopter came before his eyes, and he literally winced.

There was a loud buzzing sound.

The nurse leaned closer. "Are you having pain?"

He nodded.

She adjusted the flow from a tube above his arm.

"This will make you a little sleepy."

He closed his eyes. He was dreadfully tired.

Jack Mobus held the cup to Cal's lips. The coffee burned a little, but it tasted good, rich and strong. Cal was sitting up for the first time and he could see out the window. Rain lashed the glass and ran down in little rivulets.

Jack had come in when they were giving Cal breakfast. His first cup of coffee. Jack looked worn this morning, and anxious.

"Bobbie is dead, isn't she?" Cal said, avoiding Jack's eyes.

There was an awkward silence. Jack sat dumb for a time, looking pained. "Sure, Cal," he said soothingly, the way you talk to somebody who is non compos mentis. "You were with her."

It explained the dream.

"The doctor didn't want you to sustain another shock, so when you kept asking for her, he wanted everybody to wait, to hold it back."

The night nurse, he guessed, was out of the loop.

"Bobbie's funeral is today?"

Jack nodded. "The doctor said you can go. It's not a great idea, but the doc said he understands. Since she was your partner and all. Jesus, Cal, I'm so sorry.

"Vivian said she wants to take you to the funeral. She ordered a wheelchair."

"Did they find the guys who shot Bobbie?"

"All they have is the car, abandoned in Salisbury, Maryland."

"Have you talked to Nathaniel?" Cal asked.

Jack shook his head. "No way! I didn't want Nathaniel knowing that we're working together."

"Did Nathaniel call?"

"Vivian said he did," Jack answered. "They wouldn't let any calls through. I told them I was your brother-in-law to get in.

"The Seven-Eleven clerk told the cops that when the men came in, he gave them the money, but they didn't leave. They had been there ten minutes when you showed up."

"An ambush?"

Mobus nodded. "D.C. cops are treating it as robbery, which is bull-shit. The description you gave the state police of the men who attacked you is the same one the clerk gave the cops at the Seven-Eleven, so it ain't a robbery."

Jack suddenly stood up from the chair next to the bed and bent over, putting his mouth close to Cal's ear. "Don't go to the funeral. Listen to your Uncle Jack."

"What?"

"I've been over to your house three times. Each time I go, something's different. Somebody has been there."

"State cops said they went in."

"That was the first day."

"Vivian was there."

"That was the second day."

"Jeremiah?"

"He said he just goes in the stable to take care of the horses. I'm talk-ing about the house. I went over there last night to get your clothes and ID and stuff."

"And?"

"And the desk was open, and everything in it was strewn around."

"The state police told me the whole place had been trashed."

"*Yes!* That's my point. I put everything back in the desk and closed it after the police finished!"

Jack flopped down in the chair after his furious string of whispers as though he felt he was getting too excited.

"There was a wire on your telephone too."

"No shit?"

Jack nodded.

"Down on the relay, just the hookup, like some guy was parked there and had a monitor and left in a hurry. There's no transmitter, no moni-tor, but he left two alien leads. By the way, where's the little item I made for you?"

For a moment Cal couldn't think. "Stoneys!"

"Stoneys?"

"Yeah. I left it with Claire. I told her to put it under the bar; I didn't want it in my car tailing James around."

"Jesus, Cal."

"Take it easy, Jack. Think about it. That's the best place for it."

"In a bar that serves cops?"

"Exactly. The way Claire drinks, she won't even remember who left it."

Jack got up from the bed and walked around the room to look out the window. Suddenly he turned back and bent down close to Cal's ear.

"If it was an ambush, why wouldn't they try again? You have to disappear for a while."

"Now?"

"Today."

Cal sat dazed for a moment, and it must have shown on his face.

"I know a guy who has a cottage in Ocracoke," Jack whispered. "No one will find you there. I'll tell Vivian something."

"Don't tell Vivian shit."

"But she's coming to get you, to take you to the funeral." Jack looked warily at Cal.

"Don't tell Vivian *anything!*"

"Okay, okay. Calm down. Don't get excited. It's not good for you," Jack said anxiously.

"Find me a place, get me a rental car and a gun before I leave."

"I looked for your guns; they're missing."

"Vivian took them out the other day, but don't ask her! Loan me one of yours."

"Okay. I have one in the trunk. I'll be back in an hour or two."

"Look who I found in the lobby!"

Jack and Vivian came in together, Vivian sort of towing Jack as a prize. Vivian patted his arm. "Jack, honey, you sit right over there. I want to give my old love a kiss."

Vivian was dressed all in black for the funeral, a silk dress and hat.

"Jack says you can recall what happened now," she whispered throatily. "I am so sorry, Cal, you know that. Bobbie was a beautiful person." She kissed him long and hard.

Vivian sat down and started chattering about Bobbie.

"Edward was thunderstruck. He got the president to order the FBI to form a task force. I mean, my God, a woman police officer shot down without provocation. Edward said they're trying to find out how many other robberies these men are responsible for."

Cal watched Vivian's exquisite face. It was Vivian at her best, part television news anchor, part loving onetime wife, part what else?

"Edward got Winston to come to the funeral. He's going to use it for a major crime message. He told Edward that Bobbie shouldn't die in vain. I so hope you feel well enough to go."

Jack started to speak, but Cal shushed him.

"I'll be there. Bobbie was my partner!"

Vivian nodded as if she understood and leaned over and brushed his cheek with another kiss. "Poor Cal, you almost saved her. That's what Nathaniel said. He said that they found a blood trail from one of the men."

Vivian and Nathaniel?

"Its got to be more than mere coincidence that you would be attacked in your own home not twenty-four hours after Bobbie. Unbelievable. Nathaniel said they were going through the records of your convictions to see if anybody you two ever sent to jail could have it in for you."

Even in his weakened state, Cal knew Vivian wasn't making any sense. Or was she? Maybe he was hearing the party line?

At that moment Cal's doctor, the Woody Allen look-alike, bustled in. "Mrs. St. Denis, the White House called for you again." Dr. Woody Allen was obviously impressed to have the White House calling. Cal and Jack exchanged glances.

Vivian got up and went out to take the call, Woody Allen following her.

"Come here!" He motioned Jack over to the bed. "You didn't tell her about me going to ground?"

Jack shook his head vigorously.

"Okay, don't. Just bring the rental car downstairs. Put the gun and a map to the place in the glove box. Give me your handcuffs too. If you've got any cash, put that in there. Lock the box and give me the keys!"

"Are you going to the funeral? When I came back about eleven o'clock, she was talking to your doctor. He told her he thought you were well enough to go, if you wanted."

"Did you get the place?"

"It's all set, but it's a seven-hour drive this time of year. Can you handle it?"

"Just get the car!"

"So you'll drive down after the funeral?"

Before he could answer, the doctor was bustling Jack out of the room.

"How are we doing today?" Woody Allen beamed.

Cal managed a grin. "Great."

Dr. Woody Allen was pleased with himself. "Modesty demands that I tell you that the OR team was great." He glanced down as he said, modestly, "We were done in under an hour."

Cal fixed a big beaming smile on his face. He didn't feel all that good.

"Just ten years ago, if you had a hematoma that size, reducing it would require a five-hour operation and a two-week hospital stay."

Woody Allen lapsed into medical history. Cal let him go on.

"But the incision last night was no bigger than this." He held up a beautiful gold pen and indicated the point. Cal guessed the pen sold for $400, easy. Being a surgeon in a suburban hospital wasn't all that bad. "Then we snaked a probe with a small camera down and took a picture. Once we knew what we were dealing with, we had the fluid out in twelve minutes."

"You didn't take any of my brains, did you, Doc? I don't have all that many."

Woody Allen laughed as if it was neurosurgeon joke number twenty-four.

"You'll have no scar, a little white line, nothing more, and your hair will cover the incision on your skull. Your ribs are healing nicely. You can see the bruises are fading. The kidney was bruised, but not injured. That's a big plus."

A pause.

"Remember Joe Namath?" he asked.

What was this, Cal wondered, an American Football League trivia contest?

It was like Joe Namath, he said. "The knee is a peculiar part of the body, very intricate, very fragile. I'm not a knee man, but the knee guys told me that the nail you ran into that night went right through muscle. When you pulled it back, you tore the muscle away from the cartilage." His description made Jack wince. "We've ordered a course of therapy, but frankly, only time will give us the answer."

"What answer?" Cal asked.

"Whether you're going to have a limp the rest of your life." The police surgeon had been in touch with him, he said. He knew this was important.

The police surgeon! Cal knew then where it was going. Nathaniel couldn't call him, but he had time to get the police surgeon to force him out on disability. The one thing he had done well since flying helicopters — shit, for that matter, the one thing he had done well. It wasn't much of a job, $43,800 plus overtime, but without it he had nothing, nothing but the farm.

"If you feel weak or faint, call me at once. I approved your going to the funeral of your friend, but afterward I want you right into bed. We want you using a cane when you walk, but you shouldn't be walking very much right now. Just around the house for now. Understood?"

"Understood."

The nurse helped him dress. Jack had brought his best suit, and Vivian had bought him a new white Oxford shirt from Brooks Brothers along with a dark blue tie.

When they were finished, the nurse handed him a mirror. He looked like a multicolored raccoon wearing a sand-colored fez. Yes, the nurse said, he could get rid of the fez, and she fixed him up with a small bandage on his temple. He had a large purple bruise on the left side of his face, and there were yellowish bruises on the right.

The nurse took Cal out in a wheelchair. The rental car was at the front, a blue four-door Taurus.

Vivian came out from the telephone bank in the lobby.

"What's up?" Jack said.

"It was Edward. I said we'd meet him at the church at three P.M. because it's getting so late. He said he'd have someone to park the car."

The nurse and Jack helped Cal get into the car's passenger seat. Vivian got behind the wheel.

"I don't know why you needed a rental car. We could have taken my car."

"I'll need this later," Cal said. "I'll never be able to pull myself into my pickup truck, and I don't have the city's Cavalier anymore."

Vivian waved gaily at Jack as they drove out.

"We'll see you at the church."

Vivian was watching traffic as Cal opened the glove compartment, and she didn't notice the gun until he pulled it out.

"Do you think you need that?"

Cal worked the slide and chambered a round and pointed at her midriff.

"Actually, yes. Now turn it around."

For the first eighty miles, south across the Potomac and over to Hampton Roads, she harangued him, but Cal didn't answer. She grew more and more upset as the car headed south.

"Would you really shoot me?"

"In a heartbeat."

There was something in his voice that made Vivian lapse into silence. They were crossing by the Dismal Swamp when she spoke again. "Edward will send the Secret Service."

"You may be right." Cal made her go off Route 17 and find a call box near a gas station in Suffolk. "What's your home number?"

Cal dialed it and got a recording of Vivian's voice saying they could not come to the phone right now. "Tell him that you've decided you should spend some time with me and not to worry. You'll keep in touch. Say nothing else!"

She did as she was told.

"He'll raise a ruckus anyway."

"You know you don't believe that, Vivian. You know your job is me."

23

He was hardly able to stand up when they got to the cottage. He wondered how long he could keep going. It was dark and rainy, and a howling wind was coming off the Atlantic. Maybe Jack had let his destination slip? Maybe Ocracoke was where they planned to trap him? Maybe he was going to die in Ocracoke? Paranoid thoughts born of fatigue; on the other hand, even paranoids have enemies.

Cal locked the front and back doors and put their keys and the car keys in his pocket. He found the telephone, unplugged it, and put the connecting line in his pocket. No calls out, no calls in.

Vivian was shivering with cold and trying to build a fire. She looked ridiculous in her high heels and pearls.

"How about a whiskey?" Cal said, pointing to a liquor table by the fireplace. "At least our host has good liquor."

"Cal, you don't want that, not on medication."

"Honey, I've been shot at, beaten, operated on, and thoroughly terrorized; why wouldn't I want a drink?"

She poured two fingers of Wild Turkey into a glass. He stopped her from getting ice. He noticed she made one for herself as well.

"Do you want something to eat?" Vivian asked. "Somebody stocked the refrigerator."

She made scrambled eggs and buttered toast and brought it to the sofa while Cal surveyed the cottage.

The big open room had a fireplace and two old matching sofas at one end, a kitchen at the other, and a large dark oak table and chairs in between. Cal was thankful that he could lie back on a sofa and still be able to watch her cook.

On the long drive down the Outer Banks, Vivian's mood had shifted erratically from anxiety to fear to hostility to resignation. But now she looked calm, as though arriving alive had reassured her.

Cal was ravenous, and Vivian too ate hungrily. The food made him drowsy. "Get some coffee, will you?"

"Why don't you take a nap? You shouldn't even be sitting up."

"Make some coffee." His tone made her glance warily at him.

She made the coffee, and he drank it black. It revived him. Cal took out the pistol and pointed it at her stomach. "Get the blue bag."

"What are you doing?"

"Buying insurance, honey."

"I don't believe you would shoot me!"

"Why wouldn't I?"

"Cal —"

"Don't 'Cal' me! You were in my bed the night those two men came. Hurried down there after Bobbie died. Was that to find out if I was still alive? Or was it to set me up for the hit team? Did you make the call too? Disguise your voice?"

"What call?"

"The call meant to lure me outside, that call. You put the picture on the windshield."

Vivian's calm slipped away quickly. She looked confused and dazed, but she never took her eyes from the pistol. "I don't know what you're talking about."

"You didn't know a hit was going down that night? Come on, Vivian!"

"Cal, I swear I didn't. I came down when I heard about Bobbie. I knew you'd need someone to be with. I left you to get back to Great Falls, so Edward wouldn't get suspicious. Edward didn't know we were sleeping together, that wasn't in the deal!"

"The deal?"

Vivian put the whiskey on the mantel and ran her hands through her hair. She looked wild, not cool now, but pale and frightened.

"Cal, I never thought he was going to hurt you! I would never have gone along with that. I never thought it would end with Bobbie's death! Never!"

"Do you know who killed Bobbie?"

"No."

Cal motioned with the gun. "Get the blue bag."

She stumbled across the room and brought it to the couch.

"Open it."

The handcuffs were on top in the little case with the extra key. He held the gun in one hand and made her drag the sofa to over by the radiator.

"Sit down and handcuff yourself to the pipe."

When Cal waved the gun, she submitted. Vivian's arm was stretched out, and he went over and pushed the sofa closer with his knees. He put the little key in his pocket.

"Why are you doing this?"

Cal didn't answer.

Vivian now looked thoroughly frightened. It startled him to realize that she was terrified of him. Once she had told him that he made her feel safe.

"Could I have my whiskey?"

Cal brought her the glass, and she took a big swig.

"Now, who's trying to kill me?" he asked.

"Somebody you put in jail?"

"What are the odds, Vivian, that the very night after Bobbie was shot in a robbery, somebody attacks me on my farm?"

"Cal, I —"

"That the men who attacked me wore the same kind of face covering as the gunmen? Let's try again. Who is trying to kill me?"

"I don't know."

"Not good enough."

She sat in silence for several seconds. "Edward or his man Valasquez may know something. But I've known Edward St. Denis since I was in college. I can't believe —"

"Let's suppose your dear Edward did this. Why?"

"Because you wouldn't stop investigating that girl's death." She answered quickly, without hesitation.

"What the hell does the White House care about a nineteen-year-old restaurant worker?"

"I never knew for sure. I swear it! But it had something to do with that trip on Moray's boat in August."

"Where do you come in?"

"You guessed right about that. Edward sent me to watch you! He said you were handling a case that had major national-security implications. Edward said he needed to know what was going on. I said, Why don't you just call the chief of police. He said they didn't trust the local authorities. If he did something officially, it would be in the *Washington Post* in the morning."

"I still don't get why he picked you."

"Edward said it was 'great luck' the case was assigned to you, because you were my ex-husband. 'You can do a real service and keep Cal out of problems.' If Edward thought it was going to get into national security, I could discreetly warn you off."

"That's ridiculous, Vivian."

"I realize now it is, but back then I was eager to see you, to talk to you. Edward's always so self-important. I didn't take any of this seriously."

"Come on. Come on. This is Cal. You agreed to spy on me because you were eager to see me? Try again."

Tears were welling up in the corners of her eyes. Vivian could do that, he remembered. She could make tears come and go.

"Edward offered me a five-million-dollar fee," she finally said in a flat voice. "What I told you about our marriage is all true. Edward's so damn smart. The prenuptial agreement really cuts me out of any of his money. I said I want *my own money*. He said, 'You'll have to work for it.'"

"But you have money," Cal interrupted.

"Not real money."

Vivian stopped talking for a moment, letting the greed sink in. "Edward owes me. I've done a lot for him. . . . Give me another whiskey!" Her voice was shrill and tremulous.

Cal rose slowly and got the Wild Turkey. He poured it straight into Vivian's glass without making eye contact.

"Why don't I think that's the whole story?"

Vivian took two more gulps of the whiskey.

Cal sat watching her drink. "Let me guess what really happened," he said. "You found out Edward was interested in this case and you said, 'Edward, darling. I can help you there. Good old Cal will do anything for me. He still wants me. I can control him. How much is it worth?'"

Vivian took another gulp of whiskey. Her gaze was cold now.

Cal continued. "So that was all crap about still loving me, the day we went riding, that stuff about wanting me to help you leave Edward. That was all nonsense, wasn't it?"

"It was half true."

"Which half?"

"Think what you want, Cal. I couldn't change your mind anyway."

"What was Edward looking for?"

"Who you were talking to and what you were finding out."

"Did you tell him?"

"I told him what little you told me."

"Did Edward suggest you sleep with me?"

"Christ, no! He hates you. No. I used my own initiative," she said bitterly.

"Where does the *Potomac Fever* come in?"

"The girl was on the boat."

"Do you know who killed her?"

"No."

"Then how did you know she was on the boat? Were you there?"

"For a while."

"What do you mean, 'for a while'?"

"There were two parties. One was a big cocktail party at Maine Avenue before the *Potomac Fever* cast off. Edward was the host. It was for Cameron's reelection. We stayed there an hour."

"Did you see Mary Jeanne?"

"Just at the end. She was with Virgil James. I noticed she and Virgil had a pin for the second party."

"Pin?"

"Little porcelain ID pins the Secret Service gives out."

"What do you mean, 'two parties'?"

"There was a private overnight dinner and cruise party to Kent Narrows, just a few people. Edward set it up, but we weren't going. They kept it off Winston's schedule."

"Off the —"

"It's a little trick they do. The cocktail party was a public event; the press pool was there. Then they moved the press way back. We were all leaving in a big crowd. Some Secret Service took the limousine and the motorcade back to the White House, but the president stayed. They do this every once in a while. Edward made those arrangements that night."

"You mean the president of the United States spent the night on the *Potomac Fever*?"

Vivian nodded.

"Mary Jeanne, James?"

"I guess so."

"Cameron?"

"I think so."

"Who else?"

"Valasquez is the only one I'm sure of."

"Why Valasquez and not Edward?"

"Valasquez's area is international narcotics. Maybe there were discussions on D.C. drugs."

"What was the cruise for?"

Vivian shook her head. "I'm not sure. Edward said it was to give Winston private time to bring Cameron around. I'm not clear on the details. This I know: Cameron has been holding out for nearly a year on granting D.C. public land to Moray. Edward is furious. Moray and the president have been raising money for Cameron, and they are pissed that Cameron isn't playing ball."

"What was the girl? An hors d'oeuvre?"

"I have no idea."

"Could she have been with Winston?"

"Philip Winston." Vivian laughed harshly. "If that were true, they should have issued a press release. It would reassure the world that he was human!"

Cal smiled, trying to appear perplexed.

"You think you're confused. The first I knew about Mary Jeanne even being important was after her death was in the paper. Edward was very upset about it. He had a lot of drinks and put Wagner's *Valkyrie* on in his study. I knew then that I was in for a wild night."

"What?"

Vivian blushed deeply. "Don't be dense, Cal."

"Jesus, I don't want to know about your sex life! Why was Edward upset?"

"He kept saying, 'How could that have happened? It was just a few hours on a boat.' Things like that. I asked the same thing you did. What in the hell has this kid got to do with the price of eggs? He said, 'Winston can't afford to be drawn in.'

"I asked whether Winston had anything to do with the girl. Edward snorted at that. 'There are national-security implications,' he said, but he wouldn't tell me more.

"If I had to guess, she was for Cameron. That would be Harry Moray's way. He called his yacht *Potomac Fever* for a reason. He would indulge Potomac fever among his guests, whether the fever was power, like Winston, or sex, like Cameron.

"The funny thing was that Edward didn't seem to know much about her at all."

Cal stared at Vivian, still the pedantic, still lecturing him on Washington.

"You know, you're a piece of work. Let me get this straight. While you're having sex with your husband, you offer to stop my investigation for five million dollars and you don't even know why he wants it stopped?"

Vivian shook her head.

"If that is what you want me to say. Yes!"

Cal poured another black coffee and drank it down. He got up shakily and washed his face with very cold water.

"Cal, you look awful. You're very, very pale. This can wait. Please try to get some sleep!"

"It can't wait! I have to get whoever killed Bobbie!"

Edward had given her no real instructions, just to watch Cal.

"What could the national-security implications be?"

"I have no idea. Cameron's reelection and D.C. are totally domestic."

Vivian's face was flushed from the booze, and Cal saw that her hands were shaking. Vivian's hands had never shaken before. Vivian had always been Ms. Cool.

"What is the connection between Edward and Moray?"

"Money. Winston has no real political money left. It cost thirty-five million dollars for Winston to carry California alone. Now he's running for a second term, lots of controversy, it could cost him twice that!"

"And Edward raises the money."

"And Edward raises the money. My brother, Charley, calls Edward 'Winston's evil twin,' " Vivian snorted.

"Edward does the things Philip Winston wants to do, but is too squeamish to do. Charley says that Winston and Edward don't even have to discuss them. Edward has a sixth sense for things Winston desperately wants."

"What do the president and Edward really care about Rivergate?"

"Cal, truthfully, I don't know."

"How come Moray offered me the police job?"

"That was me. When Edward was railing about you, I said you were fed up with the police, that you had had enough. I told him he could get more with honey than he could with vinegar."

Cal looked at her, shaking his head. "You've certainly proved that! Only if they were going to buy me off, what made them decide to kill us?"

"I don't know. I thought this was just politics. I would never have thought Edward capable of that in a million years!" Vivian shook her head to emphasize disbelief.

"But why try to kill us? We had been thrown off the case. Nathaniel suspended us. Did you know that?"

"No, I didn't. Maybe Edward didn't know you were suspended either.

All I know was, Virgil James really set them off. Whatever you did to James drove Edward ballistic. He made James leave the country."

"Leave?"

"Winston appointed James special emissary to Nigeria. He left yesterday."

"What about Nathaniel? Wasn't he Edward's man in the department? Why did they need me?"

"I don't think so," said Vivian hesitantly. She looked genuinely perplexed. "Edward didn't know what you were doing until I told him. That was why I had to stay with you."

Vivian was silent for a long time, then she sat up as straight as the handcuffs would allow. "I remember one thing! They think you have an inside source, maybe in the White House. They think that's why you wouldn't quit."

The thought made Cal wince. He had used the secret-source bluff with Ophelia, and he and Bobbie had used it on James. Bobbie died because of a bluff?

"They asked me who was feeding you information. I said I didn't know. Do you have a source?"

Cal didn't answer at first.

"Why didn't you just explain that I'm stubborn and stupid," Cal finally said wearily.

"Because you're not stupid, Cal," Vivian said in her most serious voice. "Because once you set your mind to something, there's no stopping you."

Vivian looked wiped out, and her head was nodding. Cal decided to let Vivian go to sleep just as she was, fully clothed, chained to the radiator and lying on the couch. He unlocked her and took her to the bathroom first, but he made her keep the door open.

Sitting on the toilet, she looked forlorn. "Cal, this is silly. I never would have gone along with hurting you or Bobbie. Take these awful things off." She raised the arm with the cuffs dangling.

"I can't sleep like this."

He got a cover and a pillow from the bed, put the pillow under her head, and covered her.

"Please, Cal."

Cal started to chuckle.

"What is so damn funny?"

"When we were married, I used to have a recurring dream that I had you shackled in bed."

"That's very sick, Cal."

Cal was now laughing quite uncontrollably, the tension of the day slipping away and the ludicrous picture of Vivian chained to the radiator for the first time fully apparent. Suddenly, his faced hardened. He leaned down and whispered in her ear: "If I hear you even move tonight, I'll kill you."

Cal awoke and lay there, watching Vivian through the open door to the living room. In her sleep, she looked as she must have as a child, innocent and fancy-free. He realized that this was the end of the story of Vivian Welldon and Calvert Terrell. He wondered how much of last night was true.

By 10 A.M., the weather had not improved much. Cal left Vivian chained and went down to the general store on the main drag and bought them coffee. "Is the ferry running to Cape Hatteras?"

"Call that number." The clerk pointed to a card on the cash register. Cal got change and called.

"Channel seas are running eleven feet," said a woman's recorded voice. "Ferry service will be curtailed until further notice. "

Cal bought a pair of sneakers in what he guessed was Vivian's size and a windbreaker.

The wind was roaring up the spine of the island and trees were beginning to bend when he came out. He saw two cars down by the diner. One was a station wagon full of clothing and baggage, but the other one Cal didn't like. It was a new white four-door Ford with two guys in winter jackets sitting in it. He wondered why they didn't go in for breakfast.

He walked back to the cottage by a different route, watching to see if the Ford followed.

Vivian was grumpy and disheveled. He gave her one of his shirts and a pair of pants to put on and let her close the door to the bathroom. When she came out, she looked like a 1950s teenager in the baggy shirt and too-large jeans and new white sneakers.

After they finished the coffee, Cal cuffed her to the radiator again. He felt much stronger this morning and did not need to, but he realized it had a cathartic effect.

"So, Valasquez may be my man?"

"Please, Cal. Get out of this. I know Valasquez has done despicable things, I can feel it. There is no remorse, no warmth to him. He reminds me of a panther. Black. Poised all the time to leap."

"You don't like him?"

"I told you once. Carlos is a cruel man."

"So he could be the one who is trying to kill me?"

"Cal, these are greedy and power-hungry men. Winston didn't get to be president because he was nice. Until Bobbie, I wouldn't have thought murder, but when you asked me, I told you the truth. Carlos wouldn't shrink from it."

"When I was in the hospital and you were reporting to Edward, what did he say?"

"That's when I became frightened, Cal. That's when I suspected something awful. I remember when I said that you had been injured so badly, you couldn't talk. He and Carlos were relieved. It was obvious."

"But you were willing to deliver me to the funeral in a wheelchair."

She looked at him intently for several seconds.

"You won't believe this, but that would have been the safest place for you, Cal. You would have been safe in front of all those people. I thought the hospital was being watched. I thought if you didn't go, it would alert them. I was going to warn you on the way to the funeral and then help you and Jack get away."

The telephone ring startled them both. Cal had not remembered to re-attach the line until midday.

"Jesus, I'm glad to get you." Jack's voice sounded anxious and distant.

"Hold on!" Cal made Vivian go into the bathroom and turn on the shower. "I have to whisper," he told Jack.

"I picked up some little friends at the funeral."

"What?"

"Big Chrysler New Yorker. Two white guys in suits and ties. I've got to tell you, they look like feds."

"Where are you now?"

"Tysons Corner. It's raining like shit here, and when I got up, I saw another car, different guys. A couple of hours ago I drove over here and finally lost them in Neiman Marcus."

"How did they connect us up?"

"They either saw me go to your farm or they made me at the hospital. My guess is the hospital. They really expected you at the funeral. I saw Vivian's husband waiting out front with a couple of guys until right after it started."

"Anything public about Vivian's being missing?"

"Nothing. Funeral was all over local channels, but nothing else. What have you done with Vivian?"

"Just talked."

"And?"

"She was assigned by Edward to watch me. I probably got out of the hospital yesterday only because she was driving. She said they had surveillance on me for at least a week, so those guys you see are working for Edward."

"Oh shit! What now?"

"I'm going to try to buy us some insurance."

"What should I do?"

"Go to ground if you can. If they were on you that fast, I'm afraid you may be in trouble."

There was a long silence on the line. "You sure I should go?"

"Yes. You've done enough already. Bobbie wouldn't want you to do another thing."

"Call and leave a message at my office if you need to reach me. Secretary answers to the name of Phil. Don't talk to anyone else. Okay?" Jack said.

"Okay, partner."

Cal felt sudden, overwhelming loneliness when Jack clicked off. He suddenly wanted to be free, free of the whole thing. He called the ferry terminal.

The ferry was running, but seas were heavy.

He made her drive like the wind to get the last ferry, watching for the white Ford and thinking about insurance. The Ford never appeared.

They drove up through Hampton Roads, having taken the long way from the Outer Banks to the Virginia mainland.

"Where are we going?" she asked when they got on 64.

"D.C."

"Why?"

"Just drive."

"Please, Cal. Why won't you trust me?"

He turned so he could see her as she drove. She was really a smashing-looking woman. He wondered how it had all gone to hell. They should be driving back from a great vacation, not dodging killers and brooding about betrayal. Sometimes it is better not to focus on the forest, but concentrate on the trees.

"Would you go with me to the U.S. attorney? Tell him what you told me? They shouldn't be able to walk away from Bobbie, not scot-free. We could do it together."

Her head spun around and her eyes were stricken. He knew what she was going to answer before she spoke.

"I can't do that, Cal. I don't know any more than I told you. But even then, if I do something like that, I'm finished. You were right last night. Edward and Winston own me lock, stock, and barrel. They took my measure years ago. The Welldons can be bought."

They drove the rest of the way to Washington without exchanging a word.

"Go up to Union Station. You can get a cab there," he said when they got into town.

"Give it up, Cal. You're one man. These people have all the money and power in the world. Sell the farm, take the horses, go to Montana. You always wanted to go to Montana."

He didn't answer until she pulled in front at the off-loading zone.

"Maybe I will," Cal said. "I sure am tired of my life. When you get out of the car, I'm all alone. You're gone. Bobbie's gone."

"Cal, listen to me, even if you hate me. We had something a long time ago. You can't doubt that."

Cal nodded slowly.

"Then run as hard and as far as you can. This is all over. Find a life."

He nodded slowly, looking into her eyes to try to see whether this was a warning or a threat, but Vivian had drawn a curtain over her thoughts, and her eyes told him nothing. She got out and he slid behind the wheel.

Suddenly, at the last moment, before she closed the car door, she leaned down and kissed him again, holding his head in both her hands so he couldn't twist away. It was a long kiss, moist and warm. It was good-bye.

24

He had gone to Carol's in the middle of the night, after two nights in a motel. Twice in the motel he had fainted and another time fell against the door, nearly hitting his head.

Carol lived in a windswept little cottage behind Mallard Boat Works, the air filled with the smell of paint and caulking and marsh gas. He had not wanted to go there, but he couldn't think of anywhere else. She wasn't home, and he pulled the rental car across the grass behind her house so it couldn't be seen from the road and went to sleep.

"Well, aren't you the one."

It was Carol. She had an old terry-cloth bathrobe on and was peering through the car window. Her hair was all frizzy, and she looked sleepy and hungover. Shards of dawn light were above her head.

She helped him into the house and put him in her bed. "What are you doing here?"

"Hiding."

"From the people who attacked you?"

"Yes."

"Should I call the sheriff?"

"No. No. Tell no one."

He slept for two days, sometimes feverishly. He could feel Carol's warm body next to him at night, and several times she kissed him to quiet him when he awoke.

When he finally came wide awake, he wanted to leave, but Carol demanded that he stay.

"This could be dangerous for you and dangerous for members of your family," he warned.

She looked at him despairingly. "My daddy was a waterman. He had no truck with the government. He never paid a damn cent to the IRS, hated the marine police, and ran bootleg in the skipjack. Nobody can come up this old creek either direction without passing my relatives. You came to just the right place."

Cal was in constant pain. Sitting down was impossible. To bend his midriff was punishment. He either lay in bed or stood by the second-floor deck steadying himself against the doorjamb.

His initial confidence after the operation must have been due to drugs. He fell once trying to stand up from the toilet and had to crawl to a place where he could pull himself up. For days his urine was filled with blood, and the kidney blow meant each attempt to pass water was still pain filled. He stubbornly resisted medical help, despite Carol's urging. Cal was a Christian Scientist at heart. He hated doctors and believed strong will could fix anything.

Carol's cottage was small and confining, and they decided that he should not go near the front windows, so he stayed in the back, in the kitchen or the laundry room or upstairs in her bedroom.

Once during the first week, he awoke to the serious eyes of a little girl. "There's somebody in Grandma's bed!" the child screamed.

Cal heard a woman's voice from downstairs. He guessed it was Carol's daughter.

"You come right out of there! That's Grandma's boyfriend."

A week after he took refuge at Carol's, he called Jeremiah from a pay phone. "Where are you, Mr. Calvert?"

"Montana," he said. "I'll be back for the horses."

"You'd better come quick. Somebody's lurking around there at night. I can see flashlights."

"Be careful," Cal said. "Just take care of the horses. If anybody asks about me, you tell them I called you from Montana. Okay?"

The next day Cal made Carol take him in her outboard down the creek and up the Chesapeake shore to the farm. They tied up on the Montaigne beach and made their way on foot in the darkness up to the house. Carol had to hold on to his back to steady him as he felt his way along the vine-covered way.

"It sure looks vacant," she whispered as they got to the clearing.

A light had been left on over the stable door, and they skirted wide to avoid it. Just as Jack had said, the state police had put a great big crime-scene sticker on the house and there was a sign to deliver all mail and parcels to Jeremiah Watkins at the Stables of Montaigne.

Cal could see the horses, but he didn't enter the stable, because the light would frame them like a target. He didn't want to enter the kitchen either. The stable light was strong enough to spot anyone in the kitchen as well.

In the darkness he pulled Carol around the house to the outside cellar doors, opening one just enough to slither in.

"Cal, I hope there aren't spiders. I can't stand spiders," Carol whispered.

Cal almost laughed out loud. "Honey, there isn't a basement in southern Maryland that doesn't have spiders."

Inside, he turned on his flashlight, keeping his fingers over the lens so only a shard of light shone. They found the kitchen stairs and, turning off the flashlight, went up on their hands and knees, crawling on the floor well below window level. The house was silent and chill and smelled of mildew.

"I want to check the telephone tape," he whispered. "Keep close behind me, so we don't get separated in the dark." He felt his way to the phone table, but it had been moved. Why had it been moved?

He turned on the flashlight, keeping his fingers over the lens so only a dull red of the light came through his fingers. The telephone had been moved three feet. He let the light follow it.

The mine was a PMA 2, Italian or Yugoslavian, Cal guessed, the greenish plastic rotary on top making it look like a macabre little Christmas toy somebody had left under the telephone table. He reached back, and his fingers touched Carol's face.

"Freeze!" he hissed.

He opened the flashlight lens a little more and cast white light on the phone. Someone had attached the anti-personnel mine's little rotors to the base of the telephone with thin piano wire. If they hadn't been lying at floor level, they never would have seen it. If you shifted the telephone while talking or jarred it, the mine jumped up three feet and *kaboom*, eight ounces of tentex would blow outward. In a confined area it would take your legs and genitals for sure.

Probably untraceable, he thought, half the goddamn armies in the world had a version. PMAs come packed in boxes of fifty, nobody plants just one of them. For all he knew, they were all around him. He tried to remember the old acronym from the mine courses, SLTP: stop, look, think, probe.

He let the light swing around the room, but it picked up nothing else.

He turned to Carol. "Booby trap! Move backward just as we came in. Even when we get downstairs, don't turn around — just creep back toward the doors." He handed the flashlight to her.

He was struck by how calm Carol was. Years on the water. You don't panic in a storm, you work your vessel, you think clearly. Carol never spoke but carefully began slipping back down the kitchen stairs.

They saw no more mines in the house, but they had to use the light to get to the beach, and he wondered if they were being watched. He crawled with Jack's pistol at the ready. The brambles were cutting them both, and he could hear Carol's sharp gasps of pain.

He was thankful he had agreed to her coming; he barely had the strength to pull himself up into the boat.

"They must have set the mine after Vivian dropped me off, or Jack or someone else would have triggered it," he told Carol as they went back. "And the stable must be clean, or Jeremiah would have set one off."

"You've got to call the police, Cal."

"But that tells somebody that I'm in the area and I've been to the farm! That gives them a trail."

"I'll call them," she said.

"Shit, don't do that! That links us for sure. The people we're dealing with can get anything they want from the cops."

In the end, they drove to Baltimore and reported to the police from a pay telephone. Cal told the police he was traveling and had been warned that his home might have been booby-trapped. "Use extreme caution," he advised.

He gave his number at Homicide in Washington. "I'll check the voice mail there for messages."

He called Jeremiah. "Until I tell you, don't go back on the farm! No matter how hungry the horses get, you stay away." The old man was mystified.

The state police didn't start working until daybreak, but Carol drove up and down Route 4 several times and spotted a bomb-disposal truck from the naval air station and a bunch of police cars in midmorning.

The next night there was a message on his voice mail that the police had found four military-style anti-personnel mines, and he needed to come in and sign a statement.

After the mine incident, Carol's brother said he heard that a man had been asking after Cal at the Haven Restaurant, and Jeremiah said someone came to the Montaigne estate trying to buy horses. "We don't have no horses for sale," he told them when they asked about Bristol Boy and Comet. They were foreigners, he told Cal.

The mines had left Cal doubly cautious, but finally he concluded that his adversaries didn't know where he was and were now forced to seek him openly. His voice mail at work had now picked up two calls from Vivian and two calls from Nathaniel, which suggested that they both knew of his report to the state police.

One of Vivian's messages said, "If you get this . . . ," as though she wasn't sure where he was and was trying to bring him to the surface.

A message from Nathaniel said Cal was on medical leave as of the day Bobbie died.

Carol got the D.C. papers every day, and they dutifully watched the local news on the D.C. channels at night. Bobbie's death had given way to the city's budget crisis and turbulence in Russia. There were no new details on her attackers.

Two small items caught Cal's eye. Susan Lungren, the public defense lawyer who had handled Richie's case, went to work for Vic Stein's firm as a senior associate, according to the "Movers and Shakers" column in the *Post* business section, and a local story mentioned that Mary Jeanne's mother was moving to San Diego to start a new life. He guessed that Edward and Valasquez were slowly cleaning up the margins.

Each day, Cal took longer and longer walks, painfully at first, using a cane when he had to. He used the time to think about his next move, sometimes hiking north along the bay through the woods to Scientist Cliffs, bundled against the cold, bringing a thermos with coffee, then back up by the old plantation and the highway. He would take binoculars and scan the farm from the forest along the old plantation.

He felt like bait on a troll line, wondering whether a gunman's eyes were following him, or someone's binoculars tracking him. Sometimes he tried to reassure himself that they thought he had quit, but other times he knew that Valasquez did not believe that for a minute. Without a plan, he felt vulnerable and foolish. He should go to Montana or even farther. Maybe it was time to quit.

When it rained, Cal went to the Mallard warehouse, where he had rigged a gym, pushing himself, strengthening the leg, lifting it and lowering it until his thighs had more muscles than a speed skater. But he knew in his heart that something was not mending.

In the end, Cal's knee didn't improve, nor did his fear abate. In his sleep he would see Bobbie's blood-covered face like a gruesome mask with the eyes staring through the blood. He would awaken cold and shaken. Carol now slept in a guest room because of his restless sleep and nocturnal traumas. In the daytime he found that he wanted his gun with him at all times. He cleaned it and checked it obsessively, the way Bobbie had after she was shot. Cal took Carol's 12-gauge and cleaned it too, putting it up on nails above the door in the kitchen so he could reach it.

"You have got to go to the doctor about that knee!" Carol kept harping. "At least so he can tell you if you're doing everything right. Ask him for something to help you sleep too." Finally, he let her drive him to within two blocks of the hospital, and he walked the rest of the way.

The nurse was very unsympathetic. "You don't have an appointment."

But after Cal had waited an hour, the doctor finally saw him. Running his fingers over Cal's knee joint, Dr. Woody Allen had a touch that was surprisingly gentle and far more reassuring than his voice. "Actually, your knee is doing very well. As I told you before, I'm not a knee specialist, but this looks pretty good to me. You need a little patience. Patience, Lieutenant. Reduce your exercise program a little and put hot compresses on it at night when you feel pain. Don't use Ben-Gay or anything, just warm water." He checked Cal's head, the hair patchy and spiky where it had been shaved, and pronounced it healing well. The doctor demanded a urine sample, but Cal was no longer passing blood and the cup of yellow liquid didn't seem to alarm the doctor.

Cal didn't ask for sleeping pills. He wasn't a pill guy.

At the end, Woody Allen found him healing well and wrote the name of an orthopedic surgeon on a prescription pad. "She's excellent. Takes care of all the Wizards."

"What about meeting police department standards?"

"Come back in six weeks, but it looks better than I would have expected."

Cal called Nathaniel the next day, but he was out. "Give me my voice mail," he told the operator.

There, in a string of messages, was the mechanical voice, cold and clipped the way it had been when he first heard it, the way it was the night he was attacked. "St. Mary's College sailboat marina Saturday, if you're game." *If I'm game,* Cal thought. Christ, I am the game. He put the thought of going aside.

Cal's second thought was of Valasquez. Carol thought so too. Anyway, a Saturday had passed since the message, so for a day he put it aside.

But something enticed him. He borrowed a flatboat from Carol's brother that had been disguised as a floating duck blind.

Carol watched the preparations with growing apprehension. "You are as crazy as a loon," Carol complained. "Let this thing rest. You'll be killed too!"

"It's duck season, isn't it?" was all he answered. He went down to St. Inigoes, an inlet three miles past the college, at 4 A.M. on Saturday, loaded the shotgun, and used the outboard to get east and upriver of the college's marina. There he dropped anchor and hunkered down.

By first dawn there was no sign of life, but a sky full of ducks. Cal had to chuckle. If he'd actually come down here for ducks, there wouldn't be a single bird. He fired without aiming at two flights to keep his charade up if anyone was watching, but he didn't think anyone was.

By 8 A.M., in full light, the marina parking area and docks were still deserted, and anyone who knew anything about duck hunting would know that it was too late to be hunkered down in a floating blind. He paddled to the far side of the river and sat in the boat drinking coffee, the happy duck hunter at rest, sort of idly scanning with his binoculars. One hour began to stretch into two, and he was restless and so anxious to leave that when he saw the Porsche turn into the marina parking lot, he at first paid no attention.

But when he swung the glasses back, it was unmistakably Martin Cameron's tall wife wearing a fashionable leather jacket and blue jeans who was getting out of the car. "I'll be damned," he said out loud.

Ophelia Cameron walked up and down the marina, swinging a big leather purse and turning to eye the occasional car that came down Route 2. Cal scanned the whole shore, from the main campus on the hill down to the administration buildings and marina at water's edge.

To the south Cal could see two men working on a boat up on a scaffold. To the north a black man was fishing on the bank estuary. He looked old and small. The marina parking lot had no cars, and the college's sailboats seemed battened down.

He used the outboard to cross the little river and came up on the bank about five feet from Ophelia. She looked down at him without recognizing him and turned back to watching Route 2 for cars.

"Mrs. Cameron."

She whirled around.

"You want to talk to me?"

"Terrell?"

He nodded, grinning behind the camouflage paint.

"I can help you."

Ophelia Cameron looked better than when he'd interviewed her in at the Wilner, but now she looked harried too, and very scared.

If she was bait for a sniper, Cal knew he was already dead, but what if she was bait for something else?

"Drop your purse and kick it over here." Ophelia complied, and the heavy leather bag bumped to the edge of the dock. Suddenly, Ophelia took a black plastic object out of her pocket. Cal raised the shotgun. "Careful."

Ophelia jumped back, putting a black tube to her lips.

"Terrell." The mechanical voice pronounced *Terrell* just like the strange telephone calls.

"You called me that night?"

She nodded.

"You left the picture of Mary Jeanne on the windshield?"

She nodded again.

She was clumsily climbing down into the flatboat.

"Are you alone?" Cal asked.

"I sure hope so," she said.

"Hang on."

He put the outboard on max, and they roared south toward the bay.

"I don't like being in the open like this," she yelled against the wind. "We need to talk someplace. Someplace private. Just you and me."

Cal beached the boat at St. Inigoes, hustled her into his car, and drove to a Motel 6 way over on Route 301, using every back road in the county.

At the motel Cal asked for the end unit. The clerk could see the black woman in the car outside. "Trying to change your luck?" He leered at Cal.

"In a Motel Six?"

Cal brought the shotgun in and put it on the table. He silently made coffee in the little bathroom electric pot, and Ophelia nervously prowled the room. There was still no explanation of her presence, as though she was deciding what to do.

"The night you left the picture was the night I was attacked. How do I know you're not part of that?"

"You don't believe that, or we wouldn't be sitting here."

She sat drinking the coffee for some time, looking intently at him as though taking his measure.

"It's your dime," Cal said, a hint of impatience in his voice.

"I want to show you something," Ophelia said, looking anxiously at the windows. "Something very private."

"What has this to do with Mary Jeanne Turner or my dead partner?"

"I believe my husband killed Mary Jeanne Turner."

Ophelia said it matter-of-factly, like *I think my husband has gone to the store.*

Cal didn't say anything at first. He could feel his adrenaline rise, and his breathing was in fast gulps.

"You just believe? Did you see this?"

Ophelia shook her head.

"Somebody tell you?"

Ophelia shook her head again. "I have evidence. Enough."

"Like the photo you left on my windshield?"

"More than that, Mr. Terrell. You'll understand when you see it, but *not* before we talk deal."

"For whom?"

"For me, of course."

"Why didn't you say something the day I came to the Wilner?"

"I knew then what you and your partner have found out on your own."

"What is that?"

"My husband and his friends are very dangerous."

"What do you know about my partner's death?"

"Nothing. But was it a store robbery? Come on!"

"What do you want, Ophelia?"

"I want ironclad protection, immunity, relocation, and when you hear my story, you'll see I want *vindication!*"

Ophelia lapsed into silence, as though she had made an opening bid and it was up to him to match it.

"I won't bullshit you," Cal said slowly. "It will be tricky as shit. Particularly now that I know who I'm dealing with. Hiding the beautiful wife of the mayor of Washington won't be easy."

Ophelia Cameron stood up, blinking at him with her wide-open gaze. "Get the car keys. You aren't ready for this," she said.

"Sit down," said Cal. "You've got nowhere to go. If you walk out that door, you've got no assurance that I won't call your husband two seconds later."

Ophelia sat down. "Can you help me?" she asked.

"If I do, we've got to get a major power on our side. You understand that you're up against the White House too?"

Ophelia nodded.

"So the FBI or any feds are out of the question."

"Why not a special prosecutor?"

"You'll be a hundred and ten years old before Winston's attorney general will appoint a special prosecutor. It's got to be somebody independent of Washington. Maybe Steve Green, here in Maryland."

Ophelia made a face. "Why not take it to the Hill, to Senator Belden or someone who wants to take on Winston?"

"Senators have no capacity to protect you, enforce grand jury secrecy, provide police investigation, or issue subpoenas."

She paced back and forth, not answering. "Green's too ambitious by half," she said.

"That's what you want. You want a guy who's hungry. Green wants to run for the Senate. This will give him exposure. But most important, he has ironclad jurisdiction! Mary Jeanne's remains were found in Maryland. The first thing your husband and the White House will do is attack jurisdiction, get the case back where they can control it!"

Ophelia lapsed into silence for several minutes. Cal was grateful for the time to think.

"Close the curtains," she finally said.

"No, I want to keep my eye on the parking lot."

"Close them!"

He stood up and pulled the curtains.

Wordlessly Ophelia turned her back and stood for a moment, looking at the wall. Then she undid her blue jeans.

Quickly, not seductively, hooking her fingers in both the jeans' belt and the band of black panties, she bared her buttocks.

On the upper right cheek of her opulent bottom was a brand, the ugly tissue of the burn like raised lettering on an engraved envelope.

Cal could not control a gasp.

Ophelia did not turn around. She stood straight now, looking at the wall.

"What does the *B* stand for?" Cal asked.

"Bitchin'."

Ophelia was sobbing now, great gulping sobs racked her body, and her shoulders bent forward. The smooth flawless accents of a professional woman fell away.

"Can you imagine? *Imagine. Me?* Me letting some man do that?"

She had fallen to her knees now and was bending over the carpet. "That was what Martin always said. When he made love, he'd whisper it or roar it. 'Bitchin',' he'd scream. 'Bitchin' woman.'"

"He said I was his, his *alone*. This would be Cameron's mark, and no one in the world would wear this mark but me!"

"You let your husband brand you?" Cal said in an astonished voice.

"Just like some fool. All through the pain, I said, It's all right. This is a small price for Martin. I held on to the chair as hard as I could. I knew it wasn't right. But Martin had to have it, you see. Martin had to have it!"

The sobs stopped. She remained bent, staring at the rug, an occasional tear landing on the fabric.

"Why?" asked Cal finally.

"Martin is a very sick puppy."

25

For a long time they sat on the bed. Cal knew Cameron was a womanizer but thought he would have been straight, a massive user of women's flesh — no sadism, no kink — just women, touching, pinching, copulating, and gone.

But this figured. He and Bobbie were like the blind men feeling an elephant: sometimes thinking they were dealing with one thing, sometimes another, never able to see the creature in its entirety. Cal knew he had been unwilling to understand how simple it was. Martin Cameron had killed the woman, and his political allies had to keep it from coming out.

"Put your clothes on."

She pulled up her pants facing him, looking directly into his eyes.

"Does Cameron know where you are?" Cal asked.

"He thinks I'm in New York."

"How many people know about the . . ." Cal nodded toward her back.

Ophelia shook her head. "Nobody. I've never told another human being. I've been careful. I never get completely undressed at a golf club or anywhere. I don't wear bikinis or even bikini panties. I thought if anyone saw it, I'd say it was a college initiation."

"When did he do this?"

"Does that matter?" Her tone was hostile, and Cal decided to soften his attitude, follow her lead, let her tell her story at her own pace. Although not as good as Bobbie, with fifteen years' experience, Cal had good instincts about how to question people. Ophelia needed to build her story slowly, he decided.

He tried again. "Where were you when he did this to you?"

"At the Sixteenth Street apartment. It wasn't for my business, it was for him. His little love nest. God only knows who else he's brought there; I don't want to."

For a time Ophelia didn't speak.

"Ain't this so right. Lord a-mercy, sittin' here telling a white man my mostus awfullest secret." Ophelia started a mimic, her voice high, like Butterfly McQueen in *Gone With the Wind*.

Cal started to smile.

"What's so funny?"

"Mrs. Cameron, I did my homework. You grew up in Philadelphia, graduated from Rutgers. Your father was a lawyer! You were a champion swimmer. You have a master's degree in urban planning, and you were some big muckety-muck in Baltimore."

"Director of the Habitat Urban Design office," she said in a crisp voice. "That's when I met Martin."

Cal remembered reading that Cameron was the chairman of Urban Ventures, a Republican seed-money urban-renewal firm funded by major corporations. Philip Winston had set it up when he'd been chairman of the RNC. The Republican answer to Democratic housing programs.

The first night they met, Ophelia told him, Martin had taken her to dinner at Morton's. "It was so exciting. You can't imagine. I got there first and then some guy from General Electric and then Martin. Martin was already being talked about for mayor.

"'The first black Republican with a real chance,' they said. When he walked across the room, it was like he was mowing hay, all those white hands stuck out to be shaken."

She was sitting up on the room's desk chair, her knees drawn up like a teenager, her gaze a thousand miles away.

"They were talking millions." Her voice went deep to mimic the men. "'We'll need ten million in seed. . . . Get fifty million private investment. . . . Fifty million from here . . . Fifty million from there . . . These will be historic developments for the community. Historic.' I'll bet they traded a billion dollars that night."

"What was it for?" Cal asked.

"Mainly for me," she said wryly. "Later I realized Martin had probably done that a hundred times before, reeling in the ladies." It was an exciting dinner party in an exciting city. It was not lost on her that the General Electric guy signed the check, she could see the total — $700 with tip.

Cameron made no advances that night. He was a black leader trying to lift his people from their lot by lifting up the city. He was sure it would be better if Reagan won. His mentor Philip Winston would dig in and work on Washington. The conservative Republicans were hard to deal with, but he was sure he could shame them into action. "White guilt," he had called it.

"I'd never seen such a man. Just the way he talked, quietly but clear. I wanted to join that crusade. It was all 'I was telling Jesse this' and 'I told Andy that' and 'Vernon Jordan's got to realize.' Every big name."

The job offer from Virgil James had come a week later. Special assistant on the Shaw redevelopment project, $65,000 a year to start. "I was making thirty-five in Baltimore."

By that time she knew she loved Cameron; she also knew that Martin Cameron was a womanizer and took what he wanted, but she was sure she could handle him. "I thought he just needed a good woman," said Ophelia.

"We accomplished a lot. You know that, don't you? We did accomplish things! In his first term we were cookin' — the Albermarle development, police youth program. We were cookin'."

Cal caught the *we,* as though Ophelia was as much responsible for Cameron's political success as he was.

"Terrell, you have to know one thing: they talk about Colin Powell, but Martin Cameron would be a damn good president."

But as the years went on, life with him got rougher. "It was though as pressures built on Martin, he gained a tolerance for erotica, as though he had to experiment all the time."

The Martin Cameron Ophelia now described was drowning in an obsession with sex, a man at the apogee of his career trying to hide from even those close around him the demons that haunted him.

"There would be a gossip item in the paper linking him to some woman. Stage one, he'd come running to me with all those pathetic lies. 'It's blown out of proportion. . . . It's gossip. . . . It's my enemies.' Next there would be guilt, guilt without confession. He'd pray and ask my forgiveness, but there would be no admission about the sin! And finally there was reformation." Ophelia snorted cynically. "There'll be no next time. But, of course, there was *always* a next time.

"His feelings of inadequacy were unbelievable. I came to realize that women reassured him. If he took a hit politically, he'd get some woman to tell him he was the best damn lay she'd ever had. He could never get it through his head that they said that because they wanted something from him."

"Did anyone else know about Cameron's funny tastes?" Cal asked, struggling to find a better way to phrase the question.

"Maybe the other women, but I'm not sure. Virgil knew. I could tell by the way they would talk."

"What about branding?" Cal asked. "Did you ever hear about anyone else?"

She shook her head. "Until Mary Jeanne's death, I figured this was my secret, this was something Martin had with me." Ophelia returned Cal's unblinking gaze defiantly. "You think I was in denial. I wasn't. I was in love with him."

She began to chatter now, her story ducking and weaving defensively, as though she recognized she had gone too far, elicited scorn instead of sympathy.

"When I thought about going to the police, I realized all this would come out. I knew how awful it all sounds."

"You could handle being branded?"

"That's when I got scared."

Six months before Cameron ever met Mary Jeanne, he and Ophelia had gone to New York for a big fund-raiser of wealthy rock concert promoters.

Martin didn't know them, but Winston's people had said they were worth hundreds of thousands and free concert and television promotions for the campaign.

"We're partying all over the place. Park Avenue. The Village. Harlem."

In the wee hours of the second night they'd ended up in the West Village at a private party for a heavy-metal group. "I can't even remember who they were. Things were going crazy on every floor, coke and PCP, leather and bondage, scarification. In one room they were painting a girl gold so she could be centerpiece on a fountain in the garden." The branding was in the kitchen.

"You've got to remember, this was one fine house. These people may have been quirky, but they were richer than shit. The kitchen was out of *House and Garden,* done in Spanish style, mosaic tile floors, open wood ovens built in the wall. Stainless-steel, triple-door refrigerators, a Vulcan stove, enough utensils to be a Williams-Sonoma store.

"In the middle of the kitchen there's a preparation island with a sink. They've got a woman lying on it facedown, a model or something, very beautiful, very, very drunk. She's laughing and drinking champagne and kicking her heels and looking over her shoulder.

"Everybody is kind of watching these two guys. At first I couldn't figure out what they were doing. Then I realize one of the guys is heating up this little branding iron on the grill. It was a little heart. The heart had turned red, bright orange, like an electric burner does when it's on high.

"I remember I said, 'Whoa,' like out loud. I said, 'Whoa.'

"The other guy has rubbing alcohol and is swabbing her right bottom cheek and holding her down. 'You ready for it, love?' he says with a big grin.

"The girl just gives a drunken giggle. The one guy nods at the other and *boom!* He puts it to her! She screams! I mean, screams! Her bottom bounced five feet in the air — and the smell. The smell was awful. I'll never forget the smell."

The woman had been so drunk and drugged, Ophelia said, that she was up and dancing around nude twenty minutes later, showing off her ass to everybody. Martin was enthralled. "We got back to the hotel, and he's as hot as a firecracker. Watching that girl wriggle really turned him on. He's all over me."

Weeks went by, but Cameron kept talking about the branding. "Finally he lays it on me. He wants to mark me. I started laughing. 'No fucking way,' I said. No fucking way!

"But he's really leaning on me. I am the most extraordinary woman in his life. This will be our secret ceremony, like a new marriage, and I'll wear the mark of Cameron.

"I said, 'Shit, Martin, why not a tattoo? I'll put your inaugural address right on my butt!' No. No, he wants a branding. 'I want to do it! I want to mark my woman.'

"From somewhere he's got all the stuff. Somewhere he's got a little metal tube." Ophelia held up her thumb and forefinger to show how small it was. All the while, I'm scared to death."

Cameron wore her down. He virtually made it the price of their marriage, and strangely she found that marriage was the most important thing in her life.

"I'm still trying to hold on to this man. He's really concentrating on me for a change. Virgil and everybody noticed. Slowly I was even getting his paranoia down. He was beginning to sleep regularly." Ophelia said this with a tone of pride.

So she had agreed. What would the brand be? "*B* for bitchin', 'cause that's what he said I was. Could it be worse than backing into a hot Weber grill in a bathing suit?"

Even if it went wrong, it was going to be on a part of her body she could hide. She called the Washington Hospital Center and pumped some doctors with questions about treating burns, bought burn jelly and compresses, bandages and ointments.

Martin had wanted to take her to a secluded summer house, but Ophelia wouldn't go. "I wanted to be within ambulance distance of a damn good hospital."

They went to the Wilner apartment. Ophelia put on Aretha Franklin really loud to cover the noise and bit into a couch pillow.

"Don't kid yourself. It hurt like hell. Just a few seconds and I was screaming my head off and running all around."

Martin had been incredibly aroused. "I think it scared him," she said, pointing to her scar, "how much he liked it.

"The aftereffects were awful. The first day, I couldn't walk straight. I couldn't sit down comfortably for two weeks! Every time the scab moved against my clothes, it felt like hell. I just lay on my stomach in bed."

Ophelia seemed exhausted and worn from her tale. Cal went up the road to a Roy Rogers and got fried chicken and Cokes. She was asleep before she finished.

For the next two hours Cal sat in the darkness, smoking Ophelia's cigarettes. He felt strange, as though he had passed into Alice's Wonderland. On the bed was the $200,000-a-year head of her own company, a graduate of Rutgers University, a television talk-show host, a principal in one of the city's major nonprofit projects who was branded on her ass by the mayor of the city of Washington.

Shit! This wasn't a story for the police department, this was a story for Geraldo: "Tonight's show: smart women tortured by powerful, asinine, brutal men. Join us." If this woman told her story in public, Cameron was finished even if he was never charged with Mary Jeanne's murder.

But if Cal could establish where Cameron had tortured Mary Jeanne and connect the rug fibers, the whole thing would come together. The rug fibers he collected on the *Potomac Fever* didn't match, so it must have happened somewhere else. The Wilner? Cameron's office? A hotel? If Cameron forced her, it was felony murder, nice and simple.

26

"Do you have the rest of the picture you left on my windshield?"

Ophelia took an envelope from her bag and handed it to Cal.

For being shot in early dusk, it was a great photo. The president of the United States in slacks and a Hawaiian shirt. The mayor of Washington, D.C., in a flowing dashiki, holding himself erect. There was Celeste Moray looking voluptuous. There was Harry Moray, his almost white hair swept back, dapper walking shorts and high kneesocks. There was Virgil James, lean and angular in yellow slacks and a polo shirt.

Cal studied the photo for several minutes before he picked up the questioning again. "Who do you think actually killed her? Martin? Virgil?" Cal's voice was raised.

"Martin would be alone to brand her. That's a sexual act."

"So you think Martin branded her on the yacht?" Cal asked.

"I guess so."

"With the president of the United States on board?" Cal said. "Wouldn't it be a little noisy?"

"I've been to Harry's yacht parties. They go on half the night. Celeste loves loud music. The motors make a lot of noise. You could scream your head off down below and nobody would be the wiser. Nobody.

"Anyway, I thought the papers said Mary Jeanne was gagged," Ophelia said.

Cal had been questioning her for two hours. He changed tactics and tried to diminish Ophelia, to talk down to her. The contentious interrogation was working. She kept trying to explain everything, to justify herself.

Cal hadn't told Ophelia about the carpet fibers under Mary Jeanne's toenails. They had never been reported in the papers or outside the police department. Cal didn't say that he'd run samples of every carpet on the *Potomac Fever* and there wasn't a match. He didn't tell her that.

Mary Jeanne was a sticking point for Cal. If Martin was falling back in love with Ophelia, why was Mary Jeanne more than a one-nighter? "Then why Mary Jeanne?" Cal bored in.

"I'm sure Moray and Virgil dangled her. She was beautiful, you can't deny that," Ophelia said. "She was supposed to bring Martin around on Rivergate.

"For Martin, Rivergate would be political suicide. It destroys everything he has stood for."

"Why?"

"It's Negro removal. The reason D.C. has black political leadership is that it can deliver a black majority. God, the white people hate that! The capital is run by blacks. Rivergate would end all that! Moray talks about wealthy Europeans, Asians, Arabs, fancy hotels, restaurants, a stock exchange. Read that, wealthy whites!"

"Who killed my partner?"

"I haven't a clue. I would guess gang guys working for Martin. I told you. Martin and Virgil scare me!"

"What did the White House have to do with this?"

"I don't know. Harry used to say, 'It's the president's baby.' He uses it to impress investors that he's carrying out Winston's 'urban concept.' He called there all the time. Virgil too."

"Did he ever mention Edward St. Denis or a Carlos Valasquez?"

"Harry talks to St. Denis a lot. I never heard of the other guy."

"What about Vivian St. Denis?"

"That's Edward's wife, isn't it?" Ophelia shook her head to indicate little recognition of Vivian.

"If Cameron came in on Winston's coattails, why doesn't he do what the president tells him to?"

"Winston misjudged Martin. They thought that they had poured so much money into Martin over the years that Martin would say, 'How high?' when they said, 'Jump.' But like I said, Martin can't roll over on Rivergate. That's political suicide, that's destroying everything he stands for."

"How did you come to work for Moray?"

"Moray was trying to buy Martin through me. You had it right. Harry gave me a contract worth a million dollars over five years, with a loaded bonus for completion. He told the media it was a private bid! Bullshit!

There were no bidders. He gave it to me outright to share with Martin. That's why I need immunity."

"Did you?"

Ophelia snorted. "What Harry didn't know, and for that matter, what I didn't realize, was how little control I had over Martin. When Harry found out, he wanted to pull out."

Ophelia chuckled at that. "I said, 'No way, Harry.'"

"Then along came Mary Jeanne?"

"Right on cue."

Ophelia spotted Mary Jeanne in the spring. "I was at dinner one night at the River Club with Martin and some people, and she was the hostess."

Mary Jeanne began to show up at things. Virgil brought her once to a political cocktail party. Moray and Celeste included her in a fundraiser for Martin at the River Club and at a picnic at their mansion. Suddenly she was playing on the campaign softball team.

One night Ophelia said she gave Mary Jeanne a lift. She discovered that Mary Jeanne lived very near the Wilner, off Columbia Road. "What a strange kid. She acted like she didn't know anything. She's asking me all about Martin as though I'm her sorority sister, not his wife."

Mary Jeanne had a disarming manner that had annoyed Ophelia, and Ophelia had not known how to deal with it. She found herself listening to Mary Jeanne's little problems, talking on the telephone with her and loaning her clothes.

"Did she ever say she was sleeping with Martin?"

"Oh God, no! But it was like she didn't know Martin and I were married. I suspected that Martin had told her that our marriage was over. I'd heard that one before."

"When did you last see Mary Jeanne?"

"She came by the apartment the Friday before she was found. When would that be?"

"Friday, August first?" said Cal. "She came to your apartment?"

"Yes. That's it! She was on her way to work. She wanted to borrow a necklace. I almost mentioned that the day you came to question me. But I was so frightened! I got scared the moment I saw that Martin didn't call the police.

"Anyway, she was excited. Moray had invited her at the last minute to be a hostess at a weekend party on his yacht. She wanted to look her best. She thought I was coming! I didn't even know there was going to be a party!"

"You didn't know the mayor was going to Kent?"

"I knew about a fund-raiser, not an overnight party. Nothing! Martin told me he was going to be working all weekend."

"Where were you?"

"I was in New York Saturday and Sunday."

"Where?"

"In an apartment at Thirty-fourth and Park. I used a friend's apartment. You can check."

"Then how did you get this picture?"

Ophelia hesitated, and for some seconds there was silence in the room.

Her voice faltered as she spoke. "All right. I was suspicious. I didn't think Martin knew I talked to Mary Jeanne. I figured the party thing was a fake, that Martin and Mary Jeanne were trying to get me out of town.

"I called Martin all Saturday from New York. I figured I'd get back early enough to fix him dinner, do something."

"Did you reach him?"

She shook her head.

"I called the city dispatch, called the car number, called security, called Virgil. I beeped him twice. Beeped Maynard. I couldn't get anybody. I rented a car on Sunday. I figured I'd take a chance, go back through Cape May, drive by Kent."

"You mean you just took a chance to drive a hundred miles out of the way to a shore house belonging to Moray looking for Cameron?" Cal sounded incredulous. "You knew the boat would end up at Kent?"

Ophelia shook her head. "I wasn't even convinced that there was a party. Martin has used Harry's hideaway for his little games before, telling me there was a meeting with Harry."

"You figured to catch them."

Ophelia nodded.

"I had this vision of the two of them wrapped around each other by the pool and I'd say, 'Well, what have we here, my dears?' Something cool like that."

The giant Chesapeake Bay house was empty when Ophelia got there, except for the live-in help. "The house manager said Harry and a bunch of guests arrived at dawn Saturday on the *Potomac Fever*, played tennis, had lunch, and left. She remembered that my husband was there. She didn't remember Mary Jeanne. I felt kind of good. Martin hadn't been lying.

"She brought me some iced tea, and I sat in the living room. But while I was sipping, I looked down on the coffee table and there she was in her bikini! She was in about half a dozen Polaroids somebody had left."

"Why'd you steal one?"

"I was going to confront Martin. Why she was there and I wasn't. What was going on?"

Have you got any more photos?"

Ophelia shook her head. "I just slipped one in my pocket."

"Did you confront the mayor?"

"I was going to. I tried to get up nerve. Finally, by the time I decided to face him, Mary Jeanne's death was in the papers."

"What did you do then?"

Ophelia's face now took on a perplexed look, as though she had just thought of something important or recognized something she hadn't seen before.

"I went to Nathaniel! Once Nathaniel and I were . . ." There was silence for a moment.

"Did you tell him?" Cal asked.

"I started to. I called a few days after Mary Jeanne's death was in the papers, and we met at Union Station. I said, 'Martin's been sleeping with this girl.' He looked really stunned. Right away he said, 'You don't think Martin would do that, do you?' It was a real signal: 'You don't think,' like I'd better not think. Nathaniel's very close to Martin. Martin did a lot for him.

"That night, Martin was terrified. He didn't want to talk about it. He'd completely disintegrated. I'd never seen him like that. He kept saying, 'This will destroy me. This will destroy me.'

"Right in the middle of it, they call him about the Reggae Club shooting. He said, 'They did that too.' I asked what. He wouldn't talk about it, and I couldn't ask him anything. That's why I got dressed and went with him. I didn't want to leave him alone."

"What do you think he meant, 'They did that too'?" Cal said.

Ophelia shook her head. "I haven't the faintest. Anyway, after Martin got home in the morning, I could hear him in his study, pacing back and forth and talking to himself. Then he started moaning to himself, like he was in pain.

"I was scared by then, the way he was behaving. I went downstairs and tried to talk to him, but he kept ignoring me. Finally I screamed, 'Did you hurt her?' He lunged at me as if he were going to hit me. I ran upstairs."

"Did he say anything at all?" Cal asked.

"Not until later. I really thought he was having a mental collapse, you know, or having a heart attack. It took a long time for him to calm down. Later, when he was calmer, he admitted he had been with Mary Jeanne.

"I said, 'Where?' and he said, 'On the *Potomac Fever.*'

"I tried to be very gentle. 'Did you hurt her? Did you brand her?' I kept asking. But he would not or could not answer me. 'I am so tired' was all he would say."

For quite some time Cal and Ophelia sat in silence.

"How come you want to send your husband to prison?" Cal finally said in a low voice. "You say you loved this man so much, you were willing to let him brand you. Why betray him now?"

"Martin shouldn't be allowed to get away with what he did to that girl. None of them should."

27

The *Washington Post* story was slammed across the front page: CAMERON PROBED IN HOSTESS DEATH. It was eight columns and had two bylines, with a picture of a fully robed Cameron speaking from the pulpit facing one of Mary Jeanne in her high school graduation mortarboard.

The Maryland attorney general is investigating whether Mayor Martin Cameron was involved in the torture-slaying of a nineteen-year-old restaurant hostess on a yacht in the Chesapeake Bay, according to law enforcement sources.

The body of Mary Jeanne Turner was found floating offshore near the small summer community of Bayville, Maryland, last August. Turner had been tied and branded with the letter B, according to the Anne Arundel medical examiner's report.

The sources said that after District officials tried to hush up the matter, a Washington homicide detective brought Steven Green evidence that Cameron may have been involved in Turner's death. They said Turner was last seen alive on a weekend cruise aboard the yacht Potomac Fever *in August.*

The Potomac Fever *is a Netherlands Antilles vessel that was leased by Harry Moray, the owner of the Redskins, according to Maryland marine police. Moray, a former U.S. senator from Oklahoma and a lobbyist, could not be reached for comment."*

Earlier that weekend, the 150-foot pleasure craft was the scene of a fund-raising party for Cameron attended by President Winston.

Television went bananas. The story had sex, politics, race, and violence. By four o'clock you couldn't be on planet Earth and not know that the mayor of Washington was the kind of guy who liked a little kink in his sex, and by evening the instant talk shows on cable were analyzing whether tribal history in Africa may have condoned the marking of sex partners.

Green had lived up to his reputation. He went for the case like a salmon swimming to spawn, sending state troopers out with grand jury subpoenas and letting TV cameras film him entering and leaving the grand jury in Baltimore's stately old court building.

In public, Green excoriated the press for using leaks, but behind the scenes the investigation was carefully planned to maximize innuendo and suspicion.

Green stashed Ophelia in one of those new high-rise luxury apartments at Fells Point with two women state troopers, brand-new clothes, a roomful of rental movies, and two cases of $50-a-bottle chardonnay. She had survived a brutal four-day interrogation by Green and his aides designed to trap, confuse, and defeat her. Her story shifted in the margins but held in the center.

The mayor made no public announcement that his wife had disappeared, but Ophelia's answering service at the Wilner was filled with increasingly hysterical calls from him.

For a while Ophelia had balked at a medical examination of her brand or photos of her bottom, but finally she succumbed to the inducement of the chardonnay and the promise of a black woman doctor.

Ophelia was both cooperative and obstinate. She said she wanted the ordeal to be over and complained to Cal at every turn about Green's progress. "I gave him everything he needs. All he has to do is get Martin in here and slap the cuffs on him!" But at the same time, she devoured every mention of herself on television and in the papers and embellished her story at each telling.

Two weeks after Cal brought her in, Green remained mercurial about his progress, "No grand jury returns before its time," he would joke, paraphrasing the wine advertisement.

Shortly before Thanksgiving he called Cal in. "We're ready to go forward, but I want to meet you privately before I do, just you and me."

They took deli subs to the park on Federal Hill overlooking Baltimore's inner harbor. It was sunny and warm enough to sit outside, and they took a bench at a crest over the old shipyards.

After a few minutes, Green fixed Cal with a steely look. "You want me to go into a Maryland court and persuade twelve people, many of whom are likely to be of the African American persuasion, that Martin Cameron tortured a teenage white girl to death while the president of the United States watched?"

Cal shifted in his seat uncomfortably.

"On this voyage, there were at least half a dozen or more potential witnesses, not counting the crew. After they were finished giving this woman cocaine, having some perverse and perhaps painful sex, and branding her with a hot iron, this giant group of conspirators threw the woman overboard and headed back to Washington, another pleasant weekend complete."

Cal started to speak, but Green held up his hand. "The woman floated awhile in the Chesapeake, known the world over for its crabs, and shows up *across the bay* in the South River estuary with hardly a nibble on her flawless flanks."

"I guess I came to the wrong guy. . . ."

"Sit down," Green said without looking up. "When you didn't stop investigating, you claim, they got serious. They arranged for gunmen to kill your partner and try to kill you."

Green took a big bite of his sandwich and chewed, watching Cal's face.

Cal felt angry and defensive. "Of course, there are holes. There are always holes. You don't get all your cases tied up neatly, do you?" Cal stood up and began to gather up the trash from his sandwich. "Mr. Green, is it likely that two women would independently brand their asses with the letter *B?* Wouldn't you think it a little tricky to reach around and do that?"

Green didn't look up.

"Isn't it a little strange that a woman police officer investigating this case is killed in a robbery where the crooks don't want the money? Or that the same men appear sixty miles away the next night and try to kill another police officer, but don't take his guns or any valuables?"

"Sit down," Green said, gently this time. "I can indict Martin Cameron tomorrow, but I'm not sure I can convict him on what we have!"

"Are you trying to get out of this?" Cal asked.

"No. No, what you and I have to agree on is where we're going," said Green. "This isn't open-and-shut. On the stand, Ophelia will come across as an angry and bitter woman out to destroy her husband. She drips venom. A good lawyer will make her mad, and in her anger her story will shift all over the place. I just showed that in four days of debriefing."

Cal nodded.

"Presuming Cameron doesn't have an alibi, the key word here is going to be *consensual.* Cameron's lawyers will take the tack that Mary Jeanne is a young woman of dubious sexual reputation, who was having an affair with the mayor. *Yes,* they'll say, Mary Jeanne had wild sex with the mayor. But the sex" — Green raised his voice for emphasis — "was *consensual.*" They will turn Ophelia's testimony right around on her! Admittedly, the manner of sex games preferred by Cameron is perverse and distasteful, but he got his wife to consent. He didn't have to force her! Is it beyond reason, they'll ask the jury, that he persuaded Mary Jeanne to engage in erotic antics?"

"What about the tape over her mouth? Tying her up? *Is that consensual?* Did she jump in the bay in a garbage bag? Was that consensual?" Cal interjected.

"I thought of that. Try this. Cameron will contend they played sex games all night. Bondage. Branding. Asphyxiation, out on the side deck of the master cabin. She was drunk and full of cocaine, staggering around with the bag over her neck and shoulders. She fell overboard and the bag impeded her swimming and she died. Manslaughter maybe."

"She fell across the bay? James said the yacht went from Solomons to Kent Island," said Cal.

"Who's going to testify to that? James is gone. The crew is gone. Anyway, it was night. How does James know where the vessel was on open water at night?"

Green shook his head. "Moray will say that they went up the west coast during the night and turned east to Kent later. He will suggest that Mary Jeanne went overboard when the vessel was off South River."

"Why didn't they search for her? Report her missing? After her body was found, why didn't they report it to police?" Cal was firing off questions at Green.

"Presuming the sex games were on the yacht, you're absolutely right! They've got a problem with that. If Cameron goes the consensual route, he has to acknowledge that he had a rendezvous with her on the vessel.

"If the picture holds up as being taken on that occasion, it establishes that Winston, Moray, Celeste, James, knew she was on board. Even if they knew nothing about the torture, why not contact the police as soon as they learn she's dead?"

"Why wouldn't the picture hold up?"

"Because even Ophelia agrees that these same people, including Mary Jeanne, may have been on the yacht on other weekends. The film was manufactured eighteen months ago and was sold over that time period. That's all I can prove."

Green paused for a moment. "The idea of a big cover-up bothers me. I just can't believe that all these people knew the girl was tortured and branded and sat around and agreed to cover it up. What the hell is Cameron to Winston? What is Harry Moray to Winston? Someone arranges for two policemen to be attacked — one murdered — over a love killing? Jesus, the cost of keeping it quiet was a little steep."

Green got up and walked around the park bench so he was facing Cal and standing over him.

"This is a political case. Political cases aren't about convictions. O. J. Simpson's trial wasn't about a conviction, Paula Jones wasn't about a verdict. The destruction, one way or the other, was done to Cameron from the moment the case became known. I can totally destroy Martin Cameron right now for you. Is that all you want?"

"Christ, no!" Cal said heatedly. "I want the people who ordered Roberta Marie Short killed!"

"Then I need some help!" Green was thumping his finger into Cal's chest. "Get your ex-wife to come to the grand jury and tell about the connections with her husband. Valasquez. Winston."

Cal shook his head. "Never. She'll never do it!"

"Then you'd better think of someone else. St. Denis, Valasquez, and your ex-wife can quash my subpoenas in a heartbeat. I have no jurisdiction in the killing of Short, and right now it isn't linked to Mary Jeanne."

"What do we do?" asked Cal.

"We go nasty."

"Nasty?"

"We beat them to death in the press," said Green. "They don't know my limitations. Do you see! I'm going to be the anvil, you're going to be the hammer. You hammer on the cover-up. Find the gunmen, get me something. I'll lean on the mayor. Every time you uncover anything, I'll subpoena it and I'll file the subpoenas in court with affidavits on their importance. We'll tell the cover-up story without proving it!"

Cal didn't answer right away.

"It won't be easy," Green said. He stopped a minute and gazed hard at Cal. "And you really don't look so great. But I can't use the troopers! If I send troopers out of state without the legislature, the Republicans would stop me at the pass. What I can do is protect you. You can return to your farm, and I'll get the troopers to cover you."

"You're on!" Cal said. He was thinking of Bobbie. She would have liked this a lot.

The next day, Carol took him up to D.C. in the middle of the day. He had her park on Thirteenth Street, and he walked a block to Stoneys.

Jerry the day barman was on.

"Claire stuck a package for me under there," Cal said, leaning over the bar. "A month or so ago. See if it's there."

It took awhile, but Jerry came up with it. "It's an old Walkman and some wires?"

"Yeah, that's it."

"I was sorry to hear about Bobbie," Jerry said.

"Yeah. That was a bummer."

Jerry poured Cal and himself a Bushmills and hoisted his.

"Here's to her."

The liquor was sweet and warm.

When Edward St. Denis married Vivian, they moved to one of those baronial mansions built on five-acre lots west of Great Falls. The houses sold for a million plus, but even with fancy landscaping and manicured lawns, they never looked right, like a giant had strewn houses in all the wrong places.

St. Denis's house backed up to woods that cut down into a gully and along a small stream. The stream flowed back out to the road, under a culvert, and into the property directly across from St. Denis.

Cal rented a car in Baltimore, and to the side he affixed a magnetic real-estate agent's sign that belonged to a friend of Carol's. He stopped and took Polaroids of several houses, but mainly of St. Denis's, staying way back so he couldn't be seen from windows.

He guessed the White House telephone line had been pulled through the same cable tube as the regular telephones and the television line; otherwise, there would have had to be a new utility trench, and the lawn looked old and undisturbed. The tube went into the ground and under the lawn for 125 feet, surfaced just inside the edge of the wood, and ran along the surface another forty feet to the switch box on the road.

The box was the old kind, concrete, four feet tall, on a concrete pedestal and locked with a key. Cal had spotted it from the road, standing three feet above the stream bank. He figured it would take ten minutes in and out, parking, opening the box, setting up, and being gone. Ten minutes.

In the old days he and Jack would have put the wires on in the open. They'd have worn work clothes and used Jack's gray van, taking license plates from the impound yard so you couldn't run a trace. Jack was the wireman, his deft fingers finding the connections and making the splices. "Shit," he'd tell Cal. "You're so slow, we'll get arrested for loitering."

But the night he went back, of course, Jack wasn't there. He was all alone. He hadn't told Carol where he was going. She looked anxious as he left.

Cal shut off the headlights of the rental car a quarter of a mile before the house, drove past it, over the little bridge and then down a piece of old pasture road on the far side, just flashing his lights long enough to check that he wasn't driving into soft ground. It was 2:10.

Cal got the tool bag from the backseat with a yellow telephone monitor unit and Jack's recorder. He pulled on plastic gloves and pulled on an old field jacket with big pockets. Cal covered the car with a roll of camouflage netting so the windows and chrome wouldn't reflect headlights.

He heard a dog in the distance, but the only other sounds were the crickets and soft lap of the stream. He put the little flashlight in his teeth but didn't turn it on, and found the telephone box's keyhole in the dark by feeling along the door edge.

The key opened the door like butter, and Cal heaved a sigh of relief. He turned on the flashlight and bent down so the open door hid the light, and searched for the wires. The groups of wire clusters were where the drawing had showed them. He took the yellow monitor and tied into the first two connections in the group of four and checked his watch. 2:17. Suddenly a dog barked nearby and he froze, but a voice called, "Custer, get in here!" and the barking stopped.

He made his first tap and got a regular dial tone. Shit! He tried the next and got a second dial tone. Maybe Jack's information was wrong! He'd be there a week if he had to try every cluster.

Instead of trying the next connection, Cal moved the monitor's connector to the bottom wires in the group. The line was open and silent! After a few seconds, a different dial tone clicked on, one that sounded remote. It was 2:21. He was already behind! He started to work furiously.

Cal had hoped to tape the recorder under the telephone box, but Mobus hadn't given him enough play in the leads, so he put it inside the box on the bottom and tied off the wires. He turned off the flashlight and felt around on the ground for pine needles and leaves, sprinkling them over the bottom to hide the recorder. It wasn't good, but it might survive a cursory look.

Cal detached his telephone monitor and then rewired it, a little higher, making the connection to the White House line. When he said, "Testing," into the monitor, he felt the vibration of the little tape recorder switching on. Jack had done a good job. Just like always.

The car startled him. Somehow the topography must have muffled the engine, so by the time he heard it, the headlights seemed right on top of him. Cops! He rolled flat from a sitting position, watching the headlights sweep over him like a searchlight. The car turned up the St. Denis drive, the lights moving away and leaving him in the darkness.

He started to crawl away from the box, toward his car, gently shutting the box door and collecting his tools. He imagined the policemen sitting in their car trying to remember where the switch box was. Cal lay silent, twenty feet from the box, near the culvert. If the cops were coming on foot, they were sure taking their time. Finally he got up, keeping as low as he could, and hobbled back across the bridge in a crouch.

By the time he got to his car, it was 2:39. Still no cops. Christ, he was winded, and he was sure he had reinjured his knee. He stripped the camo sheet, stuffed everything into the trunk, closing it without slamming it, and put his suit jacket back on and sat in the driver's seat with the door open.

His pants were covered with dirt and leaves. He took a pint of Jack Daniel's from under the seat and took a big swig and daubed it all over his shirt and in his hair. The sweet whiskey smell wafted over him. He took another swig and waited for the cops.

If they came, he was going into a drunk act. He poured some of the pint around, hid it under the seat, and sat in the car like he'd had too much. They'd figure he stumbled out to go to the bathroom, and the car set off the tamper alarm. They'd spend their time hauling him in on DWI. He knew cops. A bird in the hand is better than checking a telephone box down a culvert in the dark. Worst case scenario: the arrest would only show that Mrs. St. Denis's ex-husband was sitting outside her house drunk. But the woods remained silent, and no more headlights broke the darkness of the road.

Finally he heard voices, up by Vivian's front door.

"Saturday, okay," a woman said, giggling. It sounded loud, like the woman had been drinking. It wasn't Vivian.

He couldn't hear the answer, and the way his car was facing, he couldn't see. He slumped way down in the seat. He could hear what sounded like a slap and another giggle. "You're getting pretty hippy," said a man. It sounded like Edward. The car headlights swung around like a searchlight, and then he heard the engine gun and the tires skidding on the gravel. A few seconds after the car left, the St. Denis outdoor light went out and there was deeper darkness and more silence.

Forget ten minutes, he had been there an hour. It seemed like a hundred years. At 3:10, he backed his car out and headed down the road, keeping the lights off and the speed down to muffle the noise. The adrenaline had covered the pain in his leg and now he was so weak and achy, he could hardly drive.

He got the three white ski masks at an alpine shop the next morning. What was it Jack always said? When you put on a tap, think of the target as a herd of cattle: you have to drive them to make calls.

When the clerk handed him the masks, Cal found he shivered involuntarily, as though the dark eyes of the gunmen were still behind the slits. He bought two wool caps too and mittens so the guy wouldn't be suspicious.

"You expecting early snows?"

He bought the stamps in Washington's main post office and got Express Mail wrappers in Arlington and labels from a shop in Georgetown. Never underestimate the power of an FBI lab. He made two telephone calls to find out that Valasquez's actual office was in the Old Executive Office Building.

He mailed a mask to Valasquez at the White House and sent St. Denis one at his home. The notes were identical: *Don't forget us.* Cal mailed the packages from Baltimore in a receptacle.

He was betting heavily on that White House hookup. If they called each other on the regular lines, he was going to be out of luck. Cal picked up the tape four days after the mailing and replaced it.

Seven calls on the tape were useless. They were so banal, Cal had to wonder whether President Winston ever did anything important. The eighth call was not banal.

Edward's voice was actually quivering. "Do you think this is a joke?"

Cal had never heard Valasquez speak before. It was a cop's voice, hard and accustomed to authority.

"It's not a joke. I got the same thing. A white mask, right?"

"With a note that says, *Don't forget us,*" Edward said, his voice rising. "*Where did this come from?*"

There was silence for a minute.

"It didn't come from down south, if that's what you mean," said Valasquez. "I checked. They're still on ice in Miami."

"But who, Carlos?"

"Unless I miss my guess, Vivian was a little too optimistic that Terrell has given up. Does she know about the mask?"

"No," Edward said.

"*Don't tell her.* Bring everything to me. Wrapper, mask, box, note, the whole works. For Christ's sake, don't put your fingerprints all over the package."

"Why can't you stop this?" Edward asked petulantly.

"I wouldn't touch Terrell now with a ten-foot pole! Patience! Green will run out of gas."

He listened to the tape several times. It wasn't evidence, but it was proof, proof of the pudding, as his mother used to say.

Miami was great, like it always is when you come from the cold, rainy North. There was sleet and the temperature was thirty-one degrees and falling when Cal left BWI. His head and his leg felt like hell. But three hours later, driving along the ocean in the warm sun with the windows down, he began to feel a lot better.

The Dade County Public Safety building was crowded and noisy, and he had to wait an hour for a homicide official to talk to him. He had brought another ski mask with him, plus a full set of clippings on Bobbie's shooting and his attack.

The sergeant that met with him was lean, tanned, Cuban, and respectful. "Christ, I read about this. That's terrible," he said, looking through the clippings. "We got a lookout on this from your department maybe a month or so ago." He rummaged through some papers and came up with a nationwide request for information written by Collins. Nathaniel must have ordered an artist to work with the 7-Eleven clerk, because there was a sketch of both men with masks, a description of them, and a pretty good description of what the guns looked like too.

"So what are you doing, following up?"

Cal shook his head. "We got an informant who said he heard these guys were 'on ice in Miami.'" It was at that moment that the Dade County officer made the connection. "You're this guy, right?"

Cal nodded.

"I'm sorry. I should've known! When I saw you, I said to myself, 'That guy must have had his head caught in a lawn mower.'"

From that moment on, the Dade County cop went all out. He brought robbery detectives up, called Miami PD and the local FBI, and took Cal out to a big Cuban lunch; but at the end of the day, there was nothing.

"Sure, we've had ski-mask robbers, but usually the wool kind, you know," said one Dade County robbery officer.

It was a narcotics officer named Octavio who came up with something, just as Cal was leaving.

"You know who does wear those?"

Cal and the homicide officers shook their heads.

"Narcoterrorism suppression teams. I've seen them in pictures. They all go masked so the terrorists can't identify them and harm their families. Often it's like a black watch cap or black silk thing, but I've seen these too."

He clicked his fingernail against the hard white plastic. "They like them because they're cooler!"

"Where do they get them?"

"Soldier-of-fortune places. You know, like those big gun shops down on the Tamiami."

Cal stayed four days. Octavio was great. He took him to every gun shop and mercenary hangout in the area. They made copies of Collins's lookout and distributed them.

One shop on Tamiami sold to the Salvadoran army and police, mainly specialty items like night scopes and H & Ks. The owner said they would have sent the masks for free as a bonus to a good customer. "I don't have them now, but we've had this model in stock. It is sold by a Canadian ski supplier and made in Indonesia."

"You know who knows all these guys?" Octavio added as they left the shop.

Cal nodded. "DEA, right?"

"Absolutely, but they probably won't tell you a thing. In a lot of places like Guatemala and El Salvador, DEA funds the police force. Of course, so do the traffickers." He laughed.

Cal went on the telephone to Green that night. "Let's scare them a little. Send a subpoena for Valasquez's personnel record to the Drug Enforcement Agency. Countries served, assignments held, that sort of thing. Specifically ask for all counternarcotics programs financed in El Salvador.

"See if maybe Senator Sarbanes would press them too. Get it on record that you've identified Valasquez on the vessel with Mary Jeanne and that you're investigating him."

Green was as efficient as ever. Two mornings later the *Washington Post* carried a story that the president's key narcotics adviser was on the *Potomac Fever* and that his role in the case might be important.

The *Washington Post* dug up a lot on Valasquez. He'd been born in Cuba in 1956 and came to Miami with his parents as a toddler. He'd taken law enforcement at South Miami State, joined the Miami PD, where he got to be a second-grade detective in Narcotics. DEA recruiters drafted him in 1977 because of his fluency in Spanish.

From then on, the *Post* clips showed, Valasquez had stayed in Colombia or Peru for the next eleven years, an unusually long time, he admitted to one interviewer.

"I felt I was making a contribution and I've come to love Central America," he said. He loved one of its citizens too. In 1986 Valasquez married a Cartagena woman.

"She's upper-caste Castilian, one of the families who lived there before the earthquake," he boasted to *Time* magazine when he became deputy director of the DEA.

Valasquez had gone from Bogotá to the Miami field office and then to the drug czar's office under Winston. The *Post* said that Valasquez had built the Miami field office into the "powerhouse" it is today.

It was also Valasquez who was credited with making Winston's drug czar tenure successful, and they had formed a strong bond in those years. With Winston's backing, Valasquez went back to the DEA as the deputy director and then to the National Security Council with the portfolio of overseas drug interdiction.

At the bottom of the *Post* story were two intriguing points: Valasquez was described as brilliant and dedicated, but one former DEA agent implied he was devious as well. "All guys who work undercover a long time learn to live a false story. It's hard to break the habit." And another unnamed former agent said his Colombian wife was wealthy and ran hotels in Cartagena. "Her money has provided them with a very comfortable lifestyle."

The next day Cal went to Miami Drug Enforcement Agency offices, wearing his best suit.

An agent came out and asked what he wanted.

He showed him the ski mask and the flyer.

"I want to know how many Latin American narcoterrorist units use this style of mask. How many of them are funded by the DEA, and what role did Carlos Valasquez have in training and directing them?"

"Why Miami, Lieutenant Terrell?" the agent asked.

"I have an undercover informant who said he was told the men who murdered Sergeant Roberta Short were 'on ice in Miami.'"

"Those precise words," said the agent as he took notes.

"Those precise words."

They kept him waiting for two hours. He guessed there were a lot of frantic calls going back and forth to Washington. Finally the assistant agent in charge and a Justice Department lawyer met with him in what Cal guessed was an interrogation room and undoubtedly wired for sound.

The Justice Department lawyer did the talking.

"Mr. Terrell, exactly what is your capacity here?"

"I'm investigating the murder of my partner."

"Captain Bench said he thought you were on convalescent leave."

"I'm back."

"We cannot divulge information about our funding of counternarco-terrorism teams. These are crucial national-security issues. We cannot divulge details about a former agent's career without a court order. You might try the White House."

"Did the agent mention I have an undercover informant with precise information on Sergeant Short's attackers?"

The Justice lawyer smiled patronizingly.

"'On ice in Miami'?"

"That's the exact phrase attributed to a man who planned the attack."

On his way to the airport, Cal guessed that the phrase "on ice in Miami" would be on Valasquez's desk by now. He hoped Valasquez remembered saying it. If he didn't, he wouldn't get the message.

In the way of a television lynching, neither Cameron nor Mary Jeanne was getting much of a chance. He was a dirty old man and she was a sex-crazed teenager, it depended on which talk show you watched.

Cal noticed that the White House quietly admitted that President Winston attended a cocktail party on August 1 on the *Potomac Fever* but stuck with the story that he left in midevening. The president's press secretary said Winston did not remember meeting Miss Turner, but in a crowd that size, "he often can't recall each person whom he was introduced to." He said he wasn't sure whether Carlos Valasquez was there, but several White House aides had attended.

Moray's lawyer, Vic Stein, looked angry and defensive on Channel 9. "The cruise was a routine social function. Harry entertains on the *Potomac Fever* probably twice a week in the summer." Stein said Miss Turner "had been invited, but Mr. and Mrs. Moray are not sure she attended or when she left."

Stein said that after the cocktail party, the Morays, Cameron, and Washington developer Virgil James stayed aboard the yacht and sailed to Moray's home on the Eastern Shore. "Nothing untoward happened during this weekend, and they returned to Washington by helicopter." He adroitly did not mention the president of the United States.

Cameron played it smart. He refused to talk to the *Washington Post*, stiffed white television reporters, sticking with the black ones, who would at least hear him out.

"This is a white plot!" Cameron charged. "This is the big lie!"

Late in the afternoon, he sat down with a black anchor on Channel 4. "George, you've known me since Resurrection City," he said, quickly setting the stage of the civil rights movement. "I mourned the death of this young woman, as many in Washington did. Crime and drugs stalk our city, and we must put a stop to it. But linking me to her death, this is a travesty!

"This woman worked in a restaurant where my staff and I sometimes ate a late dinner. I didn't even know her name. She was just a nice likable kid who greeted you at the door."

George the anchor was pitching the mayor softballs that came in low and slow. "How does this kind of an accusation get made?"

"George, I'm focusing on the timing. Next month I've got to decide whether to seek reelection. The White House has asked me to run again. The Democrats can't win Washington without something like this. They can't beat me at the polls. They've got to knock me out with the lie!"

"Who's behind this?" George asked in the tone of a man reading from a TelePrompTer.

"White police officers," said Cameron, hitting one fist into the palm of the other. "They resent that black officers get an equal shake in my administration."

The bombshell hit Sunday morning. The Sunday *Washington Post* began, in conjunction with *Newsweek,* the serialized story of Ophelia Cameron, "the queen of an African American Camelot," who revealed that she had given the grand jury crucial testimony against her husband.

In the first-person story, she told how she had discovered too late that her husband was a deeply disturbed man, driven by perverse sexual appetites.

The confession was deftly presented to appear the tale of a woman who loves a man and has to watch, powerlessly, as a great public servant is destroyed. Ophelia told how she had discovered her husband sought unorthodox sexual behavior, how she knew about his womanizing and the identity of many of his lovers, and how she had spotted his affair with Mary Jeanne Turner.

Ophelia claimed she understood this was an illness and had pressed him for years to seek psychiatric treatment. "I accepted the humiliation of his sexual adventures because I knew he was sick." But when Mary Jeanne was killed, she said, "I realized that I should have gone public long before. It would have saved that girl's life!"

Apparently Green had made her hold back the coup de grâce: that Martin Cameron had branded her body as well. There was no mention or hint of it.

For twenty-four hours Cameron and his lawyers tried to weather the storm that had broken over them. His rebuttal was lost in the firestorm. By late Tuesday Cameron saw safety in the idea of his predecessor Marion Barry. He checked himself into a hospital in South Carolina that specialized in the treatment of heart disease. "He is suffering from exhaustion," the doctors told a news conference.

Taking Cameron out of circulation temporarily put a lid on the media.

The DEA went to court to block Green's subpoena, and the hearing was set for January. Cal dumped the recorder a week before Christmas. There were no calls from Carlos, but in one call Edward told the White House press office not to confirm or deny any aspects of Valasquez's background to CBS. "He's entitled to privacy. The act prohibits us from releasing anything. Tell them to talk to Carlos."

28

Christmas Day dawned as it often does on the lower Chesapeake, not cold or snowing, but chill, gray, overcast, and damp. With the leaves stripped from the trees, Cal could see the bay from the house, windswept and white-capped.

Cal felt alone, but not lonely, as though the past five months had pared away the humanity from his bones like it was fat. He was emotionally spare and lean, and his mind had come to focus almost solely on the case.

He had finally persuaded the Maryland State Police to halt their vigil at the farm so he could act without being encumbered by their presence, and he had even stopped seeing Carol for the same reason. He didn't want to endanger her, and more important, he didn't want to be weighted down by her.

When the year had started, Bobbie had been alive; Nathaniel had been a friend, if not a close one; Vivian had been a memory, but not a threat. His life on the farm and in the police department had been predictable if not joyful. But now he was entirely on his own — in a way, cleared for action, like a downed pilot behind enemy lines, dependent upon his wits.

At noon he called Bobbie's father. He was glad he did. The holiday had been crushing for him, Cal could tell from his voice.

"You-all getting anywhere on finding those guys?"

"Any day now," Cal lied. He didn't feel that way at all.

Late in the afternoon, after his third football game, Cal steamed a dozen shrimp and took them and a cold six-pack of Rolling Rock out to the stable. It always sickened Vivian when he ate food while he cleaned the stalls. Putting Willie Nelson into the truck's tape deck, he turned up the volume so he could hear it while he worked. Willie knew how to feel sorry for himself. Hard work sharpened Cal's thinking, and he worked furiously, letting the physical strain overtake him.

The wind was sharp. His fingers were turning blue as he shoveled out the stables, and it was some minutes before he noticed that the horses had ignored their food. They were twisting and turning, searching wildly through the stall doors with their eyes.

Whatever was spooking the horses was close. Cal drew the 9mm and slowly started walking down the farm road toward Route 4. He saw nothing and heard nothing. He was two hundred feet along before he saw the car, large and dark, pulled into the trees a hundred feet off the road, its shape hardly visible in the brush. *Shit, I just came up that road, why hadn't I seen the car?*

Seeing the car did not frighten him as much as it annoyed him. Willie Nelson, of course, had masked its noise, allowing the driver to get within 500 feet of the house without alarming Cal.

The scent of the aftershave lotion hit him and he half turned, recognizing the Burberry from Britches that Nathaniel favored. "Hello, Captain Bench," Cal said as he felt the muzzle of the pistol against his neck.

"Lord almighty, I'm in the country. Christmas with Willie Nelson and Rolling Rock." Nathaniel's dark brown hand closed with an iron grip around Cal's hand holding the 9mm, and Cal let the pistol loose.

Neither of them said anything as they walked to the house. Cal kept his father's shotgun over the door, muzzle facing right, so if he went for it going in, he'd have to fade to Nathaniel's left to get a quick shot.

As if he could read Cal's mind, Nathaniel said, "Forget the shotgun." Nathaniel pushed him as he went in, and Cal stumbled through to the living room.

The light by the couch went on a second later. In the far corner stood Martin Cameron, no longer gaunt or hollow-eyed, in a Morgan State warm-up jacket with his number and game patches, looking like a football alumnus at a reunion party.

Nathaniel moved to the kitchen door. He held a pistol on Cal, very steady, very unwavering.

Cal looked at the two men.

"This is a little stupid."

"Shut up," Nathaniel answered. But Cal didn't stop.

"Assault, burglary, impeding a federal officer." Cal tried to think of more crimes. "You're finished, Nathaniel."

"Sit down!" said Nathaniel.

Cal wearily found a seat on the edge of the couch.

"Look at it this way," Nathaniel said. "I have simply arranged for you to interrogate your suspect. I've read him his rights. He has the right to remain silent, but he wants to talk to you. He has the right to have an attorney present during questioning, but he's settled for me. . . ."

Suddenly Nathaniel's voice went up sharply. "He has a right to be heard before you and Green and the motherfuckers in the White-fucking-House destroy him."

Cameron held up his hand. "Slow down, Mr. Bench. Mr. Terrell clearly is going to graciously agree to hear me out."

Nathaniel ejected the magazine from Cal's pistol, checked the chamber, and threw the gun on the floor.

Cal watched him quietly. If Nathaniel were going to kill him, he reasoned, he would have done it right away, in the stable even, done it and gone. The big police captain looked somehow different today, thinner perhaps and tougher. When they'd been partners, Nathaniel knew his job. Street guys never fucked with Nathaniel. Never. His moves today reminded Cal of that.

"You're looking good, Mr. Bench. But it was a very amateurish ambush. The aftershave. I smelled you before I saw you. If I had wanted to kill you, you'd be dead. You wouldn't have made that mistake in the Mekong Delta," said Cal.

Nathaniel smiled at the mayor. "When we came on the job, Cal here and I were the only Vietnam veterans in Homicide. A Buffalo soldier and a Cobra killer, they called us.

"I figured the war made us better Homicide men. We were the only guys who knew how to kill people."

"Mayor, this isn't very useful. You shouldn't let this guy pull you around," Cal said, nodding at Nathaniel. "Listen to your lawyers. Make a deal."

Martin Cameron rubbed his brow. "I told Nathaniel I didn't think this was a good idea. He pointed out, adroitly I thought, that I don't have much to lose."

Cal looked sharply at Nathaniel. Nathaniel had telephoned him the night of Bobbie's death. He had called the hospital after Cal was beaten, and Vivian contended Nathaniel wasn't in on the deal. Cal was beginning to find his onetime partner's actions perplexing.

"But I have a story!" Cameron assured Cal. "You listen to it, and maybe we can help each other."

"Help each other?" Cal could not keep the incredulity out of his voice.

"Give me a hearing."

Cal shrugged. Nathaniel had the gun.

"It may amaze you, Mr. Terrell, but Mary Jeanne Turner's death may be as much a mystery to me as it is to you.

"First, I did *not* kill Mary Jeanne. I loved her, probably more than I have ever loved anybody in the world but my father."

Cameron stopped, as though thinking where to go next. "I suppose I was so absorbed with Mary Jeanne that I didn't really know, or maybe I didn't care, what was going on. It made me the perfect patsy. Only I'm not entirely sure who I'm patsy for." He paused. "The last time I saw Mary Jeanne Turner, she was alive. She was very much alive! We were in bed in my cabin on the *Potomac Fever*."

Cameron began to pace back and forth. "When I fell asleep, the woman in bed with me was full of life and verve and unharmed!" His voice rose. "After you went to Green, the White House provided me with an extraordinary archive of videotapes of our times together, mine and Mary Jeanne's. Somebody had rigged her apartment, taken shots long-distance, short-distance — the whole works. The pièce de résistance was a tape from the *Potomac Fever*.

"It was the whole evening, probably triggered by light shining on a cell. The video had a timer and, from that, I guess I dozed off about three-ten Friday night. The *Potomac Fever* was under way. You can hear the engines on the video. That was the last moment I saw Mary Jeanne in life.

"The video shows that when she realized I was asleep, Mary Jeanne rolled off me, went to the bathroom, came back, pulled the covers up to my neck, kissed my forehead, got into bed beside me, and turned out the light. The camera went off.

"At seven-twenty A.M., there was the loud noise of a helicopter. Probably the one that came for Winston. Mary Jeanne must have turned on the light. The camera starts. She's getting out of bed, and there I am sawing logs. I was dead to the world. Unaware that she was on camera, Mary Jeanne took off the man's shirt she wore as a nightie. She went into the bathroom. There was no camera there. You can hear everything; this video had excellent sound.

"She came out to the cabin to dry. The most important thing on this videotape is that her backside, that beautiful backside, is as smooth as a baby's. There is no brand. There are no bruises. She put on a swimsuit over which she wore a blouse and tennis skirt. This videotape shows a healthy, apparently happy young woman going to swim and play tennis.

"She came over, kissed my cheek, and went out the door carrying her racket. The tape shows it was seven-forty-seven A.M. when the door closed on her. I wrote the time down from the video."

Cal interrupted him. "Mr. Mayor, if this is true, you've got to show it to Green, it's wasted on me."

"Nathaniel said you are probably the only honest man in this whole thing, Lieutenant Terrell, so maybe you'll hear me out."

"The tape will be part of your defense," said Cal. "That's why they have trials."

"I don't have the tape," said Cameron.

Cal started to laugh. "You mean this vital piece of exculpatory evidence has mysteriously disappeared?" Cal asked wryly.

"There will be no trial," Nathaniel angrily interjected. "There was never going to be a trial. The White House doesn't want a trial. Winston can't survive a trial. Green can't win a trial. You and Bobbie were fools not to have come to me! Bobbie'd be alive if you had!"

Anger overflowed in Cal, like a pot of boiling water. Before he could stop, he was diving at Nathaniel. The pent-up pressure of weeks flashed out in extraordinary violence. He was not going to be blamed for Bobbie's death, not by anyone but himself!

With strength he didn't know he had, Cal was off the couch and hit Nathaniel in the midriff with his head. Nathaniel became every demon Cal faced: Bobbie's death, Vivian's betrayal, Edward St. Denis, Valasquez, and the deadliness of the gunmen. Cal came up fast, his head banging Nathaniel's chin backward. Blood was coming from Nathaniel's mouth. Nathaniel couldn't shoot for fear of hitting Cameron, and in his peripheral vision Cal could see the muzzle of the pistol waving wildly.

The big police officer staggered back and went down, trying to cover his head and his groin at the same time. Cal got up on his good leg and braced himself on the wall. He kicked and hit something soft. Nathaniel screamed in pain. Testicles. Cal kicked again. Nathaniel screamed and fell back, the pistol flying out of his hand.

Cal followed him down, falling more than diving on Nathaniel's stomach. Nathaniel was losing consciousness. Cal grabbed the pistol and rolled right, putting the gun at Nathaniel's temple, so close there would be no doubt.

"You're dead."

Nathaniel was very cool then, the trained police officer. He didn't move. His eyes were white and dazed but focused on Cal.

Cal crawled backward and crouched against the far wall. "Lay down, Nathaniel. Facedown."

He rolled over with a grunt of pain.

Cameron, despite his strength and agility, had never moved, as though this fight had nothing to do with him.

"Get my cuffs off that desk, Mayor, and handcuff his hands behind him."

At first the mayor didn't move.

"Now!"

Nathaniel was trying to wipe blood from his face onto the rug. He was groggy. Cameron found the handcuffs and pulled Nathaniel's head back gently.

Cal got himself up along the wall and stepped over Nathaniel to get to the phone in the kitchen. He kept one eye on Cameron while he dialed, but the mayor had sunk back on the couch.

"Nine one one emergency," said a woman's voice.

Cameron spoke up, loudly. "Do you want to find who killed Roberta Short? You can always turn me in."

"Nine one one emergency," said the woman's voice again.

"Sorry, I misdialed." Cal hung up. "What are you talking about?"

"Tell him the rest," Nathaniel said, from the floor. "You're beating on the wrong door! We're not your problem."

"First, Mr. Terrell, Mary Jeanne was incidental to the yacht trip, an accident, the proverbial innocent bystander. The entire trip that night was to threaten me into approving District participation in Rivergate. As soon as I approve that, some very peculiar backers of Winston will free up millions for his reelection."

Cameron stopped to let his speech sink in.

"When Mary Jeanne was killed — and I now don't believe the White House had a thing to do with it — her death became an additional way to pressure me.

"The White House has that videotape, and the price of that videotape is my silence and my endorsement of the Rivergate project."

Cameron let that too sink in for a second.

"To save myself, Mr. Edward St. Denis wants me to lead my African American flock out of the promised land, Washington, and then quietly resign. He said then and not until then will he provide me with a copy of the tape."

"Wait. I'm not sure I'm following you," said Cal. "They'll give you the tape if you agree to move all the black people out of the East End?"

Cameron nodded. "That's what this is all about. Rivergate."

"Why would they do that? If the blackmail works and you give the tape to Green to clear yourself, Green is going to demand to know who was taping and why.

"Isn't the White House creating a bigger mess for itself? If the White House gives you the tape, they've got to explain why it made secret salacious tapes of political figures. That seems like a pretty unlikely scenario."

Cameron shook his head.

"The deal is, I'll say that Mary Jeanne left the vessel alive and that when she turned up dead, I panicked and didn't tell police what I know. End of story. I will have an alibi for the rest of the weekend. Green and you are out of luck and the White House is off the hook. I'm supposed to say the president didn't know anything about the tape, never even met or knew Mary Jeanne, who was secretly tucked away in my cabin. I am to say Moray let me make the tape for a little pornographic history of the trip. That's his reputation, anyhow."

Cal tried to let the scheme sink in. It was hard. He was used to corruption. This time the scale was massive. He sought refuge in the basics.

"You mean, the president knows all about this?"

"And more," said Cameron. "You haven't heard the worst."

"If you didn't torture Mary Jeanne, who did?"

For the first time Cameron looked very pained.

"That's the rub. *I don't know!* I don't have a clue! So I can't deliver your Mr. Green another suspect."

Nathaniel groaned. Cal suddenly felt sympathy for him lying there, handcuffed, the blood still oozing from a little cut. He wondered why Nathaniel had come with a gun or even why Nathaniel had come at all.

"Lie still. I'll get you something."

He went into the kitchen and got a dishtowel and soaked it in cold water. "Bathe his face."

Cameron knelt and gently bathed Nathaniel's face, talking all the while.

"Who killed Bobbie?"

"I don't know exactly, but I think I know why and you'll see in a minute."

"Go on."

Cameron talked for forty-five minutes, sketching in precise detail a multimillion-dollar real-estate investment designed to pay back certain contributors to President Winston's campaign.

"To build the project, they have to transplant forty thousand black people from the East End of Washington in two years. Talk about ethnic cleansing!

"When they sent me the plan, I told Moray my objections in a detailed letter with a copy to St. Denis. I figured this would be no big deal, they just hadn't thought this through and they'd make some changes. That's when I first found out that this was not Harry Moray's pie-in-the-sky re-development plan, this deal was a way to make millions for the participants from all that land along the river and eminent-domain seizures. Winston will get his reelection financing, and I suspect get rich too.

"One by one, Moray, James, St. Denis brought pressure on me. Then my beautiful wife, Ophelia, gets a million-dollar contract from Moray. By this time in our lives, I have no standing with Ophelia at all, but I try anyway. 'Darling, this is a little awkward. You just accepted a million-dollar contract from a man with a big development project before me. Could you give the money back?' You know what her response was?"

Cal shook his head.

"Unless I wanted my sordid extramarital love life paraded before every African American minister in the city, she advised me to go along."

"The next thing that happened was serendipitous, but Nathaniel over there thinks it was part of the scheme. One night last spring at the River Club, Celeste brings over a new hostess. I look at her, literally just look at her, and I know I have fallen into the most beautiful brown eyes I'd ever seen, deep and cool but twinkling, as though life is great and she's happy to be here."

Cal could not smother a grin.

"Sure, I know it sounds ridiculous, but it's true. First sight! Mary Jeanne Turner took my breath away!

"To court Mary Jeanne was against all rhyme and reason for me at this point in my life. Ophelia put me on notice that she had had enough.

"'Stop philandering or I'll walk.' Without Ophelia in the upcoming campaign, my chances to get the black women's vote are slim. If it became known I was sleeping with a white woman, my chances go to none. But I could not stop myself. I really couldn't. I'll be fifty-one years old next month, and Mary Jeanne was the first woman I ever really loved," Cameron said.

Cal and Nathaniel looked with incredulity at each other. But Cameron seemed deadly serious.

"Ophelia?" said Nathaniel softly.

"She was a partner. Maybe like Hillary Clinton, a business partner. We were the first black couple that equaled the whites, the Clintons, the Doles; where a black woman was a strong professional partner for her man. The great folly is that Mary Jeanne actually fell in love with me."

Nathaniel snorted angrily. "Sheeet! Martin, that's maudlin trash. You've been fucking around all your life!"

"Don't get me wrong, Mr. Terrell," Cameron said. "Nathaniel is correct. I'm a womanizer. I've slept with a lot of women. I really don't know why. Once, Ophelia got me to go to an analyst. He said I have 'compulsive sex syndrome' because my mother never gave me enough affection. He may be right." Cameron shrugged. "But Mary Jeanne was different!"

Nathaniel made another cynical grunt.

"What about the *Potomac Fever*?" Cal asked.

"I'm getting to that! I was so dumb. I thought the White House was just playing political games. I had a plan. If they tried to blackmail me over my relationship with Mary Jeanne, I'd step down. I wanted Mary Jeanne more than politics!"

Cameron grinned wryly. "St. Denis wouldn't have reckoned on that. There would not have been enough time for Winston to groom and nominate another black by the election. The city would go back to the Democrats. No Cameron. No Rivergate."

Cameron said he planned to teach at a college in the West and take Mary Jeanne.

"Until that night on the *Potomac Fever,* I hadn't breathed a word of it to Mary Jeanne, but it was not so far-fetched. I'm as strong as a bull. Except for my heart condition, there's nothing I can't do. I mean, I wanted to have kids!"

"You told her that night?"

"Yes, but by then it was too late."

"Too late?" said Cal.

That night, I found out this was no game. If I hadn't been so damn arrogant to think I could handle these men, maybe Mary Jeanne would be alive today.

"St. Denis had arranged for a fund-raiser on the *Potomac Fever* on August first. Three hours, three hundred guests, canapés and politics. The usual.

"Two nights before the fund-raiser, I got a strange request. Would I stay on board for an overnight cruise to Kent Island? Something had come up. The president urgently wanted to meet with me privately.

"I told St. Denis that I'd already said my piece, but St. Denis said Winston still wanted to talk to me. Okay. He's the president, right?"

At first, everything was unremarkable. Cameron said the cocktail party went without a hitch; President Winston did his little flimflam; and when they cast off, Celeste provided a beautiful and sumptuous dinner as dark fell on the Potomac.

"You know the first funny thing I noticed?"

Cal shook his head.

"Everybody seemed nervous except Mary Jeanne and me." Winston was distracted. His guy, Valasquez, kept running up to the bridge. The Morays were jumpy. Virgil was jumpy. I was trying to make conversation, but everyone seemed to be a million miles away.

"Suddenly, not more than a mile from where my father's farm is, just before Tall Timber, the *Potomac Fever* started to slow, and everybody except me, Winston, Valasquez, and the helmsman were hustled below. The security detail disappeared too, except for Valasquez.

"I got my first real feeling of trepidation. What's going down here? The president seemed to know what was going on, so it couldn't be an attempt on his life.

"We drifted midchannel for a while. There were no other boats and clouds hid the moon, so it was quite dark. Suddenly out of Breton Bay roars one of those racing launches, you know, a cigarette boat, and pulls alongside. Valasquez dropped the ladder and brought a man aboard.

"There was a lot of talk in high-speed Spanish. Winston seemed to know him. Lots of 'mis amigos,' two-handed handshakes. He even hugged the president.

"It is now me, Winston, Valasquez, and this guy. He is dressed in full Miami: leather briefcase, gold pen, Rolex watch, Palm Beach blazer, white slacks, tasseled loafers. Winston finally introduces the guy to me.

"Oogo, it turns out, is a lawyer. Oogo hands me an embossed card, which said HUGO, ADVOCATE, and had an eight-eight-eight number and the locations: Barcelona, Grand Caymans, Liechtenstein.

"He is a very specialized lawyer, Winston said. Oogo smiles.

"Oogo invests flight capital. No mention of where the capital is flying from. Oogo smiles again. He has been very kind, Winston said, to the Republican Party. Big smile. To me, Winston said, pointing to his own chest. Bigger smile. To Harry. Oogo smiles. And to you.

"'To me?' I asked.

"'Yes, to you,' the president said. 'Oogo and his clients were very good to your campaign.'

"Now Oogo is beaming, nodding deferentially, like he didn't want me to applaud."

Nathaniel lay back on the couch, staring at the ceiling and slowly shaking his head back and forth.

"'Oogo's clients are the investors in Rivergate,' the president said.

"I said something stupid like 'The only ones, Mr. President?'"

Cal shifted nervously. "Mayor, let's slow down. You say this is Winston's gig? That's artful. You don't know who killed Mary Jeanne, but you give me a new crime and the biggest fish in Washington?"

Cameron looked at Cal with a patronizing glance.

"Oogo wasn't going to accept anything less than Winston. A certain kind of money demands the candidate look the contributor in the eye and say, Yes, I'll handle your problem.

"You know as well as I do that I'm telling the truth. There would be no cover-up without the president, no need to be worried about Mary Jeanne's mysterious death, no real need to halt your investigation, Mr. Terrell."

Cameron paused to catch his breath. "In Washington, the Morays, St. Denises, and the Valasquezes are dispensable. Major contributors, particularly those seeking nefarious influence, know this. The Chinese executive who visited Clinton *demanded* Clinton. He wasn't going to talk to Al Gore or Bruce Lindsey. It was never a case that some aide made a mistake and let someone unsavory near the president.

"Winston told me as much himself. He didn't want to meet with this Oogo, but Oogo demanded it. Winston knew that I would never go to a meeting like this unless he personally asked me. I would only do it for him and even then I would have never taken that boat ride if I'd known there was an Oogo.

"Anyway, as soon as Winston introduced me, Oogo sort of dismissed the president with a wave of his hand, and both Winston and Valasquez went below. That ought to give you some clue. This guy can send the president of the United States below!

"Oogo looked at me for a long time without saying anything. Finally, he asked, 'You don't like the deal?' It turns out that he speaks beautiful English, with a little accent.

"I said, 'What deal?'

"'The deal I made for you. You don't like it?'

"I said, 'I'm not in any deal.'

"'Moray did not inform you?'

"Oogo handed me a beautifully embossed folder. It had my name in gold on the leather cover."

Cameron stopped talking. Cal looked at Cameron, and Cameron looked at the floor.

"There were two documents," said Cameron finally. "One was a receipt for a Grand Cayman bank account with five hundred thousand dollars in my name. I've got a copy in the car. The other was a copy of a Liechtenstein incorporation document showing me as a partner with Harry Moray in a company that owns Rivergate.

"I told him, 'Nobody will believe these!'" Cameron said heatedly. "Oogo just smiled. 'Personal appearances are not necessary for documentation. However, I think you will find that an African American man did appear with Mr. Moray and that he did sign your name.'

"Right away I thought of Virgil down below.

"Oogo said, 'If the deal is okay, why are you holding things up?'

"I told him my concerns about people forced from their homes too rapidly, social impact, economic impact. For a while he listened, tapping the tips of his fingers together and I thought, I'm finally getting somewhere.

"But then he looked up sharply and held up his hand to make me stop talking. 'Winston was right, you are crazy!' he screamed. 'I don't give a shit about those people. My investors don't give a shit about them. Our money is perishable. It has to be kept active. What do we care if a bunch of Negroes in America have to move?'

"I said, 'That's all well and good for you. But I'm the mayor and I have to consider these things.'

"But he was talking right over me. 'You've got one week,' he screamed.

"I said I couldn't approve this in a week. I needed time to make plans to explain it to the public.

"Oogo was silent for a moment, then he said, 'Maybe you need a catalyst.' I was confused. I remember thinking *catalyst* was such a strange word in this context. 'A catalyst?' I asked.

"He said, 'Something to galvanize the situation.'"

"What was that?"

"The Reggae Club," said Nathaniel.

Nathaniel sat forward. "Oogo told him that the documents were completely authentic and would be honored immediately. Martin could draw out the five hundred thousand the next day, if he chose, and he would also have point oh five percent of pretax profits of the first ten years of Rivergate, not to be less than five hundred thousand dollars a year, banked anywhere in the world."

"Did you take the money?" Cal asked.

Cameron shook his head angrily as though Cal hadn't been paying attention. "I have never taken a cent!" Cameron said. "I haven't approved Rivergate. But I didn't come forward in your investigation either. I didn't go public. I sat paralyzed, and I paid for it."

Cameron now looked tired of his tale.

"Do you have any evidence of their connection to the Reggae Club?" Cal looked from one to the other.

Cameron shook his head. "I surmised it from what Nathaniel told me. I guessed that in part from your investigation."

"Did you try to stop it?"

Cameron shook his head. "Of course, I didn't know what was going to happen, but even on Moray's boat, before the Reggae Club 'catalyst,' I knew I was in trouble. Later, sitting there, with the president of the United States, this vicious lawyer, and an armed DEA agent or whatever Carlos was, I figured, Go with the flow. I didn't know what they meant then by a catalyst, but I knew I was being threatened.

"I knew these people were not joking. I had fallen into a very dangerous situation. I went into a complete act. I said I didn't realize how important this was, my concerns can be met. I'll work with Harry. Effectively, I got down and kissed the ass of every man on deck. I wanted to get off that boat alive, and I wanted to get Mary Jeanne off that boat."

"You mean, the president of the United States sat still for all this?" Cal said.

Cameron nodded. "I had the same incredulity you have. But as soon as Oogo left the boat, Winston came to me.

"'You're not trifling with me, are you, Martin?' President Winston asked me. 'You rolled over pretty quickly.'

"I said, 'No, no, Mr. President.'

"Winston put his arm around me and walked me out to the fantail. The *Potomac Fever* had just passed Point Lookout and we were moving up the bay. The clouds were off the moon, and it was one of those extraordinary Chesapeake nights. For a second I couldn't believe this was happening.

"Winston said, 'Oogo and his friends would not be my choice of funds, but I have no others. Do you understand? This is the margin money. We have to be practical men in politics, Martin. The only way men of modest means can be in politics is to get these backers. Otherwise, only the very rich could run for office.'

"I said, 'What if I go public, Philip?'

"Winston turned and grasped my shoulders. 'You have a valid contract with these men, made months ago. I'm sure that would become public too. I would have to deplore your conflict of interest and your involvement with them. I would have to order an investigation of your actions. It would be very sordid.

"'If I go down, you go down, Martin. There'll be no football host talk shows or board of director appointments or invitations to the PGA Open. All there will be is what happened to Clinton's people: endless trials, humiliating news stories, enormous legal expenses, and probably jail.'

"I said, 'Why did you do this, Philip?' Out of nowhere he starts talking about drug money: 'The sale of narcotics creates the largest pool of uncommitted, unregulated funds in the world today. Where else was I going to get this kind of money?'

"I said, 'Philip, you were the drug czar! You got elected president on your record against drugs!'

"He looked at me with an expression of utter amazement. 'I learned the first day as drug czar that nobody can win that war. It's already over. Everybody knows that. A drug-free America is a passé value, like Mom's apple pie.'

"I remember I said something like 'This is wrong.'"

Cameron said Winston looked at him a long time, as though he were a child.

"'Their product is no more dangerous than tobacco, Martin, a lot less deadly than chemical pollutants. They don't even want me to go slow on drug enforcement. They want us to enforce our laws! They know that the harder we try to stop drugs, the higher their prices.'

"It was all classic Winston. Cool, logical, academic. Insane. All I could think, as I listened to him, was that the president of the United States has just sold half the nation's capital to narcotics traffickers."

Cameron said he literally staggered to the cabin that Moray had assigned him. Mary Jeanne was there. "She was higher than a kite. Celeste had given her a snootful of coke and vodka."

Cameron had neither the will nor strength to make love, but Mary Jeanne was insatiable, and he went through some of the motions. Later, when he thought she was sober enough to understand, in the dark and buried under the luxurious covers, he told her of his plan. "Don't tell a soul," he said, but he wanted to marry her and take her away from Washington. "She was so cute. She started to plan our house, how she would furnish it.

"I never saw her again."

29

Winston woke him up at about eight. The president wanted Cameron to go back with him on his helicopter.

"I said, 'What about Mary Jeanne?' He said Moray would get everyone back, but he wanted to talk to me. I didn't argue: I was still afraid and I wanted to look cooperative. I sensed Winston was unsure of me. He kept asking me if I was 'all right with this.' Could I handle it?"

Cameron said he had been so disturbed by what happened on the *Potomac Fever* that it was Saturday evening before he realized that Mary Jeanne had not called him.

He telephoned her apartment over and over again, but there was no answer. "At first, I was worried but not panicky. She was a nineteen-year-old girl, after all; maybe she just got to having so much fun that she lost track of time. Maybe Celeste and Harry were still out there."

But on Sunday morning, Cameron panicked. Had they taken Mary Jeanne as insurance? Had somebody figured out how much she meant to him?

He started calling. Harry Moray was at his Great Falls home and sounded legitimately mystified. "I figured she was with you." Celeste got on the other line, but she didn't know anything either. Virgil was a blank; he had flown back with Moray. "I didn't see her in the morning."

Late Sunday night, Cameron said, he called Edward St. Denis at home.

"I told him, 'You tell the president if that girl is harmed, I'll go public with the whole thing.'"

St. Denis went ballistic. Where would she go? How much does she know? Has she ever disappeared before? Is there another boyfriend? St.

Denis claimed he knew nothing, but he would start inquiries. "Keep quiet until I can find out something," St. Denis told Cameron.

For more than forty-eight hours, there was nothing. Cameron considered calling Nathaniel. "St. Denis kept on the phone to me. Don't do anything! We're working on it!"

On Wednesday Cameron said he had a terrible premonition of doom. "I'm calling the police." He agreed to wait until evening.

"Then at six o'clock Wednesday, Valasquez came to see me at my office, unannounced. He was very tense, angry. 'Send your secretary home. Put your telephone on voice mail and lock the doors.'

"I asked him why.

"'Your little sweetie was found floating in the South River.'"

Tears were now rolling down Cameron's cheeks as he told his tale, and Cal handed him a towel. Cal wondered whether ministers studied acting.

"It was like a physical blow. I couldn't even think for a minute where South River was. My heart was racing."

But Valasquez had no time for sympathy. Valasquez was brutal. "'You killed her, you son of a bitch' was the first thing he said. When I tried to stand up from the desk at one point, he threw me down over it. He was incredibly strong. He had duct tape with him and tied my hands behind me and taped my mouth. He drew this metal baton and began to ask me questions.

"'This is like truth or consequences,' he said. 'You nod yes, shake your head no.'

"Did I brand her? Had I gone back to Kent Island? Did I throw her in the bay? It went on for maybe twenty minutes, but it seemed like hours.

"When I was slow to answer or he didn't like my answer, he hit me with the metal baton. On my back, in my crotch, behind my knees. The pain was excruciating. I was screaming into the tape. Right in the office of the mayor of Washington, D.C.

"Later, when they showed me the videotapes, I realized that Valasquez already knew when he came to my office that nothing had happened on the *Potomac Fever*. They knew I had not harmed her on the boat. I began to think that St. Denis and Valasquez really didn't know what happened to her. Don't you see! Why would they come lean on me?"

As he told the story, Cameron was getting short of breath, the way heart patients do when they're talking too fast.

"Later, I wondered if the beating was just a cover for what they'd done."

When the interrogation was over, Cameron said, he knew he was badly hurt. He went into his lavatory and threw up blood. Valasquez watched him.

Valasquez told Cameron not to call anybody about this. "'I will know if you do. Do not go to the woman's apartment,' he said. 'Do not answer any questions from any source without my permission.'

"'Meet your commitments. Approve the Rivergate project!'

"With Mary Jeanne gone, I tried to summon the courage to break with them and disclose the whole thing. I really did try. I called Nathaniel, but when I got him on the telephone, I realized that I was a coward. I couldn't do it."

"Did St. Denis or Valasquez ever talk about their role in the Reggae Club shooting?" asked Cal.

Cameron shook his head. "Nobody has ever said anything. But Winston moved so quickly to capitalize on the shooting to get Rivergate under way that I came to believe they knew it was going to happen. It was like they had a press release already written."

Nathaniel and Cal took Cameron on a racing drive to Baltimore Washington International. The doctors from the hospital in South Carolina had called Nathaniel on his cell phone. Reporters were asking where the mayor was. Cameron and Nathaniel decided he must go back immediately before anyone discovered his true whereabouts.

Cameron sat in back, and Cal sat in front with Nathaniel. Cal was going to drop a bomb on Martin Cameron.

"Ophelia thinks Mary Jeanne resisted the branding and you killed her."

Cameron dismissed it with a wave of his hand. "How would Ophelia know? Ophelia hates me more than any person alive. She'd say anything to hurt me."

"Does branding people turn you on?" Cal asked matter-of-factly.

"Jesus, no."

"Then why did you brand Ophelia?"

"Brand Ophelia?"

The car swerved, the tires squealing, forcing cars to hurtle around them.

Nathaniel's head had whirled around. "Say what?"

"Did you brand Ophelia?"

"Did she tell you that?" said Cameron angrily.

"Did you brand her?"

"No. Ophelia doesn't have a brand." Cameron was shaking his head.

"Wrong, Mr. Mayor. Big as life. I've seen it," said Cal. "It's just like the one on Mary Jeanne."

Nathaniel pulled off the parkway abruptly, the wheels throwing gravel all over, again confounding the following traffic.

He turned to Cal. "Are you shitting me?"

Cal shook his head. "Why do you think Green believed her?"

Even behind dark glasses, Cameron appeared dazed. "Where?"

"On her right buttock, just like Mary Jeanne."

"I swear —" Cameron started to say.

"Don't swear," said Nathaniel. "Just tell me. Did you brand Ophelia?"

"Christ, I've hardly seen Ophelia without her clothes on in three years, but she never had a brand!"

They sat a long time in the car by the highway. Cal did not let it rest.

"Ophelia told us in detail how you got into brands, where you did it, how you did it, and how you got off on it. Green's had the brand examined. It was burned into her skin with some kind of a hot iron. It's for real and in a place where she could not have done it herself."

Cameron did not answer him, but Cal noticed that his breath was coming in hard, short bursts. Suddenly he took two pills from a little box and put them in his mouth.

Nathaniel pulled a half-empty Coke bottle from the driver's drink holder and passed it back. Cameron took a swig and threw his head back to get the pills down.

"If you want him now," Nathaniel said disgustedly to Cal, "he's yours."

Cal shook his head. "You guys came to me."

At the airport, they had to run for Cameron's plane.

"Don't talk to anyone," Nathaniel warned Cameron. "Dr. Reynolds will meet you. Even if you're recognized, don't answer any questions."

Cameron seemed old and meek and thoroughly daunted by Cal's disclosure.

They waited at the gate until he disappeared down the loading tunnel.

"He's finished," Nathaniel said, shaking his head.

They watched the plane lift off, then started walking slowly up the Jetway.

"What are you going to do now?" Nathaniel asked.

"With Cameron?"

Nathaniel nodded.

"If I hadn't seen the brand . . . ," Cal said, shaking his head, unable to finish the thought. "He's got to be lying, but it's a hell of a story."

"It's funny, though. I know Ophelia pretty well —"

"She said, real well," Cal interjected.

Nathaniel looked sharply at him. "She's right. I knew her too well for a while. But why didn't she tell me? She came to see me after the Turner story hit the papers. She told me Martin was involved with Mary Jeanne. Why not tell me about the brand?"

"Maybe she started to, but she was afraid of you, afraid you were in Martin's pocket."

Nathaniel was silent for a moment. "I suppose I was." He put his hand on Cal's arm. "You have to believe one thing. I had nothing to do with setting up you and Bobbie. Never. Truth be known, I don't think Martin did either. Maybe he is into branding. Maybe he panicked when Mary Jeanne died, and tried to hide the body. But killing cops? No way."

Cal pulled away and started to walk to the main terminal. He needed a drink.

He had an awful feeling in the pit of his stomach. This had been a linear case. Cameron kills girlfriend. Powerful political friends cover it up. But now he felt like it had swerved, and he was reeling, a pilot caught in a tailspin.

He walked into the airport bar almost unconscious that Nathaniel was still with him. The case was confused; he wasn't sure that he could sort it out. If Cameron wasn't lying, there were three capital crimes, not one:

Provoking a gang shooting that resulted in the death of four youngsters, the purpose being to force a speculative land development, possibly at the direction of the president's men.

To cover that up, a Washington police officer was killed, probably at the direction of the president's men.

And a young woman was tortured to death. If Cameron was telling the truth, Cal realized, he was no closer to finding her killer than he had been when he and Bobbie walked out of the autopsy five months before.

The bar was packed with holiday travelers. Cal pushed his way in. "A double tequila and some lime."

The barmaid's question, "Is he with you?" reminded Cal of Nathaniel.

"Jacks on the rocks," said Nathaniel.

Cal didn't turn around, but looked at Nathaniel in the mirror. The big detective's face was badly swollen, and one eye had nearly closed.

"So what are we going to do?" Nathaniel asked.

"*We* aren't going to do anything, Nathaniel. We aren't a *we* anymore. You're the head of the Homicide Department. These guys have done everything but garrote somebody on your desk, and as far as I can see, you've done everything to cover it up."

Cal could see in the mirror that Nathaniel flinched at his words. Nathaniel downed his drink and gestured to the barmaid for another.

The woman eyed his battered face nervously as she poured. Nathaniel started talking, almost as though he were talking to himself.

"This is not the time or place for this," Nathaniel whispered, his eyes canvassing the crowd. "But you have to hear me out."

"There is no other time," Cal shot back, refusing to lower his voice.

Slowly, softly, Nathaniel tried again. "When this all started, I was about to become the chief of the Metropolitan Police Department. Can you imagine that? Calvin Bench's son, chief of the police? Calvin Bench was so afraid of police officers when they stopped his cab that he couldn't talk. For years the white cops in the hack inspector's office thought he had a stammer. He didn't have a stammer. He was just a frightened little man trying to support his family."

Cal took another swig of tequila and pulled back away from Nathaniel to let a couple of airline stews order Cokes.

"The chance to get the chief's job consumed me. I thought of nothing else," he said, looking at Cal in the bar mirror. "Can you understand that?"

"How did you plan to replace Poindexter?" asked Cal.

"Poindexter has a chronic urinary tract problem. Nobody knows about it. The doctors think it's cancer."

"Cameron was going to appoint you?"

Nathaniel nodded.

"Did he lean on you in this thing?"

Nathaniel shook his head. "He never called me once. He didn't have to. When I found out about Poindexter last spring, I decided to have a no-fault year. You and Bobbie scared the hell out of me. You always have. You've always taken everything to the limit. Nine out of ten cops would have never found that sniper site at the Reggae Club shoot. Walk a perimeter one thousand yards from a shooting at five A.M. after being on scene seven or eight hours? Uh-uh. Nine out of ten cops would have bought Richie as the girl's killer."

"But you knew all along Cameron could be involved!" Cal said angrily.

"I knew he partied with the girl. Martin's a satyr, not a murderer. No way did he kill her."

"But you didn't tell me and Bobbie anything you knew."

"Naw, I guess I've been in Washington a little too long for that. Knowledge is power in this town, and nobody volunteers everything he knows right out of the starting gate. Politicians don't. Lawyers don't. When we were partners, we didn't always tell each other everything we knew."

Neither of them spoke. Both men knew rationalizing was no substitute for the truth.

"Didn't you ever want something so badly that it hurt?" Nathaniel said urgently. "Something that leads you to defy your own good sense?"

Cal tried to think for a minute. Vivian leaped to mind, but Cal said nothing. Less and less, he understood Vivian.

"I wanted to be chief of the Metropolitan Police Department of the District of Columbia. I wanted it in the worst way!" Nathaniel looked defeated as he said it.

"Anyway, I didn't know about Cameron and the girl until after I assigned you to the case; then it was too late.

"To tell the truth, I never would have assigned it to you, if I had known. I wanted this to be just a nice, quiet year. I never actively hindered you, I just didn't help you and I loaded you down with every administrative detail I could think of." Nathaniel paused and looked down at his drink for a few seconds.

"The night after I suspended you, I went home and took stock of myself. I didn't like what I saw. Ylena didn't either. She told me I had changed. She couldn't believe that I had suspended the two officers I most admired in the department. That's when I called you, the night Bobbie was killed. I knew then, I had been going down the wrong road."

They stood silently for a while watching the crowd. Nathaniel was the first to speak. "Do you believe Cameron?"

"At first blush it's preposterous," Cal said. "But what he says fits. When Vivian was telling me how she spied on me, I kept thinking: this is a lot of trouble for St. Denis, Valasquez, and Winston. Why do these guys care? If Cameron's right, they had bigger fish to fry."

"Maybe the guy Hugo did this on his own?" said Nathaniel.

"No, I don't think so. He's an investor protecting his money. Somebody politically sophisticated had to come up with the idea that a certain kind of criminal event would be a catalyst in the Washington political scene. *Catalyst* isn't a Spanish lawyer's word, it's a Washington talk show word! Later somebody had to tell him which cop to lean on."

"Will you trust me to help you?" asked Nathaniel.

"I'm all out of trust this month. I want to operate alone. Why don't you do this. Find those gunmen. There was a gang of Salvadoran soldiers working around the Reggae Club as janitors, but when I checked on them, I found out they were still in the army and worked here while training. I thought that strange. Then I went down to Miami, and the cops there say that DEA funded Latin antidrug units that wear masks on operations, some like the masks on the guys who killed Bobbie."

He looked silently at Nathaniel. The big police officer was clearly disappointed at Cal's suspicion of him, but he didn't say anything. He just nodded.

"Can you get out of the office?" Cal asked.

Nathaniel nodded.

"Try to do a lot of the work yourself, so we know what you find before anyone else."

30

Carlos Frederico Valasquez lived very well on government pay. His condo was in one of those new multipurpose buildings, half offices and half apartments, with a health club, swimming pool, supermarket, and a white-tablecloth restaurant. Apartments there started at $300,000, with a $1,200-a-month condo fee.

The first week Cal conducted periodic surveillance, using different rental cars, identifying Valasquez's telephones, cars, and habits.

Every weekday morning Valasquez walked to the White House at 7:30 A.M., brisk, full strides, a man of purpose. Vivian had been right: his clothes were perfect, beautifully tailored, but could not hide physical force — he seemed on the alert, even when walking, ready to jump. The panther metaphor had been apt.

One morning there was deviation. Cal would have missed him except for luck. At the last moment Cal turned his head, and there was a silver Mercedes poised to enter traffic going south on Ninth. Valasquez was at the wheel. Cal did not try to follow him. Nathaniel ran the plates through DMV: 836-906, tax value $57,000, titled to C. Valasquez, 708 D Street N.W. No liens.

While Valasquez was at work in the White House, Cal cased his building. The apartments could be reached only by a bank of elevators in sight of the desk, except for a key-controlled one that came up directly from the basement.

With $300 and his police badge, Cal got the garage elevator key from the attendant long enough for a copy.

Posing as a worker, he pulled the trash in the incinerator room on Valasquez's floor and sifted through dirty coffee grounds, rotting fruit, and used Tampax. Nothing, three days in a row. But on the fourth day, Cal got Valasquez's bag. Most of it was useless, advertisements, utility-bill stubs, empty cereal boxes, but there were pieces of a travel agency itinerary. Enough to read the name of the agency and a number. They put it together on Nathaniel's kitchen table.

They got Nathaniel's wife, Ylena, to call, posing as Carlos Valasquez's secretary. "I'm doing his expense accounts. Can you give me the dates and amounts on travel transaction three eight six nine four two? His writing is blurred."

"Round-trip, business class, Air France, Dulles–Paris with a connection to Barcelona. Four thousand four hundred and twenty-eight dollars," the clerk said. "God, are you organized! The flight isn't until next week. Departs four forty-five, January fourteenth, return January six-teenth at six P.M. EST."

The stroke of luck Cal had been waiting for!

Valasquez arrived at Dulles by a White House limousine at 3:55. He checked a suitcase and shoulder bag and waited for the plane in the VIP lounge. Cal watched him board.

Cal bagged the apartment just after seven. He wasn't quite sure what he was looking for, a firm connection to the shooters, of course, or to the drug lords.

Cal entered the building from the office lobby, carrying a briefcase, looking hurried and talking on a cellular telephone. The pose of a man who belonged and knew where he was going.

When Cal got to Valasquez's floor, he stepped into the incinerator room, pulled some coveralls from his briefcase, drew them over the suit, put on plastic gloves and the white plastic ski mask he had bought to show in Miami. If there was an internal television monitoring system, it would give Valasquez a start to discover later his apartment being bagged by a guy wearing one of the ski masks.

There were two key locks and no sign of a tamper alarm. One lock gave him no trouble, the other took valuable seconds, and he could hear someone moving about in a nearby apartment, but Valasquez's door gave way just as a lock behind him started to disengage.

Inside, Cal noted it was 7:31. He waited until the other tenant had summoned the elevator, scanning at the same time for a television monitor or an alarm system. If there was either, it was hidden.

Even in the beam of a flashlight, the apartment knocked Cal's head back: it was far more sophisticated and richly furnished than Cal would have expected for an ex–Miami narcotics detective. It was decorated by someone with elegant taste and an unlimited budget.

The living room was done in light linen and tan fabrics opening onto a dining room built along one wall of windows. There was a natural teak dining table for twelve. In a study-like room off the dining room, there was a small sofa, two TV sets, a lavish wine collection in a wall bar, and a computer.

He quickly determined that Valasquez was a very neat man. There were no unusual business papers, no notations on the calendar, no banking or tax documents, and only the most routine bills for building services and utilities, all current and paid. There were letters in Spanish addressed to Valasquez's wife in Cartagena. Cal shined his flashlight closely on them and took a picture with the small camera.

The living room was so pristine that Cal guessed it was hardly used. Indeed, the whole apartment was impersonal, as though the occupant visited only once in a while.

Except for the bedroom, where Valasquez had recently dressed, and breakfast dishes in the kitchen, the apartment was spotless. On the bed table was a silver-framed photo of Valasquez on a beach with a tall, dark-haired woman in a wispy summer dress. Cal took a picture of her too.

Cal searched the nearby bathroom quickly and expertly. There were no prescription drugs, no unusual patent medicines. There were several female things: lipsticks, one a very dark burgundy, and a hairbrush with blond hair. The dark-haired woman in the picture was not the only person who shared Carlos's affections.

On the floor of the bathroom linen closet Cal found a small safe with a combination lock and an alarm cable running into the wall. He gently tried the handle to see if it had been left disengaged, but it was solid.

There were two VCRs and half a dozen popular movie tapes, but no personal tapes at all.

By 7:39, Cal was sweating profusely in the coveralls and had scanned everything but the dressing room.

The apartment had a walk-in closet/dressing room with floor-to-ceiling mirrors and wall shelves holding the clothes. Valasquez's clothes were laid out with precision along one whole wall, but on the opposite wall, a woman's clothes were piled and hung in jumbled confusion.

There were far fewer female clothes, as though the woman did not spend a lot of time there. Both wardrobes were expensive. Valasquez had tailored shirts from London, Italian shoes with Milan labels, and calfskin driver's gloves from Spain.

Cal crossed to the woman's side, quickly turning labels to the flashlight and looking behind hanging clothes.

It was several seconds before the feeling of nausea came over him. It was not one thing that brought it on, it was several. The riding boots, of course, with the vw in gold up by the calf top. A tennis outfit that he thought he'd seen before, and a leather winter coat he remembered from the hospital. Then he started wildly rifling through the drawers. There was a handful of jewelry, but one was a bracelet he'd given Vivian ten years ago with tiny gold seashells. There was lingerie in one drawer with v on each piece, just the way her underwear had always been monogrammed, with the initial on the underpants at the right hip.

He was so engrossed in her clothes that he barely heard the sirens on the street, fourteen stories below. They stopped suddenly, the way sirens do when the police arrive at the scene.

Cal tried to put things back as he found them, but he realized that he had been searching wildly now, making no attempt to hide the muss. His heart was pounding and he felt flushed and confused as he ran for the door.

In the hall he pulled the fire alarm and a terrible gong sounded as the fire alarm went off, echoing and re-echoing on the stairwell.

Cal ran down the stairs just as apartment doors began to open. He had gone two floors before he realized that he hadn't taken off the coveralls or the ski mask. It took every ounce of his will to stop his hands from shaking. He stripped the mask, coveralls, and gloves and returned them to the attaché case along with the flashlight.

The mechanical voice went seconds later, warning that the elevators were not working. Cal leaned against the stairwell waiting for the people. The alarms stopped the elevators and soon, as he had planned, the stairwell was filled with people leaving the building. They paid no attention to Cal. He joined the rush, pounding down the stairs and across the lobby, anonymous in the herd of people, pushing past the police to get to the street.

They met in the upstairs bar at the Willard. Two men having a late-evening drink. For some reason, he couldn't bring himself to tell Nathaniel about Vivian's clothes. He was embarrassed, he supposed, unwilling to reveal to a friend how bad things were. He realized in an instant that he had forgotten a truth about Vivian he had learned years before: Vivian always had an agenda. You just had to know what it was.

"Anything?"

Cal shook his head.

"There was an alarm on a closet safe; I had to scoot pretty fast."

Nathaniel opened a manila folder. "I've got some material on Oogo.

"Hugo Marin Playa is a Colombian by birth and a lawyer who now lives in Barcelona. He was one of thirteen persons indicted in a narcotics money-laundering conspiracy in Tampa, Florida, and he's been looked at for importation tax manipulations in the United Kingdom and convicted of tax evasion in Venezuela."

"Just your average presidential confidant," said Cal.

"There's more," Nathaniel said, grinning. "A federal judge in Tampa issued a bench warrant for Hugo a year ago, and negotiations for extradition are ongoing with Spain, so when he was aboard the *Potomac Fever,* he was actually wanted in the United States.

"I found a clipping in the file that said he had invested billions for narcotraffickers around the world. He's not the sort of guy President Winston wanted coming in the front door of the White House."

"Any information from Miami?"

Nathaniel shook his head. "Only one thing. The House Judiciary Committee reports show that DEA began a major drug-interdiction program in El Salvador when Winston was drug czar, and the plan was the conception of guess who."

"Valasquez."

"We're getting there," said Nathaniel.

"We're running out of time. Cameron can't hide out that long, and Green will lose his political momentum if we don't hand him something soon. We've got to —"

"Find a weak link?" Nathaniel chimed in.

Cal nodded. "Virgil?"

"I don't think he knows. Vivian?" said Nathaniel.

Cal grunted wryly. "I don't think she's a weak link."

"Then who?"

"Review the bidding," said Cal.

Nathaniel dutifully started. "The president cannot let it be known he's dealing with narcotraffickers, selling pardons, and plotting shoot-outs in D.C. Impeachable. When Mary Jeanne's body floats up, he tells St. Denis to take care of it. St. Denis is an uptown lawyer, he doesn't know what to do, but Winston has assigned him a guy who does."

"Valasquez," Cal said, nodding.

"When they can't contain it, Valasquez picks a team to find the leak." Nathaniel paused. "Only how did they know she'd be at the Seven-Eleven?"

"Cellular. We're on our cellulars all day. I said I was meeting a guy and might not meet Bobbie, but I'd call later. She went there every night to the Seven-Eleven for milk anyway."

"So they weren't expecting anybody else?"

Cal nodded.

"So they killed her in a shootout. A day later they try to get a second bite of the apple, attack you, and fuck it up. You get away," Nathaniel said.

"Only can we prove it?"

Nathaniel shook his head. "All we've got linking Edward and Valasquez to the shootings is an unusable wiretap, your ex-wife's assertion she helped them watch you and Cameron," Nathaniel said.

"Then?" Cal asked.

"So you're nearly dead in a hospital. Virgil is stashed. The Morays won't talk. For a moment it looks okay to Valasquez. Not good, but okay," Nathaniel added. "The next thing they know, you snatch Vivian and they realize that to have peace, they have to get rid of you."

"Only along comes Ophelia and Green," said Cal. "She gives up the mayor, but she can't give up the White House because she doesn't know about Bobbie or campaign money or the cover-up or the Reggae Club thing."

They sat silent for a moment.

"Why the Reggae Club thing at all?" Nathaniel asked.

"That area had pretty stable demographics," Cal said, "so the normal crime rate wasn't causing political turmoil. They needed a hue and cry, so they created their own little crime wave. How they got those two kids to shoot it out is anybody's guess, but they probably supplied the shooter with the MAC 10, and that guaranteed a lot of bullets flying around. They didn't want him talking about where he got the MAC 10, so one of the Salvadorans ambushed him."

The two men sat mulling things over for a minute.

"So, who can deliver Valasquez and St. Denis?" Cal asked.

"Martin," said Nathaniel.

"Even if you believe him, Cameron said he doesn't know!"

Nathaniel was leaning forward now, breathless and eager with a plan. "But he can spook them."

"How?" asked Cal.

"He'll tell them he's going public. He'll tell them he's got nothing to lose and he's going to Green for a deal. We'll wire him," said Nathaniel, his voice filled with growing enthusiasm.

Cal looked at Nathaniel intently. "Cameron doesn't have the balls to wear a wire."

"You've got him wrong!"

"Furthermore, after Bobbie tried it, these guys wouldn't let someone get anywhere near them without a complete search."

"Maybe, maybe not. Meanwhile, what *do* we do?" asked Nathaniel, deflated.

They sat in silence for a minute. Suddenly Cal brightened.

"Maybe you've got something! See if you can persuade Martin to try to get a disbursement from the bank account they set up for him. My betting is that the money's not there. Tell him to make a big stink with the bank people. When he doesn't get his money, it will get back to Hugo and to our guys. That will explain why he comes to the White House guys. He's desperate for money!"

It took two days for Nathaniel to get Martin to do it and another two days to get word from the Cayman Islands bank. "You were right," said Nathaniel. "The bank said Martin Cameron's account is closed, and it showed the balance had been withdrawn by Martin Cameron!"

"Okay! Okay! This just might work. Martin goes to St. Denis's house fairly late at night in a snit because he can't get the money he was promised and he can't pay his lawyers. One way or the other, Edward has to call someone on the telephone."

"Why is that important?"

"I have a key to St. Denis's telephone box."

"You what?"

"I put a wire on his White House telephone."

"Is it still there?"

"Yes, but he has two other lines. We would have to go in and tie off the others. Martin can spook St. Denis, and we'll get his next call plus anything Edward says to Martin face-to-face. If we go to St. Denis at home at night, he'll have to reach out to Valasquez or someone."

"Tell the mayor I'll take manslaughter," Green said. "The girl died during the sex games. He panicked, got rid of her body, and tried to lay low. He has to take three to five, with two years incarceration, one year of it in a halfway house, five years' probation, resign from public office, and agree to psychiatric treatment."

Green was eager but suspicious. "What Cameron may be doing is trying to deflect everything from himself. He knows that he's the only one connected to this woman, and for all I know, he created this whole goddamn secret meeting for your benefit! He doesn't have a likely suspect to give me in the girl's death. That's his problem!"

"What about what Vivian said? Clearly the White House is involved," said Cal.

Pressed by Cal, Green finally agreed to pursue it. "I'll give you troopers to wire Cameron. Even if St. Denis only hears Cameron out, it may give me a basis for the court to override a quash of my subpoenas."

Green's eyes were glowing. Cal watched him. Green felt he was finally near pay dirt. It showed in his animated gestures, in the way he posed in front of his aides, striding up and down, shooting his cuffs and pontificating. He'd set out to get a Republican mayor and a little publicity; now he was within striking distance of the White House.

Nathaniel resisted. "Martin's never going to go for manslaughter. He says he didn't even know Mary Jeanne was dead until after her body was found."

Green walked to the window and looked out over Baltimore Harbor. "If he sticks with that story, I don't want a thing to do with this. I'll take him to trial. I'm not going to end up giving a pass to a guy who branded a nineteen-year-old girl and tossed her into the bay."

They argued back and forth in Green's office for three hours.

"Look how this would play in public," Green kept reiterating. "The men who killed Roberta Short have disappeared. Even if I had St. Denis on tape with an admission, I'm going to have a bitch of a time proving anything. It is still a robbery attempt in which a police officer was shot. We have no real evidence connecting St. Denis and Valasquez to her death or to the attack on Terrell. Even the mayor doesn't know anything about that.

"My point is that *all* we'll have is St. Denis blurting out an admission, if he does blurt out an admission, which I for one don't think he will. I'll end up giving the mayor a walk on murder."

In the end it was no plea, no Green.

Surprisingly Martin Cameron was very pragmatic. "Two years is not a lifetime, and Ophelia always said I needed psychiatric care. In a way, this is no worse than Chappaquiddick."

He said it over and over again, as though to convince himself.

Nathaniel looked aghast. "You swore to me you didn't do it!"

"I didn't, Nathaniel, I didn't. But I'm a fifty-one-year-old black politician with high blood pressure and heart disease. I have no real money, and except for you, Nathaniel, I have no real friends."

"You can't do this," Nathaniel roared.

Cameron held up his palm in a quieting gesture. "Let me try to explain it. I don't know who killed Mary Jeanne. I swear to God. Maybe the Colombians? Maybe Valasquez? God knows. But you two think you know they killed Roberta Short. If I can help with that alone, Nathaniel, I will have done something better than hiding in this awful hospital in South Carolina."

Green wanted the whole thing to go down in Virginia. It would be Maryland authorities and Virginia authorities. Democratic governors and Democratic attorneys general. He advised the Virginia attorney general that he was sending a team of state troopers with an undercover informant to attempt to gain an admission from a Virginia citizen implicated in a death in Maryland. He didn't mention that the informant was the mayor of Washington and he didn't mention that the suspect was the president's counsel.

The Virginia authorities never guessed. Green got a nice note back: *Please keep us advised if you need assistance or conclude that there is a violation of Virginia law.*

The troopers used an old ruse from vice undercover cases. They put Cameron's arm in a full cast and put the transmitter in the cast with a pinhole at the wrist.

"This is ridiculous," said Cal. "Wouldn't it bother you that in addition to everything else, the mayor shows up with a broken arm?"

The captain of the troopers was offended. It had worked in the Frederick County massage parlor case. They called Green. Green backed the troopers.

Cal and Nathaniel suited up in Nathaniel's kitchen. Nathaniel's wife was there in a dressing gown. She was not happy. "Haven't you had enough, Nathaniel?" she said, her German accent getting heavier the more upset she became. "Both of you! What if you two get hurt? This is crazy, Nathaniel. It is nearly twenty years' police work you have!"

Cal wondered if she knew about Nathaniel and Ophelia. He guessed she didn't.

They were going to be hunters who had come down old Route 193, in a car with a couple of .410-gauge shotguns and three dead squirrels. Cal had bagged the squirrels out his back door. If they were seen, he hoped the hunting outfits would explain the camouflaged coveralls and the face grease.

They didn't tell the troopers where they were going.

They had a receiver for the mayor's transmissions as well as a monitor for the telephone. The Maryland troopers would be down in the direction local police might come from. They would monitor and record the mayor from a van and would stop any local authorities who happened along.

If Cal and Nathaniel were spotted from the other direction, they would be on their own.

It was cold and damp, the way winters end along the Potomac River. The ground was covered with a thick layer of molding leaves covering the reddish clay mud. *It's funny,* Cal thought in the darkness, *the mayor and I are twenty-five miles upriver from where we were born and brought up. We could both go to houses in which we were born, build a fire, have a beer, and this whole thing would probably go away.* He had a sudden desire to do just that.

They were lying facedown by the telephone box, and the wet had long ago soaked through the coveralls, chilling Cal's skin. In his heart, Cal agreed with Green. This was a long shot.

Cal opened the box and tied off all of St. Denis's lines, in addition to the White House one, drawing a single lead to a tape recorder that Nathaniel had police techs make. He checked the connection and listened to the dial tones for a moment.

"Two minutes," said Nathaniel.

They waited in silence.

As he had been instructed, the mayor gave a voice check from the road. They no more than heard his voice when they saw the headlights swing up the driveway toward the house.

There was silence. Then a woman with a heavy Spanish accent.

Then St. Denis.

"What in God's name are you doing here?"

"I've got to talk to you."

"What happened to your arm?"

"I fell at the hospital."

"We have nothing to talk about, Martin."

"Yes, we do!" Martin was very good. His voice sounded with the right note of panic. "You froze my money!"

"You have to go!" said St. Denis.

"Get my money so I can pay my lawyers!"

"They won't do that now," St. Denis said anxiously. "It's too late."

"If I go, you know where I'll go! I've waited two days to be sure you'd be home. You have to listen to me." Martin's voice was now panicky, but threatening as well, like a panhandler who will turn mean.

St. Denis must have heard it too.

"Come in." There were the sounds of rustling and movement. "You aren't recording this, are you?"

"Here, look."

More rustling noises.

Silence.

"I called to get my money, and they said it was drawn out!"

"Drawn out," said St. Denis.

"By *me!*" said Cameron.

"I don't know what you're talking about."

"Don't be a fool," the mayor said heatedly. "Ophelia's given everyone up. Do you know something else?"

"No."

"She has a brand on her buttocks just where Mary Jeanne did. She's going to be a devastating witness."

"Did you brand her too?" St. Denis screamed. He now sounded horrified and anxious as well.

"What do you mean 'too'?" said Martin. "You know I didn't brand Mary Jeanne."

"I don't know anything like that, Martin."

"But the video . . ." Martin now sounded hesitant.

There was a noise.

"What was that?" asked Martin.

"That's my wife upstairs."

The telephone clicked in the monitor, and Cal could no longer concentrate on the body-mike transmissions. There was the fast clicking of an automatic dialer.

"Yes," said a strong man's voice.

"Carlos?"

"Yes."

"I have to whisper. Do you know who's downstairs?" came Vivian's throaty tones, cool and distinct. Cal's heart raced.

"No . . . What?" The man's voice was now urgent and angry.

"Martin Cameron is talking to Edward."

"Now?"

"Of course, now!"

"Oh, Jesus. Get him out of there! It's a setup."

"How?"

"Just get him out of there."

The telephone clicked and went to a dial tone.

Nathaniel was whispering urgently in his other ear. "Vivian just came in the room screaming at Martin to get out."

Cal heard St. Denis say, "Why?" on the radio receiver.

Then there was a door slam. A few seconds later, Martin was speaking into the mike.

"I'm in the car. His wife threw me out."

31

For two days Cal was ill: a temperature of 102, aches, stomach nausea. It was strange, Cal never caught colds or the flu, but the cold ground by the telephone box must have done it. Or maybe it was failure. After all was said and done, they had failed. Cameron's tape of St. Denis was nearly worthless, Green said; the conversation was too vague and left St. Denis openings to testify that he didn't understand what Cameron was saying. The tape of Vivian's call was worth even less. They didn't need Green to tell them that.

Green immediately lost interest. He had had enough anyway. He was going to convict the mayor of Washington in the death of the restaurant hostess — not too shabby.

Green had learned the extraordinary power of a sitting president to slow and stymie an investigation. Green had also learned that the American people were growing tired of political scandal. Watergate, Koreagate, Irangate, Travelgate, Monicagate had been enough. Instead of rising to political fame in the polls, Green found himself derided as a busybody. Who cared if two relatively obscure White House aides went unpunished? Nobody ever heard of them anyway.

Cal didn't argue when Green told him. His cold made it hard to talk, and he felt drowsy. The fever made Cal dream too. Sometimes he dreamed about Vivian in handcuffs in Ocracoke, sometimes about their wedding, but just one scene: Vivian was coming down the aisle, so incredibly beautiful that Cal could not believe she was marrying him.

On the third day, still feverish, Cal sat in the kitchen drinking tea and watching television. Cameron had suffered a heart attack in South Carolina. Cal remembered how disappointed the mayor was after failing with St. Denis, weary and shaken as the troopers took him to the South Carolina plane. The doctors said Cameron was in intensive care, that the stress of the investigation had taken its toll.

The next day the *Washington Post* carried a story that Cameron was negotiating for a plea to manslaughter in the hostess's death. A spokesman for Green's office said he could not confirm or deny the story. Later CBS quoted sources in Green's office as saying that the Maryland prosecutor had vacated his subpoenas for material on Carlos Valasquez, President Winston's narcotics advisor.

Nathaniel called on the fourth day and suggested they meet to try and form a plan. "I have a plan," Cal said. His abruptness silenced Nathaniel, and he hung up, saying he'd call later that afternoon. Of course, Cal really didn't have a plan; he had instincts.

Cal called the real-estate agent in the afternoon. The farm would bring at least $600,000. Bayfront acres were hotter than firecrackers. The agent didn't handle furniture, but he'd send up an estate sale guy.

Cal traded in his Ford 150 for a big, new F-250 with a hitch. He also bought an almost new horse trailer and a brand-new Beretta 9mm pistol. He drove over to Wythe County, Virginia, and bought a gun without a wait by using his police ID.

He used up a box of ammunition sighting it in. Personally, he liked a Glock, but his Glock was at Vivian's. Anyway, the Beretta had faster action. He might need fast action. Valasquez looked like a man who could take care of himself.

Old Mr. Claggett, his mother's lawyer, revised Cal's will, grumbling the whole time. Cal took Vivian off the will and put on Carol, her daughters, and Jeremiah. Jeremiah had been a fixture in Cal's life since childhood; a quiet, gentle fixture who seemed to communicate with horses better than with people. Cal wondered whether, like Jeremiah, he should have stuck with horses.

"Jeremiah is sixty-eight years old, Cal. He didn't make a hundred thousand dollars in his whole life," Clagget grumbled.

"So now he may," said Cal. Cal provided for Comet and Bristol Boy. The executor was charged with guaranteeing that when the horses died, their remains would not be sold for animal food.

He spent a lot of time thinking about killing Edward and Valasquez. He knew that was why he had bought the gun. From boyhood, he had been brought up not to shoot anything except with a camera, but he had gone to a war where he shot all kinds of things and into a job where he killed a twenty-three-year-old man and wounded another. Now, he certainly knew how to kill. He was competent and strangely unafraid of the consequences. But it was not the epitaph that Roberta Short would have wanted. It would let her killers off the hook; their death would overshadow their crimes. They would become the victims of a crazed police officer, not the perpetrators of her murder and the Reggae Club shooting.

Cal selected one of Vivian's pictures from his scrapbook with care. She was coming out of the water in a bikini, laughing as she ran up the beach, a fantastic body. He drove down to Solomons and got Carol to write the message in a female hand. *To Carlos: What a grand weekend, Vivian.* He developed the picture of Carlos and the black-haired woman, blew it up, and cropped out the frame. He mounted both pictures on paper and then had Carol write: *To Magdalena. Have you met Carlos's latest?*

He went to Purolator's office for overseas delivery. "It will be in Cartagena in two days," they promised.

It took three days to spot Edward. Cal got up the first morning and staked out the White House parking area for the official cars. He told Nathaniel he was still nursing the flu. Nathaniel's wife was anxious when he called. "You're not asking him to do anything more, are you?"

"Never again," Cal said.

The sunny early-spring warmth made it natural that somebody would be lounging on the benches across from the Corcoran Gallery, even at 7 A.M. Cal wore a running suit. He brought a Walkman and listened to Willie Nelson as he watched. Willie was doing "Momma Don't Let Your Babies Grow Up to Be Cowboys." Cal thought that appropriate for the day's activities. He appeared the jogger, taking time out.

The first day, Cal either missed Edward or Edward never came at all. The second day, Cal spotted Edward in his car, but it went past the Old Executive Office Building, up Seventeenth Street to the new offices at H Street.

On the third day, Cal posed as a biker fixing a tire near the White House offices until he saw the car coming north on Seventeenth.

Edward was just closing the door as Cal approached him. The driver looked at Cal nervously, and the White House police officer inside the big doors started to rise from his seat.

"We need to meet, Edward."

"Its all over, Cal. Forget it."

"I could go to the *Post*."

"What will you tell them that you haven't told Green?"

"About you. About how you arranged for teenage killers to go on a rampage. I'm going to tell them you personally masterminded everything. The Reggae Club massacre. Sergeant Short's death. I'm going to hang it all on you, Edward. You'll be holding the bag. Be at the Washington Hotel rooftop restaurant alone at twelve-thirty."

Edward did not answer; he sat there shaking his head back and forth.

Cal smiled. "Have a nice day."

He put on the earphones and rolled the bicycle, the happy biker who had exchanged pleasantries with the prominent public official. The chauffeur and the guard had turned to other things.

Cal didn't go to the restaurant at 12:30. That would have been stupid. The previous day Cal had rented a room directly across from the elevator bank on the seventh floor. He changed into a blue suit. He fitted the recorder at his waist, and ran a pinhead wire up behind his tie. He tried it twice. It was okay for homemade, not as good as Jack Mobus, but "good enough for government work," he said out loud.

He waited, working the slide of the new 9mm and checking the load. He didn't care whether it was Edward who came or Valasquez, or both. He would be ready. They could call the turn.

That morning Edward had been wearing a Swiss-cut dark double-breasted gray suit with a white shirt and blue tie with tiny white dots. Cal remembered that his shoes looked British made and had a high shine.

With that description, the headwaiter spotted him at once.

"Is he with another man?" Cal asked.

"No, he's alone."

"Ask him to come to the seventh floor. Don't give him the room number, I'll meet him at the elevator," Cal said. Edward had come, as Cal knew he would. Edward was a man who solved problems.

Cal could see the elevator door through the fisheye. He watched. Edward came out after a time. He was still alone. He had no briefcase now, and he didn't seem to know what to do with his hands.

Cal neither saw nor heard anyone else.

"Over here," he finally said through a crack in the door.

The room was awkwardly small. It had a giant bed and two chairs so big that he and Edward only had room to face each other over the bed. Edward looked very friendly and curious.

"Cal. I'm here, but this really is silly. What is it about?" Cal edged himself to the farthest corner, crouched down, out of the line of fire of the door, and put the two pistols on the bed. Edward paled slightly when he saw the guns.

"Why are you crouched down like that?"

"I find this position comfortable."

"What is this about?"

"It's about dead young people in a parking lot and a dead police officer. It's about using Vivian to set me up."

"Setting you up?"

"With Vivian. Was that necessary?"

There was no pretense then.

"She tried to reason with you, Cal. You could have made a lot of money." Edward smiled. It was a smile of a man who controls his destiny, but is prissy too, the smile of a 72°F guy, a guy who didn't like getting his hands dirty. Suddenly Cal knew what had happened to Vivian. Despite everything, she didn't like inside guys, even rich inside guys. She liked guys who were physical.

"Did you know Vivian slept with me?"

"I thought as much. We took that possibility into consideration in the planning. She said she would have to pretend to be dissatisfied with me and raise the idea that she was coming back."

"Pretend?"

"May I sit down?"

"Sure."

Edward slipped into one of the chairs. He was smiling. It was the same smile he used at Senate hearings, as though he simply had access to more information than others. It was the smile of a man who thinks he can handle the situation.

"Vivian is a brilliant woman. I know you agree."

Cal felt a pang of pain. He had brooded since he saw Valasquez's apartment, but like all lovers of all time, he had not really accepted the truth.

"I don't think you ever understood her. I knew Vivian and I were a matched pair when I first met her in California, but she had to work through her infatuations. She had to mature, like a good cabernet. It meant I had to wait years in the wings, but her brother, Charley, was right, she came around. It was a question of money and breeding."

He kept his gaze riveted on Cal. Cal must have looked unconvinced. Edward seemed to want to explain.

"The price of being with you was too high. That's why she let you leave without a word. Her destiny was with me."

Cal knew then, for the first time, that Edward didn't know that Vivian had taken Valasquez as her lover.

"Edward," Cal said softly. "Did you come alone?"

Edward nodded briskly. "Of course! I knew you wouldn't hurt me. I've read your record. You're the kind of man this nation relies on. You once crashed your helicopter rather than kill innocent civilians in a war I'm sure you despised. You play by the rules."

"Where is Valasquez?"

Edward seemed legitimately amazed at the question. "He's in his office."

They left together, two businessmen. Cal hailed a cab. "Seven oh eight D Street," he said, taking his seat with one gun out, held below the driver's rearview vision.

"Whatever you're doing, Cal, this is ridiculous," said Edward.

He was probably right.

When they got to Valasquez's building, Cal ignored security and appeared to be in an animated conversation with Edward. The clerk did not think to disturb two well-dressed men in the middle of the day. At the apartment, Edward watched in fascination as Cal disarmed the two locks and let themselves in.

Edward was nonplussed at the sumptuous interior. He stood stock-still for a moment just looking around as though he had not guessed that the lesser people lived so well and so tastefully. "This is Carlos's apartment?"

Cal nodded.

"Why are we here?" asked Edward. "It's Carlos you want to talk to."

Cal beckoned to Edward. In the dressing room it took Edward a lot longer than Cal would have expected to grasp what he was seeing, even after Cal pointed out the clothes.

Edward stumbled back and forth, fingering the material, looking at the monograms.

It was the tennis outfit that enthralled him.

"She must have two outfits exactly alike. She had the same dress on this morning," Edward said, touching the material. Cal had to smother a smile. "Vivian adores tennis. It keeps her figure trim. I just don't understand! Her girlfriends set up the appointments; I often talked to them."

Cal almost had to guide Edward to a seat on the couch. They sat in silence.

"Vivian certainly has an eye for color," Cal finally said, nodding toward the rich green African tapestry of gazelles on a savanna.

Edward followed his gaze, and his face showed that he understood.

"She despised Carlos!" Edward suddenly screamed, shaking his head. "She thought he was totally uncouth. I could hardly get her to join us when he came for dinner."

"Who killed Bobbie?" Cal whispered.

"Once Carlos ogled her in the swimming pool, and she wanted me to have him fired! I tried. But Winston wouldn't fire him," Edward said miserably, ignoring Cal.

"You ordered the Reggae Club shooting, right?" Cal whispered again.

"Carlos," Edward said bitterly. "I couldn't believe one person could make such a mess of things. Not personally. Those awful men. 'Mis amigos.'" Edward mimicked Valasquez. "The Colombians."

Unblinking, Edward began to chatter, almost feverishly. The whole thing was Valasquez's plan. "There was supposed to be a big shootout. A couple of drug lords would be killed. The next I knew, it was like World War Three. Seventeen young people shot!"

"Why, Edward?"

Like Clinton, Winston had hoped to take in overseas money as soft money, run his television campaign out of soft, and pay for the nitty-gritty out of direct contributions. But the reformers had scared away legitimate foreign contributions.

"I was thirty-six percent behind in my quota," Edward said. "I was desperate. Carlos told Winston that he knew of some people who would help. We learned later that Carlos had been on their payroll for years. He said they could handle everything without a ripple."

Edward laughed. "Without a ripple! One of the biggest shootouts in the city's history. Later one police officer dead and another hospitalized! A nobody cook murdered. Scandal all over the papers. White House subpoenas.

"What I didn't know was that Carlos's friends had already been bankrolling Harry Moray, working through Spanish cutouts and Swiss banks."

"Who are the Colombians?" Cal finally interjected.

"Narcotraffickers who got to Spain before the crackdown. That was how Carlos helped them; he took certain names and identities *out* of

DEA intelligence computers, so there are no records of their new identities and name trails. But they wanted more."

"What else?"

"Several of them had been convicted here before Carlos was on the payroll. They wanted pardons and they wanted Winston to get Rivergate under construction before he leaves office, so they could sell it. The money washes when they sell."

Edward looked around at Valasquez's grand apartment. "Carlos had his own financial interest."

Cal gave a harsh laugh. "It's my guess Vivian does too. I would bet you a dollar she decorated this place. Her services don't come cheap," Cal said.

Edward started to say something, but Cal cut him off. "Edward, I think you're far too modest. I don't think some cop like Valasquez or a Colombian money launderer could work through the idea of creating violent crime to permit the president to take action. That was your idea, wasn't it? Right out of a political seminar, crime as a catalyst. It shapes public opinion. That's not my man Valasquez."

Again, Edward's face took on a look of real pain. "It wasn't me. I swear! It was . . ."

Edward hesitated, and in a flash Cal realized why. It wasn't Edward. "Vivian," Cal said out loud. Cal could see her in his mind's eye on the Sunday morning talk shows, pontificating on the impact of crime on politics.

Edward nodded.

"Let me get the picture." Cal was now enthralled and he let the heavy pistol waver for a minute. Edward gulped hard.

"You're in charge of a very tricky deal for Winston. You've got money in this yourself and you plan to share five million dollars with your wife . . ."

Edward seemed surprised that Vivian had told Cal so much. "Valasquez said it gave the investors confidence to know that we all had an incentive — me, Winston, Moray, all of us."

"But now you realize maybe Vivian had a share with you and a share with Carlos?" Cal said helpfully.

Edward grimaced, but he didn't answer.

Cal stopped grinning and leaned close to Edward. "Why did you order the killing of Sergeant Short?"

"I told you, I didn't order it!" Edward screamed.

"Show me!" Cal said, his voice filled with steel.

There was absolute silence for forty seconds.

Finally, Edward answered. "It was all a mistake. The Colombians went crazy when the Turner girl came up dead! Valasquez had persuaded them to take a risk. He told them to go to Winston on Moray's yacht, put the pressure directly on Cameron.

"It was a long shot, but Hugo figured it would clear the logjam. He was under pressure himself. Anyway, he agreed to come and have a face-to-face with Cameron, show him some steel. The next thing the Colombians knew, a party girl on the same boat is dead.

"We couldn't give them any answers. The surveillance camera in Cameron's cabin showed her leaving alive. We didn't have a clue what had happened to her. It was insane!

"We searched everywhere. We couldn't even figure out how she got off Kent Island. Later, Valasquez cleaned out her apartment, took out the surveillance cameras, took all the mayor's stuff, anything that would connect her to Cameron.

"We thought probably Cameron killed her, but Valasquez leaned on him and he swore he didn't."

"When are we going to get to Sergeant Short!"

"*Wait, I'm explaining!* The Colombians already had operatives working in Washington. They were Salvadoran soldiers posing as restaurant workers at the Reggae Club. They were here to keep an eye on Moray and the money.

"Valasquez told me the Colombians use these men as muscle all over the world. Valasquez used to call them donkeys. He said they would do anything for a few dollars.

"When the girl showed up dead, it complicated things. I still don't know why Carlos went ahead with the Reggae Club plan. After the Turner girl's death, I thought it had been shelved. Everything was happening too fast —"

Edward suddenly stopped mid-tale. His look suggested that he now fully understood. It was Vivian and Carlos, not Vivian and Edward! That's why he didn't know about the Reggae Club. He only thought he was in charge. Edward shook his head back and forth as he went on.

"It was Carlos who got the idea that Vivian should keep an eye on you in the first place! 'Cal has a soft spot for me,' she said."

Cal looked at Edward with distaste. "I still want to know why Bobbie got killed," said Cal.

"Vivian was sure that someone inside was helping you and Short, but she couldn't get you to tell her. We wanted to find out who was helping you. We suspected it was Cameron. Valasquez had you followed by friends of his to see if you'd lead them to the source, but you didn't. You just wouldn't leave it alone. After you picked up James, it was out of our hands." Edward was weary.

"Why Bobbie? Why not me?"

"Vivian said she would crack. She said the woman had never recovered from being shot, and she would not stand up under pressure. Carlos passed that on. Carlos figured they sent two of the Salvadorans from the Reggae Club. They were supposed to pick her up, smack her around, search her apartment, get the name, and disappear. Nobody was supposed to get killed. James also reported that you and your partner had a secret informant. We had to know who it was."

Edward sat there looking fearfully at Cal. He was no longer convinced that Cal was the civilized man he had first thought. He was no longer the man in control.

"They were only supposed to get the name . . . get the name of the source," he pleaded again. Edward was watching Cal's face. He didn't like what he saw. "Are you going to kill me?"

Cal could feel the little recorder under his shirt whirring. He wondered if it was working properly. He had never trusted body mikes; they often fucked up. "You killed yourself, Edward."

Cal looked back as he closed the apartment door. Edward was sitting in a peculiarly stiff pose on the couch, the way a dog does when commanded to stay.

Cal made four copies of the tape. He took one to the White House parcel office, addressed to President Winston. He also sent one to Valasquez at the White House.

He took one over to Nathaniel's office. Nathaniel was out. Cal sat at his old desk. His stuff was still there, but somebody had been using the computer. Bobbie's desk was clear, and there was another detective's nameplate at the front. Cal typed the note: *Listen to the tape. My guess is, Valasquez will run to give himself time. See if you can get flight and departure location. I'll try to get Green to go to a judge and get a warrant. Okay?*

He took a police car to Baltimore, keeping it floored and using the dashboard light and the siren.

"It's not voluntary," said Green.

"I know," said Cal. "You can sort that out later. That's why I sent Carlos a tape too — to spook him, get him on the run. Let's think of it as they thought of the Reggae Club shooting. Let's think of it as a catalyst."

Green said he'd get the warrant and send out a Teletype that Maryland authorities sought Carlos Valasquez for questioning in the Reggae Club shooting.

When Cal got to St. Denis's house, it was dusk. He could see Vivian's Mercedes, but no other car. He had called Nathaniel, who still had no information on Valasquez. He wondered where Edward was. It had been four hours. He rang the door, and a Filipino man came. "Mrs. St. Denis, please?" Cal smiled his Fuller Brush salesman smile.

Finally, she came. She was wearing a sweater and slacks but with pearls and heels, a rich lady at home.

"What did you do to Edward?" she said. "I couldn't make head or tail of it on the telephone. He said you tried to kill him?"

Cal kept smiling. The Filipino looked anxiously at him. "Could we go in the living room? I wanted to play you a tape."

He followed Vivian through the house. God, she loved to decorate! The sunroom was breathtaking, not in the league with Moray's, but built to be part of a Japanese garden beyond. Vivian avoided his eyes as they sat down. She riveted her gaze on a little waterfall that was the centerpiece of the garden. "What do you want?"

For some time Cal just looked at her. He realized that she was a total stranger. He tried to reconcile the warm, alluring woman in the Paris hotel fifteen years ago with the woman before him now. He remembered Athos in *The Three Musketeers*. When Cal read the book as a child, he could not conceive of how Athos could kill the woman he loved, but now Cal understood.

Vivian didn't speak either, but watched curiously as he set up the tape and turned it on. A servant silently padded in and placed a tray of San Pellegrino, lemon, ice, and crystal glasses in front of Vivian, and she waved him away absentmindedly.

The little tape recorder made Edward's voice sound squeaky, but it was clear. There was no sound in the room except his voice.

"I never . . . ," Vivian started to say once, but she didn't complete the thought.

There was silence when Edward had finished.

"Why Bobbie?" Cal asked softly, shaking his head. "She was just doing her job."

Cal found that he wasn't angry, but sad. He had never believed in evil. In all his years as a police detective, evil had never been a factor. There was sanity and insanity, the civilized and the uncivilized, but never evil. Now he realized he had been unable to recognize something he didn't believe in.

"Edward is dissembling," she said. "I think he is having a breakdown." The beginning of the defense. "Whatever he said was under duress," Vivian said next in that grumpy way she had of saying things that she wished as though they were facts. "It will be inadmissible."

"It has been my experience," Cal said, rising to his feet, "that in these cases, the first person to make a deal with the prosecutor has the best chance of surviving."

He opened the garden door to leave.

"Don't you want your tape?" she said.

He shook his head. "That's your copy."

In the movies, the hero confronts the antagonist. There is closure. In the real world, things just peter out, sometimes ending without your even realizing it.

Carlos Valasquez left Dulles Airport on Continental's Mexico City flight with a connection to Bogotá two hours before Cal and Nathaniel got there. It was in U.S. airspace over Oklahoma when Green faxed the Maryland court order to Continental's traffic manager. But Continental's legal office scoffed at the notion of the plane landing in Houston or Dallas and asking Valasquez to deplane. "We only recognize the FBI's procedure in flight to avoid prosecution. Take your order to a federal court and get the FBI involved."

32

Unlike Clinton's legal counsel, Vincent Foster, Edward St. Denis did not kill himself in a public park. Fairfax County police said that his body was found in the living room of his Great Falls home, surrounded by pieces of his wife's clothing and jewelry.

According to the *Washington Post,* he used a Glock 9mm semiautomatic pistol that belonged to Lieutenant Calvert Terrell, a Washington, D.C., homicide detective. Terrell, the paper said, was Mrs. St. Denis's former husband.

Mrs. St. Denis said Terrell had asked her to keep the gun months before while he was in the hospital, and she had forgotten to return it. "I've always hated firearms, and I wish I had never seen this one."

The day after St. Denis died, Steven Green, the Maryland attorney general, disclosed that he had agreed to accept a plea of guilty to manslaughter from Washington mayor Martin Cameron in the death of the restaurant hostess. He said Cameron disclosed that a gangland shooting in Washington had been provoked by two of President Winston's advisers, counsel Edward St. Denis and Carlos Valasquez. Green said he was referring Cameron's allegations to the United States attorney for the District of Columbia.

The plot, Green said, was hatched to destabilize a large residential area of Northeast Washington and make it easier for a private developer, Harry Moray, to acquire the land. Harry Moray and "others," Green said, had fed money into President Winston's campaign and Mayor Cameron's campaign. The cover-up of this plot, Green said, resulted in the murder of a D.C. police officer. The plot had been devised on

Moray's yacht, *Potomac Fever,* on the same weekend the Turner woman was tortured.

Vivian hired one of the top criminal lawyers in Washington, a veteran of Watergate. He was one of those Washington lawyers who knows how to slip a client out between a criminal prosecution and a congressional hearing.

Two congressional committees immediately announced investigations. "St. Denis and Valasquez could not have done this without the president's knowledge," said one committee chairman. Vivian's attorney submitted a proffer for immunity to this committee as soon as it was constituted.

Cal found Cameron's plea strange in the face of his denials. According to Green's news release, "Turner had agreed to be 'marked' with a *B* during a party in which she had large amounts of alcohol and cocaine. During the 'marking,' the Turner girl stopped breathing, and Cameron could not revive her. Cameron said he panicked and disposed of her body."

Had Cameron been lying about Mary Jeanne? If he wasn't, he was pleading guilty to a complete fabrication.

The plea agreement said Green would recommend jail time for Cameron and treatment for what the papers called "compulsive sexual behavior." Cameron would resign and agree not to engage in political activity for five years.

Coincidentally, they buried Edward St. Denis from the same church where Bobbie's service was held. It is one of the most historic sites of worship in Washington, sitting as it does across from the White House. Presidents have prayed there before and after wars, before doing good and after doing evil. Vivian looked absolutely stunning. She had picked out a dark blue silk suit for the occasion, a string of blue pearls, navy blue leather gloves, a veil without a hat, and those three-inch heels that made her legs look terrific.

Cal did not know why he had been invited. Nor did he know why he went. Maybe he went to remind Vivian of Bobbie, who died because greedy and ambitious people consorted with the devil.

There were very few people at the service; more had clearly been anticipated. Washington can be a very cruel city. What was it Harry Truman said? "If you want a friend in Washington, get a dog." Edward had not liked dogs.

The day after the funeral, the *Washington Post* reported that Carlos Valasquez was killed by a hit-and-run driver in Cartagena, Colombia.

The paper said that Valasquez had been riding a bicycle from his home to a nearby bakery when he was hit by a car that sped away. Colombian police had no leads on the driver. The article mentioned that Carlos's wife was the sister of Hugo Playa, a notorious lawyer and money launderer for narcotics traffickers.

Cal surmised that she and her brother had not been understanding about Carlos and Vivian. Some women take things better than others.

Cal knew that the men who had actually killed Roberta Short would probably never be caught or even identified. Strangely, he found that the thought did not disturb him. He suspected that life as they knew it was punishment enough.

Not long after Edward was buried, the gossip columns said Harry Moray and his wife, Celeste, were now living permanently in France.

Virgil James was diagnosed with AIDS while serving in Africa and was being treated in Paris.

The River Club folded. Two months later Rivergate collapsed. In bankruptcy court filings, it was disclosed that the primary funding for the whole Rivergate plan came from anonymous offshore bank accounts.

The *Washington Post* reported that business entities controlled by Hugo Playa had made numerous soft-money contributions to both the Republican and Democratic National Committees, to the D.C. committees, and through an official of the now defunct Reggae Club, to Mayor Cameron's campaign.

President Winston issued a white paper after an investigation by his new White House counsel. He artfully put it out late on a Saturday in March during the college basketball tournament. He said that St. Denis had once arranged for him to meet a foreign national who he later learned was wanted in the United States and Germany on money-laundering charges. "Of course, if I had had any idea who this man was, I would have never met with him." The meeting was "at a social gathering with numerous other guests," the president said. The president provided his report to the attorney general.

As Cal had predicted to Ophelia, Winston's attorney general, like Janet Reno before him, painstakingly examined whether Cameron's allegations deserved a special prosecutor. He took the maximum amount of time and then concluded that these charges did not warrant appointing special counsel. There were those in Washington who believed that provoking gang murders was clearly under the statute. The U.S. attorney in Washington solemnly delayed his investigation until the attorney general made his decision. The congressional committees too waited in the wings, the members afraid they would be accused of throwing a monkey wrench into potential prosecutions.

Cal and Nathaniel wrote endless prosecution memos and were interviewed by an endless stream of congressional investigators and FBI agents. But at the end of six months, in the way of Washington political investigations, nothing had happened, nobody had been charged with anything, and only Cameron had gone to jail.

Nathaniel was removed as chief of homicide and accused in the media of trying to help Cameron avoid prosecution. There were no formal charges, just the nasty jibes of his enemies in the police department delivered through the newspapers and television. It was certainly not the conclusion of his law-enforcement career that he had imagined. He had been one of those black success stories. He had risen from private to captain in the U.S. Army, gotten a college degree in night school, joined the police, and become head of the department's best investigative division, Homicide, and now the news stories painted him as just another crooked cop. Invariably, Cal noticed, when they ran a critical article, they also ran an awful picture of Nathaniel in uniform, one of those academy shots, in which he was looking out from under his uniform cap in a startled glare. Considering all the other pictures the papers had of Nathaniel briefing reporters in his tweed suits or receiving commendations, Cal had to figure this was designed to gall.

In late spring the U.S. attorney advised Nathaniel that he was a target of the investigation. He hired a well-known Fifth Street lawyer, and Cal guessed that even though the attorney and Nathaniel were friends, it was probably costing a pretty penny.

Their chance encounters at hearings and interviews grew fewer and fewer.

One day the *Washington Post* reported that Nathaniel had been called before the grand jury. Cal called Ylena. "How is he taking this?"

"Not well." Only Ylena said *vell*.

"I said we should go to my parent's house in Gelsenkirchen, but he said he would not run away. He said that he was glad his father hadn't lived to see this."

"What's he doing?"

"Doing? Sitting."

"All day?"

"All day. He writes his testimony over and over. Then he will say, 'How does this sound?' It always sounds the same. When he is not writing, he stares at the computer. We hardly even talk anymore."

Cal took only what he could easily pack in the back of the pickup and in the loft of the horse trailer. His best saddle, his clothes, family pictures, his mother's portrait, sketches his father made of migratory birds. He gave the Smithsonian the rest of his father's library and his own books. The estate-sale guys took the rest, agreeing to clean the house too.

The house and furniture brought $656,000 — not a bad nest egg for a retired police lieutenant.

On the morning he was supposed to vacate the farm and start out for Montana, he went down to the bay to watch the dawn. Sitting there, he realized that he had lived on or around water all his life. He had even once crashed a helicopter into the South China Sea. There was no water in Montana.

The next week Cal bought the old marina down at Point Lookout. He couldn't leave the Chesapeake after all. The marina wasn't much, but the owner threw a beautiful old Herreshoff in the bargain. Hard by the wind, he told Cal, it would heel right up and go like lightning.

33

In the warm winds of the bay that summer, Cal cleared much from his mind at the helm of the Herreshoff. He would work on the marina's decking and rental slips in the morning and take the Herreshoff out in the afternoon. He named it *Roberta*. *Roberta* was fast and agile and loved to fly through the water. Even though the wind in the afternoon was not as good as in the morning, the *Roberta* would find it; and most days she would skip along, showing a little hull.

One day he came about to let a fifty-foot motor yacht pass. On the foredeck a voluptuous young woman in a bikini was taking the sun. In the glare he couldn't see her features, but he was reminded of Mary Jeanne Turner. It was a nagging thought. He tried to push it out of his mind, but it came again that day and that night and the next day.

It was funny, he had no interest in the outcome of the rest, in the Senate committee or the House committee or the grand jury. Cal no longer watched television or got a Washington paper. But Mary Jeanne gnawed at him. Nathaniel was right. Martin Cameron never harmed her.

Nathaniel answered the telephone the way people who are waiting for it to ring do, a trifle too quickly. "Bench."

"I need your help," Cal said.

It wasn't like old times, but it was a fair imitation. Mary Jeanne's death had been bothering Nathaniel, and together they began to work the case as they would have a decade before. On the first day, Cal thought Nathaniel didn't look well, but as Bench got into the simple routine of organizing material, studying maps, and reviewing files, he brightened.

To Cal's amazement, Collins had become chief of homicide. Jesus, Bobbie would have laughed her head off at that! Out of affection for Nathaniel, Collins released all the file materials to them.

They started by testing the premise that Mary Jeanne died as the Cameron guilty plea recounted, falling overboard after a drunken party.

Carol got Cal an introduction to the Maryland Marine Research team chief at Annapolis, who laid out the maps for him in the coffee shop of the Hilton Hotel. Cal and Carol had plotted an approximate course for the *Potomac Fever* using the times they had and her knowledge of the captain's cruising habits and fuel consumption. Carol said even with radar, the captain would be afraid of shoals and floating objects and would have stayed in the main shipping channel up the center of the bay, turning to anchor north of the Bay Bridge because of the location of Moray's estate.

The marine research guy studied the course inch by inch, shaking his head. "No way! There is no way someone fell off a vessel at Kent Narrows and drifted across the bay," he said. "The movement of water is inshore. The body would have beached south of Kent on the Eastern Shore. We've done research on that for erosion studies. You put something in the water either side of the main channel and it will ultimately drift inshore."

Next they tried to obtain the videotape that Cameron had told them about, but no investigators on what the press now called Reggaegate had ever heard of it.

"Did Cameron make it up?" Nathaniel asked.

Cal shook his head. "No. Edward admitted they had complete surveillance of Cameron."

Cameron had said it placed Mary Jeanne alive and well at Kent Narrows at 7:47 A.M. "That's a place to start," said Nathaniel.

The woman who had run Moray's Kent Narrows home now lived in Cambridge, on the Choptank River. She was as big as a house from tasting her own good sauces and Eastern Shore canned crabmeat.

They sat in Tina Thompkin's chintz-filled living room and went over the morning of August 2. The president had been expected. Mr. Moray had said they would arrive on the *Potomac Fever* sometime during the night. The Secret Service had come four days before and done a security search. Bell Atlantic came with them and set up several temporary telephone lines. This was all old hat to Tina. The president had been at Kentland before, sampled her she-crab soup and declared it the best he'd ever tasted. He had sent her a nice little note, and she was hoping to see him again that weekend.

When Mr. Moray was at Kent, Tina and her "girls" stayed over in the servants' quarters. That morning she awoke at 5 A.M. to start the breakfast for Moray's guests and noticed that the *Potomac Fever* was lying offshore in the mist. She remembered it looked ghostly and silent.

To her disappointment that morning, the president never came into the house. She saw him and Mayor Cameron, who had also admired her crab soup, having coffee at a garden table she had laid out for the guests and the Secret Service agents. She said Winston and Cameron left on a helicopter with another man she didn't recognize. She guessed that was shortly after 8 A.M. She had never met Carlos Valasquez, but she identified his photo as possibly being the other man on the helicopter. Virgil James was also a regular guest at Kentland, and she remembered that much later that morning he played tennis with Celeste. Maybe 10:30. About the same time, Mr. Moray came ashore and went swimming.

She had never seen or met Mary Jeanne Turner. Never. Not that morning or any other morning. Mary Jeanne had never been a guest at Kentland. Where was Tina between 7:30 and 9 A.M.? Nathaniel asked. Tina admitted that she was hard at work in the kitchen and could have missed Mary Jeanne. She took a smoke at the back door, and that's when she saw the president. Could she see the swimming pool from where she had the smoke? No. It is on the other side. She could see the helipad in the distance and the bay.

Tina had not seen Ophelia Cameron that weekend at all. She knew Mrs. Cameron from previous trips. "On Sunday? Nobody was there on Sunday but the servants."

"You never saw her the whole weekend," said Nathaniel.

"Never!"

Nathaniel and Tina went back and forth. Could one of the other girls have let Ophelia in and given her iced tea on Sunday without Tina's knowing about it. "Not if she wanted to keep her job!"

Were there a Polaroid camera and pictures left lying around on a coffee table?

"Nothing is left lying around in Miss Celeste's house."

Tina finally got mad at being badgered. "There were no colored at Kentland after Mr. James left."

Cal and Nathaniel exchanged glances. If there was one thing a white, sixty-five-year-old Eastern Shore woman was going to remember, it was African American people who had attained status.

In the car they looked at each other. "Where the hell was Mary Jeanne?" Nathaniel asked.

"And what was she doing up at seven forty-seven, if she had a snootful of cocaine and drinks?" Cal echoed.

"Maybe the helicopter woke her up? Remember, she's a kid with energy. She can't get the mayor up, but she's excited and doesn't want to miss a minute. She decided to go for a swim and maybe find someone to play tennis with," said Nathaniel.

"What about the Secret Service?" said Cal.

"They already told the House committee that they have no information on how Mary Jeanne left the official party."

"Where did Ophelia get the picture?" said Cal.

Nathaniel just shook his head.

They canvassed the marinas and yacht basin, the discount stores up off Route 50, and houses as far away as two miles, showing Mary Jeanne's and Ophelia Cameron's pictures. It took a week. No one recognized Mary Jeanne, though most had read the news stories.

But on the seventh day, a clerk at the Shoals Motel, "vaguely" recognized Ophelia. "We don't get many African American guests, especially ones that look like models. I remember she was traveling alone and she had every credit card in the world."

The motel's manager, a woman, let them review the registration records. "You're lucky. We keep them one year." She was kind of excited to help two private detectives, and she set them up with coffee in one of the meeting rooms.

Nathaniel found the card: August 1 at 8 P.M., paid by American Express, room 120, one guest. The reservation had been made by telephone on July 31. Ophelia scrawled her signature with a flourish. She did not check out until Sunday morning, August 3. Two towels were missing and billed to American Express at $15 apiece.

"She never went to New York at all. She spent Friday and Saturday night in Kent!"

Nathaniel wanted to brace Ophelia and confront her. Cal restrained him. "We don't understand this. She's lying, but why? What was she doing there? What does it have to do with Cameron pleading guilty?"

The manager let them into room 120. She guessed 300 or more guests had used it since the previous August. "Has the rug been changed?" Cal asked.

She shook her head. "Those were installed new last year."

Green was astounded when they told him. "Why in God's name would I want to order lab analysis of rug fibers that would prove I accepted a fabricated guilty plea?"

"Because you're an honest prosecutor," said Cal.

Eight days later, the samples came back positive: the same texture and color of the ones from Mary Jeanne's body and presumably the same manufacture. They went back to the room with a state police laboratory team, but found nothing else. At least they had a crime scene. Mary Jeanne Turner's life had ended in this room, but why and with whom?

Green subpoenaed Ophelia's credit-card and telephone toll-call records, grumbling as he did so.

Ophelia's American Express showed that she had rented a car in Washington at the airport Avis on August 1 at 3 P.M., and the car was driven 147 miles before being turned in at the airport Sunday night.

"Between National and Kent, using Route Fifty back and forth, is a hundred and thirty miles. The car had a hundred and forty-seven miles on it."

Nathaniel handed Cal the map. The distance to Bayville, where Mary Jeanne's body had turned up, was nearly nine miles from the Bay Bridge, just a seventeen-mile round-trip detour.

Cameron was in a minimum-security facility at Garrett Park. Prisoners had to work on a vegetable farm. He looked like a million dollars, slim and robust. "I used to hate working the fields for my father, but now I see that is what God wanted me to see: those were the best years of my life."

Nathaniel told him about Ophelia.

"Why did you go and do that, Nathaniel?"

Nathaniel looked crestfallen.

"I guessed something like that the day Cal told me about the brand on Ophelia. She had warned me she had had enough. I just didn't heed those warnings."

"So you think she killed Mary Jeanne?"

Cameron nodded solemnly. "I've had a lot of time to think. . . ."

"How did she get ahold of her?"

"I don't know. I don't know how or why she branded Mary Jeanne either. Vengeance, maybe. But I never branded anyone."

"You can change your plea," Cal said. "We've been working with Green on this."

Cameron shook his head.

"But you'll be free," Nathaniel said.

Cameron gently put his hand on Nathaniel's arm.

"What is the definition of *manslaughter*, Nathaniel?"

Nathaniel seemed confused by the question.

Cal softly answered. "The killing of a human being by another when the killing is unlawful but without malice."

"I'm the one who really killed Mary Jeanne. You understand that, don't you? Why don't you just drop it? Your friend Mr. Green needs this conviction to get the Senate seat."

"We can't," said Cal. "That's not how it works."

"Have you talked to Ophelia?"

Nathaniel shook his head.

Cameron smiled a faint, gentle smile. "You may want to do that first."

"What I can't figure out is how in Christ's name Ophelia branded herself," Nathaniel said as they drove back to Washington.

"Where are Bobbie's notes?" Cal asked.

They found them in storage.

Cal went through all of the scarification experts that Bobbie had called and from them got a list of people who did body marking in the Washington area. It took three days of calling to locate the parlor. It was off Charles Street in Baltimore. The guy had been a navy corpsman and advertised that his body piercings and brandings were medically safe and painless. He used a localized painkiller. The guy didn't really recognize Ophelia's picture, but he had done only one mature black woman in the whole time he'd been into scarification. "She was very precise; she brought a sketch of how she wanted it to look. My business is really teenage white kids and hookers. I've got to tell you that was an outstanding ass. I've never seen anything hotter."

He had all the paperwork. A signed release from an O. Brown, a Polaroid before and a Polaroid after. O. Brown signed them as being photos of her anatomy. "I got sued once when a man claimed he didn't like the brand," the shop owner explained.

Green had not kept track of Ophelia. "She moved to New York." But Cameron gave them an address, a rural address, just outside New Canaan, Connecticut.

It was an estate, one of those big rolling pieces of land that the extremely wealthy enjoyed before property taxes. On the main road the sign said simply, TOLBERT MANOR. DR. MORRIS ROTHBERG, next to an electronic gate with an intercom.

The woman's voice on the box refused even to acknowledge that an Ophelia Cameron was there. "Tell her Nathaniel Bench wants to talk to her." They waited five minutes.

"Do you have a court order?" asked the voice.

"That's a strange question," Nathaniel said.

Fifteen minutes later the gate buzzed. It was nearly three-quarters of a mile to the house, a large stone building that had been modeled on a nineteenth-century English country estate.

A woman in a white coat came out to the portico. "Which one is Bench?"

Nathaniel nodded.

"I called Dr. Rothberg. He said if Ophelia wants to see you, he has no objection. But if she becomes upset, I have to stop the meeting."

"What is this place?" asked Cal.

"This is a private sanitarium," the woman said.

They sat on the stone terrace and watched a hawk circling over the field. Thirty minutes passed. The hawk had left when Ophelia came out.

The woman in the white coat said, "Do you want to meet with Mr. Bench alone?"

"It's okay," Ophelia said, putting her hand on the woman's arm. "These fellas aren't going to do me any harm."

Ophelia looked awful. Cal guessed her weight had exploded to nearly 300 pounds, and her once beautiful face was so bloated that her eyes had become tiny slits. She or somebody had shaved her head, literally shaved it, and her scalp glistened in the sunlight. She was wearing a white hospital gown, and a cigarette dangled from her lips. The ashes were falling next to the food stains on her chest.

Cal heard Nathaniel suck in a shocked breath.

They followed her into a parlor. It had been done in awful French provincial furniture, the cheap kind that institutions and offices buy. Ophelia lowered herself heavily into the center of a white sofa built for three and plumped the pillows around herself. She made them wait while the woman brewed tea and then sat there pouring just like in *House and Garden* magazine.

Nathaniel did the talking. Ophelia listened demurely.

"Did you tell Martin all this?" she asked at one point.

Nathaniel nodded.

Ophelia smiled. "You boys are a day late and a dollar short."

"We'll set this right by the campaign. This is all the media saying this because Martin is the vice-presidential nominee. That's all."

She chattered about the conventions, then suddenly looked sad. "Dr. Rothberg made me miss Martin's speech."

Nathaniel became exasperated. "There is enough evidence to prosecute you, Ophelia. This isn't the media."

"Honey, Martin's lawyers are handling everything. Go talk to Martin," she said.

Nathaniel tried again, but now Ophelia sat sphinxlike with her eyes closed. The only indication that she was awake was the glow of her cigarette when she inhaled.

Finally Cal cut in.

"Ophelia. We're working with Martin. He wanted you to tell us everything so we can help the lawyers."

It was like turning on a light switch. She smiled at Cal. "That motel man thought we were going to sleep together. Remember? You did want to touch me, didn't you!"

Cal knew now it was a game. "I sure did! You're a beautiful woman!"

She made a gesture as though brushing her hair back, but there was no hair.

"Why did you kill Mary Jeanne?" Cal asked softly.

"I just wanted to teach her a lesson."

"What was the lesson?"

"Not to lie."

"What did she lie about?"

Ophelia smiled. "Every time I touched her, she'd yell and wiggle, just like she wiggled for Martin."

"How did she lie to you, Ophelia," Nathaniel said, now keeping his voice as Cal had, at a low whisper.

"*She wasn't supposed to fall in love with him!*" Ophelia screamed.

The woman in the white coat came to the door. "Now, now, Mrs. Cameron."

"What was she supposed to do?"

"She was supposed to get him to approve Rivergate! Virgil and I paid her a lot of money!"

"You set her on Martin?"

"I know what Martin likes. He likes big-assed women." Ophelia giggled and thumped her backside.

The story came then, twisting and turning in Ophelia's disoriented mind. Harry wouldn't pay Virgil and Ophelia until ground was broken on the project. Virgil noticed Cameron was drawn to the hostess. Ophelia quietly sounded out Celeste.

Celeste was high on her. "She's as smart as a whip. Tony Frohlo signed for a million below contract demand when she got through with him!"

Ophelia cultivated Mary Jeanne like a sister and drew her into the plan. "My husband can be Winston's vice president. Probably the first black president, but he has to approve this project to free up campaign financing."

Mary Jeanne struggled with the idea that Ophelia wanted someone to cozy up to her husband and sleep with him if necessary. "Think of us as a team," Ophelia said. "He needs intimacy, he needs enormous amounts of sexual companionship. You be his bed partner and I'll be his political partner. We'll go all the way."

Ophelia helped Mary Jeanne seduce Martin. She advised her on how to fix up her apartment to be a love nest and how to dress for him. She bought Mary Jeanne the right CDs and videos, told her what to talk about and what turned him on.

Mary Jeanne began to warm to it. It was like a great movie role: consort to the first black president. But Virgil thought time was running out on them. Harry never confided in him, but by late July Harry warned that the whole project could go down the tubes. Ophelia saw her whole life crumbling. Martin kept stalling.

Two days before Martin's fund-raiser on the *Potomac Fever,* Virgil found out that the president was going to have a night meeting with

Martin to pressure him. Virgil suggested to Harry that Mary Jeanne help out. Harry liked the idea. Virgil would come as a beard.

"Ophelia, did you know that they were taking secret pictures of Martin and Mary Jeanne?" Cal asked. She looked bewildered. Either she had not known or could not remember.

Ophelia now started to chatter, making herself a second cup of tea and absentmindedly spooning sugar into it.

"I told her just what to do, how to act with the president and what to wear. I told her the moment to get Martin to do something is right after you have sex. He's like a pussy cat."

Ophelia loaned her jewelry and bought her a new bikini and a tennis outfit from Neiman Marcus. "This is it, kid! Do your stuff!"

"Why did you drive out there?" asked Nathaniel.

Ophelia smiled. "Mary Jeanne and I decided that if Martin came around, we were going to reward him. I was going to show up and be real nice and show the president that everything in our lives was going smoothly. Mary Jeanne and I were going to do our sister act.

"I said I'd be in the motel and she should walk over early so nobody would see me. Later I could just drive up like I had been on the road from New York and thought to stop."

But as Friday wore into the night, Ophelia got more and more nervous. She took a lot of diet pills and drank a lot of coffee. When dawn came, she hadn't slept a wink.

"Did Mary Jeanne come like you asked?" Nathaniel said.

Ophelia's face darkened. "You know what?"

Nathaniel shook his head.

"She said she and Martin were in love! Martin never loved anyone but himself! She said he wanted to get rid of me!"

Mary Jeanne's ingenue act dropped away. She derided Ophelia for her age, her insensitivity to Martin's needs. "He doesn't care about the election. He wants to teach, to live again. He's going to tell the president that he's through. We're going away together. He never really loved you! He married you for politics!"

Ophelia knew that Mary Jeanne was telling the truth. "Escaping Washington was his dream. He talked about it all the time." Now, Ophelia said, after all the pain and humiliation of seventeen years, Martin was going to abandon her. He was going leave her to controversy and notoriety and slip off with this girl.

Ophelia struck Mary Jeanne again and again with all her strength.

The younger woman staggered and fell to the floor, gasping for breath. After several blows, Ophelia managed to tie her with panty hose and put a towel in her mouth, but Mary Jeanne kept spitting it out. She got tape from the trunk of her car.

The brand was to teach her a lesson, like *The Scarlet Letter*, only *A*, adultery, wasn't in Ophelia's lexicon that Saturday morning. "You imagine the little bitch, lecturing me about Martin." Ophelia was screaming again, saying the word *bitch* over and over. Nathaniel looked nervously at Cal. This time the white woman appeared at the doorway with a frown. Ophelia lowered her voice.

She recalled that she heated up a butter knife from the kitchenette and touched it to Mary Jeanne's buttocks as she enumerated her angers. Mary Jeanne wriggled and screamed through the gag, but Ophelia ignored her. She was concentrating on the beauty of calligraphy. "Every time I touched her, she bucked up and down. I said, 'You won't be wiggling your butt around for a good long while.'"

When Mary Jeanne went quiet, Ophelia thought she had only fainted. She finished the drawing carefully. When she tried to arouse Mary Jeanne, she found no pulse. At first she panicked, sitting there on the floor with the body, but late in the evening she remembered a little black community across the bridge where she might not be noticed pushing something into the water. She dragged Mary Jeanne over to the corner so she wouldn't be noticed if someone came to the door.

Then she had a pizza and Cokes delivered and watched a pay TV movie. "You know, the one where Tom Cruise is a sport agent." The pizza man couldn't see Mary Jeanne's body.

"You ate a pizza?" Nathaniel said.

"Pepperoni. Double cheese."

She waited until early Sunday morning to be sure she wouldn't be seen, rolled Mary Jeanne in a garbage bag from the motel's maid's room, and dragged her out across the gravel to the car. "She weighed a ton."

At first she was sure she would be confronted and arrested, but later she realized that neither Cameron nor anyone else seemed to have a clue to what had happened to the girl. She went to Nathaniel fully intending to surrender. "I got scared."

Suddenly Ophelia noticed that Cal's cup was empty. "Can I pour you a second cup?" she asked Cal as she finished. He shook his head.

"Martin called me yesterday."

Nathaniel looked surprised.

"He wants me to make a series of talks to black professional women in the campaign. I got a lot of notes."

She took a sheaf of papers from her bodice.

"The greatest challenge facing black women is to have the respect of their men," she started to read.

Nathaniel and Cal slowly stood up.

The woman in the white coat must have had a peephole, because she came right in.

Nathaniel looked down at Ophelia. "Do you have any remorse for killing Mary Jeanne?"

Cal thought it was a stupid question. Ophelia thought so too.

"Honey, except for that little bitch, you'd be the chief of police."

Dr. Rothberg was a small, wizened man with a very gentle manner.

"How did Ophelia get here?" Cal asked.

"She was brought in by Norwalk police. She barricaded herself in a room at a Ramada Inn off Ninety-five, shaved her head as you see, and began ordering pizzas. For some reason it was three days before the motel called the police. They brought her here. They identified her officially only a week ago, but I knew who she was. She told me she will someday be the First Lady of the United States."

"She told us she killed Mary Jeanne Turner," Nathaniel said.

"She told me that too, but it doesn't make any difference."

"Why?"

"In my opinion, she will never be competent to stand trial."

If you really are a small-boat sailor, the best time on the Chesapeake Bay is late October or early November. For a vessel as agile as the *Roberta*, the heeled-over ride on a sunny October afternoon is as close to heaven as one is likely to get without a funeral.

Nathaniel was indicted on six counts of obstruction of justice in the last week of October.

Cal took Nathaniel, Ylena, Carol, and Jack Mobus out the week after. Nobody did much talking. It was one of those crystal days, so perfect that you think there never can be another one like it. Nathaniel sat forward, behind the cockpit hatch, and let the spray wash his face for an hour while the others watched him in silence. On the way back Cal anchored where the Patuxent empties into the bay and brought up a couple of bottles of Asti Spumante. They hoisted a glass to the two Robertas, one a sailboat and the other an absent friend.

Cal looked at Nathaniel. "Remember the time . . . ," they both started to say at once. Soon they were all laughing, a little hysterically maybe, but long and hard. The sailboat bobbing at anchor, Cal thought, looked like a lifeboat and they were the survivors.